Wanted

Love United Series # 3

Wanted – Love United Series #3

Melyssa Winchester

Copyright © 2014 Melyssa Winchester

To one of the women that despite hardships continues to inspire me each and every day through her strength and determination. Jennifer Hicks, this one is for you darlin'. Never give up and never surrender, ever.

PROLOGUE

Serenity

There are moments in your life when you're moving along, going through the motions and it can feel like you are living in the darkest parts of hell itself. Your heart is weakened, your body is torn apart and the will to survive, that light we all have inside of us, is on the verge of being blown completely out. It appears that nothing can feel quite as dark as that moment and you feel yourself giving into it believing there is no way out.

You become lost in the despair and you truly believe yourself to be living in hell.

That moment is beautiful compared to the reality of what Hell really is. No matter how dark of a path you take in life, it cannot prepare you for what you will experience once your fate has been decided and you end up here.

It may feel this way to me because I'm not meant to be here. I am still very much alive and still very much controlled by the light that I was born into when I was created in Heaven. Where darkness, pain and torture abound around every corner here and it's accepted, I just can't seem to allow my mind to embrace the normalcy of it.

Innocent souls, ones that were taken before their destiny can be reached are being tortured here with each passing second. The screams are so common place that even when it's not happening, I can still hear them in my head. Even in the darkest moments there are still souls praying for a Savior. To be saved from the pain they now have to endure. Strong souls, ones that normally would not break are being forced to and it's sickening.

Ryan tried to warn me that I would not be able to handle Hell before we walked into the church in Green Haven and while I had taken his words to heart, I didn't give it much thought past that. He's right though, even Heaven's brightest light would eventually break under the darkness that's apparent here.

It's obvious from the way everything has happened since I got here that Lucifer is thankful to be home again. The one place in all of existence where he can truly be himself and not have to worry about the way he is perceived or hiding under the guise of a helpless human. He is in his element and it had taken affect almost the minute we touched down.

He hadn't been lying to me when he said that he wanted me to rule with him. The minute we appeared, he immediately separated from me and began to partake in the deviant pleasures that are blindly accepted here. While he didn't lie to me, it's obvious that in making sure I witness everything he does, he wants to torture me.

Admitting that he's succeeding in his goal makes me sick.

I am supposed to be stronger than this. I am made of Heaven. Seeing the way he tortures helpless human souls should have been easier to take but I found myself looking away on more than one occasion. I couldn't handle it. My heart bled with the agony each and every one of his victims felt as he used his power on them, draining them of their very life force all in an effort to garner more information for his sick plans.

Any curiosity I might have had in terms of what Ryan dealt with during his time under Lucifer's control has been completely wiped as I experience it first-hand. Souls that had previously been blue and bright the first time I came upon them were now glowing dark red, the darkness taking over, effectively destroying the very thing that made them who they are.

It is only a matter of time before the same thing happens to me. I know that. There is no way he would want me to rule over Hell beside him with the light that resides in me. He would drain me of it much the same way he did with Ryan and Graham and no matter how strong I am and what I'm made of, I would be powerless to stop it.

I would bend to him and his will and when I did, it would be then that he would achieve the very thing he wanted from the very beginning.

I would be his bride.

It's far worse than just becoming his partner in the darkness because the minute I become that, it's only a matter of time before he would achieve the other part of his plan.

Owning me completely.

CHAPTER ONE

Ryan

I really can't take the looks and the questions anymore.

For the last two months I have gone out of my way to avoid her as much as humanly possible yet somehow she still manages to find me and badger me in a way I can't handle. I don't have the answers for her and even if I did, I wouldn't even know where to begin.

Emma Daniels has been Serenity's best friend for as long as I've known her but she knows absolutely nothing about who her best friend really is. It makes dealing with her that much harder. Maybe if she knew even a little about what all of us have been dealing with the last year maybe I could explain why I didn't know as much as I want to about where she is.

I've been trying to hold it together since Serenity vanished but the more time that passes the harder it is for me. The plea that I let slip every night before I finally go to sleep isn't working and I don't know if it ever will. I don't want to give up but I'm running out of options.

Breaking down isn't an option. I know what will happen if I allow that to happen. No one will be safe. Despite the newfound knowledge I have about my beginning, I am still what Lucifer made me to be. I can still create a level of destruction previously unknown to the world around me if given a reason to and the loss of Serenity is a pretty strong reason.

"You just need to tell me. Did she run away with Graham? Is that why you always look so hurt when I bring her up?"

It's been this exact way ever since Serenity disappeared two months ago and Graham was mysteriously gone too. I know where he is though and he is most definitely not with her. He will eventually be making his way back to school and I could easily wait for Emma to get her answers then but I just don't have it in me.

I understand how much she cares but I really wish that the angels could have just swapped out her memories again. The constant barrage of hearing her name repeated over and over does nothing to help the emptiness in my heart at not having her here with me the way she should be.

"No, she isn't with Graham. I have no idea where he is but you know Serenity, she wouldn't just take off with Graham and not tell anyone."

That had to be a good enough answer for her right now because I didn't have anything left I could give her. I just want to get back to my room, put my headphones over my head and drown out the world and my mind for a while. That is the only thing that can ease the turmoil that burns inside of me. I don't want to let the anger build but if this girl asked me any more questions I wasn't going to be responsible for what happened. I may have it under control but I'm not against slipping. Even the strongest alcohol survivor has those and I am no different.

"I don't know what I know about her anymore..."

No, definitely not going to let the conversation take this turn. She would not doubt the woman I love, not when she sacrificed herself for the sake of the very person standing in front of me now.

"Yes you do know her. You know her better than anyone. I have no idea where she is Emma but she would never just up and leave without saying goodbye. You know this."

God, everything is such a fucking mess. I should be the one that isn't here anymore. Not her, never her. She should be here with her best friend, going to class and then to stupid parties and having the time of her life. Instead she is god knows where with no tangible connection to me or anyone else in her life that cares about her. This is all wrong.

"You're right. I'm sorry Ryan...I just don't know what to do anymore. I went to see her mom, and she hasn't seen her. No one on campus has seen her and Graham is missing too."

"This isn't the first time Graham has taken off though Emma. You know he did this once before. Maybe not knowing what happened to her got to him too and he needed to get out of town for a while."

"Maybe," She shrugged. "I just wish she would come home already."

I understood that sentiment. Nothing was right as long as she's missing. I can't eat, sleep or breathe right knowing that she is out there somewhere I can't get to her, going through god knows what alone. I want nothing more than for her to come home safe and sound. Then maybe the hole in my heart could finally start healing.

"I want the same thing Emma. I wish there was more I could tell you but I really have no idea where she is."

I have to extricate myself from this situation and I have to do it right this second. I am dangerously close to breaking in an emotional way and given how my control of my emotions has been slipping as of late, the last thing I want is for Emma to be on the receiving end of it.

"Look I need to get going but if I hear anything I'll let you know okay?" I say hoping she gets the hint and I'd get out of here with minimal issues. I still had to make it all the way across the quad without cracking so I really need to get a move on.

"Yeah thanks and Ryan, I'm sorry. Pretty sure I'm not the only one who misses her."

Missing her is putting it mildly. I was beyond missing her at this point, having passed that stage only a day or two after she vanished into thin air right in front of my eyes. Emma most definitely wasn't the only one that felt Serenity's absence but I couldn't exactly explain it to her. There is still too much she doesn't know and most likely wouldn't understand even if she did.

I have to remain indifferent.

"Yeah, you're welcome. See you around Emma."

Making my way across the quad, desperate for the confines of my room and the utter mind quiet that losing myself in the music would bring I turned around one final time when I was sure I was far enough away from her to go unnoticed. It was then that I saw it, the last thing I'd been expecting.

Graham is back.

Graham

9

A few months ago I never would have thought I'd be standing here again.

I had come to terms with everything that happened to me and the end that I would inevitably reach and was ready to move on. As long it meant in the end Serenity would have been able to continue living on, there was nothing left for me to do here.

It had taken me a little longer to come back here because I couldn't resist stopping in Green Haven once I had been given the all clear by the hospital and saying a proper goodbye to my mother. Lucifer had taken so much from me in the short time that he had been with me but my mom had been the biggest loss. I needed to be able to say a proper goodbye to her and finally begin to mourn her the way she deserves.

I only hoped that in passing she is in a better place and the angels she would encounter would take good care of her the way I hadn't been able to.

There seems to be a pull inside me to repeat the steps I had taken before in the way I'm coming back. I find myself standing again under the very same tree that months ago I watched Serenity from as she made her way into the English building with her best friend at her side. Even with the time passing it still manages to center me and give me a sense of purpose that until now has been non-existent.

The only issue is I'm back here without her. In saving me she somehow put herself at risk and now she's gone. Gabriel tried explaining it all to me but given that he was just as out of the loop as I am, his explanations did nothing for me. Michael and Ryan had experienced Serenity's final moments and since neither of them has spoken to me since I recovered, I would never get the truth of what happened to her that night.

Lucifer had been right where she is concerned. She did choose to save me over herself but she just never realized that in doing so she would be leaving behind a person who would have chosen to die then do this life without her. The sacrifice she made is huge but without her here to share it with given that it appeared as though everything has gone back to normal, it just wasn't worth much at all.

The only thing that kept me going while I recovered and learned about what happened to her was the fact that Gabriel said she had not passed on. She is still alive though we have no idea where she is. I had been a pawn for Lucifer before and knowing that he had her now meant that she could be just about anywhere but what she isn't is here with me where she needs to be.

*****

"Don't you guys know anything? What use is Heaven when you leave us all to our own devices anyway?"

Gabriel has been visiting me in the hospital every night since he dropped me off at the door of the emergency room. I could tell he was carrying what happened to me on his shoulders and I wanted to make that right for him but given that he couldn't tell me anything and wasn't allowing himself to show any real emotion I'm having a hard time doing it for him. I wanted answers and I wanted them now.

"Contrary to what you believe of me Graham, I do not enjoy entering a humans mind without their consent. Serenity was in the midst of a pivotal moment and she had to come to terms with it on her own. There is no other way that it could have been handled. If I had known what she was planning in that moment I would have done everything in my power to stop her, you must realize this."

Yeah I realized it alright but it didn't make it any easier to stomach.

"I don't wanna blame you man. I know she made the choice to save me and what happened after isn't what she expected but I just don't get how God could have let it happen. Doesn't she mean anything to him?"

It's obvious from his pained expression that any mention of his father is upsetting to him. I had no idea what happened in Heaven but I could only imagine it was the same way with angels and their father as a human and their dad. Going against them was never easy and you lived with the effects for a lifetime.

"I cannot speak on my father's motivations any longer Graham. I am still processing the information that he withheld

11

from us. Everything that I once believed as it pertained to him has been shattered."

"He has her doesn't he?" I asked knowing Gabriel would know exactly who I'm talking about. "He's going to kill her."

"She is with Lucifer yes but in what capacity at this time I have no idea. He has not ended her life, as she would appear in Heaven at such time and that has not happened."

I felt better knowing that she isn't dead but nothing short of her coming back home would ease my concern completely. She should never have been in this position at all. I was torn between being angry with her for sacrificing herself when I was ready to die and worrying for her because I know what Lucifer is really capable of.

"He wants her to rule Hell with him. He told me that before…"

"I know what he wants and it would appear he has gotten that now. I am working under the assumption that when Serenity disappeared she was taken back to Hell."

"Then what do we do to get her out?"

"An angel has never walked through hell before so there is no method we can employ currently to rescue her from the result of her decision. Michael and I are working on it but given that Father no longer wants to be a part of it, our resources of knowledge are limited."

God was giving up? Just like that?

"Graham there is much you do not know as it pertains to our father and his choices and when the time is right I will inform you but just know that the choice we made to go into the church that day went against his overall picture and he is most displeased with us."

"So you guys are in what…a time out?"

"In a sense that is exactly what we are in. He will not let us in any longer because we broke his trust and until that can be earned back we are on our own. He could have cast us out as he did Lucifer but he is choosing a different tactic."

"No offense Gabe, but your father is a dick."

12

"You are entitled to your opinion and as much as I would like to deny it, it seems to be the overall consensus as of late."

"So what am I supposed to do in the meantime? Just sit here while she's rotting away in Hell or wherever he took her and do nothing?"

"No. You are to heal yourself completely as I do believe that is what Serenity would want and then we will all come together and move forward."

"Move forward how?"

"Gather as much information as we can and save Serenity. It is the very thing that each of us wants to do on our own but it has to be done together or it will fail."

"Do you think we can do this?"

"It is not a matter of whether or not we can do it, there is no other alternative. This will not be Serenity's end."

*****

I have had my doubts about Gabriel in the time that I've known him but there was a moment during our conversation where I couldn't doubt him anymore. He wants to save Serenity as much as I do and I know that he would do whatever it takes to make it happen even if it meant going against Heaven and his father again.

So I'm back here now, doing as he asked me, preparing for the moment when I would come face to face with the man Serenity had loved and left behind. I knew that it was going to be inevitable but it didn't make me enjoy doing it. I know that everything that happened had been Lucifer's doing but I still couldn't entirely let Ryan off the hook. I still want to blame him for putting Serenity in this position to begin with. No matter how wrong it is.

"You need to get out of here."

Looking up I came face to face with the very person I had just been thinking about and he didn't look at all happy to see me.

"Maybe you're the one that needs to back off and leave."

Before I could react I felt his hand tighten around my arm and my body being pulled. I'm still not healed completely but if he didn't let go I was going to have no problem using what strength I did have to make him regret putting his hands on me. As I'm about to make a move, he spoke.

"I'm not gonna do anything to you man so lighten up. You just haven't been here for the last couple months. Emma is looking for answers and if she sees you then she's going to go into overdrive."

I didn't want to lower my guards with him but given what he said it was hard not to. If he's bringing up Emma and her need for answers than this really did have nothing to do with the animosity between us.

"Gabriel didn't alter time for her?"

"No and I've been paying the price ever since. She's starting to think that Serenity ran off with you because you weren't around either so you need to stay under the radar unless you wanna be on the end of Emma on the warpath."

That's most definitely something I didn't want. I'm still not fully up to speed with everything that happened before Serenity vanished. I'm completely clueless for everything after it. I wouldn't be able to give Emma anything other than possibly upsetting her more.

"Someone needs to tell her the truth."

I don't know why I said it but I knew why I felt it so strongly. Emma from the moment Serenity met her had known about her differences and always accepted her as she was, not for what she could do and if there is anyone that could handle hearing everything that Serenity had been through over the last year it was her. She needed to know but more than that she deserved to.

"I know that and I've stopped myself every single time I see her from doing it because Gabriel doesn't want it happening. He's afraid it will only put her at risk but I think she's at risk whether she knows or not. At least if she knew everything she might be able to prepare herself for anything."

Agreeing with Ryan is something I never expected to do. I'm not sure if it's the bond between Serenity and me or the fact that he is a demon but I hated him on sight. There is something about him that didn't sit right with me which made agreeing with him now confusing. I want to hate him and I can't, not when what he's saying makes perfect sense.

14

"Gabe wants me here which means I can't hide away forever. I'm going to have to deal with her at some point but thanks for the concern."

"It has nothing to do with concern for you."

"Of course it doesn't. Anyway, thanks."

As I pushed my way past him in an attempt to create some distance, he spoke again.

"She loved you."

Turning around to face him again, this time my feet frozen in place at what he said, words I never would have expected him to admit to knowing, I really took him in.

He looked worn, his eyes weaker in color though still complete with the black rim that signaled the demon side of him. If the way he looks is any indication I can easily see that we are both experiencing the same things with Serenity's disappearance. We were going through the motions but barely surviving. It looked like neither one of us had much left in us to fight anymore.

"You're wrong." I whispered. "She loved you easily, with me it was always just the bond."

He looked shocked at my words but not nearly as shocked as I was hearing myself say them. I wanted to believe that Serenity loved me and that it was more than just the soul mate bond between us that made it happen but I couldn't. She did love Ryan in a way she could never love me because there is no bond between them other than what they created themselves.

"It was never just the bond Graham."

"How do you know that? Do you have some info I don't? I saw the way she looked that day you know, when we were together in her room. The minute her eyes locked on yours it all became crystal clear."

"The only thing crystal clear is how blind you really are. You were her first love Graham and not because of some stupid bond the two of you share but because you were the first guy to see past the typical bullshit to what really matters. You saw her."

The feeling I got when I agreed with him is growing stronger by the minute and I wasn't sure what to do with it. I want to continue hating him, blaming him for everything that happened

15

because it's just easier than admitting that maybe he is just as much a victim as I was. I just couldn't allow myself to do that.

"Please just stop."

"Stop what? Telling you the truth? Would you rather I lie to you?"

No, I didn't want him to lie to me, there had been more than enough of that going on since I came back into Serenity's life but I really couldn't handle liking this guy right now.

"None of that matters anyway. She's gone. It doesn't matter who she loves or who she's bonded with. She's gone and we're just left here to deal with the fallout."

"Is that really how you look at this? Jesus man, you're even more screwed up then I thought."

He has no idea how close to the truth he is with his statement. I am screwed up. I mean it's hard not to be when you're the reason why the person you love isn't there with you anymore. Everyone could give me a ton of reasons why this wasn't my fault but it didn't change the facts. Serenity had chosen to save me and in doing so was taken away.

I caused this. If I hadn't gone back into the church that day in an effort to save her I wouldn't have been taken and she would still be here now instead of being spoken about like she's long dead.

"Yeah well I think I'm entitled to be a little screwed up don't you? How are you coping with everything Ryan…already moved on?"

It was a pot shot I know but I don't care anymore. Just based on the way he looked he wasn't taking care of himself either so he had no right to accuse me of being something that while true, he was too.

"I'm going to ignore that."

"Yeah you do that. Ignore me. It's better that way anyway."

I start to move away again but not before hearing his final statement and feeling the effect as it shot me straight through my heart.

"It's not better for Serenity."

Michael

For as long as I can recall I have always been put off by anything remotely human in nature. It is this way of being that made it easy for me to stay in Heaven watching from a distance as my fellow warriors dealt with anything Earth related. Somewhere along the way though something changed within me and ever since it has caused me nothing but trouble.

Serenity Richards, the ball of light created of Heaven but turned human through multiple trials my father put her through. Everything in my existence had been just fine until she had come crashing into it.

When I had been tasked with watching over her recovery and then that of her demon companion I looked at it as nothing but another job that needed to be done. I never once thought for a second that I would come to care for either one of them or worse than that, develop actual feelings and opinions on what they did with their lives. That is what has taken place though.

I have not been able to focus on anything since my return to Heaven. I have lost my coveted place at Father's side and there is no play I can make to get it back. I made choices based on my own free will and in the end turned the very man I idolize against me. It should upset me but I find that it does the complete opposite. I have no feeling at all regarding my loss of position. My only real thought has been about her.

That silly, most stubborn, absurd little ball of light that I am not supposed to give a second thought to other then caring for her during her time here. She has invaded every sensible part of me and made it impossible to think about anything other then what fate has befallen her.

Speaking to Gabriel about it has done nothing but create a disconnect between the two of us because he is so entangled in his own grief and pain that he is not witnessing mine in the way it should be. He believes me to be in love with the ball of light, as he is but he couldn't be farther from the truth. I do not love her in the way in which a Beloved loves their mate, a fact that I cannot seem to get through to him no matter how hard I try.

17

The way I am feeling now is like that of a father to a daughter or a brother to a sister. I feel a loss in my chest like no other one I have ever experienced and I know there is no way to rid myself of it until we find her again. I want my brother to see that so we can aid one another in achieving what we both want even though our reasons for wanting it are drastically different.

When Father made her, he did it with the soul intent of her being the very thing to change the world at which he is so proud of. I don't think he gave much thought to the fact that not only would she change the world when it was her time to but she would also change everything that the angels have ever believed in.

The world is right again, at least as right as it can be with Lucifer still out there somewhere, ready to strike at any moment but Heaven is not. Gabriel is ripping apart at the seams and I am unable to function at all. With all of the power I have available to me there is nothing I can do for myself to end the misery I've felt since the day I watched her disappear in the church. I cannot help Gabriel and I cannot help myself.

All I do is fail.

Gabriel has been leaving Heaven quite frequently as of late and heading back down to where Graham and Ryan reside going through much the same things we do here and in one of the times when he was conveniently out of the picture I decided to take my worries and concerns to Father. If Gabriel would not help me locate and bring Serenity home then I was going to go to the only other person that would.

*****

"You seem to be especially troubled today my son."

"I am Father. There is something that I wish to do but I need to discuss it with you before embarking."

"Would this happen to have anything to do with our little ball of light?"

Of course he knew it was about Serenity. He knew everything though he put on a good show a lot more times than I realize pretending he didn't.

"It pains me to no end that we are unable to locate her. I want nothing more than to bring her back where she belongs and I do believe that out of everyone in Heaven you want the very same thing."

The undertaking that had been put into motion twenty one years before in which Serenity would reach her full potential and save the world had to be paramount in father's mind and I was hoping that in bringing it up I would get him to agree to help me in locating her.

"Have you not seen the world as I see it now Michael? There is finally a sense of peace that we have not known for centuries. Where you believe me to be on the same page as you, I am afraid I am not."

"So you do not want her located even though she is made of the light?"

"I want her found but what you do not realize is I already know where Serenity is and there is no way we can penetrate it given the limited resources we now have. Without the pure angel on our side no matter how strong of a force we put together we will fail."

For as long as I have ruled side by side with my father I have never heard him speak this way and I am most unsure what to do about it. He is the Almighty, not just some random human. There is nothing above or below that he could not penetrate.

"I don't understand you. I have tried in as many ways as I can yet it still makes no sense to me. Since when has a member of heaven residing in hell stopped you from taking action?"

"Since now Michael and you would be wise to watch your tongue with me. You are walking a very thin line as it is."

"Someone is always walking a thin line with you it seems. First Lucifer did when he questioned you about your creation, then it was Gabriel and now me. You cannot blame us for not knowing how to interact with you when you act the way that you are."

"You came to me in an attempt to garner support in locating Serenity did you not? Well she has been located. I have explained to you the situation yet you still sit here arguing with me. You are *not listening nor actually hearing me Michael, so leave me now. Your presence is no longer wanted."*

"You're right father. I came to you in order to get help in finding her and bringing her home where she belongs. I thought of all of the beings here you would be the one that would understand my need most. I can see I was wrong."

"Yes you were."

"There is something going on with you that none of us are important enough to be made aware of. I noticed it with Ryan and now it is appearing again. Whatever it is, you need to deal with it before more than just Gabriel and I are the only supporters you have lost."

*****

I have always been the upstanding being that my father needed me to be but after that conversation with him I know everything I said was correct. I couldn't be what he needed me to be anymore because he wasn't who he is supposed to be. We were falling further and further apart from the original objective and try as I might to put us back on the same path, I am failing at every turn.

There has to be something more that he is not telling me, or any of the residents of Heaven that would make him behave the way he has been. When he told us the truth about Ryan, admitting the grave error we made twenty one years before, something changed within him and it only seemed to be getting worse the more time that passed. I wanted nothing more than for him to explain himself but it is obvious that at this time, it is a pointless endeavor.

Father would keep everything hidden under lock and key until he was ready to share and not a minute before.

This left me with only one alternative moving forward. Because the little ball of light had forced her way into my system in the way she had and I now felt an overwhelming need to bring her back where she belongs, I am going to move forward doing just that.

With or without Father's help or even Gabriel's, I would bring Serenity Richards back home to the life she deserved to have. The very life that I promised her during her first month here in Heaven and there is nothing anyone can do to stop me.

Not even God himself.

CHAPTER TWO

Gabriel

Dissention in the ranks is difficult no matter who the participants are. It is practically unheard of in Heaven as we all just follow what Father wants without question. Since Lucifer disappeared before being destroyed, taking Serenity with him, there has been disagreements but nothing that caused this level of desertion.

Sides were being taken as they would be in war, yet there is no war on the horizon. There were people that stood by Father, believing in his end goal and following it no matter what the cost. Then there were the others. The ones that want answers yet weren't getting them in the way they were accustomed and were siding with Michael and me in an effort to see change occur.

If only they could see that not everything is kosher between Michael and me, they might not want to follow us so blindly.

It all started with Michael's reaction to Serenity's disappearance. While I had been expecting him to feel something given the time he spent with her while I had been off in search of her soul mate, I hadn't been expecting it to be quite as powerful as it was. I wanted her found just as badly as everyone else but with Michael it is as if it was all he could see.

There is only one time that I am aware of that one can be so blinded by rage and anger and only see one path available to take and that is when one soul falls in love with another. The way in which Michael has changed since that moment in the church, left no doubt that he loved her, though getting him to admit to such a thing would be the equivalent of pulling teeth. It just would not happen, at least not overnight.

He will admit to caring for her but to what degree he remains tight lipped. It only makes me read into things more and try as I might I can't help but distance myself from him because of it. I am attempting to not let the bond I share with Serenity override what is most important but it would seem that when Father made me he didn't make me without flaws. I feel almost human in my response.

I've been working with Father more lately in an attempt to garner information. I may not agree with the way he has been running things and there may be issues between us but anything that brings me closer to finding out where she is and what happened to her that fateful night, I will do it. Father may already know that this is my sole intent but he hasn't mentioned his displeasure with it so until that moment I will continue on in much the way I have been.

She has been located in Hell. A place created solely by my fallen brother for the darkest souls of the world to reside upon their passing. It is not a place for the living or the ones made purely of light the way Serenity is which just makes the need to save her from there much more urgent within me. One can only go so long before being affected by what happens there which means we have a timetable to get her out.

Hell is not a place that beings of light travel to often. In fact it's practically unheard of. The one documented case of an angel walking straight into the bowels of Lucifer's darkness is not a fairytale. The angel did not make it out alive. It has made any future visits impossible. There is too much risk involved and while I should heed the past as a vision of what could happen to me in the here and now I find that it is something I cannot do.

I need to get her out and whether I do that with my brother by my side, or even with the help of the half demon Ryan and the soul mate Graham is irrelevant. We would be stronger in numbers and this is a fact I have made Graham aware of but I will still proceed forward regardless of the help and extra abilities. It is the highest order of business for me and nothing can persuade me away from it.

As focused as I have been on getting her out alive, I have not given myself the proper time to process everything that did happen. I was not there to physically witness what happened but I did get a firsthand account the minute Michael returned. Given the way everything happened it really is no surprise that he's different.

I'm not sure I would have even been able to survive it given everything that had already taken place between us.

Lucifer possessed her when she finally freed Graham, something I am sure she did not give herself the chance to ponder before making her final decision without us. She went into it blind, only concerned with saving her soul mate and not thinking of the long term effects. That was Serenity at her finest, always thinking about others and preparing herself for personal sacrifice at every turn.

If she had informed me of what she was planning I would have protected her against the possession as that is one thing I have the ability to control. He would never have had the chance to become one with her in the way in which he has and she might even still be here with us now. I want to be angry with her for that but I find that I can't be. In any given situation where lives are on the line, you think less with the rational part of your brain and more with the overall survival prospect.

Graham needed to be saved more than she needed to be protected from Lucifer.

With my end goal in mind and now in the stages of putting it in motion it has given me time to really think about what she will be like when I finally reach her. I know what life on Earth can do to the humans that inhabit it and also what Heaven can do but I can't imagine the horrors she will witness being in Hell and being by my fallen brothers side.

Will she even be the same Serenity when we get her back or will the light that she is known for be stripped and only a shell remaining of the girl we all knew and loved?

What you believe to be right for another person isn't always the case so while saving her seems like the right thing to do, I have to wonder if that is what she would really want by the time I am able to reach her. Will she want to come back to her life on earth or will Lucifer have gotten to her in such a way that she will want her life to remain the way that it is?

"Gabriel..."

This is not the first time he has come to me wanting to speak. I have been putting him off as much as possible given what I believe about him but at some point I know I am going to have to deal with what I am feeling inside and there is no better time than now if we are to move forward.

"Michael."

"I am aware that you have been doing everything in your power to avoid me for reasons that make no sense but we need to speak."

"My concerns are valid but this is not the time, nor the place to discuss them. What do you wish to speak about?"

"Serenity is in hell."

"I am aware of where she currently resides Michael. Who do you think found out the information?"

The silence in my mind could only mean one thing. He learned of Serenity's location and is now questioning why I hadn't come to him with it first. It was a valid question but one that I felt didn't need an answer. He would know if he just admitted it to himself.

"It is going to have to be the time to speak of this Gabriel because we cannot move forward without it. Serenity is exactly as you always wished she would be to me. She is my sister and only my sister. I love her in that regard even though you believe it to be otherwise. That is only the bond between you appearing. You must hear me and understand my words."

"One does not react the way in which you have been when it is just a sibling bond between you."

"Again that is the bond speaking and not your common sense. She needs to be saved. That is the only thing that is important here and if you can just put the other things in the background I do believe we may be able to do just that."

Could it be true? Am I able to put everything out of my mind the way that Michael wants me to and move forward with him in saving her?

"What do you have in mind?"

"We need to infiltrate Hell and we need to do it soon."

Well we were in agreement there but until we had an actual plan of attack I didn't see us making it past the first few levels of Hell, let alone where Lucifer himself resides.

25

"We need to begin planning now but more than that we can't do this alone. Father is not an option given that his priorities seem to lie elsewhere, so we need something equally as strong."

"There is no being above or below as strong as father and that includes Lucifer himself. Who exactly do you have in mind for this?"

He has piqued my interest now. As much as I want to appear disinterested in anything he has to say, I couldn't help but wonder just how much thought he had given this and who he thought the right person to go into hell would be.

"We need to go back down to Earth brother because the only two people that want her out almost as badly as we do are there and we can be damn sure one of them will go to his grave to save her life."

"You want to go to Ryan?"

"Ryan and Graham yes. They are the only two beings that know things about our brother, things that we will need in order for this to succeed."

This is something I cannot argue with. Ryan is a pure angel, one of the first created, before being sent down to the woman who fraternized with demons and becoming one himself. He is also the only being that could take on the power that Lucifer now wields and end him for good. While the plan may not have been one we were willing to accept before, in saving Serenity it might just be the thing that turned a loss into a win.

"You wish to use Ryan to save Serenity even though you know what that would do to her?"

"That is exactly what I'm proposing and I promise you, given what I have seen from the boy, he is going to want to be a part of this."

Michael is right. Ryan would not settle for sitting on the sidelines while we went into hell in an attempt to rescue Serenity from Lucifer's clutches. He would want to be on the front lines, pushing himself in whatever manner needed to get the job done, gladly giving up his life in the process. I just wasn't sure how I felt about taking advantage of that even if it is something he would want.

26

"I will not send him into the lion's den without first speaking to him about it."

"Then brother, what are we waiting for? The clock is ticking."

Serenity

I can't do this.

I know what he wants me to do and I was determined to follow his orders a little bit so that he didn't decide to grow tired of me and sentence me to a life in this cesspool but I just can't do it.

I've been following him around for what feels like days, watching him drain the life forces out of various victims and then feeding on them all in an effort to make the power inside of him that much stronger but now it's my turn. I have to stand before a non willing victim and do as he has done. In fact he is overjoyed at the prospect of watching me do it for the first time.

"You must do this Serenity."

"How can you just do this to people and not care? Doesn't it bother you at all seeing the very light that you came from being extracted from their body? Isn't there some sort of solidarity you feel with the people that are still your family?"

I know it's a long shot, bringing up his previous existence in Heaven but I have to do something to stall this. I know how badly he wants me to join with him and rule Hell but this is really not my thing. I've remained strong since coming here but if I did this I know the walls would begin to crumble and there would be no going back for me. I would never be able to live with myself once this happened.

"That is not my way of life anymore. In order to achieve my ultimate goal, of which you were one, I need the power that these bodies contain and soon you will as well. In order to survive down here Serenity this is something you will need to do."

He explained all of this to me before. I'm not strong enough on my own, even with the light inside me to maintain living in hell for any long period of time and that was his ultimate goal. He wants to keep me here until I am perfected enough for entrance to the world again. I know what he's telling me now is the truth but it

27

didn't help with the sickness I feel at having to do it at all. I want out of this and out of here already.

I don't want to become the cold hearted killer that the being standing beside me is.

"Place your hand on his chest right here." He snapped, pulling my arm and placing it gingerly on the chest that is now lying dormant in front of me. "Close your eyes and allow your mind to do the rest."

There's no getting out of this now. Closing my eyes I immediately began to feel the pull of the man's soul. The very light that swirled around inside of him standing at attention with the feel of my hand. It's only a matter of seconds now before I drain him of the light which would mean it was only a matter of seconds before Lucifer would proceed to drain his blood in much the same way as he had done with me.

"You feel it rising don't you? The tremendous level of power that it brings to the surface within you? Embrace that feeling Serenity, as it will be the very thing that makes you viable."

That's the thing. I don't want to embrace it. I know the minute I do that everything will change forever. The last thing I want to do is listen to him and do the very thing he wants me to. I just want to keep fighting it even though I know I'm fighting a losing battle.

It's surrounding us now, the goodness of this poor man's soul and I immediately felt the wetness on my cheeks as I accepted exactly what I was doing to him. My heart physically hurt even though the rest of my body seemed to be growing stronger by the minute. God I just want this to end already!

"I always knew you were special Serenity but in seeing the speed in which you handle this very small task, I now see you as so much more. It is truly a sight to behold, the power that you wield when you are focused on a goal. Now the fun can begin."

I watched in horror as he bent down to the now still body and pulled the athame, taking his time and making slow almost delicate looking slices in the man's arms. While he may no longer be the man he was when all of this began I still wasn't ready to accept the reality. I want to remember him as this man as long as I can, because the alternative is just too much.

I remember the way the blade felt when it pierced my skin, what it felt like so long ago and watching it happening again now, thankful that I'd been able to pass out halfway through, is hard to stomach. I can smell the blood as he collects it in the goblet and as much as I want to turn away from it, I find myself oddly fascinated and can't.

It's starting, I can feel it. The change in me. There is no going back now.

"I am aware of your displeasure for this act but you know what comes next bellissimo angelo. You must partake of the life blood."

He has been doing that a lot since we came here. Calling me his beautiful angel but doing it in as many different languages as he could. It never came out the same way twice. When Gabriel came to me as a voice in the beginning and called me an angel it had been comforting which is the opposite of what it feels like now. There is nothing comforting about this.

As he raised the goblet to my mouth and pried my lips apart the only thought I have is if in doing this I could be forgiven. If there is ever a chance that I could get out of here and away from him and the horror I am experiencing, could God or even Gabriel ever forgive me for what I had to do.

The real question though is can I forgive myself?

CHAPTER THREE

Ryan

I don't know what's worse. Knowing she's missing or finding out that my worst fears have come true and she's in Hell.

Coping has been extremely difficult for me since she vanished but I somehow still manage to get up and keep going. I refuse to believe that we wouldn't find her and that eventually she would make her way back to me. I wanted her to see that in her absence I hadn't completely given up. There wasn't anything I wouldn't do for her and continuing to live when every part of me wants to do anything but seems like the right way to honor her until she comes back to me.

Being told that she's in hell, a place that I have been on more than one occasion just made all of what I am already feeling that much worse. When people speak of a fate worse than death they aren't just coming up with a line, it's very true. Hell is the fate that is worse than death and as much as I want her to be found alive and have her come back, I wanted death for her more because there is no way even with as strong as she is, she would survive that fate.

I spent a good portion of my life topside because of my differences, or at least that's what I like to believe given that Lucifer made a point of not letting me spend much time at home with him. I wasn't like the other demons because I still had a soul and a very human purpose where they did not. All they had to do is complete tasks handed down by the man himself and go on their merry way.

So while I might not have spent a great deal of time there, I was aware of what went on once you enter and it is something I never wanted anyone I know to see, least of all Serenity. Even with the knowledge I have now about my true heritage, she is still the brightest light that Heaven has ever created and she was not meant for the horror and darkness her time in Hell would instill in her.

What disturbed me even more was the Almighty not wanting to do a damn thing to change her fate. I realize that things hadn't exactly gone according to plan and that if blame were to be placed it would fall on Serenity but it doesn't mean she needs to be completely written off which is essentially what he was doing. At least that's the way Michael made it sound. No, it didn't sit right with me at all. Just what kind of God is he?

When he appeared to me, I had been reminded of the last time he'd shown up in front of me, when Serenity had been by my side. It didn't matter how crazy things had turned after it, I still looked at that memory and smiled. She could never handle the full magnitude of the angels appearing in front of her and the reaction was always entertaining. I found myself wanting that again instead of the emptiness I have now.

*****

"Don't you guys ever knock? I mean I could have easily been naked here."

"I assure you, we make sure of that before we arrive so there is no need to knock. Have I mentioned how thankful I am that you finally moved yourself out of Serenity's dorm room?"

"Yeah, I think you've commended me on that more than once. I still don't see why I had to leave."

It's no secret that when Serenity vanished I'd taken up residence in her dorm room. It didn't make Emma very happy at first but the longer Serenity seemed to stay away she became used to it. I guess she was finally able to see it for what it is. I needed to be there in order to remain as close to her as possible. Moving away would mean disconnecting and that is just something I couldn't do. Being away now is hard but necessary.

"You told me on more than one occasion that at any given moment Emma Daniels could make her presence known and I am not like my brother, I refuse to remain locked in someone's mind for any extended period of time."

"Well making an appointment in my head could have worked that out."

31

"When did you become a doctor's office Ryan? When I need to speak with you I will appear to you and do as I need."

"Yeah I know which is why I'm in my own room now. So what brings you here?"

"Serenity has been located."

For as long as I could remember I have been longing to hear those words. For Gabriel or Michael to come to me much the way the elder angel is now and tell me that all of my prayers were answered and she was found safe and sound. It's only recently I began to lose hope that I'd ever hear it.

"Where is she? Is she alright?"

"I am afraid it is much worse than we expected. She is indeed alive, as you already know but she resides with Lucifer in Hell."

"She what?" I ask unable to properly process his words.

"When she disappeared from our vision in the church that evening Lucifer took her to Hell."

"No, No, No. She can't be in Hell. She's not meant for that. Your father has to be wrong or he's being duped. Serenity is not there with him."

I could not allow myself to believe in this. When she wanted to sacrifice herself for Graham I knew it was a possibility which is why I tried so hard to get her to see reason. She was too good to be in hell. She wouldn't survive it.

"As much as I do not want to be the bearer of this news I am afraid it is very true. Gabriel has also confirmed it for me."

"Well we have to get her out. We can't let her stay there."

"I agree. I attempted to garner our father's assistance but it appears as though he wants no part of it."

"Okay wait…you're telling me that God knows she's trapped in hell and he doesn't want to do everything in his power to get her out?"

It isn't often you witness an angel expressing sorrow and pain but Michael was doing it now. I could tell with the way he bowed his head that what he said was the truth and he wasn't having the easiest time dealing with it. His father had turned his back on Serenity, something that until this very moment I thought would be impossible.

"Our father has not been right for some time now. I should have known where he would stand on this issue but I hoped to be able to get through to him."

"So if God himself isn't going to help us, how the hell are we going to get her out? You do know that there are levels to hell right and that they are extremely difficult to penetrate when you are not one of them?"

"I am aware of all of that Ryan but I do not care. I have to do whatever it takes."

Well at least we agree on that. It didn't matter if anyone helped me but I would do whatever I had to do to get her out of there before she really was lost to me forever. Knowing Lucifer the way I do, I knew it wouldn't be very much longer before that came true.

"Well, what do you need from me? I won't let you go through this alone."

"I was hoping you would say that because what I need to ask of you, well really what Gabriel and I both need from you is quite extensive and could threaten the very life you lead in this moment."

"I don't care about my life here. I care about bringing her home before Lucifer kills her. What do you need?"

"We need you to be the one to infiltrate hell. No one knows as much as you do about it and given your heritage, your true calling, we feel that you are the very person we need in order to achieve what we all want."

"You want me to do what we should have done in the church that night?"

"No, well yes, though not in the way that we would have done that night. We will all be going with you and we will all have our roles to play in saving Serenity but you are the knowledge base and we need to use you so that we can prepare accordingly."

"Who do you mean by all?"

"Gabriel, myself and though you will not like it, Graham Hudson."

He's right, I didn't like it but what Michael wasn't expecting is that I understood it. I know why Graham needs to be there just

33

as much as I know the reasoning that it had to be these two angels side by side with me. We all cared about her in our own way which made us the only ones suitable for the job.

"When the time comes Ryan we will need you to be the one to end Lucifer once and for all, even though I realize that goes along with Father's destiny for you and will end your human existence. I do not want to ask that of you now though. For now we just need to make a plan for getting her out. Everything else can come later."

"When do we start"

*****

There was a time not so long ago where I lived for following Lucifer and the thought of him being defeated was something I could just not process. It still managed to amaze me how quickly things changed. All it took is the love of a beautiful ball of Heavenly light and I suddenly knew what side I really wanted to be on and what needs to be done.

I know that in ending Lucifer's reign over Serenity and the rest of the world it would end my human life. It would secure the world in a long term way but it would essentially put an end to any real living I might have with the girl of my dreams. I came to terms with it months ago. I couldn't allow myself to be selfish all because I finally found what I spent my entire life searching for.

She wouldn't want me to do that, it isn't the way she operates. As much as she might hate to say goodbye to me, at some point we would have to and in the end I know she'd understand why I had to make the choice I did. The life of millions has to mean more than just the life of one. I would do whatever needs to be done to make that happen.

Even at my own expense.

I have the knowledge of the levels of Hell. What we would need to go through and defeat before finally reaching where Lucifer no doubt held her prisoner. I would guide the angels and even Graham through everything that I could remember of it and we would put our lives on the line in order to save her. That's the right thing to do even though God seems to think otherwise. We were about to exert our free will and there was no room for failure.

We would succeed in bringing Serenity out alive and I would spend every minute living and loving her until it was time for me to finally put an end to Lucifer once and for all. He has roamed the earth for far too long, it's time that someone put an end to the horror he lives to create.

I only hope that when the time came for me to come face to face with Serenity again that she wouldn't be too far gone. I needed to save her and know that I was doing the right thing. That I would be saving the light I had fallen in love with and not the soulless being Lucifer would no doubt leave behind.

I couldn't and wouldn't settle for anything less than my Serenity.

CHAPTER FOUR

Graham

I have a lot to make up for now that I'm back even though I wasn't entirely sure the things I'd done six months prior can be made up for.

Sure there is the argument that I wasn't exactly myself and that I couldn't be held responsible for the things I had done and put people through while under Lucifer's control. I can't accept that though. The only place the blame should land for everything that happened is at my doorstep. In control or not I still did it all.

There's a tie for worst thing I have ever done between the way I treated Emma and all of the random girls I fooled around with. I have no idea where to even start making up for my actions with the girls I used but I definitely wanted to try with Emma. I didn't just owe it to the girl herself but Serenity as well.

Ryan telling me what she suspected bothers me. Even though I'm positive Emma knew everything that had taken place between Serenity and I before she'd gone to school and after she had to know that I wouldn't have just run off with her. Even being possessed by the devil himself I never would have done that.

Watching her as she made her way into the Arts building, I know this is my chance. I wasn't entirely sure how I would handle it if Emma were to approach me first so I have to be the one to do it. I can control the outcome better that way and maybe even begin to make up for all the damage I caused the last time we'd been together.

"Emma! Wait up!" I call out and watch as she stops before spinning around on her heel to face me. Where she looked almost calm before I spoke, now she looks anything but. It's obvious that what happened between her and I when Lucifer had control is still paramount in her mind. Something I hate but have to dispel.

"Graham, I thought we'd seen the last of you."

"Sorry to disappoint."

She rolled her eyes at my comment and despite not wanting to let her reactions get to me; I found them doing just that. I didn't want this girl to hate me but it was inevitable. I had practically raped her the last time we were this close. It wasn't exactly something one could easily brush off.

"What do you want Graham? I really need to get to class."

Well it's now or never. When you've got nothing left to lose it's easy to go all in with any given situation and this was me about to go all in.

"I'm heading that way too, English Lit right? I thought we could walk together."

"You're kidding right?" she asks, leveling me with her distrusting eyes.

"Dead serious princess. Look I know the last time we were around each other didn't exactly go the best but I'm hoping you'll let me apologize for it and maybe we can move on."

Where she had been ready to turn and run from me minutes before, she seems conflicted about her approach now. I can tell she sees the truth that I wasn't trying to bullshit her but she isn't quite where I need her to be yet. I still have a move I need to play.

"I know how much Serenity means to you and I think you know that she means that much to me, if not more, so for her sake, can we please just move past this? I was a complete jackass to you and I would really like the chance to make up for it."

She's softening to me; I can see it as her face begins releasing the tension that had been held there when she saw me coming toward her. Name dropping isn't exactly my style but if I want to get through to Emma I know I'm going to have to use drastic measures. Nothing else would work.

"Well come on, let's get going or we're gonna be late. As legendary as I am for my lateness, I'm actually trying to be better about it."

"English Lit is where you wanna try being different?"

"Better then Psych. At least the English professor doesn't try and get inside my head."

"I hear you." I say with a laugh. "I've already got enough things going on in my head. I don't need any more."

We walk in silence to the class but where I would expect it to be uncomfortable due to the history, it isn't. It's probably the most peaceful walk I've had since before Lucifer had taken me over. It didn't stop the ache in my chest knowing that I was walking with Serenity's best friend and not Serenity herself but it did numb it just a little which given the way I've been feeling, I need.

"Graham..."

Well it was comfortable anyway.

I am not going to do this now. I had finally gotten Emma to a point where she is trusting me enough to walk with me, the last thing I want to do is give her a reason to doubt my sincerity and talking to an angel, whether in my head or not is just not going to help.

"At your earliest convenience we need to speak. Please contact me when you are free."

Just as easily as he had been in my mind he seemed to vanish from it, leaving me to breathe a small sigh of relief. As awesome as it might appear to other people to be able to communicate with angels, it is definitely annoying that they never seem to check before just popping in for a visit.

"Graham, are you alright?" Emma asked, bringing me back to the present and the fact that sometime between walking to class and Gabriel appearing in my mind, I completely stopped walking. No wonder she's concerned.

"Yeah, I'm fine, just a lot on my mind."

"You sure you don't want to start taking Psych after all?" she answered back with a smile.

I've never noticed it before but Emma has a really nice smile. Considering every time I'd been around her it had been because of Serenity it's no surprise I hadn't noticed until now but no weirder then the fact that I'm noticing at all. With everything going on the last thing I need to be doing is checking out her best friend.

"I've had all the head shrinking I can take thanks." I say chucking. She has no idea what I've gone through over the last year. That was more than enough for anyone to take. "Come on, I don't want to screw up your chance to look reformed of prior bad habits."

Leveling me with the brightest smile I've ever seen, complete with a punch on the arm she began jogging toward the class, leaving me no other choice but push the way it felt out of my mind and run to catch up.

Just what the hell is going on with me?

Gabriel

When I agreed to split up from Michael and leave him to speak with Ryan while I did the same with Graham I had not expected to come across what I am now witnessing.

Graham and Emma speaking and neither one of them displaying any awkwardness is definitely something I had not seen coming. The last time they had been around one another Graham had been under Lucifer's control and it had not gone well. Not only had he gone out of his way to make her feel uncomfortable but he also admitted to admiring her in a way that she was unaccustomed to.

He may believe that he hadn't actually been in control of the way he acted but that is not accurate. While Lucifer did have him under the strictest control he had still given Graham free reign in regards to dealing with the people around him. If he hadn't felt it then it wouldn't have happened. He had been attracted to the Daniels girl; it is as obvious as the bond between him and Serenity.

Given the way that Emma looked at him the day Ryan had shown up in their dorm room I would never have expected her to soften the way in which she is with him though it was also common knowledge that while she had done her best to spurn his advances, he had been right on the money when he accused her of being attracted to him. As it is with Emma though her loyalty won out.

It would seem that in Serenity's absence, both of their ways of being are changing. I know I should be taking more care with this given what I am about to ask him to do but right now leaning on Graham where Emma is concerned is not high on my priority list. All I need is for him to agree or disagree in helping us bring Serenity home.

There is no doubt that out of all of us he is the most at risk if he does agree to help. He is strictly human with no trace of the previous darkness that was inside of him remaining and his skill level is limited. There is one thing about Graham that could not be disputed though and that was his bond to the very person we were about to go in and save.

Ryan would do everything in his power to get us where we needed to be but it would be Graham and his hold over her that would bring her around to us if her time with Lucifer had changed her in the way I imagined. Michael and I may have the power to do anything we wish but in this regard, no matter how much mind control we manage to wield over her, the final decision will still be hers alone.

If her light is gone than her decision would not be one that is favorable to us and in order for this to work effectively we need it to be that way. I could only hope that Graham would be willing to walk into the fire again, especially after the ordeal he just started recovering from.

When I had taken him out and healed him to the best of my ability, proceeding to leave him in the hospital in Green Haven I was positive that this would be the last time I would ever need him. That finally he would be safe from Lucifer's clutches and would be able to move on with his life, Serenity being missing or not. After putting him in the position to begin with it is the least I could do for him. Yet here we are again and he is integral to what we want to accomplish.

"What did you need Gabe?"

His voice came to me crystal clear and I was thankful I hadn't had to wait too long for a response. If Michael and I were to move forward then time really was of the essence.

"There has been a new development and it is imperative that I speak with you about it. Is your location safe?"

"No, I'm in class. Do you really need to appear to tell me what's going on?"

It is a valid question. I do not have to appear in order to pass along the information I learned but I wanted to so that there could be no doubt in his mind of the validity of what I would be telling him.

"No I suppose it is not imperative that I appear to you but what I have to say will change everything."

"Then just tell me man. I need some good news right about now don't you think?"

While this could be considered some form of good news I know it will not be the news he wants or needs to hear. While we were one step closer to locating Serenity it was still not a done deal and the last thing I want to do is get anyone's hopes up. While we have a basic plan of action, there is still no guarantee to its success.

"It is regarding Serenity."

"Shit, I really do need to leave class don't I? What about her?"

He is eager there was no doubt of that. He needed to remain where he was though at least until we were ready to move forward. It would be then that we would need to come together and begin and not a second before.

"She has been located."

CHAPTER FIVE

Ryan

Hell is not that much different then Heaven, at least with the way that things appear once you have been allowed entrance. You see what is the most pleasing to your eye when you're in Heaven and while there isn't a pleasing thing about Hell to anyone who isn't a demon it's much the same there. You see it almost in the way you see the world except darker and more broken down.

There is nothing made of light there, except the people that were dragged down against their will. Lucifer wanted it that way. Everything had to be shrouded in darkness in order for it to be a true home for him. Where you see brightness and beauty when you're high among the clouds, you see the opposite there.

I haven't been there in a long time but the one thing I know is that it never changes. While more demons might begin to occupy the space, the way it's run always remains the same. We would need dark magic in order to reach it, something I wasn't entirely sure Michael and Gabriel have much experience with but something I am more than willing to teach them if it means getting Serenity back.

What would await us wouldn't be pretty but it wouldn't be a problem until we passed through the first few levels we needed to pass in order to reach the man himself. He has lower level demons guarding the entrances, which never really made sense to me but I wasn't stupid enough to question it during my time there. If anything that would work in our favor as we made our way forward.

Gabriel followed through with his end, reaching out to Graham and securing his place in the plan. I am not a fan of them using the soul mate bond in order to save Serenity but there are just some things I have to accept and realize that without them we wouldn't have a shot at all of getting what we want. So as much as I hate it, I also embrace it. He would get through to her with the bond if it came up and in the meantime, we would all do what we had to in order to make sure he stayed alive.

Graham is completely human which means that his experience with Hell will not be a good one. He would crack quickly if we didn't remain vigilant in watching over him, guarding from the true evil he would witness the moment we touched down. I have no doubt that it is much the same with Serenity even though we all knew she isn't entirely human. She relied on her humanity more than the angelic parts of herself which meant that in the end, she would be tortured just as badly as Graham would be.

"I've got a question."

Once classes let out we all agreed to meet in my dorm room and after going over everything we knew, it's time for the true planning to begin. Graham has taken everything he's heard with a grain of salt which I can't help but admire but now he had questions. If he needs answers then that meant he isn't entirely comfortable with what we are going to do which means that while he might have the light in him, he wasn't entirely prepared for everything it would bring.

The more I thought about it, I wasn't either. I don't think anyone can every truly be prepared for what we're being dealt.

"How does power work in Hell? Will Michael and Gabriel be able to use it or are they cut off once they enter?"

With as much information as I have about Lucifer and Hell, I have to hand it to Graham. He asked the one question I don't have an answer for. There has never been an angel that I witnessed with my own eyes entering the darkness and using their power. I have to assume that Lucifer would have guarded against it but nothing is clear with the fallen angel anymore.

Turning to the angels, I wait for them to give the answers Graham wants and that I find myself wanting as well. Having angels that were able to use their powers going forward is something we definitely needed.

"It would appear as though our brother has not guarded himself against our power in the place he considers home. We are able to use our powers there but they are in a decreased capacity."

Michael answered, his answer almost rehearsed as if he'd been expecting it.

"So you're not running at full power but at least you've got some. That's a good thing right?"

Both angels nodded and I just shrugged. I do believe that power of any kind is great but going in with full power is always still the better option. While we still might be able to pull this off without full usage, it wasn't going to be easy.

"We are going to reach the lost souls first, the wanderers. Those that while inherently dark have not accepted their fate. They will be easy to eliminate. As will the lower level demons that will be waiting for us after that. It's only when we reach the stronger demons, the ones that Lucifer has actually spent time grooming that we run into the issues."

"What kind of issues?" Graham questioned. "I thought Lucifer would be the worst of it."

"Demons have a thirst like no other being before them which is why they feed so willingly on humans. When we enter the third level we are running straight into those types. They haven't fed in a long time and we're like juicy steaks. They have strength of which the earth has never seen before and they will use it for just a small taste of any of you." I answer motioning around the room to both Graham and the angels.

"If we can defeat them, we're only two steps away from Lucifer. The next level is not as driven by thirst and hunger but they are by hatred and pure evil. They appreciate the art of torture like no other demon in the world. Lucifer planned it that way. In order to get to him you must get through the torture chambers he has set up down there. This is the place where any being of light that has ever tried to pass through failed."

"Not making it through is not an option." Michael stated simply. It's a statement I agree with whole heartedly. We had to get through all of the death and destruction hell offered to get Serenity. Failure is not an option. We were to succeed where every other being before us has failed.

"The only real issue I see is keeping Graham safe throughout." I admit. "Don't get pissed at me man but you are human and what you're about to go through is going to do things to you that will make Lucifer possessing you look like a walk in the park. If you're going to help us with Serenity then we have to make sure none of it affects you."

"That is where we can come in." Michael spoke up. "We have the power to level you in protection, at least as much as possible in order for you to remain guarded throughout the ordeal."

I nodded in agreement. I know what the angels were capable of. I may be one of them and capable of the same things, at least according to God but it didn't seem real to me, so for now they would most definitely be needed in order to protect Graham the way we need him to be.

"So after the torture demons, we get to the man himself right?"

"Yes Graham. There are many layers and levels to hell but with the way we are planning to go, it would be after that where we would reach Lucifer's main base of operations. This is where he enjoys his own brand of maiming, torture and killing. I have no doubt that is where he's keeping Serenity."

Just thinking about the way he was when I had been with him turned my stomach. Serenity witnessing any of that didn't sit right with me. I had barely been able to stomach it and I'd been a part of it for a very long time. Someone who has no real knowledge of it and has spent the majority of their life sheltered from all things truly evil would break much more quickly. I really hate that this is what happened to her.

"She isn't gonna be the same is she?" Graham whispered quietly, obviously going through the same motion of thought as I am in regard to just what the girl we both loved is handling in an effort to keep the world level.

"No. I know we all want her to be the same Serenity but she won't be. Graham wasn't himself when Lucifer was inside him and did things completely out of character. If he is forcing Serenity to do the same then I have no doubt that she will never be the same again. The only good thing is that maybe he hasn't broken her yet."

"She is stronger than most and she will withstand a great deal before he gets his way." Gabriel agreed, stating what everyone in the room already believed to be the truth.

"Well I believe now that we know what to expect we need to move forward. Any extra time spent here is just sealing her fate even more. We cannot let Lucifer do any more damage to our ball of light."

I could tell by the way Gabriel's light shifted in the room that what Michael said upset him. I'm not entirely sure what's going on between the two angels but whatever it is, we needed to deal with it before going into Hell. If they went in acting this way than we wouldn't make it out alive. The darkness would feed on it and make it worse until it wouldn't be demons killing us but each other.

"We're not going anywhere until you two sort out your shit."

Graham threw me a look of confusion and I motioned toward the angels in explanation. I knew that he wouldn't get it but given what I'm seeing, we need to deal with it now even if we didn't entirely understand it.

"What do you think they need to sort out?" he asked.

"Michael just said something and Gabriel reacted. There is something more going on that we're not aware of man and until they get it out and handle it, we're not going anywhere. I'm not putting my life, your life or even Serenity's life on the line because these two can't get along."

I could tell he agreed with me as his body language changed as he faced the angels, braced for whatever would happen next. I wasn't looking to draw battle lines, especially when we were on the same side but I wasn't about to sit here and lie about what I'd seen either.

"There is nothing going on between Michael and me."

"There was a time when I thought angels weren't able to lie but I swear to god man the more time I spend around you, it seems that is all you do. You lie and deflect. That isn't going to fly here."

"He's been like that since the first time he came to me." Graham spoke, which only proved my point even more. I'm not the only one that's aware of the fact that the angels didn't operate in the most upright way.

"You don't want to be like your father, you want to run on free will but all you're doing is proving just how alike you all are to him and to the way Heaven is really run. So you wanna tell me what the hell is going on here, or do Graham and I move forward with the plan without you?"

It was a risk, pushing them this way but if there is one angel I would get through to with it, it's Gabriel. There is no way he was going to let us go through with saving Serenity without him. He cared about her as much as Graham and I did combined. He needed to be there.

"You are correct Ryan; there is a disconnection between my brother and me." Michael stated, taking me off guard, expecting Gabriel to be the one to break first.

"Well then fix it because if you don't then those demons we're about to go fight are going to sense it and use it until you are unable to handle it or yourselves anymore. This isn't about some petty beef between the two of you. This is as life and death as it gets."

Graham

There are a lot of similarities between the angels and us. There is the most obvious one of us being connected because of Serenity but there is also the one less obvious in that we all had feelings in our own way for the girl affectionately known as Heaven's little ball of light. Add that into our need to do the right thing for the world and by her and the four of us teaming up the way we are isn't entirely surprising.

I didn't realize it until Ryan called them out but there is most definitely something going on between the two brothers. They had each come to us separately instead of together the way I would have assumed they would have and now Gabriel could barely look his brother in the eye. It might be hard for a human to take in the light when in the presence of an angel but when in their own company that wasn't a problem.

47

When it comes to the power contained in the room right now, I seem to be the odd man out. I'm just as Ryan and even the angels have referred to me, completely human. I can offer nothing to them other then my knowledge of Lucifer from my time with him and the bond that Serenity and I share. I might have superior strength against other people like me but in terms of taking on the full load of hell, I'm a weakling.

There is one area I'm not weak in though and it made me the most knowledgeable person in the room. Ryan didn't realize what was going on though the way he spoke to the angels meant that he didn't much care. Just knowing something is wrong was enough for him. I knew the reason why everything was turning out the way it is. I wanted the angels themselves to be the ones to admit to it though.

It all comes back to the way I feel about Ryan. This guy despite being part demon, managed to work his way into Serenity's heart and earn not only her trust but her love as well. The very human part of me wants to hate him for it and being driven by that particular feeling makes it extremely difficult to hear anything he has to say, no matter how right he is. I am jealous of what he shares with her because it is exactly what I want, just without all the pain that comes along with it.

I see that exact thing in Gabriel now. He is angry and jealous but it isn't directed toward Ryan and me the way I would expect it to be given our relationship with Serenity. It's directed at his brother which means that for whatever reason, he believes Michael to have feelings for the little ball of light and he is unable to handle them the way the rest of us seem to be.

There is a connection between Serenity and Gabriel, one that surpasses human existence and is strictly meant for the other side. They have been bonded together for as long as they have existed in much the same kind of way that her and I have been. Where I can be with her in this lifetime, and any other lifetimes we may live together, he is resigned to waiting until it's his time and I think knowing that, especially given everything that is happening now is finally getting to him.

Angels are supposed to be strong warriors, not being guided by emotion, instead focusing on the task at hand and seeing it through to its conclusion. Gabriel is wired differently. I knew that from the very first time I met him in Green Haven and it's exactly the same now. He isn't human but he seems almost guided by the same things I am. I'm sure that is why I was the perfect host for him, just how alike we really are.

"Gabriel is jealous." I said, allowing what I believed to be the truth fall from my lips no matter what the reaction might be. If Ryan isn't fearful of what the two angels might do then I wasn't going to be either. They needed us whether they like what we have to say or not.

"He's what?" Ryan asked looking up at the sound of my words. "Jealous of who?"

"I gotta figure Michael. If it was us he would have already thrown eye daggers our way and so far, I'm still standing."

"Eye daggers huh?" Ryan laughed. "He done that to you before?"

"Yeah, it's his thing. I don't mean to make light of it but it's obvious."

"You have no idea what you are speaking about Graham and I would suggest you keep your nose out of things you do not understand."

"Yeah okay grumpy pants. You're just pissed because I'm right. You wanna know what the truth is? Michael cares about Serenity, maybe the same as we do, or maybe differently and it just pisses you off because just like with me and Ryan, you want her all to yourself and can't handle anyone else having feelings of any kind in her direction."

By the look on Ryan's face it's obvious he didn't expect me to voice my opinion. Gabriel could tell me to butt out all he wants but I'm not going to do it. Not when the very thing I'm talking about could mean our death moving forward.

"Gabriel, do not be upset with the human. He's only speaking a truth that you cannot."

"See? Your own brother knows what this is."

"Someone wanna fill me in on just what the hell is going on here?" Ryan asked, his eyes continuously going back and forth between the angels and me in an effort to figure out just how out of the loop he is.

"It's pretty clear with what I just said. Gabriel's need to see this through is nothing more than selfish because he wants to be the one to save Serenity so that he can be with her. It's the whole beloved bond coming full circle or whatever. Michael wants to save her for probably the purest reasons out of all of us yet he's the one getting shit on for it."

"Though Graham is using wording in which I am not accustomed nor enjoy he is correct. Gabriel believes me to be in love with Serenity but what he doesn't seem to understand is, I've gotten to know the girl after spending time with her over the last year and I have come to view her as a sister. I want to save her the same as I would want to save Gabriel himself."

"So I was right then." Ryan interjected leveling Gabriel with his angry glare. "You two need to work out your shit."

"Yes it would appear that we do." Michael replies.

"Then do it. We'll get out of here but guys work it out quick, we got a girl that needs our full attention right now."

If it wasn't happening right in front of my eyes I never would have believed it was possible. Ryan and I working together in an attempt to mend fences between the angels makes no sense. We both love the same girl and we despise each other for what we mean to her but in the moment it's as if we are on the same page the way it should be.

Maybe it's time that the way we are with each other changed. The angels aren't the only ones that need to rectify their issues. We do too and this seems like a pretty good place to start.

CHAPTER SIX

Serenity

I can feel myself slipping away.

Despite all the strength I've shown in my attempt to keep myself grounded it's happening and I am starting to feel powerless to stop it. He said it was only a matter of time before the way of life here would change me and while I'd done my best not to believe him I'm beginning to realize it's impossible to deny.

The more he puts me through, both with the blood and the taking of each soul's power I feel myself falling away. The parts of me that make me who I truly am are beginning to fade and are slowly being replaced with the darkness Lucifer wants me to embrace so heavily.

It's in these moments where I try to get back to the core of who and what I am. I picture the way my life was as a young girl before my father left, how happy I'd been and I use it to combat the sorrow I'm drowning in.

My parents never had the perfect relationship but from the pictures I've seen, the love letters I've found and read over the years growing up, I know that at some point they were happier than I ever thought possible. There isn't much I can remember about my time with my father given that he left when I was so young but I do remember the encompassing feeling of being adored. He did love me like no other. Even if in the end he did take off.

This is what I want to focus on, the happy feeling of childhood where anything that went bump in the night could be taken away with a few small words from a parent that loves you unconditionally. Right now it is the only thing keeping me level and I pray that it lasts for just a little longer.

I know that there are people out there, both in the world itself and in Heaven that are looking for me and they won't stop until I'm found again. It's what makes all of this almost bearable. Even after going against the plan that day they won't give up on me and it has nothing to do with the fact that they love me or because I'm special. It's because it is just who they are.

My family.

I've been having this conflict lately with what I chose to do and what was actually accomplished. Like whether or not it was a good thing overall. Could I have handled it differently and if so would I be where I am now if I had?

Being able to free Graham from his grasp is something I will never feel bad for. I did the right thing for him. I didn't realize what would happen next but how many people do when they find themselves in a life or death situation? I just knew I had to save him and I would gladly do it all over again if it meant that Graham could be free to live a long and happy life. He deserves that.

Coming to terms with my choice and where the real conflict comes into it is that I lied by omission in order to do what I thought was the right thing. I hid my real intention from not only Gabriel and Michael but Ryan too. I've always prided myself on not being a liar, even if it is by omission so now, living with the decision I made that day is hard.

Will it stop them from doing whatever it takes to save me? No. They will come for me; it's only a matter of when that's going to be. I want to stay strong as long as it takes and come back to them as strong as ever but with the way things have been happening lately I'm starting to think that might not be possible.

I'm enjoying myself even when I'm using all of my power and strength not to. Whatever Lucifer is trying to do in bringing me with him and forcing me to do these things in order to be a true dark princess, it's actually working. That's the last thing I want. I want to hate this but the more time that passes I'm finding it harder and harder to do.

I just hope I don't have to wait too much longer because if I do, I know I won't go back the same person I was when I came here. I will be forever changed and that scares the ever living shit out of me.

"You must stop fighting the inevitable Serenity. It will only make things harder for your moving forward."

This isn't the first time he's said this, I knew it wouldn't be the last either. He was right in that giving myself over would be easier for both of us but it doesn't mean I have to do it. In fact that is the very last thing I want to do, despite my body telling me otherwise.

"I know what you get out of seeing me do all of this but what I don't get is the reason why."

"You want to know why I have chosen you as the one to stand beside me to rule all of this?" he asks motioning around us.

"I guess so, yeah. I know that you want my power and even though you failed you almost had it once already. So what's stopping you from just taking it that same way now? Having to drag me around with you and watch me change slowly can't be what you signed up for."

"I could easily just drain you of your power dear Serenity. I find though that the more time that passes both here and on Earth, I want something more. We have had this conversation before have we not? You believe my every move to be inherently evil but I assure you, it isn't."

"So I'm your something more?"

"I want someone to share this life with. It does become quite lonely after a time. I thought I had that person in Ryan but it would appear I was wrong as it pertained to him."

His expression is pained and I felt the sympathetic part of me rise up in response, immediately starting to push it back down. He is the last person I want to feel sympathy for. All he's ever done since the moment he entered my life is create death and destruction and more than that, pain. He didn't deserve sympathy.

"You want to feel for me, I can sense it in you. Embrace it Serenity, for it is not as wrong as you believe it to be. At one point you must remember that I was one of Heaven's most trusted. There is nothing I would not have done for my father and brothers. I may have questioned things beyond the normal scope but I loved unconditionally, much like you do."

Damn it.

I do not want to feel for him even if he wants me to. I need to remember he is the sick bastard that had almost taken my life and actually had taken Ryan's. The person that possessed Graham and made him do unspeakable things while under his control. I could not bend to this but damn do I want to.

"So you chose me for this because we love the same?"

He seemed to think over my question before answering which did nothing for the feeling of unease growing deep inside me.

"Yes…partially. You and I are not that different overall Serenity. We love and care deeply for those few people we let close enough to truly know us. Our strength is unmatched even though sometimes we may appear to be different then the world around us. We were both born of the very same light and even now when we are at our darkest point we still have it burning deep. There could be no one but you for me."

"You make it all sound so perfect yet I think you know that it isn't."

"But it can be and the more time you spend here with me, you will see it just as I do. I do not bring you through these trials with me because I wish to torture you Serenity. I just want to share my life with you and prepare you for what it means to be my other half."

I waited to feel the bile rising in my throat at being called his other half but it never came. I don't know if it's because his words are getting to me on a level they couldn't before or because my sympathy button has been activated but whatever the reason, the sickness I should have felt wasn't there.

Ryan was right when he said that Lucifer is better than the angels just based on the fact that you always knew up front what you were getting. He is nothing if not brutally honest, even if he went about it in the wrong way.

"Do you want me to admit that draining the life force from these victims is getting to me? That drinking the blood does things to my body that as much as I want to control it I can't? Is that what it takes to get you off?"

"You will soon lose the vulgarity that your human existence instilled in you. It is most unbecoming of someone of your stature but to answer your question, it does please me to hear that you are

54

reacting to what I have been putting you through. It means that we are one step closer to the overall goal."

"What's the overall goal?" I question as I prepare myself mentally for his response. Up until now I thought the end goal was to rule Hell with him but the way he sounds now there is something much more sinister on the horizon and I can't go another step forward until I know what that is.

"Do you hear me?!" I snapped. "What are you going to make me do?"

"You will be mine in every possible way and you will be the very thing that ends what is left of the world and the light that still inhabits it."

Gabriel

I have never been good at hiding my feelings. They always seem to bleed over into every single facet of my existence so it is no surprise that Graham and Ryan had been able to pick up on it so easily. It appears as though Michael was right in his earlier assessment of what my true worth was. I am the one that was made to feel and experience life both when on Earth and otherwise. I would always be this way no matter what happened next.

Explaining in any detail why I held onto the belief system I did as it pertained to my brother and Serenity would be impossible because there are times where it doesn't even make sense to me. Michael had explained to me on previous occasions what he truly felt for her and while I want to believe him with everything in me, I am just unable to do so.

"The humans are right brother. We need to handle this before we move forward."

"You know my belief Michael and try as I might I am unable to entirely let go of it. How can we move forward if that is the case?"

"It's easy Gabriel. You trust in me and what I am telling you and we move forward. I want her home again, not because I am in love with her as you believe but because it is where she belongs. She is not meant for this fate and I know that you know it."

I do know it. I want her home possibly more than the others given that I had known something was off with her before we put the plan in motion but I'd blocked it in an effort to trust and believe in her. She did deserve much better than the fate of Hell.

"I have a Beloved and our connection runs deep. I would never dream of breaking that bond with Faith in order to pursue something that is against what has been written. You are aware of my belief system so why fight it so hard?"

"I do not have the answer to that question Michael."

The way in which Heaven operates dictates that each of us has a Beloved. It could be likened to the soul mate bond a great deal but was not entirely the same. Each of my brothers has found theirs. Michael did indeed have Faith; Uriel had his in Aurora and Raphael with Mary. I am the last remaining brother to experience it.

Michael speaking of Faith and witnessing the way his heavenly light seemed to grow infinitely brighter at the mere mention of her name brought to focus the real truth of the matter. My brother was not trying to get with the being destined for me, instead he is doing as he admitted and caring for her the way a brother does with a younger sister.

I need to accept that for the reality that it is. I just wasn't at all sure how to begin. What should just be known and realized is not happening for me in this regard.

"I believe I know why you feel the way in which you do."

If he has answers then even though I am still experiencing the on edge feeling around him I am more than open to hearing them. In fact, I definitely need to hear them. It really is the only way we would be able to move forward.

"I am as they say, all ears brother."

"When we all came into contact with our other halves, it happened in Heaven and there is nothing that stood between us and them. In your case it is not that cut and dry. You have two other suitors for her hand and I believe because of that you perceive everything that pertains to her as a threat to the bond between you two."

"I do believe you may be on to something there Michael. I want nothing more than to have the connection that our brothers have with their beloved and you as well with your counterpart in Faith. It appears though that achieving that ultimate goal is impossible for me."

"I might have the answer to that as well little brother."

"Since when did you become as all knowing as our father?"

Michael has always been the one in Heaven that works side by side with Father in whatever endeavor crosses their paths but I have never seen him quite this knowledgeable. Even though we were on the outs where the Almighty is concerned, he was channeling him strongly in this moment. There could be no denial of the things he brought to light.

"It was only a matter of time before everything I have learned while working with him paid off Gabriel. As it pertains to your situation though I do believe I have the answer. Finding your beloved has been harder than most because I do believe Father wanted to teach you a lesson before being able to obtain it."

"You think our father set it up this way?"

"Given everything that we now know about him can you really believe anything else?"

Michael made a valid point. Things with Father have become increasingly difficult as of late and I really couldn't discount the theory that in an effort to teach me some kind of a lesson he had taken the road he did in terms of Serenity and the bond we share. It didn't make sense but then nothing he has been doing lately seems to. My hope is that Michael is incorrect, at least in this regard.

"I am sorry. I am beginning to believe that you may have a point and the reason for my overreaction has more to do with the hand that I have been dealt and less to do with you as I have made it seem."

"The time for apologies is long past Gabriel. I understand the position you are in and I hold no ill will toward you. My only goal throughout this entire process has been to make you see the truth and I hope that now, you may be able to do that, at least enough so that in moving forward we can remain as one."

We needed to remain as one cohesive unit just as Ryan alluded to earlier in order to get Serenity out from the literal hell she found herself in and it all depends on me. I know that and with everything that Michael and I have discussed after being given the time alone I felt confident moving forward that I could now do just that. We would get her out alive.

We would not fail.

"Call them back brother. It's time we got started."

CHAPTER SEVEN

Ryan

From the second I heard where Serenity is being held I've wanted to go and get her. I want to do the very thing Michael says seems to be engrained inside of me and sacrifice myself in order to bring her home again. It's almost compulsive, I can't ignore it, even knowing how potentially dangerous it is.

Truthfully, I have always been like this, leaping before thinking things through all the way. It started as a kid when I would attempt things believing I was invincible and then carried over during my time with the devil himself. He called me on it more than once. Where the angels may believe that everything happens in its own time, I want it on my own terms and in my own way, which usually means quickly.

Do I want to jump in head first and save her? More than anything but can I actually do that when it means risking the other three people that are willing to fight alongside of me in order to save her? No.

Gabriel and Michael might have their own issues they need to deal with but they weren't the only ones. I had to confront my need to want to leap before I look and make sure I got it under control before heading into a situation that could potentially end me. I might know Hell better than any of the others but out of all of us, Graham included, I am the one in the most danger heading in.

I have not been back there in a long time and by now I'm sure Lucifer has informed the other demons, ones I used to call brothers just how far I have fallen away from the original plan as far as the world went. That means that now I am public enemy number one and I'll be going in with a big red target on my back. The demon that ends the traitorous half demon will definitely be revered by Lucifer.

I can't let that happen.

"This has to suck for him."

Since we hadn't said much to each other since exiting the room I actually forgot that I wasn't alone. With so much information passing hands and plans being put into motion I actually preferred the quietness of my own head and not the constant chatter around me. I'm not alone though, Graham is here and it seems that now he finally wants to talk to me.

"It has to suck for who? Gabriel?"

"Yeah. I mean think about it man. He's got this whole beloved bond with Serenity, something that was planned in Heaven before she even came down here and now that he knows about it he has to hold it together while she attaches herself to us."

I would be lying if I said that I never thought about the bond that both Gabriel and Graham held with Serenity. I focused on it a lot more then I want to admit but where before I would have let it eat me alive and react based on it, I won't now. They had a bond with her that couldn't be broken but the last moment we spent together I had something much stronger. I was the keeper of her heart.

"I think this situation just sucks all the way around Graham. It isn't just all on Gabriel."

"You're right; it's not all on Gabe. We all have our place where Serenity is concerned but between you and me and now Michael, I think he's dealt with enough."

"Michael isn't in love with Serenity. She's like a baby sister to him. I can see it in his eyes when he talks about saving her or even about what she did in order to save you. He wants to protect her but that's as far as it goes."

Before Lucifer called us to Green Haven to save Graham it started happening and I just went with the flow. I identified with Michael more than Gabriel so when push came to shove I was able to see his point of view more so than any other. I understand his motivations and I think it makes it easier to follow him when he bases his decisions on rational thought and less on emotion, something Gabriel just can't do.

So while Graham could identify with Gabriel because of the way they both think from the emotional end of things, I'm on the

Michael side even though I have the ability to want to run purely on emotions just like everyone else.

"Maybe he's not in love with her but we are and that's double trouble for his bond with her."

"You're pretty obsessed with Gabriel for someone that has his own selfish stake in getting her back. Don't you think we should be dealing with that while they deal with their shit so that we don't have the same problem once we get started?"

It's true. We need to confront this head on. When Graham had come back to school after healing from the Lucifer effect we had almost come to blows in our hatred of each other but from that moment on we bypassed dealing with it. Now with what we face it's the right time to confront it. We both need to go in knowing we are on the same side and not have anything lingering between us.

"You really want to get into this now?"

"It's been almost three months. When do you think would be a good time to confront this? If we go in and they sense we're harboring any residual hatred or upset towards each other then we're as good as dead. The way I figure it; there's no better time than now."

The last thing I want to do is get into a fight in the middle of a college campus full of students but what I told him is right. We need to deal with this now. It meant our life or death.

"Fine, we'll do it your way." He answered, taking a deep breath before continuing. "You know how I feel about her. You're aware of the bond between us but I'm not talking about that. I genuinely love her regardless of any stupid bond Heaven thinks we share. I saw that girl at her worst and all I could focus on was making everything right for her again. I don't want the Serenity that is in constant flight mode because of her differences anymore. I want the one that's not afraid to stay and fight. I want to be the one that stands and fights with her. Happy now?"

I know he's being sarcastic with his final words knowing full well no one would be happy to hear the woman they love is loved so deeply by another man. I had to hear it though because if we were really going to do this then I had to listen to the worst of it and accept it before I could affectively do what I really want.

Saving her.

"Blissfully happy Graham."

"Just remember you asked."

"Let me ask you something and answer me truthfully."

I expected his face to register something, whether it be fear of what I'm about to ask or a look that would show his plan to be dishonest but looking at him now, there is no expression other than his need to get this over with.

"I'll answer whatever you want if it means we can get on with this."

"What's going on with you and Emma?"

The minute his eyes went wide I knew I had him in something he didn't expect. He didn't realize that I caught his little performance with her or that Serenity had explained to me everything that happened in the room with him that day before I'd come back. This is definitely a topic he isn't going to enjoy talking about.

"Nothing is going on with her. I treated the girl like shit and I want the chance to make up for it. End of story."

There is more to the story of course but he wouldn't realize that I knew given that it was just part of the power that still lingered in me. While I might not be as strong as I used to be in terms of what I could actually do, this part has never failed me yet. I could easily sense when there is more under the surface. I wasn't about to push it though.

"Fair enough."

"You don't sound convinced."

"Honestly, I could care less whether it's the truth or not but I was curious."

"What does any of that have to do with Serenity?"

"It's simple. If there is something going on with you and her best friend she is going to sense it the minute we bring her home. If you really claim to love her as you admitted and you want her to stop running then I want to be sure you've really thought everything through."

"How many times do you want me to repeat it? There is nothing going on with me and Emma Daniels, other than the both of us loving her and wanting the best for her. So can we get back to the original topic now?"

Oh we most definitely can, you just won't like what I've got to say. I thought as I listened to him speak. It had been hard enough for me hearing him speak of Serenity the way he did. I could only imagine what he'd feel the minute I spilled my guts about the girl we both cared for.

"There is a lot that you need to know about me and what actually brought me to her. You sure you're ready to hear it?"

I needed to be sure before moving forward. He might have the soul mate bond with her but he did not have this and I wasn't entirely sure he'd understand it once it was out.

"I can take it. Lucifer was running around in my skin not that long ago remember? I think I can handle anything."

Well he had me there.

"I've been hearing voices from about the same age as Serenity. I reacted pretty much the same way she did in that I pulled away from everyone and everything and lived my life in solitude. What no one knows is, I prayed for someone to come along that was like me so I wouldn't have to be alone anymore. I don't wanna waste your time telling you how often I did it but the end result is the prayer was answered."

I studied him for any reaction and when none came I continued along. There is still so much that I needed to put out there and by the end I could only hope the look of stone on his face would change into something more reactive.

"I wasn't the only one praying, at least according to Michael. By the time they put us on the path toward each other I already joined with Lucifer and I was in a very dark place, which you already know about. The point I'm trying to make here is we were the answer to each other prayers."

"You're kidding me right? Heaven thought answering her prayer in the best way would be to send her a demon?"

"No, that isn't it at all Graham and if you just think about it you know that. Lucifer put me on her trail at that point. I knew everything I thought I needed to know about her in order to get close to her for him and reach our end goal. I just had no idea what

I would be in for the minute I came face to face with her. It only took that one day in class for me to know she was different. The times with her on the campus only solidified the pull that was growing inside me. She owned me and I still can't explain how."

"Was it this hard to stomach when I told you how I felt about her?" He asked and I couldn't help but smile as I nodded. I had to hand it to him though, he might be finding this hard to handle but he wasn't showing it, at least not yet.

"I fell in love with her then but didn't want to admit it to myself. I was still following Lucifer's plan. I wanted nothing more than to please him. When I kissed her that first time, everything changed. I couldn't logically be a part of a plan that took her away from the world or selfishly, from me. I know I'm giving a bit too much information but you gotta know how it is for me man. I might not have the bond with her that you have but what I do have is a love like I've never known for her and an inherent urge to do whatever it takes to make sure she stays happy, healthy and in one piece."

"You also married her. You forgot to twist that knife in."

"I'm not doing this to screw with you Graham. I'm giving you the facts. The truth as I know it. Yes I married her. Did I want to do it when it happened, no but it did happen and whether Heaven acknowledges it or not, it isn't changing. It's real and it's binding until the day she tells me otherwise."

"You wanna know a secret?"

"It's probably not a secret but sure man, I'll all ears."

"I always imagined that when she got married, she would have been doing it with me. It totally reeks of estrogen man but I actually planned it all out in my head. I think I've been doing that ever since I saw her in that pink dress at the school dance."

Hearing about their past together should have bothered me but it didn't. I actually found myself interested to hear more about their time together. He has experienced her in so many ways that until this point I haven't and the more he says the more I want to know in order to truly understand the woman I'd fallen in love with.

"She does have that effect doesn't she? You can see your entire life flash before your eyes as long as she's with you."

64

"Yeah that's exactly how it is. I know how you feel about her Ryan and I also know that in the end the person she ends up with is her decision. I would never push myself on her. I know her heart is with you and going into this, saving her, it's not something I'm going to forget."

"Can you handle what we're about to do? What I mean by that is, when we finally get to her, can you handle it if she isn't the same girl you knew when you two spent time together in Green Haven?"

"You mean can I handle her not being the Serenity I love?"

"Yeah that's exactly what I mean. I just want you to be prepared for everything."

I want nothing more than to comment on what he said about knowing that Serenity's heart belongs to me but I didn't want to rock the boat. This is as open as we had ever been with one another and I knew it wasn't easy. So instead I chose to focus on what would happen moving forward. I needed to know he's ready for whatever we found when we got there.

"I remember what it felt like for me having that asshole riding around in my skin and I can't imagine what it is going to be like for her but even if she comes out and she's the complete opposite of the girl I know, I will handle it. I just want her back."

That was all I needed to hear. We had put the way we felt on the table and gotten it out of the way, both of us agreeing to move forward with our knowledge and focus on the end result as a whole. While we still may not like the way things are, at least we were on the same page. It looked like as far as Graham and I were concerned, we were ready to move forward.

"Then I think it's time we go and talk to the angels. It's time we got this show on the road. No more waiting."

It's time to go to hell and back in order to save the girl that had found the lost boy in both of us and forever changed us.

It was time to save Serenity.

CHAPTER EIGHT

Lucifer

There has never been a doubt in my mind as to Serenity's perfection.

From the very first moment I laid eyes on her as a young girl I knew that she would be the one for me. She embodied everything I could ever want in a mate. She was strong yet silent, a devotion level unlike any other and power that knew no bounds. She was the ultimate prize and I have been determined to have her from that second on.

There are issues of course as there are with any viable candidate. Her heart while truly beautiful caused more problems than solutions as did her stubbornness. The light within her while problematic was not my utmost concern. Just as I had with Graham months before I could eventually break her of it.

That moment is upon us as I watch her feeding off of the blood of yet another helpless victim. She is bending to my will, turning to the side of the darkness and embracing it. She is more than ready to be the princess to my prince. The only thing left to do now is to taste of her myself. Something that should have happened during our time together on the useless planet but that had not been afforded me in the end.

When she turned on me, releasing Graham from his bond to me I looked my death straight in the eye. The way her eyes turned black, I thought it really would be my final end. I would die at the hands of the woman I wanted nothing more than to rule the world with.

As it happens, she was not as knowledgeable in the ways of true exorcism and banishment as I first assumed because once Graham had been released she left herself wide open for the very same thing to happen to her. I saw the opening and I took it knowing that in the end I would have the result I craved from the start and she would most definitely be my dark princess.

She had not seen it coming and even once I joined with her continued to fight me tooth and nail for control of her body. At least she did until she saw the man she loved standing before her with the blade at the ready. Something inside of her in that moment gave up and she broke completely, giving me the control I craved and just as the blade sliced through her, I began the extraction process.

We were in hell before she realized just what her earlier actions caused. Where her human body should have eventually died from the impact of the blade piercing her, it did not and now we roam the bowels of hell together, separated but still as one.

When Graham developed his first taste for the blood it had been almost orgasmic for me because it was the culmination of him becoming one with what came next. Watching Serenity do much the same, well there just isn't a word romantic enough to describe the feeling that burns inside of me. I just want to stop her as she swallows the pints of blood in her hands, bring her to me, and devour her.

I have spent years pushing down reactions such as these but with her I find myself unable to stop them. She is my counterpart, my equal, she is everything. We are now connected on a level that not even Heaven can take away from us. She understands me and my impulses now more than ever because she experiences them herself.

"I have never tasted something so amazing in my life. I want more!"

I understood her eagerness. I want her to have more, as much as she could possibly withstand because I know with each drop she drinks she will become even more the dark princess she was always meant to be. Oh yes, I am definitely enjoying every minute of her transformation.

Surrounding her body with my presence, and bringing her into my arms I see the stray blood drop that slipped out past her mouth and is now running down her lips. In a moment I can only explain as desperate need, I bend down until my lips are a mere breath away from the corner of her own. Wasting no time I put my lips to the edge of hers and sliding my tongue out just a little I lick the blood droplet away, taking the taste of her sweat and the scent of her skin with me.

I have never been so driven to take another being this way in all of my existence. Even after being bonded to Lilith in the manner at which I had been centuries before.

It was in these seconds of time as I pull back up and away from her intoxicating scent that she surprises me. Grabbing me and pulling me to her, making me thankful that my form here at home is at its most solid, forcing her lips on mine in a moment of hungry passion.

This is most definitely not the Serenity of old. This newer, more improved version made my blood boil and my form quake with need. My princess is completely mine. Her change complete now that we have finally come together partaking of one another.

Pulling away from her embrace I allow myself the chance to really take in the vision standing before me now. Her eyes though darkened red still manage to shine and draw me in. The way her lips curve up into the new version of her smile makes me go weak at the sight.

This is the happiest day of my existence to date. The way she is looking at me now could never be taken from me even if she was. I would treasure it always.

"It would appear as though someone is enjoying themselves."

She nods and the pink crept across her cheeks which only made the need inside of me to take even more of her stronger and harder to contain. There is nothing about her that I didn't find absolutely breathtaking.

"Enjoying it doesn't seem right." She replies, her smile growing even bigger. "I am overdosing on it. Even now knowing that the blood is finished, I still crave more. Please tell me that we get to do this often."

She seemed to be adapting to the change so well that her speech is even making the appropriate changes. Where as a human she had been brash and loud, she was now more subdued and regal with her words. It was all coming together just the way I planned it. She is exquisite.

"As often as you would like my queen. You do seem to have taken quite a liking to it and I would like nothing more than for you to enjoy your time here with me."

The wicked gleam that appears in her eyes speaks volumes as to where her mind is now that she has finally crossed over. As she levels her gaze on me, making her way toward me, the crooked smile still pasted beautifully across her lips I knew what would happen next.

"I can think of only one other thing that could happen now that would make me enjoy my time here. The question is...are you eagerly awaiting it as I am, or do we need to continue on with the rest of the tour?"

Pulling her body to mine and lifting her up into my arms I gave her the answer she sought without speaking. If what she wants is time alone with me, there is no way I am going to make her wait for it. With everything coming together so perfectly there was only one thing left to do for me and I cannot wait to begin.

It is definitely time to become one with my bride.

Serenity

I'm not sure why I fought against this as hard as I did.

Every single being both human and otherwise is flawed and I don't mean that in the purely physical way. We all have in us the ability to make mistakes, choose a path that may not have been the original design and live our decisions in ways that may not be acceptable to others. No matter what road we choose to take there is always going to be someone that in the end we disappoint, it's inevitable.

Lucifer is flawed. He has made choices for as long as he has been around to do things his own way and in doing so he was not only cast out from his family but vilified for feeling the way he does. I have spent so long fighting against him that I never really gave myself the chance to truly understand him.

Some might say that I feel the way I do now because of everything I have gone through during my time here with him but that's wrong. The blood didn't change me, the torture didn't and

69

even his words didn't. It was just plain and simply the realization that in not giving him a chance I am actually no better than the place I am born of.

There is a connection between the two of us now that wasn't there before. I truly believe that I understand him now, at least the parts that he allows me to know anyway. I want to know so much more, itching to spend hours or even days inside his mind learning of everything he has been through so that I can adequately support him the way he wishes of me but until he realizes I don't plan on leaving him, he won't ever open up.

The truth is, the day in Green Haven when he said that he wanted nothing more than to just have one taste of me, to feel my lips pressed to his even if he was in Graham's form at the time, something began shifting inside of me. The words got to me in a way that I didn't think at the time was possible yet here we are, after coming together in the most primal of ways and I am left feeling nothing but true satisfaction.

What I experienced that day in the church, I have since felt during our time together here in Hell and now that we have both acted on it, we've become one and bonded on a level that transcends everything before it. With the blood of the innocent running through both of our veins we are ultimately satisfied and more than that, we are together.

I wanted nothing more a short time ago than to be saved from what I believed to truly be the worst place on Earth and now I can't imagine ever leaving. I know he can feel it inside of me, the desire that I have to stay here for all of eternity with him. I'm not sure how he feels about it but I do know that on some level it must please him because he is getting exactly what he's wanted for as long as he can remember.

It's time for me to know more. Now that we're together in this way, our bodies in sync together I want to crawl inside of his mind and have him open up to me fully.

"It appears that my princess is deep in thought."

"I want to know more about you."

"Then ask that which you must know. There are no secrets between us any longer Serenity. Anything that I am or have ever been is yours to have and to know."

"Why did you choose this path when you were cast out?"

This topic of conversation whether we are comfortable with one another or not is going to be difficult. I have no delusions of grandeur in that regard. It is either going to remain a neutral topic or it is going to get heated very fast. I wasn't entirely against either one. The power level between the two of us could not be matched so if it did turn deadly, I know I can hold my own.

"I was a petulant child who had been kicked out of my home. I wanted nothing more than to get revenge on my Father for that and my brothers for not standing beside me."

Holy crap, that wasn't what I was expecting.

"You really believe that?"

He raised his eyes to mine and I knew beyond a shadow of a doubt that he did believe it, though he looks shocked that I would even question it.

"You expected a much different answer did you not?" As I nod in response he continued. "I could tell you that I chose the path because it was the one I was destined for, or some other such nonsense but as I told you before, there are no lies or secrets between us my belle."

"Do you ever think about going back?"

"In the beginning before I allowed the darkness to completely consume me I thought of nothing but going home. The only issue with that is, I was not then nor am I now prepared to apologize for my beliefs."

I sympathized with his answer. During my time in Heaven I had felt much the same way. I towed the line and did everything as I was supposed to for the sake of Ryan and the other angels but I would never apologize for the choices I made. In fact I would make all of them over again if it gave me the same end result.

"You are seeing the ways in which we are alike easily now my belle. This pleases me."

I couldn't argue with that. I did see how we are similar now and it is happening in ways that have nothing to do with how he sees us.

"It is my hope that you can see now why I wanted you to be the one here with me. Why it had to be you and only you. It was never about taking your life away even though in my haste to reach an end result it did appear that way for a time."

He tried to end my life in an effort to gain the power he wanted so much. That moment in time did hang between us and could present itself in an unfavorable light moving forward but it was not enough of a concern to me now given everything we have experienced together. He didn't succeed in his plan and because of that we could be here now.

"I am here with you now and that is what matters."

The smile that crept across his hardened features had the ability to take my breath away. I had seen it on more than one occasion during the times we had been against each other and even admired it for a time given the way he has always been depicted but now it meant so much more. It is beautiful and bright and I wanted nothing more than for it to remain there as long as possible.

"You do not know how long I have desired to hear those very words fall from your lips my belle. There is nothing that can stop us now. It is our time."

There was a time where I wouldn't have agreed to what is being said but looking forward I can't help but be in complete agreement with it. We really were unstoppable.

"Yes, our time is now."

CHAPTER NINE

Graham

This is definitely not the way I pictured Hell.

Sure it felt like we were underground, which I figure makes sense since it's always been spoken of as being under the earth but it really isn't all that different then Earth. The same way you walk into certain neighborhoods and find destruction and darkness, the same is evident here. I have to take points away from Lucifer for originality.

I want the fire.

It wasn't entirely easy getting here but now that we are, I'm more than a little ready to find Lucifer and hopefully give him a dose of what he gave me months before. I understood better than ever now what true revenge feels like once you're hit with it. I want nothing more than to end the bastard.

Between Michael and Gabriel's power and Ryan's knowledge of the spell needed to allow us entrance we have done everything to the letter in order to get here. I wasn't expecting the use of animal blood though. That is definitely something I wouldn't be itching to repeat anytime soon. The knowledge of the sick ingredients needed to get into hell might have been great for some people but it wasn't for me. Now all I have to do is forget it.

"Do you remember when I told you to clear your mind? You might wanna get on that now. I can sense it from here and if I can, they will."

Of course I remember when Ryan said that before we started working on the spell. He wanted to be sure that nothing got between us and bringing Serenity home and I agreed. I fully intended to clear my mind but I couldn't help thinking about things with everything I'm seeing now. It was impossible to stop it.

"Ryan is right Graham. You must not let the rage inside of you for our fallen brother guide you or you will fall victim to the true evil that resides here."

Great, now the angels are on my case about it.

Well if they are so concerned that I'm going to screw the entire thing up, why don't they freeze my brain or whatever it is they do when they block you from thinking?

"For someone who read about us on the internet, I would have thought you would have filtered out the bullshit Graham. We do have the power to alter your mind but we do not prevent you from thinking. It looks like someone needs to go back to school." Michael stated as Ryan laughed.

I should be more annoyed that everyone seems to be picking on me but I'm just not. I didn't have the knowledge any of them did so of course I'm going to come across like a first class noob. Maybe when this was all said and done I would be able to teach some other poor schmuck the rules of entering hell. Until then, I would take whatever comedy that came at my expense.

"Real funny Michael. So you said the first thing we'd run into were wanderers but so far the only wanderers I see are the four of us." I offered up hoping the change of subject would work.

"To be honest, we should have already run into some of them. It's weird that we haven't come across anything. Maybe it's changed since I was here last time."

If something didn't seem right to Ryan then I'm pretty sure it didn't mean anything good for us in the long term. He's the only one out all of us that has been here before and if he is already noticing differences we have to be on guard more than ever.

As we continued moving ahead I wondered if Hell is the same way as Heaven. When Gabriel grabbed me from the church after Serenity saved me, I spent a little time upstairs healing and the angel explained to me then that everyone viewed it in a different way. If that's the case then I wonder if the way I view Hell is different then what Ryan and the angels are seeing.

All I really know is that the smell left something to be desired. It wasn't the brightest place in the world either but the smell makes me wanna turn around and head right back on home. It's like a mixture of old garbage and wet socks. If this is what turns on the locals than it's no secret why they call most places on earth hellholes.

74

"Someone needs to invest in some air freshener. You should bring that up at the next town meeting man." I laugh directing my comment right at Ryan.

I know it's probably not a good idea to turn into a smart ass with where we are but considering what he is and who he had been aligned with up until recently I figured it was a comment that was true if nothing else. This place really is the pit it's been made out to be.

"Yeah I'll do that and when I do, I'll offer you up as the person who gave me the idea." He answered back with an eye roll which only made me laugh harder. "Ignore the smell Graham; it's only going to get worse."

Before I could ask him just how much worse I saw what we had been expecting from the moment we touched down. The wanderers, as Ryan referred to them, were indeed doing what their name implied as they began moving toward us. They're transparent and completely different from what I pictured. They only way they can be described that makes any sense to the average human is to say they look the most like ghosts.

I figured the closer they came to where we were standing they would just pass through us. It was too bad Ryan didn't want to let me hang on to that illusion, choosing instead to bark orders at me, though I couldn't be sure he wasn't doing it for everyone's benefit.

"You may be able to move through them but they are still powerful. Make sure your weapons are ready and dispose of them as quickly and quietly as possible."

Weapons. Of course we've moved on to that part of the program now. I've never been a violent guy and more than that I have never used a weapon before in my entire life. It just isn't something that appealed to me. There were other people I'd been friends with over the years that either had permits to carry guns or chose to carry knives as a form of protection but not me. I preferred either talking my way out of situations or using my fists if it came to it.

This is definitely new territory for me.

When Ryan gave me the blade earlier before going ahead with the ritual, I wasn't exactly dying to take it. I wanted to find another

75

alternative around actually hurting someone. Even if the things we were going to face weren't people at all but something much more sinister. Of course there is no other way around it but it didn't mean I wanted to use it now.

"Did you hear me Graham? If you don't pull your blade right now they will attach themselves to you and drain your very insides."

I heard him loud and clear so I did as he wanted and pulled the blade, taking care of three as I stepped up my speed before they could reach me and do as Ryan explained. As they disappeared I thought I would feel the loss but with each passing one I slammed the blade into all I feel is relief.

Maybe I could do this after all. No more super noob.

Gabriel and Michael seem to be making fast work of the wanderers they encountered as I saw the shine of both angel blades moving in quick succession around me. This was obviously something they are very skilled at, even if they were supposed to be beings of the light.

After making our way through thirty or more of the same transparent and seemingly empty looking wanderer ghosts we seemed to reach what looked like a long empty hallway. Exhaling a deep breath and taking in the surroundings around me, I waited for some form of instruction moving forward.

"That seemed easier than I thought it would be."

"Yeah, that's what I told you. They're just wanderers. They haven't accepted their fate yet and because of that they haven't harnessed the real power that runs through here."

"I feel the need to ask, how is everyone holding up?" Gabriel interjected before I had a chance to respond to Ryan's know it all comment.

I realize he knows more than even the angels do but does he really have to sound like such a jerk?

"Do not let yourself go down that road Graham." Gabriel admonished which only made me feel even worse. I forgot he had the ability to read my thoughts. Damn host aftermath. I didn't exactly want anyone knowing that I'm beginning to let all of this get to me.

76

"What road?" Ryan questioned.

"The road at which he is becoming annoyed with the way you speak to him. Are the two of you sure you worked through your issues in their entirety?"

"Yeah Gabe, we did and the next time you wanna go into my head like that, you mind giving me a bit of warning first? I feel like I've been body snatched." I answer, switching gears again in an effort to drop what I didn't want to get into.

"As fun as all of this is, I think we need to keep moving if we want to actually save her sometime today."

I couldn't agree more. Whatever I did or didn't feel where the half demon is concerned didn't matter right now. Getting to Serenity and getting her out alive did and I didn't want to spend any more time being driven away from that primary goal.

"So what can we expect next?" I asked, wanting to prepare myself as much as possible.

"Lower level demons. Not much stronger than the wanderers but they can pack a punch if you let them get close enough. Let's not do that."

As we made our way forward, me and Ryan in front with the angels following closely behind I couldn't help but think of just how much more darkness I was about to witness. When Lucifer had been inside of me I figured that to be the worst of it but being here now, I knew that isn't the case at all. Given the levels of demons we have to make our way through I knew it was going to get ten times worse.

I only hope that in making my way through the levels of dark power that radiate here, I didn't become part of it myself.

Ryan

I know I'm being a dick to Graham but considering where we are, I honestly feel that I have to be.

The true levels of angst and evil haven't even been reached yet and I could already see Graham attaching himself to what surrounds him. He might not know it but I did. I spent more than a little time that very same way and the last thing any of us needs right now is for Graham to be like me. I have to be rough and realistic in order to make sure I kept him safe.

It's true; we did work through our issues before coming down here even though I always knew there would be something on the surface regardless. This has nothing to do with that though and everything to do with the fact that he meant a whole lot to the woman we were here to save and if something happened to him again along the way, especially on my watch, I will never forgive myself for it.

I have to keep him and even the angels in one piece otherwise Serenity may never come home at all and even if she did, she would only be half the woman I know and love so deeply because these other people with me are her family and she needs them just as much as they need her.

"Alright guys this is where your power is going to come into play. There will be demons and a lot of them. Lower demons make up the majority of hell as they aren't special enough to become Lucifer's pet projects. Whatever you can't take with the blades, you gotta use power for."

"Even though our power is limited?"

"Limited is going to be better than none at all. Use whatever you got at your disposal Michael."

I noticed the grin come across Graham's face. What he has to smile about is beyond me but I wasn't going to waste time wondering about it.

"What's so funny man?"

"I was just thinking about all of those pictures of Saint Michael I was shown as a kid. He always had the most badass armor. I guess I expected that if I ever got to fight beside him, he'd be wearing it."

"Shut up Graham." Michael snapped from behind us.

The depictions of Michael are some of the most recognized all over the world though I had to admit, it's more than a bit of a letdown that they didn't do him justice. He might not have the armor but he sure did have the attitude and strength.

"No fire use down here because even though we still need to go up against the blood seekers, we don't need them coming before we're ready." I said steering the conversation back on course.

"Energy should be enough to annihilate them?" Gabriel questioned.

"Yeah, they're lesser demons. We're still more powerful than they are. Like I said, just don't let them get too close. They can still pack a pretty bad punch if given the chance."

I can sense them around me though we aren't close enough to come into their line of vision. I hate dealing with the lesser demons, especially after being promoted up the ranks so easily the way I had been during my time with Lucifer. They hate the fact that they aren't good enough to get behind his velvet rope and the fact that I did, well it was enough to make me a marked man by more than just a few of them.

The smell Graham mentioned earlier getting worse with each step I took; I know we are only a few seconds away from coming face to face with the reason for it. When a demon possessed a human, especially one that had already passed on at the time of possession there was always the smell of decaying flesh. I can smell it easily now which means there is more than just a few waiting around the bend for our arrival.

"Be ready guys." I call as we began making our way around the corner. It looks the same for me as it does for Graham. Hell is interesting that way. It's a series of hallways and dark areas that look like alleys there to meet us every second. In a way I always believe that Lucifer made it that way so that he could have his own personal maze should humans ever enter.

There is nothing better to a being made of evil then a game of cat and mouse. Hunter and prey is definitely how Lucifer liked to obtain every soul he encountered. I could only hope that Serenity hadn't already become the prey. At least more then she had been when he possessed and taken her from us.

Before we knew it they were upon us, hundreds of lower level demons all coming together at the scent of Graham and me as we made our way in their direction. Weapons were at the ready and our movements almost synchronized in the way we came together to fight. Bodies fell to the floor, possessed humans that now could finally meet their end as we sliced and diced our way through the throng that just seemed to keep coming.

Where I had been worried about Graham more then I wanted to let on he seemed to actually be holding his own. He moved with a speed I was unaware he is capable of as he backed up not only Gabriel and Michael but me as well. He may have had his reservations about killing at first but now he seems to have come into his own and realized that he's only doing what needs to be done in order to save Serenity.

Every few seconds I would see a flash of light whiz by my head and I knew instantly that Michael and Gabriel had heeded my warning and were using energy induced orbs to finish off the demons that they were unable to reach with their angel blades. They also seemed to realize that with each one they used they were draining themselves so the light appeared only minimal at best. It meant good things for us moving forward. They would still be able to fight even when things became much more dangerous.

Focusing on the task in front of me I didn't realize at first that Graham was no longer in my line of sight. It's only when I scanned quickly around me in an effort to locate him that I saw just why he had gone missing in the first place.

He had been caught by one of the lower demons we hadn't been able to adequately get to in time. Not wasting a second I ran over and with one short, swift motion I brought the athame deep into the corpse that the demon inhabited, bringing it to its knees as the essence of the demon disappeared from its body.

As Graham slumped to the floor I again took in the scene around me and grabbed the stray demons that were now beginning to surround me. It appeared they had finally realized just who I was and were going to work together in order to bring me down. Too bad it isn't their lucky day. I'm not going to be taken down quite that easily.

Once secure that I had a few seconds to check on the fallen man in front of me, I got to my knees and began checking him over for signs of injury but even more than that, signs that they had gotten into his mind. While he looked out of it, his eyes rolling into the back of his head from the impact, he looked fine which meant I realized what was going on before they could do anything long lasting to him.

"You alright man? You gonna be able to continue?"

"Yeah…I don't know what happened. I had the bastard and then out of nowhere there was another one on me."

"That happens. Even to the best of us. You did good man. Are you sure you're good to move because I figure if I don't get you up out of here in the next three seconds we're going to both become demon mind food."

My intent in telling him wasn't to freak him out or to get him to get up and move himself but that is exactly what he ended up doing which surprised me. This guy is definitely a lot stronger both inside and out then I gave him credit for originally. I have to hand it to him. He is a better man then I am that's for sure.

"Let's go. I've got this."

I found the bravado impressive but I knew he didn't have it. At least he didn't have it entirely the way he might have fifteen minutes earlier. What happened with the demon had taken a lot out of him. Unfortunately I had to take it at face value for the time being as they were beginning to pile up around us again and I was going to need all the help I could get in order to make it out of this in one piece.

"For the record, you're full of shit Hudson but come on, we don't have time to argue about it."

Grabbing his arm and pulling him to me, I flipped myself around until we were back to back and ready to take on what was slowly beginning to move in on us. Injured or not, while Gabe and Michael handled their own mess, he was all I had. It's time to put on the show of a lifetime and pray it works.

True to his word Graham moved and began slashing through demon after demon without even a breath between and I found myself taking seconds at a time during my own battle with them to watch the way he moved. He did seem to have this even though I could see the drain on his body that he was so willfully trying to push away. There is no doubt in my mind as I watched him that he is definitely made of something more than just humanity.

It was only when we finally got a break in between the fighting that I saw the grin on his face. I couldn't help but match it with one of my own. There is something to be said about the rush one gets from a fight and it was apparent that not only am I feeling it but Graham was as well even though I knew he probably didn't want to.

That's the thing about guys. We will push past any pain we might feel in order to reach the goal we set, even when it's our own demise on the line as it is now. We will give it everything we got even if we are on the losing end because we don't wanna ever be seen as the one that goes down without a fight, the one that just gives up. That was us now. We were tired, we felt our bodies draining of energy fast yet we kept bringing everything we had to the table because there is just no room for failure.

Michael and Gabriel appeared at our side and it was in that moment that I knew we had gotten past the onslaught of demons and free to move on to the next stage. Seeing the way they looked as they gathered around just made me jealous. They didn't look any worse for wear while I was positive Graham and I both looked we were ready to lay down and sleep for a week in order to heal the damage that had been done to us.

Lucky sons of bitches.

"How are you two doing on the power supply?" I questioned, wondering just how much of that aspect had been taken out of them. What we were going to face next was going to be a million times harder then what we had just been through and we were going to need that power more than ever.

"Despite the way I am sure it appeared we did not use much of it at all so we should be more than ready to face what awaits us next Ryan."

"It did seem like the world was lit up a lot while we were fighting. You sure you got enough left in you for the next stage?"

"More than positive. You must not doubt us. We cannot afford to lie."

There it is. The staunch nature that I have come to know and expect from Michael. It seems that whatever he'd been going through before coming here in terms of adapting to the human way of life was now pushed to the background in favor of his natural way of being.

"It appears as if Graham may be needing assistance." Gabriel stated motioning toward where Graham was leaning loosely up against the dirt covered wall.

"Yeah he probably needs to be healed. One of them got the better of him before he realized what was happening. I stopped it but I'm pretty sure he took a beating in the process. Though good luck getting the guy to admit it."

"Takes a licking and keeps on ticking baby." Graham choked out in between intakes of breath.

"Yeah, yeah we know. You're a tank man but you still need to take some time before we go forward. You definitely won't get out of the next part alive with the way you're looking now."

"I look fucking fabulous. It's not my problem you can't look as good as me."

"Does he always joke in this way to avoid the issue?" Michael asked, genuinely perplexed with the way Graham was acting.

"Yeah man, he does. It's the human guy code."

"There is a code? Do the females also have such a code?"

I want to laugh at how literal he seems to take my words, reminding me again of the time where he assumed we all turn green but one look at Gabriel and I knew that it wasn't going to be the right thing to do. It was a first for me but I could finally see that even his own brother was getting annoyed with him.

"Michael it is a saying that is all."

I couldn't help it, I let out the laugh I'd been trying hard to keep in and it was only made worse when I heard Graham's own chuckle come from his place on the wall.

"Hanging with angels never gets old." He stated, the laughter fading off and leaving only a grin behind.

I couldn't agree more. Even facing a situation like the one we found ourselves in, the way the angels act is still a source of entertainment. It would make getting through the final two stages that much easier. With as dark as things are about to get we needed to keep ourselves light.

"Michael, I know you wanna believe that we literally mean things the way they come out but man, we don't turn green and there is no code, well other than a few common sense rules you just don't mess with. Don't over think it so much."

"I will heal the Hudson boy and we will catch up to you both. I think it is imperative you move on ahead so that we know what we are walking into next." Gabriel said quietly bringing us all back to the reality of what lay ahead.

If he was willing to stay behind and heal Graham then I'm more than happy to move forward with Michael. What the angel lacked in common sense he made up for in spades with his ability to go to war. If anyone had to be standing by my side moving forward I'm thankful it was him.

"We will inform you of what we learn brother. Take great care in moving forward." Michael replied back, his face again all business.

As I began walking with the Archangel, I found it hard to tame the now quickening beat of my heart. We had gotten through the first two stages of demons and now we were on our way to the third and fourth before reaching Lucifer himself. I couldn't help but feel excited that we were closer to Serenity again. It has been far too long since I've seen her and even my heart couldn't seem to wait, no matter what way she would be when we found her.

"Hang in there pretty girl, we're on our way."

CHAPTER TEN

Gabriel

As I walk through the bowels of the place that my fallen brother calls home I find myself conflicted.

I know that we are doing the right thing, going in this way and attempting to save Serenity from the fate at which he leveled her with but at the same time I can't help but feel that in doing things this way I am betraying Father in a way that I may never be able to recover from.

There is no way that he will look upon this favorably. We have gone against him and everything he has taught us in taking this drastic of an action. I know he isn't the same anymore, that somewhere along the way he changed his course but I am still a host of heaven above all else. I want nothing more than to please him even with the change of direction.

Can I really live with being vilified further and maybe even losing my powers when everything is said and done?

It didn't only bother me in my own regard. I am also concerned for the fate of my brother. It is no secret that out of all of the angels that Father chose to have created in his image, Michael was the closest one to becoming him at least on the surface. I have seen subtle changes in my brother since our descent to the planet and even here in Hell but it could not be denied that he is still very much his father's son.

Loss of power for Michael would be tremendous and I am not sure he would ever recover from it even though he claims otherwise. If we rescued Serenity we would have done the right thing but at what cost in the end?

"You alright man?"

I turn back to face the man that is now no longer leaning against the makeshift dirt encrusted wall and is instead back on his feet. Yes I have to focus on what lays ahead of us and less on what would happen once it was over. Graham Hudson has been nothing but the perfect warrior in our time here and it is about time I do what is needed in order to repair him to continue on.

"Yes. I just found myself lost in thought."

"About what, the next step?"

"In a manner of speaking yes but not in the way you imagine. I am thinking of the grander picture."

"What happens after we get out of here?" he questioned easily, almost as if he was able to see inside my mind.

"Yes."

"This isn't going to go over well for you and Michael is it?"

"That would be putting it mildly Graham. Right now though I would much rather focus on what is happening around us. Any other thought process could be deadly. So may I heal you as Michael requested?"

"Yeah man, do your worst."

"I would never dream of doing anything wrong with you Graham."

"It's a saying Gabe, jeez. Heal me; we need to catch up to the others."

As I placed my hands over the area at which he signaled to have the most pain I focused on the power within me and let it overtake me. It was in moments like this one, where I am doing the right thing and using my power in a pure way that I felt most at peace with who and what I am. While I may never be the way that Father wants me to be, at least I would have the ability to heal and see life better because of the actions I'd taken. It is something no one could ever take away from me.

"How do you feel?" I ask as he brought himself back up to his feet again, a dazed expression across his features.

"Alive."

"Then it has been a success. Let's find Michael and Ryan."

"Gabe, wait a sec." he called stopping me before I could turn to leave. "I feel like there's something I gotta say."

"You do not have to say anything if what you are planning on is a thank you. It is my pleasure. You are quite the warrior Graham Hudson."

He laughed lightly as I complimented him which only confused me as I am unaware of anything amusing in the words I've spoken.

"Thanks for that but that wasn't what I wanted to say. I figure the thank you is implied."

"It is."

"I just wanna say you're doing the right thing. I know Heaven isn't exactly a fan of going against the status quo but what you're doing here right now, it is the right thing and when we get out of here, don't let anyone tell you any different."

His words should not have gotten to me but they did. It wasn't often that in my travels I interacted with the human populace quite the way I have been since becoming involved with Serenity and it is even less likely to have one of them thank me and tell me what I am doing is a good thing. There could be no denial of the effect of his words.

"I will do my best not to. Now we must go now before we find ourselves in a situation my limited power cannot get us out of."

I want to say more to him, to inform him of the magnitude of his words but I am unable to do so. I may be the angel that interacted best with the humans but in the moment I find myself in I am not able to find the right words and actions to adequately display my true feelings. I am for the first time at a complete loss.

"So even the angels are tough guys huh?" he asked with a laugh while motioning to the path in front of us, showing me that he was indeed ready to move.

"It would appear to be that way but thank you Graham Hudson. You consistently find ways to restore my faith in the human race. For that I am grateful."

"Shit Gabriel, you keep that up and you're gonna make me cry."

Left with only a grin we began moving forward, no other words in that moment needing to be spoken. We knew what we had to do next and we were focused on that goal but now we both knew that we were on the same page more than ever before. The advantage is now with us because as long as we remained this intact, nothing could stop us.

Ryan

I wasn't sure what was taking Gabriel and Graham so long but if they didn't hurry and catch up with us soon then we were all going to be in a world of hurt the minute we turned the corner.

The closer we seemed to get to the man himself the more I seem to be changing inside. I didn't want to call attention to it but the part of me that still very much worshipped Lucifer is beginning to grow inside me and if I'm not careful all of the work I've done at keeping it dormant all of these months is going to be for nothing.

I can feel the burning in me for the blood that I could now smell clear as day. We are only a few steps away from some of the hungriest demons that inhabit this place and all I want to do is join with them, forsaking this undertaking all together. As much as I tried to be different and be made of the light the way Michael and Gabriel believe me to be, I can't. I'm still very much a victim to what resides at my very core.

I would always succumb to the darkness that burns in me.

"You look uncomfortable Ryan, is there something that I need to be made aware of moving forward?"

I could easily lie to him though I'm pretty sure he'd see right through it but I won't. We had come this far together as a team and there is no way I could go back on that now, especially with what we're about to face. We need to be on the same page more than ever. He needs to know this almost as much as I want to tell him.

"Being here, it's bringing up things better off buried."

"I see." He stated, his eyes never once leaving mine almost as if he is searching for a hidden truth behind them.

"I've been working really hard on pushing this down but being here brings it all back up. This is the one place in all of existence where being what I am is accepted and it wants nothing more than to come to the surface and be accepted."

"Are you strong enough after the trials we have already faced to continue forward?"

"Yes. I just need to fight harder and keep my mind focused on her and nothing else. I just don't want to lie to you about it."

"I appreciate your candor with me Ryan; it will help me immensely moving forward but worry not about my reaction or even that of my brother. We are here for you in any way we can be, so if you need us to be of assistance you just need to speak the words."

It's the truth. I don't want to admit that I'm concerned about the reaction from the angels to what's happening to me but I definitely am. We were sworn enemies, whether I am a pure angel or not. I had been born of a demon and a human and I couldn't deny it. I just wanted him to know I had no plans to turn on him, no matter how much the hunger grew inside of me.

"Is there really anything you can do for this?"

"To be quite honest I am not sure. I have never worked alongside a demon before, half or not. I suppose given my lack of knowledge in that regard I would have to say no."

"Well thanks for at least wanting to."

"Of course. I will do whatever I can to help you with your trouble. How much distress is it currently causing you?"

"It's mild but it's there and it's only getting worse the closer we get. So can we just hang back here for a few minutes and wait for the others? I think if I have a little more time to get a grip on it I can push it down where it belongs."

"As you wish Ryan."

I do not like showing weakness and having this happen now is exactly what it felt like. In not being able to control what burns inside of me I am letting down the people that were here with me to save Serenity and proving what a weak human I really am. Despite not wanting to believe it before, it's just proof that Lucifer was right all along. I am a weak link, whether for his side or that of the angels.

"You are more alike than I thought."

"What do you mean?"

"My brother for all of his strengths seems to revert back to the very thing you are doing now. I will tell you the same thing that I told him. Do not let doubt consume you. It will end up being the very thing that ends you. Ryan. You are much stronger then you realize. You must continue to focus on that and not on the ways you believe you are letting us down. You are not doing that at all."

"How are you able to do that?" I ask, putting what he said out of my mind in favor of focusing on how he knew I was thinking it to begin with. "See into my mind that way. I thought I had the ability to block you."

"You do but it would seem that in our travels together we have become close to one another and I am able to see past your walls where I was not able to before."

Well that's new. All of the power I controlled before, the ability to block the angels being the strongest of it all is now changing because of my time with them. It isn't that I want to hide from them but knowing that I am slowly losing the power that made me such an asset to Lucifer is actually kind of depressing.

"You are realizing the light within you Ryan. You must not allow that depression to consume you."

Damn it. He needs to stop doing that. It's actually starting to creep me out now.

"My apologies."

"Don't worry about it, I guess I just need to get used to it. Everything is different now."

"Sometimes, different can be a good thing Ryan. Embrace the changes inside of you because they will bring you closer to your real heritage and away from the darkness that has been eating you alive for years. It could spell good things for the future."

"You sound so sure."

"That is because I am sure. I may not be all knowing and seeing the way that my father is but Ryan I can see it inside of you just dying to get out. The urge to be different, better then what you have been before. I want to see that come to fruition but if you let the doubt continue to build that will never happen."

Again he's making a good point. Giving into the doubt is only feeding the beast inside of me and would do nothing in terms of moving forward both in the moment and long term. I have to do the very thing he wants me to, embrace the changes and roll with them as best as I can. That's the only way we would get through the next stages of our plan.

90

Before I could respond to him, letting him know how much I appreciate having him be the voice of reason for me when I want to do nothing but be completely unreasonable, I heard the steps behind us and immediately prepared myself for what might be coming around the bend.

"It is only Graham and my brother Ryan. Relax."

My body immediately evened itself out as the angel and Graham came around the bend both of them looking stronger and brighter than before. Whatever Gabriel had done for Graham really had done the trick. He looked great. More than ready to fight again.

"Are we ready to do this?" Graham asked as his eyes landed on me. I could feel them burning into me, just the way Michael's had done only minutes before. He was searching me much the same way to see if I am ready for what came next.

The concern from the very beginning has always been him and whether or not he would be able to handle himself the deeper into hell we managed to go but now everything has shifted and I'm the main focus of concern. I thought in coming here I would be able to handle it and had even made it appear as such to the others, so it has never been brought up but it looks like it needs to be.

"Ryan needs a minute or two to collect himself. It would appear as though even though he hasn't been here in a long period of time, this place still has the ability to get to him."

"I'll be fine; I just need to shake this. Now you see why I hate coming here."

They all nodded at once and it was in that moment I knew that despite my own fears there really is no judgment. They all seem to understand what being in this place is doing to me and were more than willing to give me whatever time I needed to put myself back in the right frame of mind to move forward.

Even with the demon growing inside of me and wanting release I still feel it clear as day.

Total acceptance.

CHAPTER ELEVEN

Serenity

Something is happening. I can feel it.

I can't explain why it is that I know it but there is something inside of me that just speaks to its knowledge. I haven't felt a pull this strong since I've been here and it has nothing at all to do with the growing closeness between Lucifer and me.

The open and honest conversation we shared earlier was an eye opening experience for me. When I arrived here I had been so against him and everything he planned but the more we actually opened up to one another I felt myself finally seeing a side of him that not many others got to see. I saw him for the angel he is not the fallen one he had become. He is filled with so much darkness not because he always wanted to be that way but because there really was no other way for him.

I believe that he never wanted to hurt me even though it took a lot of time for me to completely come to terms with it. I still held on to the belief that in draining me the way he had that he wanted nothing more than for me to end up dead alongside of the man he believes to have betrayed him in falling for me. That isn't the case anymore. He just didn't see any other alternative at the time to achieve what he wanted so badly.

There is this small part of me that still fights the way I feel now. It fights so hard because it wants me to continue believing that all of this is evil and that in accepting it I am also accepting my own damnation but honestly, with everything I managed to learn about the man that I now stand beside, I would gladly accept eternal damnation because at least then I would always be getting the truth and not just information they thought I needed to know whenever they felt like telling me.

Do I still ache to be back with Ryan? Of course but with each passing hour that need seems to lessen and I embrace what is in front of me even more. I will always love Ryan despite everything that has happened since meeting him and not only because he was my first in so many ways but because he opened my eyes to a whole new world around me and never gave up even when it might have been better to do just that.

I can easily care about the both of them now. I can be what Lucifer needs and wants me to be and remain loyal to his side despite the fact that I love and care for the very person he wants to see destroyed forever. He's allowing me that. This is definitely not the way I imagined things being when joined together with the King of Hell. I really am amazed I didn't agree to this sooner given how well it just seems to fit.

*****

"When you possessed me why didn't you wipe my memories the way you did with Graham?"

"I know that it appears as though I want the opposite with you Serenity as my actions have proven but I never wanted to entirely take your choice away from you even though it seemed easier. That is why I didn't remove your memories. I want you to always have them even if they are about beings I would rather not speak about."

"Can you handle how I feel about Ryan and even Graham?"

"I want you to rule the darkness with me. I want to reside in Hell for as long as we are permitted and I want you to do so willingly. Yes, I want to remove that light within you that will make you turn from me but in doing so it would change who you are and I cannot bring myself to do that, at least not fully."

"You didn't answer my question."

"I believe I did. The light is the reason you have such feelings for both of the people you mention therefore I would never want to take the way you feel from you."

The more I spoke to him the more confused I became. I still want to hate him even though my body and minds reaction to him is shifting with each passing second. I want to hold onto the hate and loathing I had for him despite hearing the caring tone in his voice toward me now but I am failing at it. All I feel is sympathy.

"I can feel your confliction Serenity."

"I'm sorry for that."

"Do not be sorry to me for anything. You are here with me now willingly. Maybe that is because of the paces that I put you through in order to have you reach this point, or maybe it is because my words speak to you now where they didn't before. Whatever the reason for it, I treasure every second with you and do not want it filled with apologies."

"They are going to come for me, you must know this. What am I supposed to do when that time comes?"

"Make a choice."

"Will you actually give me the choice this time? I know that you've said you never really wanted to take my ability to choose from me but that is exactly what you have done every step of the way. How can I believe you mean what you say now?"

"You must trust me. There is no other way for me to prove it until the moment you speak of actually materializes."

"If they come for me and they succeed, are you just going to give up?"

His answer here was extremely important to me. I wasn't entirely sure that if Ryan and the angels came for me that they would win given the magnitude of Hell itself and what resided here but if it did happen I want to know what he is going to do next. I needed to know.

"I cannot give up Serenity. I believe you already know that about me. I will never give up until the earth is destroyed. I need to make my father see what an abomination he created."

He was right, I did know that would be his answer but that wasn't the part I wanted to know about. If he saw me as so important to his plan moving forward, I needed to know what losing me would mean to him. Would he willingly let me go and not pursue it again, using my very human friends against me?

"It is not the big picture you are wondering about is it? What you want to know is much more personal in nature if I am reading your responses correctly."

As the final few words fell from his lips he reached across to me, pulling me into him and pressing his lips to mine. As we just

94

lingered in that position both of us enjoying the feel of one another
he pulled away, speaking again.
    "I will never give up on you."

*****

There was something final in his words that only made me gravitate toward him that much more. It wasn't as if I hadn't felt that way with a person before because it is the very thing I experienced with Ryan so strongly but hearing it from Lucifer, a being born purely of evil yet somehow softer with me than anyone else, it pulled me in deeper.

I found myself not wanting to leave him. I know it is only a matter of time before the cavalry I called for shows up for me but now when they came I'm not entirely sure I want to leave. It is the same way I felt when my mother picked me up from the center to take me home. I am enjoying my life the way it is turning out and I don't want anything or in this case, anyone to interrupt it.

There is one definite drawback to being here that I haven't wanted to bring up but that gets to me a lot as we make our way around, doing much the same routine as every other day. I miss the light. While the darkness has its advantages there is still a part of me that misses everything that came with the light. My old life, my friends and even my family though thinking of my mother didn't exactly inspire the bright spot it should have. I miss moving from one day to the next and not knowing what to expect.

He must know that I've been feeling this way because lately he's been giving me more and more time to myself. As if in some small way him letting me process everything will make the longing hurt less. I can tell he doesn't want to subject me to the same routine day to day, that he wants more for the both of us but in this moment that's just not possible. So I have to accept and take what I'm given and somehow adapt.

"My belle, may I have a moment of your time?"

I can't help it. I absolutely love it when he calls me his belle. I've never been much of a nickname girl even though Graham wanted nothing more than for me to be but this one, I could definitely get used to it. There is just so much emotion behind it and for someone that until recently I believed to be devoid of it, I find myself welcoming it with open arms. It means there is more to him than meets the eye.

"Of course. It wasn't as if I was doing anything of real consequence anyway."

"There seems to be a disturbance, multiple ones and I am wondering if you've gotten any sort of feeling as to what it might be."

There it is again, just further proof that something isn't right. If Lucifer is telling me that there's something going on in Hell and he isn't aware of what it is then it can only mean one thing. What I wished for forever ago is actually happening and they have come for me. There are only three people that I am aware of that could get anything past him. It is the only logical explanation.

"I feel a shift as well. At least I did earlier but since then I haven't given it much focus. I think you know what it is otherwise you would not be here asking."

"They have come for you."

"That is how it appears yes."

With the distance between us it is hard to make out his face and it didn't help that it seems to be hidden in the natural dark shadow of the room. I want nothing more than to see his expression because I know it will tell me everything I need to know about what is about to happen next. A lot changed since I came here but the one thing that didn't is me wanting to know everything before proceeding.

"Tell me what you're thinking. I think we've reached that point now." I push, knowing I might not get anywhere but hoping that our connection over the last little while has earned me enough trust.

"Serenity you do not want to know my thoughts on this matter. They are not the most pure."

Since when does pure thought matter to him? What the hell is going on and why is he acting so weird? Is there something else going on that he isn't telling me?

96

"I don't care if they're pure and nice or not. I want to know."

"I do believe that you have come to enjoy your time here and as such when they arrive I will defend myself and you. I do not think I can allow them to take you. I know that goes against my earlier statement of wanting to let you make the choice but you did ask for the truth always."

He's right. I did ask for the truth because unlike the times I dealt with the angels, he always seemed more than ready to give it to me. I couldn't fault him for the way he feels. He had every right to want to react in this way.

"I know this might sound weird but do whatever you have to do."

"It does not sound weird to me Serenity but I do have to admit I am quite confused by your response. Just what do you mean?"

"It's simple. Do whatever you have to in order to keep me here because I don't think I want to be saved."

CHAPTER TWELVE

Ryan

Going deeper into hell especially when you are on the side of the light is always going to be a risk and it's one that I've been expecting but in trying to prepare myself for the eventual feeding frenzy my body would undergo the closer we got to the man himself, I really didn't think about how that would affect the others in the long term.

Both Gabriel and Michael need to keep their attention on Graham since it is his blood that the demons are most likely to go after. Sure, I have human blood running through my veins but not on the same level as he does. He is pure human where I am something much more sinister, something that these demons can sense the difference with.

They are not the only ones that could smell, crave to taste and almost feel Graham's blood. Given my true nature, at least the one that I've been born with, I am suffering through much the same experience. I could feel it pumping in his veins, hear the pounding in my head and I wanted nothing more than to grab him and just take a taste. The difference between them and me is I am still somehow able to control it.

I've hated this level of hell for as long as I can remember. Even when embracing the darker side of me, I always hated the sight and smell of blood. The urge is so powerful though that even with as much as I hate it, I still want to be a part of it. It is undeniable in its intensity.

This isn't the strongest level of Hell. These are most definitely not the strongest demons that inhabit it but Lucifer is by far most proud of this particular level. He enjoys the feeding frenzy that he fosters here and visits it often in the times he has come home, me by his side for the ride.

It was during one particular visit that he explained why he enjoys this level of hell so much and why he wanted me to embrace the hunger that he knew was burning inside of me. As much as I don't want to focus on that now as the angels, Graham and I make our way forward, it's hard not to. Being back here only floods my mind with the memories I would most like to forget.

*****

"Ryan, it has been such a long time since I experienced this place through the eyes of the unenlightened. You must tell me what you feel as we move through these levels. I want to see everything through your eyes."

He is excited. He's been excited from the minute he brought me here but the deeper we went the more it just seemed to grow. He is unable to hide his pleasure now as the smile on his face can attest to. Some may look at the smile as evil but I can't. It looks beautiful.

I couldn't tell him everything I was feeling. He would most definitely not like hearing my distaste for the smell that lingered throughout the dank hallways he kept bringing me down. I hadn't been expecting flowers and perfume but the smell of decay that kept wafting by was almost too much for my fragile stomach to take.

I am a kid after all. The last thing I want to experience is death in quite this way.

"There is burning inside of my chest father and I don't know what to do about it."

"That is the hunger building in you my son. You must embrace that hunger the more it presents itself, it will serve you well moving forward with our plans."

"Will the pain of it ever stop?"

"Yes, the more you embrace it and answer its call the pain will fade and become more pleasurable to you."

"What will I have to do?"

"You must feed but not right now. That will come in time Ryan, as will everything else that I am about to show you. It pleases me to no end that the hunger is already presenting itself

*inside of you. You are your birth fathers son, of that I am quite
certain."*

I'm alright with everything he says until he mentions the
sperm donor. I didn't wanna know how similar I am to him,
especially since he bailed early on and left me with the mother that
I was sure was born of the very place I'm standing in. I hate him
and hearing about him now just made me want to turn around the
way I'd come and go home.

*"My son, the anger you feel is strong and pure but you need to
direct it better. I understand the hatred you have for the demon
that made you what you are but you must push past that and
embrace everything he has actually given you. Your human mother
will be dealt with in time. Of that I give you my solemn promise.
She will not damage you any further."*

That made me happy, knowing that he knew the torture I was
going through with my mom and was going to help me. I might not
entirely understand everything going on around me but when he
said he would do something he always followed through, so I
trusted that he would do it again. He really is the father I never
had.

*"This level of hell will be hard to take at first my son. The
level of hunger here is unmatched. All of these demons will smell
the human blood that resides inside of you and they will do
anything they can to get a mere taste. I will protect you this time
but on further visits you will have to learn how to deal with it
yourself. Embrace the dark side of you and let it carry you
through. It is the only way you can make it through this level
alive."*

"You seem to enjoy it here, why is that?"

*"When I fell the first thing I began experiencing was the
hunger inside of me much the way that you are now. It was
dreadfully painful at first but over time I found ways to manage it
and after completely embracing it, everything became easier. I
enjoy the hunger, the way it burns, the way it feels throughout your
form so much that I created this level of hell in order to always
carry a piece of it with me."*

"Do you not feel the hunger anymore?"

"Not at the level of which you do Ryan. I have mastered the true art of dealing with it and one day you will as well. You must always remember though that until the day of mastery comes, you must remain in your demon form in order to make it through. It is my hope that as you grow and become one with the evil inside of you that you will enjoy it as much as I."

I had no doubt given everything he described that I would be like him in the end. That I would do as he wanted and embrace it, enjoying it and mastering it much the same way as he had before me. I could feel in it me now as made our way slowly through, passing the demons as they searched for the smell they were intoxicated by. I am beginning to enjoy it already.

*****

Remembering the darkest times of my life is never easy for me but it did give me a knowledge that until now I had forgotten about, choosing instead to be guided by the light. I have to heed his words now if I want to make it through this portion and I'm going to have to make sure that the angels and Graham knew exactly what's coming. I can't let them see the change in me after the fact. It would spell certain death.

"Ryan, are you alright?" Michael asked as he paused in his movements, noticing that I had frozen in place.

"Yeah Mike, I'm fine but there's something I need to make sure you know before we face them."

"What would that be? Is there something you have recalled that may help us in making it through this level of depravity?"

"I don't know if it's going to help you but it's the only way that I can make it through alive."

"What is it that you remember?"

"I need to let the demon side of me take over. I warned you before that these particular demons will smell the human blood and even your power given the pure nature of it but I didn't really focus on me. I remember the first time I was here now. Lucifer told me something in order to help me make it through and I'm going to have to use that now in order to keep going."

"When you accept the change within you, are you able to control yourself as it pertains to Graham?"

I'm glad he understood what I was trying to say and what it would mean for all of us moving forward. He was asking all the right questions and I felt secure in the knowledge that even if I had to go dark side in order to make it through, this particular angel would bring me back before it went too far.

"Yes. I've learned enough since accepting what I am to be able to control myself around the humans. I just need to make sure you know going in that I will most definitely be acting like the very demons we are trying to defeat. If it gets out of hand I need to know that you will do whatever it takes to stop it."

"You have my word Ryan. I do not want to hurt you but if it goes to a point where I think that is the only way to prevent something far more sinister I will handle it."

"Thank you."

"You are most welcome."

Now that I know Michael would have my back and be able to guard against anything I might end up doing, I'm more secure moving forward. I will keep myself in control as much as possible and I would get all of us through this because I know that with what comes next, I can't afford not to.

As we rounded the bend I saw them. The very beings that just like me desired the blood of a pure human more than any other delicacy above or below. They are strong, hungry and would stop at nothing to get what they desire. Allowing the hunger in me to rise up, the anger coming right along with it, I felt the change in my body. In a few seconds I would no longer be Ryan the human but Ryan the demon.

I have to make sure before the change occurs that Gabriel and Michael know that this is the phase they were needed most.

"You must make contact with each of them and you must touch them. Your touch alone will bring them down. Graham can use the blade to injure the ones that come at him but he will not be able to end them."

"What will you do?"

"Give them something to feed on." I answer my voice flat. I would give the angels what they need in order to get past this stage even though it was going to hurt my human form to do so.

Bringing the blade to my wrist, I sliced it across, opening up the skin until the dark red color of my blood began rising to the surface. Yes these are the demons that demanded blood and as such I'm going to give them exactly what they want.

"Are you sure this is what you should be doing Ryan?" Michael called to me. His voice came through hazy as I was losing even more of myself to the darkness and before it completely took over, I answered him.

"It's the only thing I can do."

Gabriel

Ryan has done something for us that though knowing him, I never expected of him. He sacrificed his own human form in order to give us the upper hand with the demons we just finished defeating.

Not only did he open his body up to give them the scent of his blood but he also had given Michael and I exactly what we needed in terms of weaponry to be able to defeat them. As the demons drew away from Graham and the scent of his much protected blood, choosing instead to make their way toward the blood that was now slowly making its way to the ground below we were able to take them out one by one, just with the power of Heaven that we held so strongly in our fingertips.

Father had been right when he said the being we knew as the half demon was really made of Heaven. That he is the purest angel that he had ever had the pleasure of creating. I could see that clear now as he gave himself up in order for us to move forward in our effort to save the woman he loves.

"Are we really going to let them feed on him?" Graham called, his face a mask of horror as he watched the remaining blood driven demons sucking away at the marks Ryan placed on his skin.

103

"No we are going to do away with them as we have the others." Michael stated, quickly making his way up behind the feeding demons and placing his arms across their forms.

I didn't want to admit it but it is empowering watching my brother work in the manner he did. This really is the element that Michael is most comfortable in and I am thankful he didn't need my assistance now because I was more than happy to watch from the sidelines and see him at his strongest. While our power levels may be decreased in this place, the fight within Michael is not.

As the last of the demon forms disappeared before our eyes, Graham and I immediately moved in to where Ryan's drained form lay. I only hope that in allowing us the chance to get the upper hand, he had not fallen too deep into the darkness he had been born of.

"Gabriel, you must begin to heal the boy. I fear he has lost far too much blood in doing what he did."

Michael didn't have to explain that to me. I could tell by the color of his skin, the faded pink that it was now becoming that he is not in his top form. I also knew from seeing his eyes as he opened himself up to the demons before him that he was also not the human he had been only a few short minutes before. He is now one of the very same members of the darkness we just annihilated.

"He warned me of the way he would be in this form brother. If he makes a move on you I am to handle it accordingly. Please do as I ask."

With Michael's words reverberating in my mind, I kneeled to where Ryan lay and placed my hand on the wrists he had openly marked minutes before. Using whatever power available to me, I forced it forward in an effort to not only heal the cuts but also strengthen him again. As the light surrounded his body I watched the color begin to come back to its normal state through his body.

Content that what had been done is working, I rose again and made my way back to where Graham stood frozen in place, his face a mask of concern for his fallen partner and horror at having to see it at all. I should concern myself with his mental state but given everything we had already been through, I knew it was better having him come to terms with everything himself. It is the only way it would make sense for him.

"I want to hate him but I can't."

"I know Graham. You want to believe him to be the inherent source of all the evil that you have been through over the course of the last year but seeing the way in which he sacrificed himself to save you, you are unable to do so."

"Yeah, that's it exactly, though I don't think I would have used that many words."

"Of course not."

"Is he going to be alright?"

"In time he will be his normal self again but until then we wait."

The truth of the matter is that while I want to give Ryan all the time he needs in order to gain his full strength and power again, time is not on our side. We are dangerously close to the last level of demons that we have to pass through in order to come face to face with my brother again and we need to move quicker than ever now.

"Did...it...work?" Ryan choked out as he began moving from his position on the ground.

Before I could reach out to help, Michael stepped forward blocking my way. Reaching out to him I watched as he helped him to his feet and surrounded him in his light, one that given the use of the healing power I just used, was infinitely stronger then my own. Michael is now showering him in protective light, just the way I wanted to.

"It worked Ryan. We have defeated the level of blood thirsty demons just as you knew we would when you made your bonehead move." Michael answered, his voice giving away nothing of his true feelings but his words speaking volumes.

"Did I hurt any of you?"

"You did not. The only one hurt in what came next was you, something that my brother fixed."

"Thanks." Ryan said, his eyes lifting only slightly in my direction.

"You are most welcome. My only hope is that my power was strong enough to heal you to maximum capacity again."

"You make him sound like a robot man. Just say you wanted to heal him so he was normal or something." Graham interrupted laughing.

"He's right man. You do make me sound like a cyborg but just so you know, I feel fine."

While I did not enjoy the two of them picking at my choice of words I understand what they are getting at. It is always going to be one of the ways we differ. I would never speak like one of them but I was more than pleased that I had healed him to where he sounded more like himself. That is what I am choosing to focus on.

"When we get out of here, I want to know what a cyborg is. For now, let's just focus on the last phase." Michael stated bringing our true reason for being back to the surface. The time for joking over.

"Ryan I do believe you need to go over the last phase with us again. Given everything we have been through over the last few hours, we need to have our minds refreshed. With the trauma of the last wave we need to know if we can expect much the same again."

I watched as his face contorted, obviously remembering just what is about to come next. Whether it is memories of a time he had been here before or just the realization of what is to come, it was more than obvious this is a trial he was not looking forward to. Not that one could look forward to any of this, demon or not.

"We're about to walk into the true meaning of hell. The torture chambers. Pure torture demons who do not feel anything but the pleasure that comes from torturing the very light out the beings they drag down here. This is where the cat and mouse game Lucifer designed stops. The mouse has been caught and it meets its end."

There is finality in his explanation that is not lost on me. This is the one area at which a being of light has never been able to pass through. We were always caught in this place and we met our inevitable end. None of us wanted to focus on that fate being possible but unfortunately we had to if we want to move forward with the ultimate amount of knowledge.

106

"There are actual torture chambers here?"

"Come on Graham, this is hell. Who do you think came up with them on Earth? Lucifer was the original designer, so of course he would have them here."

This is one area I know Graham will have the most difficulty with. A few months before he had been a victim of Lucifer and his torture techniques. Walking into what we were about to is only going to spark the memory of that time and if we are not careful we might lose the boy again, which is something I am just not comfortable with.

"This is where the protection that we have put on Graham has to be at its strongest. This is your weak area Graham."

"You don't need to tell me Gabe, I get it. I was tortured so seeing it again could trigger something in me. I'm a risk. I know that."

"No man I don't think you are a risk here." Ryan answered. "You having gone through it with Lucifer already might actually make you the only one that can handle it."

"How do you figure that? He broke me once before, what's stopping me from breaking again?"

"Your experience." Ryan answered back immediately, leaving no room for doubt in his belief.

"I thought that just makes me the weak link, like Gabriel said."

"Honestly, it should make you the weaker one but I've seen you fight man. Lucifer may have broken you but it wasn't easy and look at you now. You're back to normal. No residual effects of what he did which means no weaknesses. You're going in at what Gabe calls full capacity. You've got this. It's the rest of us that need to be concerned."

"How do you mean?" I asked, wondering just what Michael and I had to fear as it pertained to the torture demons given the beings that we are and our defenses against such things.

"You're on limited power supply for one and for two; I've only been the one doing the torturing. I'm still human and I can be manipulated. This is where the demon side of me again comes into play. It's the only way I can make it through this alive. I'm not

107

doing it though. I will fight this without the damn demon inside of me."

I could not argue with his assessment of our power supply but I was not going to agree to let him face this without using the power he has at his disposal. Even if the power is made of inherent and pure evil it could still prove useful.

"You do not want to do that Ryan. You must face this using whatever method necessary."

"You don't get it. I'm like Lucifer. I enjoy not only the blood draining but the torture. Ripping the light from someone for me is the same as scoring a hit is for a drug addict. If I allow myself to walk in there with the demon guiding me, I will turn on you even knowing that we're doing all of this for Serenity. It won't matter. I will deviate back to what drives me underneath it all."

"You will do this even knowing it puts us at a disadvantage?"

"If it means keeping you safe from me then yeah, I will."

"Then let us go and pray that we make it through what no other being before us has."

Serenity

I can't let him see this.

I'm not even sure how I can explain it considering that up until a few minutes ago there had been nothing there. I had been resting, as Lucifer asked of me and suddenly I felt the most excruciating pain and pulling myself from the dream I found myself in I saw it.

The stain of blood on the sheets below me is the first thing I notice and then in my search to find out where it originated from I notice the cuts. Two delicate slices across both of my wrists, an eerie reminder of the markings Ryan gave me when he drained the life from me.

Why are they appearing now? Is it happening because as Lucifer said they were here and prepared to rescue me the way I prayed for? Or is there something more going on?

For a bit after I noticed the cuts they continued to spill my blood. No amount of wiping at it or even sucking the blood in an effort to stop it worked. It just continued to spill and then just as easily as the pain had shown up and the blood began to spill it stopped. What had been an open wound slowly began to close until now they were just two delicate scars that could only be looked at as a reminder of days past.

I need answers but the only way I can get them is to take the issue to the man I just asked to fight for me. If I took this to him now then I would also have to take the doubts that are now flooding my mind to him as well and that is something I just can't do. He could not find out that whatever was happening to me physically is also affecting me emotionally. That I feel a pull I can't explain drawing me away from him.

Ryan's here. I feel him and I know that is what the pull really is though I'm not entirely sure I'm ready to face it. Whatever is happening to him out there I can't allow myself to feel for. I chose to be here with Lucifer and whatever happens from this point has to continue the way it will without interference from me. Just as I made the decision that day to give myself over to save him, I have done so again only this time for the opposite side.

The prayer I made early in my time here has to be forgotten. Time and knowledge have changed my mind and despite the strength of the pull in me now to walk away from my choice I cannot allow it to win. I will not turn my back on Lucifer no matter how much Ryan wants me to.

"Serenity we must speak."

Shit. Not now.

"What do we need to speak about?"

"Well I think it imperative we speak about what is about to come but I also see that we have other more pressing issues to deal with first."

Looking across the room at him I could see just what the pressing issue is. He sees the blood stains on the floor in front of me and also on the bed. As much as I don't want to deal with this now, I know there is no way around it.

"I don't know what's going on. Something is happening to me and it just doesn't make any sense." I sigh. "I think you might know what this is though."

"I cannot say with any degree of certainty that I do. You must explain everything to me my belle and then maybe we can make some sense of this together."

This is exactly what I don't want to do. Telling him what happened to me and also what I'm beginning to feel is only going to spell trouble. I can feel it. He is going to end up changing on me, pulling away or whatever he does when he's upset and that is definitely not something I want to experience.

"Serenity my belle, you must tell me even if you think it will hurt me."

"I was resting and woke up to the blood on the bed. When my attempts at trying to stop the flow didn't help I stood, thinking that a movement change might but it didn't, which is why there is trails of blood everywhere. I have no idea why this is happening to me but as you can see, it stopped." I say holding up my wrists to show him exactly what happened in his time apart from me.

The scars are light brown now, as if they have healed completely and they look more like the marks I had after the incident in Green Haven and less like something that happened only minutes before. It's a phenomenon I can't even begin to understand.

"I sense there is more that you are not telling me."

"You are aware of the pull between Ryan and me. I am feeling it much stronger now and it is becoming harder to ignore. I feel myself being pulled away from you and the life you want for us and again moving in his direction, something I do not want."

"Do not fight it. Let whatever is occurring happen naturally. You are bonded to my protégé in a way I am unfamiliar with but in order to come up with a way to combat it, I need to see it in its natural way. Can you do that for me?"

"I will do whatever you ask of me. I just do not want anything to change between us."

"Oh my belle, nothing has changed, of that be assured. This is not something of your design, it is made of the light and I will find a way around it."

As he made his way over, pulling me into him, I immediately felt my heart begin to steady. The fears I had in telling him were slowly being washed away as his arms around me gave me all of the answers I need. He may be affected by what I told him but he is not going to let it tear us apart the way I assumed.

It is in the moment standing completely still that I feel it for the first time since my time here began.

True peace.

CHAPTER THIRTEEN

Graham

Confronting the torture that I had been victim to during the time Lucifer held me captive is not something I ever want to do.

Even during the time where my body was healing, both through Heavenly intervention and that of the local hospital I didn't focus on it. It's something that I thought I could face at a later date when I healed completely and I was on more stable footing with my actual life again.

Ryan's belief that I'm stronger because of what I endured is insane. If anything, all I can see it doing is making me weaker. If we're going to be going head to head with demons that spent their entire existences doing exactly what had been done to me there is no way I would be able to defeat it. I will fall victim again no matter what anyone else thinks.

I've always thought myself to be a pretty strong guy. I can handle anything thrown at me and come out on top of it. All I need is time to adapt to it. Going through everything the way I did with the King of Hell, it taught me that I'm not exactly as strong as I believe I am. In fact, I actually believe he was right when he said that humans are weak compared to the angels, especially the fallen ones. I'm no better than any other human he used his power on. I broke as easily as a porcelain tea set.

It's not something I like to admit but I'm still screwed up by what he did to me all those months. I can still smell the blood he made me drink and sometimes even find myself craving it. I can still see Serenity as the life was drained from her and the look on Ryan's face as he did it. I can still taste the blood as he drank it even though it has nothing to do with me. Those memory dumps he did on me still get to me too. I always know when I'm being affected by it because the headaches become more then I can handle.

This is what I face going forward. All of this is coming to the surface and I'm being forced to confront it all. In order to save

Serenity I have to. I'll do it of course but I'm not about to share it with the people I'm fighting with. They can't know the doubts I have or even the fear I have with reliving everything that I am. It would only mean that things would be more dangerous going forward.

I have to stay strong no matter how much it's getting to me. Anything else is just unacceptable.

"How do we deal with this moving forward?"

"You mean how do we fight?" Ryan asked, his focus remaining on the steps he was taking yet still turning just enough to acknowledge he heard me.

"Yeah."

"Gabe and Michael are gonna use their power like they did with the lower level demons and we are going to use our weapons as much as possible but we have to avoid letting them touch us. This time not because of the mind tricks."

"Then why?"

"The minute they touch you, they will put you in a chamber, or at least have you chained. It's immediate and you don't even get a second to get yourself out of it."

Okay so I couldn't let these demons anywhere near me. Where I failed before letting them get too close to me, paying the price, I can't do the same here. I have to get them before they get me.

"Will it have the same affect on the angels?"

"No. They get touched and their power drains. Then after that they are like humans to the torture demons."

Shit. It's even worse than I thought. If Gabriel or Michael fall victim to anything they will lose the only defense they have and would become no better than me going up against Lucifer. Not only did we have to protect ourselves from being caught but them too because we need their power.

"How many are we looking at dealing with?"

"That's where it gets kind of funny. While he locked and loaded the others levels of hell with as many demons as possible there are only fifteen torture demons. At least that's how many were here when he brought me the last time."

"That doesn't seem so bad."

113

"Yeah that's what they all say until you're face to face with one. Be ready Graham, that's all I can say."

He has no idea just how ready I am. I can just make out the beginning of what looks to be the area where the torturing happens and just the site of the bindings attached to the wall made my stomach tie up in knots. I remember those metal bindings more than I want to admit. I'm going to make damn sure I wasn't caught in them again. Once had definitely been enough.

"Tame the anger. I'm feeding off it." Ryan snapped which caused me to take a step back falling right into line with Gabriel and Michael who had taken up the rear in the travels.

"He's right Graham. You must remain clear of any and all emotion now more than ever. We have you protected as much as possible."

"Easier said than done Michael." I mumbled, shooting Gabriel one final look. With only a nod in response I again focus on what lay ahead. If Gabriel is in agreement with Michael and Ryan then I know I have to be too. I have to do what they tell me. It's the only way.

"Michael you go in first and then Gabriel should join you. You need to take as many of them out with those orbs of power as possible. It's going to take more than one per demon. If you can break them up enough, Graham and I can take out the rest with the blades."

"I was hoping you would say that." Michael said grinning and immediately moving forward toward the very chamber I was dreading. It looks like I'm about to get a bird's eye view of Michael in his element.

"Be careful brother, do not go in blind." Gabriel called as Michael drew even further away from us, his intent more than clear."

"Do not worry brother, I got this."

I'm not sure what's crazier in this moment for me. Facing torture demons or hearing Michael's voice in my head even though he isn't speaking to anyone but Gabriel.

When did this become my life?

"The minute you were split from Serenity." Gabriel said his voice barely a whisper.

Jesus. He needs to stop doing that. I thought shaking off the truth of his words.

Watching as Gabriel moved himself forward, ready to join his brother in the fight against the demons that waited for us; I stood and watched as the torture chamber around me began to light up under their power. Limited or not it was amazing to see.

"You ready Graham?"

Steeling myself for what we were about to walk into I let Ryan's question sink in. Am I really ready to do this? Face my own demons head on?

There was only one answer I could give, ready or not.

"Let's do this."

Ryan

There are many forms of torture that one can use when draining the light from an unwilling victim. Lucifer taught me each way in graphic detail and all stages were visible the minute that Graham and I enter the chambers.

The way that Lucifer dealt with Graham during their time together only showed two types but in reality there are more like five that can be employed for maximum impact. The use of memories is the first form and one that I know the man standing beside me knew better than most. Taking all of the good memories and then combining them with the bad did a great deal of damage to the beings that are truly born of light.

Add to that the manipulation of the senses which from everything I learned had also happened during Graham's time with him and it is usually more than enough to bring even the strongest to their knees.

The physical beating came next if the other two methods didn't work. The part where the torturer would cut and burn their victim until they gave themselves over completely or at least until they had nothing left in them to fight with. As much as I hate to admit it, this was always my drug of choice in terms of torture.

115

Even now I can remember the thrill of cutting into the flesh and watching the blood run freely from it, the smell so intoxicating it usually ended with me drinking of it even though it's never part of the plan.

Possessing them when they are on the brink of death is the next form of torture. Making the human soul do things in its body that they had no control over and watching as it ripped itself apart from the inside out was probably the worst form of torture other then the last which is death itself. I enjoyed possessing but never as much as the man that taught me everything there was to know about it.

It's evident with the amount of bodies lying throughout the room that death seemed to be the only method of extraction for most of them. It appears as though the torture demons had gotten a batch of strong souls to deal with this time around. As such death is the only way for them to get what they ultimately wanted.

If I wasn't so used to it by now it would have turned my stomach, something that I could tell by Graham's face now that it did with him. He's seeing something even darker then what he experienced and there is no way I can shelter him from it. In order to move forward he has to come to terms with this and handle himself accordingly.

The minute he moved I realized that whatever had been said before we came into the room worked because he seems to have shed all signs of fear and loathing for what he is about to do and immediately gone on the offensive. As his blade tore through one demon after another, as mine did following suit I realized that when we all made it out of here, we were going to have to make sure Graham more so then the rest of us made it out in one piece.

He is reaching a point now where the level of darkness he is surrounded by is definitely making its way into his psyche. He was going to feel the effects of this, especially this portion for a long time to come.

The room was bathed in light as Michael and Gabriel used their power to bring down the demons that had them surrounded. Where I had warned them of only fifteen it appeared as though Lucifer had bumped up the tally over the years as the room was now filled with at least 50, not counting the ones we had already managed to do away with.

It's only when I heard the scream from across the room that I realize our worst fears for this mission are coming to light. As strong as the angels still are it appears as though Gabriel had still managed to fall victim just the way I described.

"Michael, use your light and protect your brother before they can touch him again." I yell slicing my way through the two demons that are now blocking my path. Making a run for it, praying Graham is able to handle the load around him on his own I watched as Michael did exactly as I said and wrapped the protective light around his fallen brother.

"What happened to him?" Michael called to me as he shot another blast of energy at the demons around him.

"One of them touched him. Drained him of his power. He's as good as human now, at least until we can get him out of here and heal him."

"I am not the healer. I am the warrior."

Shit, that isn't going to be good.

"Just keep doing your thing then Xena; I'll handle your brother. As long as he's protected with whatever you just did he should be fine. We just have to keep them off him again for the duration."

"Is he able to still fight with the blade?"

"Yeah." I answered turning to Gabriel and using my strength to pull him back to his feet. "You got this man?"

"Yes. Those bastards might have taken my power but I will have the last laugh."

If we weren't in the heat of it I would question every word that just fell out of his mouth but as it is, we needed to put our focus on finishing what we started. There could be no more breaks. It was time to fight.

Glancing back at Graham and seeing him coming toward us, the demons that had been surrounding him now piles of ash on the floor, I couldn't help but smile. He's proving exactly what I knew the entire time. He can handle these more than any other demon because of his experience. He knew what was coming before it even reached him.

He is the real champion.

When he made his way to where we stood, in a line formation we all began moving forward, determined to finish the rest off once and for all. It was in that moment as we all looked the worst of death in the face that I knew we were going to make it past this and get to the man himself.

There really is strength in numbers, especially when those numbers want the exact same thing.

"We're coming pretty girl, get ready. You're coming home."

CHAPTER FOURTEEN

Serenity

Yes I am most definitely connecting to him now. With his words reverberating in my mind and my heart wanting so desperately to grab onto them for dear life I can feel the light inside me beginning to grow again. Where it has been dormant for what feels like days, now it is coming to the surface again and I am powerless to prevent it.

There is still a part of me that was fighting against it, wanting nothing more than to stick to the plan at which I had come to terms with before. I accepted what was to be my life here with Lucifer and despite the pull from Ryan now I still want to stick to it. Even if everyone else wants me to do something different.

When he came to me earlier and explained exactly what it is that he wanted me to do I was against it. I fought him tooth and nail and even now I still wanted to even though he had eventually broken me down and gotten me to agree to his terms. I understand what he wants me to do and why but there has to be another way around it.

Knowing Ryan the way I do, I knew that if I just explain everything to him and why I felt I need to do what I am going to do that he would bend to me. He would have to accept it because of the way he felt about me but Lucifer wants no part of that. For whatever reason, he doesn't want this to come to a head the way that it appears it's going to with each moment that passes.

He is so close. I can feel his heart beat from here and while I don't understand how that is even possible, I'm allowing myself to hold onto it. To let that pull that has always been between us to grow. My body is reacting but so is my heart and it is that reaction that I most want to embrace now as his words repeat over and over in a loop in my mind.

"We're coming pretty girl, get ready. You're coming home."

All of the darkness, pain, torture and inherent evil that I have been starting to embrace is fading away in favor of the light that

119

being around him gave me. The way I felt waking up to him the morning after we made love for the first time paramount in my mind and guiding me even more towards the heart that beat inside of his chest.

The one that beat for me and me alone. Just as mine beat for him despite the way Lucifer has gotten to me.

I can see it all so clearly now, the haze of earlier lifting. There is still a conflict within me but it isn't nearly as strong as it had been hours before. No, now I am allowing the light to win, the very light that Lucifer had chosen not to strip me off this time around. It is allowing me to see and experience everything that I forced to the background.

Ryan's eyes and the way they crinkle when he smiles. The wicked way he grins at me when sharing a private moment between just the two of us. The way he smelled the day we had our picnic and how intoxicating it really had been for me then. So powerful is everything running through me that I could smell him, taste the way his lips felt when they were pressed against mine and the way his body felt as it curled itself around mine during our last moments together in my dorm room.

He's definitely close now and guided by a force stronger then one of my own making, I made my way to the door, fully prepared to walk through and meet him halfway, making the dream of him sweeping in and picking me up into his arms that much more of a reality.

I am more than ready for him.

Before I could make my way out the door of the room, Lucifer appeared before me and gently pulled me back in, making sure the now opened door shut tight behind him.

"I know what is happening Serenity but before they come for you, I just need one more moment alone with you."

Considering the plan he laid out during our time earlier I was more than willing to give him the time he requested. He is sacrificing now just as I was known to and as such deserved to be heard.

"I just want you to be aware that I will not fight them as I promised you earlier. I will let them take that which they are here to save. It is why I did not attempt to stop them as they made their way closer to us. I know that you do not fully understand why I am making this choice but all will be revealed in time."

He was right, I didn't get why he is going to give me over when I asked him to fight for me but given the level of sadness in his eyes now, I knew I would bend to whatever he wanted me to. I might be leaving Hell and leaving him behind but I am leaving with knowledge now that no one would ever take away from me.

"Are you sure this is what you want?" I ask, wanting to make sure before whatever came next that he is secure in his decision. The look in his eyes told me a completely different story and I was hoping that he wouldn't try and hide it from me. I need his honesty more than ever now.

"I am positive. I do not want to let you go, you must trust me on that but in an effort to secure what will come next for the both of us, I have to do it."

"What do you mean by that? You have to do what? Let me go or something more?"

"My sweet belle, I am so sorry. Please forgive me for what I must do."

Before I can react to his words I feel the world begin to go hazy around me as I fall to my knees on the floor, desperately trying to fight whatever he's doing to me but failing. Where I felt his hands only seconds before on my head, I now feel nothing but the air around me and it is then that the darkness sets in.

As my eyes begin to close I allow myself one final look at the man kneeling by my side now and am touched by what I see before everything goes dark.

There is a single tear, slowly making its way from the corner of his eye down his cheek.

Ryan

I wasn't sure what to expect when I saw Serenity again after the hell both her and I have been through over the course of the last few months but it is definitely not this.

Lucifer making his toward us, Serenity tightly held in his arms, her limp body appearing as if she is just sleeping peacefully, something I know better than to believe. If he is bringing her towards us this way now it means that he's done with her. Whatever sick shit he wanted her for, she no longer held the appeal. I only hope he didn't actually kill her.

We all stood together, the angels, along with Graham, seemingly transfixed by the vision taking place in front of us. It's obvious from the look of fear Graham wore and the confusion on the faces of the angels that I'm not the only one who didn't like the way this looks.

"Stand down Ryan; I am not here to fight you. I am here merely to give you what it is you want most."

His calm reaction and what the words he said meant only made me question his end game even more then I did before we came here. How can he be calm coming face to face with me again when he knew I was here to take her back from him? Isn't Serenity the point of all of this? Since when is he just going to willingly give her over?

"At what price?" I spit out, not hiding my distrust for a second. He had to know by now that I wasn't just going to take anything he said at face value, not when I knew him so well.

"There is no price. I am aware of the war the four of you have waged during your time here and I know the reason behind it. You want Serenity back and I am going to give her to you. I only have one request."

Of course he has a request. No price my ass. Everything he did always had something attached to it and this is going to be no different. Too bad I'm not in a mood to barter.

"Ryan, hear him out. I sense no ill will from my fallen brother." Gabriel spoke, taking my attention immediately away from Lucifer, still holding Serenity's limp form and instead putting it all on the angel.

"You're kidding me right? In the same breath as he said there is no price he's putting a price on it. Just like always. I'm not listening to it. If he won't give her to me willingly then I am going to take her by force."

122

"You would be wise to listen to my brother Ryan. The request I have is not malicious in its intent. It is pure and both Michael and Gabriel can attest to it."

Gabriel had been taken for a ride by Lucifer before so there is no way I am willing to trust anything he has to say but with Michael, he has never done me wrong at any point. If he told me that what his brother was saying is true then I would stand down but not a second before.

"Listen to him Ryan. He is telling the truth, though I am as shocked by it as you."

Taking a step back and gaining control of the anger that's building in me, just itching for a fight, I did as Michael requested and I waited for Lucifer to state his request even though I wanted to do anything but.

"My only request is that you let me hand her off to Gabriel. She is in need of healing and he is the only one that can give her the adequate care she needs."

Healing? What the hell did he do to her?

"What the fuck did you do to her you sick son of a bitch?"

"I did only what needed to be done. When you take her from this place she will remember nothing of her time here. It is my gift to her."

"She doesn't need any of your so called gifts. All you do is damage and destroy everything you come into contact with. You just better pray you didn't do that to her or I'll come back and this time I won't rest until you're lying dead at my feet."

I meant every word I said. If there is even a hair out of place on her head I would come back here again and I wouldn't leave until I had gotten what I came for. His head on a platter the way it should have been a year ago. I would make him pay for the havoc he created, not only for me but for the very woman he held in his arms right now.

"In order for us to grant your request Lucifer, you must do something for us in return." Michael said stepping forward and motioning toward Gabriel. "Your torture demons removed his power and as you well know that means we cannot grant your request unless you reinstate it."

I expected him to actually think about what his brother was saying but before I could prepare myself for the typical dragging out of the situation he was known for, he spoke again and took me completely by surprise.

"Of course. Whatever needs to be done in order for her to be healed, I will do. Bring Gabriel to me."

"Is this really happening?" Graham leaned in and whispered. "Since when is he this helpful?"

I couldn't answer him, at least not with anything that made sense. I had no idea why he was acting this docile to us given the hell he just put us through. I expected way more of a fight in coming here to get her away from him but instead was being met with nothing but kindness. It's something I know that the King of Hell just doesn't have. I was just as confused as Graham watching Michael walk towards his brother with Gabriel in tow.

Things became even weirder as I watched Lucifer restore the light inside of Gabriel. He is standing by his word. With as crazy as it all is, I still waited patiently for the other shoe to drop. Things really couldn't go this smoothly. There has to be something up his sleeve and it's only going to take another few seconds before I'm sure we find out what it is.

"You may take her now brother. Please be careful though. While she is merely sleeping at the moment there may be damage I am unaware of as I was unable to catch her as she fell."

When she fell? Fell from where? How? What the hell is he talking about?

The questions flooded my brain until I couldn't handle them anymore and it's only then that he spoke again and this time he again directed it back at me.

"She wanted to remain here with me as I predicted when I brought her with me but I cannot allow that to happen right now, not when the bond with you is so strong within her. So I am giving her over to you until such time as I believe she needs to come home again."

"This will never be her home." I seethed. "The minute we take her from here it will be over my dead body that you see her again."

124

"You know how easily that can be arranged Ryan but I do understand where the burst of emotion comes from within you. You love her, it is plain as day. Please take her now before I change my mind."

"Michael, take both Gabriel and Serenity out of here. I'm not done here."

I know the request is a long shot but I have to take it. I knew Graham wanted time with Lucifer even more then I did and the sooner they got Serenity out of here the sooner she would be able to heal. It was a win for all of us. I would worry about getting Graham out of here later. Right now I still wanted face time with the asshole in front of me.

His little act wasn't going to continue any longer because I see right through it.

"As you wish Ryan. Call for me when you are topside."

He vanished then, taking both Gabriel and the sleeping Serenity with him and once they completely disappeared I finally let out of the breath I had been holding. She is safe and she is free. We succeeded with what we had come here to do.

It's a good feeling.

"We have nothing more to say to one another. I will allow you exit from here easily if you leave now but push it any further and I will make sure Serenity sees neither one of you again."

"I'll risk it." Graham spoke up as he moved toward Lucifer, his face now a mask of anger.

"It is nice to see you again Graham and even more pleasurable to see the anger of past lifetimes alive and well inside of you burning bright but I am afraid I stick to my earlier statement, if you do not leave now as I have requested, you will meet your untimely end."

Grabbing onto Graham and pulling him back with all the strength I had left, I got him close enough so that I was able to whisper to him. While Lucifer still might hear us I was willing to take the risk.

"Remember what the angels said Graham. We can do this another time. Right now we need to get back to Serenity."

Given that I wanted nothing more than to stay here and fight right alongside Graham and take him down once and for all, I was starting to see just what Gabriel and Michael had been trying to make clear from the beginning. We succeeded in our goal and right now nothing else mattered but that. We could have a shot at Lucifer another day.

That is definitely a promise I intend to keep. I would get revenge, not only for Serenity but for Graham and myself as well.

"That son of a bitch rode around inside of me for months, making me turn my back on everything that was right. I am not leaving until I make him pay for it."

Lucifer stepped forward and I immediately put myself between them. If this was about to come to blows then Graham wasn't going to be one taking the attack. I would.

"I merely want to apologize to the boy Ryan, you can relax."

"You'll excuse me if I don't believe a word of that."

"You always did doubt me far too much. I would have though my record of truth spoke volumes about my credibility."

"It does but it's everything else you've done that I question."

"Well then let me say it from here then. I am sorry for what I put you through during our time together Graham. You were a means to an end. I did enjoy our time together and will always look back on it fondly. You were more than just a suitable vessel for me."

"Graham, let's go. I know you want to pound the shit out of him but it's gonna have to wait. She needs us more."

As he looked up at me and really took in what I said he immediately backed down the way I wanted him to. It seems that just like I do, he also reacts most when the topic of Serenity is brought up. Minutes before he wanted to waste the King of Hell now he wants to just make our way back to Serenity.

"Fine, we'll go but I promise you. This isn't over."

"I'm counting on it."

CHAPTER FIFTEEN

Gabriel

There hasn't been many times over the last year where we've had any cause for celebration but seeing the sleeping form of the woman now, I know I have been given one. We have all been given one. Serenity is indeed home, though not in a bed of her choosing and she looks no worse for wear.

I am aware that time with Lucifer does not always manifest itself in the physical way especially after our dealings with Graham but I would focus on anything going on internally with her later. I was just pleased to see that physically she was still very much the same Serenity she has always been.

"It is seeing her in this form that reminds me that she is definitely an agent of heaven brother. Has there ever been a more peaceful being then the one we find ourselves in front of?"

In watching her as intently as I was, I had almost forgotten that we were not alone in the room together. That Michael is there with us and is just as pleased as me that we had succeeded with our task where all others before us failed. The animosity I held before our trip into the dungeons of hell is now replaced with the utmost love and respect, much the way it has always been.

Of all the people that I could share this moment with I am content that it is Michael. He understands what I am feeling most of all.

"I do not believe I have ever seen a more accurate vision of Heaven then the one before us now." I reply in kind, finding myself choked up at the sight of her now resting form before me. There is so much I am feeling in the moment but there are no words I am aware of that can adequately describe it. It is beautiful in its simplicity.

There is an underlying issue that needs to be given the proper focus but I am against being the one to bring it up. We both know what would come the minute Father is able to locate us again, which shouldn't be much longer and we were going to face his

127

wrath the minute that occurred. While we had done the right thing, it was definitely not going to appear that way to our father who specifically warned us from this very thing before we began.

"Do not let Father and his displeasure with us ruin this moment Gabriel. We will deal with him in due time. Until then I suggest we just enjoy this gift we have been given and focus on how to make it even better from here. Are you positive that your healing will have the desired results?"

Michael informed me of what needed to be done in order for me to be able to heal Serenity and I was none too pleased. Allowing my fallen brother to be anywhere near the light inside of me was a dangerous move but it appears as though he had done what he told Michael he would do and had indeed put me back the way I was meant to be. It enabled me to heal Serenity in the way she needs in order to face her human life again and I am more than content that the healing would work the way it is meant to.

"The healing will have the desired affect but it is Lucifer's words to you that concern me more at this stage Michael."

"What exactly concerns you about them brother?"

"He made mention of erasing her memory did he not? There is no way of knowing just how much that will damage her and it concerns me to no end. Without knowing the full extent of her memory loss I am unsure how to proceed."

"We have to proceed as we normally would Gabriel. Until she wakes and we are able to ascertain just how much has been done we can only work the way we have been trained to. We will adapt as we see fit. I know this concerns you on more than the angelic level and it is completely understandable but you must not jump the gun."

Michael was correct in his assessment of the situation. I am indeed concerned for Serenity's well being on more than just the celestial level. I knew that I would do whatever it took with the power I commanded to make sure she healed and is able to get back to life in a timely manner but as it pertained to her memory loss, I was afraid just how that would affect us all moving forward.

Would she recall the bond that had been forged between us before her time in Hell? Would she recall anything of her time there or had Lucifer really been telling the truth when he claimed to have taken that time away from her as a gift?

"Brother, we are being summoned."

Michael's words cut through me like a knife. We had just gotten her home and while I expected to be summoned, couldn't Father have chosen a more opportune time? Serenity is in a dream like state but will wake at any moment and if she woke up alone I fear for what she would face. I want to be here for her when the time comes so I can guide her appropriately.

"You go Michael. Explain to him that I need to be here right now. I know that he will not enjoy that explanation but it is all I have to give. I do not want her going through any of this alone. She has been alone for far too long as it is."

"Gabriel, you know that I cannot do that. It has to be the both of us or the end result will be far worse. You must come with me now and we must receive whatever Father's true punishment is and only then can we make our way back down here. The last thing we need now is to be forbidden from her forever."

Again my brother is the pillar of knowledge. Father would most definitely forbid us from Serenity should I do as I want and stay here with her. It is something that at this point I cannot afford. She needs me now more than ever.

"Fine, let's get this over with."

"Spoken like a true human. Nicely done brother, it's time to face the music."

Graham

Ever since we made it out it's been bothering me. I didn't want to tell Ryan but it was getting to a point where I'm beginning to have no other choice. Lucifer's words continue to play on a loop in my head and he's the only one that can answer me. I only hope he isn't as lost by what had been said as I am.

"Can I ask you something?"

"After what we just went through? You can ask me any god damned thing you want. I can't promise you the right answer though or even the one you wanna hear."

129

It still amazes me, how the two of us interact with each other now. Where months before we had been on opposite sides, both of us vying for the affection of the same girl we'd both fallen in love with, now we were on the same side, fighting the same root of all evil. The urge to lay the guy out replaced with a need to pick his brain. It's amazing what going through hell could do for a relationship, even one as conflicted as ours.

"What do you think Lucifer meant by Serenity not remembering? I know he said that she wouldn't remember her time with him but do you think he did something more or was he being on the level?"

"Nothing Lucifer ever does is on the level Graham. You of all people know that. I honestly don't know what to believe. With the way Michael gave Gabriel over to be fixed it makes me think he's actually on the level."

"Yeah I guess…"

"Okay you got my attention now man, so why don't you just tell me what you're really thinking."

"What if he took more than just her time in hell from her? What if that's his end game. Stripping her completely of her memory so that we all have to fight tooth and nail to really bring her back to us? If we've gotta make her remember than that means she won't reach her destiny which only works more in his favor."

I can tell that what I said got to Ryan and he's questioning everything the same way, if he hadn't been before. I might be reading way too much into the situation given that Serenity had been given over to us without so much as a fight but after having the bastard climbing around in my skin I had to believe he didn't do anything out of the goodness of his heart.

"Honestly Graham, it's possible. Anything with Lucifer is possible. I wouldn't put a damn thing past him but right now I can't think that way. I have to believe that after Gabriel is done with her that she's going to be the way she was. It's all my heart can allow me to believe."

"What happens if she's different?"

I don't want to admit it but facing a Serenity that isn't the girl I know and love isn't something I'm sure I can handle. For years

130

she had been a certain way to me and imagining her in some other way, or even seeing it firsthand, playing out in front of me scares the hell out of me. I need her to be the same girl. It's the only way I can cope with everything we've been through.

"Then we do whatever it takes to help her." He responded which did nothing to help the sick feeling building in my stomach. "You wanna tell me what this is all about?"

"I think what we just went through screwed with my head."

"That's probably the most honest thing I've ever heard you say. Thank you."

"I've never lied about anything."

"No you're right, you haven't. You just haven't come right out and admitted when something is getting to you either. We're a lot alike that way. Too damn pigheaded to admit when something leaves us less than perfect."

Before it would bother me being compared to him but now hearing him say we were alike, especially given that he had abilities and strengths that I could only dream of having, left me feeling less alone. I actually welcomed it. Maybe if we were processing things the same way then I could get through this after all because I wasn't the only one.

"Let's just get to Serenity alright? Nothing is going to feel better or make sense until we see her again. I know that's how I feel and given everything that I know about you I'm willing to bet you feel the same way. So store your shit for now Graham, we'll deal with it all soon enough."

"Yeah, alright."

"For the record, you're not the only one worried about her. If she's going to be the same or different and what if anything Lucifer did to her head before he brought her to us. I'm dealing with that too but I can't go there, at least not all the way, until I see her again."

There it is again. The two of us being on the same page. It's something straight out of an alternate universe. I want to enjoy it, because at the very least it means that we were doing what we know Serenity would want but I can't help but have one final question linger in my mind.

131

Just how long is it going to last?

Gabriel

There was a time where coming home excited me. It is even more apparent during those times where we are away for extended periods of time without being able to check in. Stepping through the gates and seeing our brethren created such a calming stillness within me that there is nothing above and below that could compare to it.

I missed it more than I was able to adequately express, especially now as we stood before our Father and we were hearing nothing but just how much trouble we caused. We were not children and the reprimand was not needed but it didn't seem to matter to the Almighty. He wanted us to hear it which meant we were going to hear it, children or not.

I often compared my life to that of the humans because with the way we interacted with our father, especially lately, it is as if we switched places and were indeed dealing in a purely human capacity. The similarities were endless it seemed and by the look on the face of my angelic brother, I could tell I am not the only one that felt that way.

Though with Michael it appeared as though on top of being annoyed at having to be on the receiving end of Father's endless barrage of upset at what we had done, he is also bored out of his mind. If we weren't in the middle of being verbally accosted I definitely would have laughed. As it is, the urge was strong and almost pointless to fight.

"The two of you remind me more and more of Lucifer every day. It is as if you have no respect for what you have been told and you want to follow the same path as he did before you."

"What is it that you expect us to say Father? That we regret going against you and your wishes and doing the right thing and bringing Serenity home? If that is what you are after taking us over your knee the way you are currently, you will not get it."

"You disappoint me most of all Michael, not only in your tone but the words you use. You are becoming more like the humans

132

that your brother is in charge of then the son I have kept by my side all of this time."

"I made a choice and while you choose to believe that I did it to spite you, it is not the case. You only see what you want to see. Saving Serenity from the fate that she found herself in was the right thing to do. It is that cut and dry."

"Do you not believe that I would have gotten her out of that predicament myself?"

"Actually now that you mention it, I don't believe you would have done whatever it took to bring her back to us even though you claim she is your most precious gift. You want nothing more than to see the most treasured son dead and that is where your focus has been."

I want to interrupt and stop Michael before he took himself down a path he would be unable to come back from but I knew it would fall on deaf ears. This has been brewing between him and Father for awhile and there is nothing that would come between it now. It had to take place otherwise it would just be held in until something far worse happened.

"Lucifer has never been the most treasured."

"That's really all you want to comment on? I thought given your statement a few seconds ago that you would most want to comment on the Serenity business but of course you don't. It all comes back to Lucifer. Are you that blinded by him Father?"

"How dare you question me? You are nothing more than a petulant child!"

"Then I guess that's what I am. I'm done with this and with you. Take my damn power away, cast me from Heaven, I don't care anymore. What I do care about is going back down there and making sure that your most precious gift is still in one piece, which is what you should be focusing on."

"Do you feel as your brother does Gabriel?" Father asked, turning to me. I didn't want this to turn around on me but I know where I stand and it wasn't going to please the man standing in front of me now. I was in agreement with Michael.

"I do Father. I know how much that upsets you but we have bared witness to your decisions as of late and they all seem centered around Lucifer with no thought to the people that he hurts. You know that Michael and I both have the utmost respect for you and your decisions but as of late we are not as secure in them as we wish to be."

"We can't accept what you tell us on blind faith anymore. We need answers." Michael added once I finished.

"The only answer you need is that you must trust in me. Up until this moment in time have I ever led you astray?"

"No you have not but Michael is right. If you want us to continue to follow you blindly then you have to give us something to go on and more than just the standard, everything will reveal itself in time. The time has long past for us to know everything, at least as it pertains to your plan regarding Lucifer and Serenity."

Speaking to my father in the way I am doing now only reminds me of the day Serenity said the very same words to me. After following along with Father's orders and staying away from her for a short period of time, she had spoken to me much the same way. I couldn't help but smile at the memory. It seems we were already having a positive effect on one another.

"I cannot give you the answers you want."

"Well then I guess we all know what happens now." Michael snapped before turning to me. "I'm leaving. We have a ball of light we need to take care of. You stay here and listen to this, or you come with me but make a choice Gabriel. I've heard enough."

It was in that moment, when Michael spoke his final words before vanishing that I realized exactly what was going on here. I don't know why I didn't see it before but now that I had there is no way I am going to keep it to myself. There has been far too much of that over the course of our time together and I wasn't going to stand for it a minute longer.

"Father I think I know what is going on."

"What do you mean my son?"

"What is the one thing that Lucifer wants above all else?"

"This is not regarding your beloved again is it?"

"No, as much as I focus on her this has nothing to do with her specifically. This goes much deeper than Serenity. It affects all of us."

"You need to explain yourself son, while I am adept at following your thoughts, at this time I seen to be unable to."

It is common knowledge that the Almighty is the seer of all things but his inability to read me when everything seemed rather calm confused me greatly. Is it possible that it is manifesting itself in this way already?

"Lucifer wants nothing more than for Heaven to be punished. He wanted to do that with Serenity but when that didn't work out the first time I think he put something into motion with the power he has at his disposal and now it is showing itself by tearing us apart from the inside out."

"You believe your fallen brother to be behind the discord between us?"

"Can you tell me that you do not? Knowing him the way that you do, is he not capable of such a devious act?"

He couldn't argue with me. He knew that Lucifer is in fact able to do exactly what I am accusing him of and he is probably more than shocked that he didn't realize it sooner. If he is able to reach us in this way there was really no limitation on what he is capable of. It could very well be the reason that Father was acting so strangely.

"If that is indeed what is happening here then it stands to reason that we must formulate a plan to rid the world and heaven of him once and for all. Once we take care of him then we can focus our efforts on taking on the remainder of hell. Without their leader they will not stand for long."

This is the father I know and love. He may be focused on taking care of Lucifer more so then anyone else but in this moment now he has every right to be that way. It is what he did from this moment on, with the knowledge I have given him that would determine what I did next and more so then that, what Michael did.

"You must go and speak to your brother about this immediately and when the time is right we need to have another meeting, all of us. If Lucifer is indeed using the old power to manipulate Heaven then we need to go on the defensive and we need to do it soon."

"Yes Father."

"Go my son, be with Serenity and keep me abreast of any changes or issues. Given the information you have just given me I feel that I need to put my focus into other pursuits so I am leaving the care of her up to you and your brother. I trust that the both of you will not let me down."

"No sir, we won't."

"Gabriel?"

"Yes Father?"

"I'm sorry for my behavior. Please tell your brother that he is right. From now on, things will be handled differently."

CHAPTER SIXTEEN

Ryan

There are only three times I can remember where I did the unthinkable and opened myself up to prayer. It's no secret given who my parents are that the advantages in such a thing were never discussed with me. What I've noticed about the times when I have done it is I've reached the end of my rope. I've done all I can logically do and in doing it am laying it at someone else's feet for awhile.

The first time I did it was when I was eight. I was lonely and unable to manage it productively anymore. At eight years old I didn't grasp that I was the son of a demon, at least not the way I did as I got older and I thought that in doing it the man upstairs would hear it and would give me the only thing I could ever really want. He would give me someone else to walk through this shitty life with, someone who understood what I'm going through and would help me find better ways to cope.

As it turns out I got that and so much more. I didn't realize it at the time but Serenity is exactly what I had been praying for and although it took thirteen years in order for it to happen I'm so thankful it did. She came when I needed her most and brought so much with her that I am changed forever because of it. I don't regret that prayer and no matter what we went through, good and bad, I don't think I ever would.

The second time I remember praying is the day in the church when I had to take her life. I prayed for a miracle, a way out of this, not for me but for her. I did not want to condemn her to a life like the one I had been living before I met her. I wanted so much better for her. I was ready to say goodbye to my life and the world as a whole as long as she got to live on and bring the happiness and light to others that she had given to me.

Again it would appear that the prayer was heard and granted. More happened then just what I prayed for though because in the process of wanting her saved, I had also been saved. It is in the sacrifice I made for her that I was also redeemed in the eyes of Heaven and even though the majority still view me as the demon I am, they can't deny that I'm different then all the others they've come across.

The third and final time I prayed had been during our time in Hell. I prayed that I would find her and I would be able to do what I desperately wanted to and save her, bringing her back to the life she still very much deserved to live. I don't know if it was my prayer being answered or just the will of the four people that had been there to save her but we succeeded and now she's laying in the bed and I'm watching her sleep peacefully. I like to believe that just like the other times my prayer was answered. It makes it easier to cope with and judging by the look on Graham's face as he watches her the same way that I am, he wants to believe the same thing.

It's time to pray again. We might have succeeded in saving her but there is still so much more to go through now that we had. I wasn't going to pray for me or even for Graham. This prayer was strictly going to be for her and what I want for her moving forward. She might be sleeping peacefully in bed right now but when she finally did wake up, I prayed she would wake and be herself. The strong woman I had come to know and love so deeply. I want her to be okay, not for the rest of us but for her alone. She is going to need things to be as normal as possible.

I wanted that for her so badly that I was going to push my prayer envelope and hope this one would also be answered. I couldn't focus on what would happen if it wasn't. If Heaven had been so good at answering me before, then I know they will be again. They would not let me or Serenity down, especially given what she means to them.

Of course I wanted her to wake up but that isn't something I'm going to selfishly pray for. She would do that in due time and I would just have to be as patient as possible until it happened. Whether Graham is praying for her to wake up is completely on

138

him but what I want would always be much bigger then my own selfish needs.

With all the time that passed after she vanished from the church that night I had almost given up hope of ever finding her again. I was walking a thin line near the end and while I didn't like admitting that I'd gotten to that point I couldn't exactly deny it because then I wouldn't be entirely truthful and now more than ever I wanted to live my life strictly by the letter of the truth. Watching her now there are moments where I can swear I'm dreaming because this is just too good to be true.

I can't wait to tell her how much I love her and how hard it's been living without her. I want to look into those hazel eyes and make her see that my life would always be better as long as she is a part of it, even if she is changed from the time Lucifer held her captive. I would take her in whatever form I'm given as long as she's here.

If I'm honest there is so much more that I want to say but I know that when she does wake up I am going to have to give her time to adjust and not drop everything on her right away. It's a struggle though, making my heart understand what my mind already accepts. There have been so many moments over the last year where I didn't say what I should have said and now that I have her back I'm going to damn sure make up for every single one of them. She would never go another moment without knowing just how treasured she is.

Graham feels the same way; I can see it on his face. He wants her to wake up so that he can say and do the same things. So much has happened during her time away from us, I think we both wanted her to wake up so badly just so that she could see all the changes we made during our effort to find her. The two of us went from being in what seemed like the worst kind of competition with each other to finally being on the same page. We understood each other now and Serenity needs to see that even more than the rest of the world does.

He knows how I legitimately feel about her now and he isn't going to push his way into her heart anymore. He made that very clear before we got here. While the way he felt about her hasn't changed at all in the time we all spent apart, at least I felt secure that he wasn't going to use that to his advantage the way I assume he would have in the past. We reached a level of mutual respect and when I wasn't amazed by it, I was thankful for it.

Serenity's destiny was still in play even when she isn't aware of it. If Graham and I could come together the way we did then it's living proof that just because of her affect on our lives, the world is being changed. It might be happening at a slower pace but she was definitely making a positive impact and on a half demon no less. The one person she shouldn't have been able to touch.

I know what I'm supposed to be, or what I would have been had there not been a heavenly screw up twenty two years before but I'm still not there in terms of accepting it as fact. With the demon still very much alive in me I don't think I would ever be able to fully accept it. What pure angel walks around with the darkness inside them? I might have been an abomination before but now I am something else entirely. A true anomaly.

Right before my eyes I saw her start to shift her body in the bed and I swear my heart nearly jumped out of my chest. What we've been waiting for seems to be happening now and if we both found it unbelievable, her even being here, well now we were confronted with just how real it is.

"Did she just move?" Graham whispered motioning to the bed, his eyes a mixture of true happiness and mild disbelief. It's exactly what I was feeling as I watched her move again, this time her eyes fluttering open ever so slowly.

Serenity began sitting up, her eyes now wide as she took in her surroundings. As I watched her eyes flutter from one side of the room to the other, my heart stopped in my chest when they finally landed on me. Not wanting to waste another second I began moving toward her and it's only when she began pulling back on the bed, wrapping her arms around her body that I realize she's scared. Definitely not the reaction I'd been hoping for the first time she looked at me again.

Just what did she have to be afraid of? Didn't she realize she was safe now and there was nothing alive that would ever hurt her again? Didn't she know she had nothing to fear with me?

140

"Serenity, it's okay pretty girl, you're safe now."

Where my words were meant to soothe, they seemed to have the opposite effect as the reaction her body had to me finally reached her eyes. There was no denying it, she is scared of me and I had no idea why. All I do know is I never wanted to see that look in her eyes again, especially directed at me.

Not wanting to risk moving toward her again, I just held my hands up in surrender, attempting to let her know that I meant her no harm. I only hoped that it would have the desired effect and she would finally relax and stop looking at me this way.

"Who are you? Where am I? What have you done with me?"

What the hell? She doesn't know me?

I had no idea what to do with the information. It made understanding the fear based reaction easier but it did nothing for the way it felt in my chest knowing that she didn't know who I was and what we meant to each other. Just what the hell did Lucifer do to her?

"I'm Ryan, you know me. We know each other. You're in my bedroom and I swear to you pretty girl, I haven't done anything to you. I would never even dream of it."

She began to relax but the wariness was still there in her eyes and it turned my stomach. She obviously believes what I told her about not wanting to hurt her but that look meant that she didn't believe the rest of it. She really didn't know who I was.

"Son of a bitch, I knew he did more than he said." Graham snapped and not taking my eyes off Serenity I watched as her gaze shifted from me to the other person in the room. In that moment I watched as her entire expression changed before my very eyes and the light complete with the slight twinkle I had come to love about her directed itself completely at Graham.

"Graham Cracker, thank god!"

Gabriel

When I made my way back down to Ryan's dorm room, the new base of operations as it pertained to watching over Serenity, I

141

expected to find my brother watching over everyone inside but I was met with something quite different and unexpected.

It had been my goal to appear in my true form but the minute I touched down and realized that Serenity was indeed awake I switched gears. With everything she had been through I felt it unnecessary to add to her troubles by appearing in true angel form. She had issues with my doing that before she was taken, I could only imagine how much harder that would be when her mind had been toyed with.

I don't trust my brother. When he had spoken of only taking away the duration of time in hell from her, I knew him well enough to know that something far more sinister had been done. Given the look of shock on her face as I watched Ryan and Graham interact with her my assumptions were confirmed as fact.

She had no memory of the man standing before her now and it was obvious given the pained expression on his face that he was most definitely not taking it well. Even after all of the time he spent in Lucifer's company he obviously put trust in the fact that nothing more had been done to the woman he loves and now he was being confronted with just how wrong he had been.

The healing seemed to take hold in much the way I expected. She looked healthier than ever, a nice change given her coloring when Michael had taken us home from the darkness. Her cheeks were again their normal rosy shade of pink and her eyes were no longer a dry brown, instead a very lit up hazel, the way God himself intended when he gave her the features she now displayed. Physically she is the Serenity Richards we all know and love.

Emotionally is a different story though. She was most definitely not the same woman as before but it would take some time to find out just far gone she was and what we would all need to do in order to bring her back.

As the room lit up around me, I immediately cast a look around to the other occupants to gauge whether or not they had seen his entrance or if he remained much like me and under the radar. Secure in the knowledge that the temperament of the room hadn't changed with the shift of Michael's arrival, I turned to face the brother that had only mere minutes before walked out on me.

142

Serenity may be the more pressing issue at the moment but we were definitely going to have to speak about what I had come to learn during my time with Father. It might not change anything in Michael's mind but he is due answers and explanations just as much as the rest of Heaven. If our fallen brother is really controlling the way we are behaving then we needed to mount a defense and we needed to do it soon.

"It appears that the spitfire has awoken from her slumber finally. I was wondering just how long she was going to remain in the sleeping beauty fairytale."

"Since when have you been reading up on the human fables brother? It doesn't seem like your style but yes it appears as though our little ball of light has finally come back to us."

"You did not appear in your true form Gabriel, is there some reason for that or do you just enjoy eavesdropping as much as I do?"

I would have assumed that Michael knew the reason behind why I am cloaked but given that he had appeared and immediately turned to speak to me, it was no real surprise. It just means that now I am going to have to explain everything I witnessed since my arrival.

"It appears as though Lucifer was not entirely truthful with us brother. Serenity has indeed been damaged during her time with him and while he may have wiped her time in hell from her memory it appears as though he did much worse."

"What do you mean?"

"Do you not see what is taking place before us? Serenity has indeed awoken and that is something to be joyous about but she has done so with no memory of the very man that she pledged her life to only a few short months ago."

"She doesn't remember Ryan?"

"It would appear that she does not but she does have memory of the Hudson boy which means that while our brother did far worse then he spoke of, he didn't erase her memory entirely."

"This is not good Gabriel. You know what resides deep within the being that is supposed to be the purest of angels. If Serenity does not recall him, I am afraid something terrible will occur."

Michael was concerned that Ryan would revert back to his demon side and he had every reason to be. While he had been doing better at controlling that part of his nature and had even gone so far as to pull away from everything he possibly could in an effort to keep everyone around him safe he was still a ticking time bomb until that part was removed from him. Serenity not remembering could be the catalyst to something far darker then what we had all just been through if we didn't get a handle on it.

"We need to find a way to separate Ryan from the others and speak to him privately and in our true forms. We need to gauge what he is feeling and whether or not we have to be concerned about what comes next."

"You really believe he would turn now Gabriel? Now that he has the woman he loves back in his life, even if she can't remember him or their time together, you fear he will embrace his darker side?"

"Wouldn't you if you lost your Faith?"

I could only liken the way Ryan felt about Serenity to that of what we all shared with our beloved. If we were ever forced to part ways with them we would die inside which would open the door to us following down a much darker road even though we were strictly built for the light. With them being the better parts of us it made it entirely possible that we could turn just as easily as Ryan himself.

There is definitely a flaw in Father's design.

"I will reach out to Ryan and pull him away from the current situation he finds himself in. You continue to stand guard, watch and inform me of anything that takes place in my absence. We must not let this situation get out of hand before we truly know everything we are dealing with."

As I watch Michael disappear I turn my attention back to what is now taking place in the room. I could feel Serenity's unease almost as if it were my own and I could tell that in each passing second it is becoming that much stronger both for her and Ryan as well.

We most definitely have to get a handle on this or it could spell disaster before we even began. Lucifer was not going to win this round. No matter how well he set it up to do so.

CHAPTER SEVENTEEN

Serenity

There is something about this guy in front of me. Ryan. I feel like I should know him yet no matter how hard I try I can't seem to place just how and where I know him from. The pleading look in his eyes tells me that he wants me to remember him and that in doing so it will change everything but I just can't give him what he wants.

His eyes, blue with the slight black rim around them speak volumes to what he has been through even though I am not quite sure what all of that is. They seem almost tortured as they look at me now, searching me for some sign of recognition. It's like he can see right through me and if I didn't find him as attractive as I seem to, I would most definitely be freaked out by the intensity of his gaze.

I know these eyes, I can feel it inside of me but because my mind can't place it, I'm fearful of it even though my body seems to know it has nothing to fear from him.

The only thing keeping me remotely grounded right now is the fact that I'm not alone with him. I'm here with someone I do remember, fondly even and it's because of that connection that I am able to keep my wits about me when all I want to do is scream out and cry in sheer terror.

I want to remember. I don't like the way my brain feels fuzzy and I don't like the way my body feels since the moment I sat up in bed. I feel like I've been out cold for a week even though I'm sure it hasn't been that long. What happened to me and why do I feel this out of sorts? Was I in some kind of accident? Is that why both Graham and this Ryan guy were staring at me the way they are?

"Ryan, do you think you can give Serenity and me some time alone?" Graham asks as his body turns to face the other man, the one with the eyes that I can't place.

I don't want to admit it but I'm so thankful for Graham right now. He seems to know how uncomfortable all of this is for me and is doing whatever he can to ease it. I might not remember much but that is something that hasn't changed in all the time I've known him. He is always looking out for everyone else, even if it means going above and beyond. He would protect me here even if there is nothing to protect from.

"Yeah that's fine. She hasn't eaten anything for at least twelve hours so I'll just go grab her something."

I can't explain it but as I watch him turn from me, his penetrating eyes no longer on mine but fixed on the door in front of him, a feeling of emptiness comes over me. Whatever we meant to one another it's obviously stronger then I first thought. There is actually an ache in my chest watching him take the steps to leave the room and a part of me wants desperately to call him back though I don't understand for the life of me why.

"Serenity, how much do you remember?" Graham speaks as soon as Ryan has safely exited the room. "You've been out for awhile so I wanna know whatever you can remember about what happened to you."

That's the thing. I couldn't tell him what I remember because I can't remember anything. The last thing I remember is going to classes with Emma and somehow here I am now in a strange guy's room with no memory of how I got here or what happened to me. What's even worse is that I don't understand why Graham is here when the last time I saw him had been when I said goodbye before coming here for school.

"I don't remember much other than saying goodbye to Emma and heading to classes but Graham Cracker, what are you doing here?"

The level of confusion that registers on his face tells me more than his words ever could. Obviously he's been here for awhile and he's been expecting that I would remember that. Just how long have I been out and why can't I remember any of it?

"You don't remember me coming here?"

"No. The last time I saw you, we were in Green Haven."

He sighs and I immediately follow suit. I can tell that he wasn't expecting what I dropped on him but given that I'm the one with the extreme bout of memory loss I figure I have the right to exhale the breath I've been holding even more than he does. He knows more than I do about what happened to me and he's the only one I could trust to give me the answers. I only hope that he would.

"I've been here for months Ser. I came here for you. You really don't remember that?"

He came here for me.

I let the gravity of his words sink in around me. Could they really mean what I think or is my over active brain just reading too much into it?

"You came here for me?"

"Yeah, I mean I came for more than just that reason really but what happened between us three years ago, it never sat right for me so I came here to find you and explain."

"Did you explain?"

He nods and I sink back into the bed with a moan. I need to remember all of this. I get the feeling that everything Graham told me had fixed a lot of what happened between us three years before and it's imperative that I remember it now. As happy as I was to see him the minute I woke up from whatever this is that I'm going through, it is quickly turning into something more because of the fact that I can't recall anything other than the loss I felt after walking away from him.

"I don't remember any of it."

"I can see that."

"What happened to me? Why can't I remember anything?"

His forehead creases and I watch as he lifts his hand up and rubs at it. It didn't take a brain surgeon to see that he's struggling with what I just asked him. He knew what happened to me and from the looks of his reaction, it isn't anything good. Am I really ready to hear about it if it sparks this kind of reaction in him?

"You had an accident Ser. A pretty bad one. Ryan brought you here because of the way you feel about hospitals. I want to tell you more but right now, you need to heal."

I wanted to press him for more but I knew he was right. If I had been in an accident the way he claimed then I did need to heal. I need to focus on healing not only my body, which from the way

148

it ached seemed to have been put through its paces but also my mind so that I could open it enough to remember all of the things I've obviously forgotten. I wouldn't be getting anymore answers right now.

"Ryan brought me here? I don't get it…"

"He's the one that found you and brought you here. That's all you need to know."

No actually I needed to know a lot more but for now I wasn't going to push it. The only thing I wanted to know anyway is what happened between me and Graham since he had come to Stephenville for me. Did we finally talk about what happened between us the night of the party where I kissed him or was it something else?

"Graham…"

"Yeah Ser?"

"That night of the party…"

"Stop." He says, raising his hand up in an effort to silence me. "We've already talked about that night Serenity. I know everything now and deep inside even though you can't remember, you do too."

He knows everything. Holy shit.

"You know everything and you're still here?"

Reaching across the bed and taking my hand into his, covering it completely, he looks me in the eyes before speaking again. His eyes go soft, the way I've seen them do on so many occasions before during our time together, I watch as he inhales a deep breath, preparing himself to speak.

"There is nowhere else I should be Serenity."

It was then that I knew all that I needed to know, at least for the time being. His statement along with the way his eyes look as they stare into mine told me everything I needed to know as it pertained to us.

He came back for me because I wasn't the only one that felt something. He felt it too, finally coming back to tell me. I knew it beyond a shadow of a doubt. We were together the way we we're meant to be.

I'm Graham Hudson's girlfriend.

Graham

I'm definitely going to hell for this.

I knew it was wrong but when she woke up and looked at me for the first time, recognizing me and not Ryan, especially given everything that happened between them I was beyond happy. The excitement running through my body at seeing her awake and looking much the same way she had always been quickly turned into me being overjoyed at being the only one she really knew.

I could tell by Ryan's reaction that he wasn't taking her memory loss well. That he'd been hoping at least a little bit that the man he followed blindly for years told him the truth and that she hadn't been affected any further then just her time in Hell. Serenity waking up and not remembering him meant that Lucifer did something far worse and now Ryan is going to be the one paying the price.

He shouldn't be feeling that and I want to be able to take it away for him but the way it felt for me when she thanked god that I was there made me switch gears. I want to be the one she remembers and I want to be the one she relies on to get her through everything that is going to come now. As much as I feel bad for Ryan, it's hard not to find myself being a little selfish with the way everything turned out.

I haven't completely lost myself though. I know that I'm going to have to give her answers about what happened to her and why she isn't able to remember anything and I would do that but not before enjoying this for just a little while longer. I'm not sure how long it's going to last and I want to keep her with me as long as humanly possible before everything goes back to normal and I lose her again. It was hard enough handling that the first time around, I'm not entirely sure I can do it again.

"Graham I know that you want to be selfish in this moment and I understand why but you must not go down that path. Do whatever you need to in order to keep her calm but do not put something in motion that you cannot come back from."

Gabriel as usual is right. As much as I wanted to enjoy the moment I did need to put my focus on Serenity and what she needs, what would help her more in the long term, not my own selfish needs but damn the way she's looking at me right now, it's hard.

The way her hand felt in mine, after months being unable to even reach out to her at all is my own personal heaven on earth. There had been times during the last few months where I thought I would never even see her again much less get to touch her, so right now, as I held onto her hand for dear life; I was letting that feeling guide me. The softness of her hands in mine, all of the fear that had traced her face only seconds before gone, replaced instead with a look I had been dying to see for years after she walked out of my life.

She remembers me, us and everything that had happened in between. More than just remembering all of that she seems to genuinely want it, something I had not been expecting when she came back to us again.

I would listen to Gabriel and I would do whatever is easiest for her and I would do it easily given that it appeared as though what she most wants in that moment is me.

"You and me…you said that we talked about everything but does that mean what I think it means?"

This was my chance to tell her the truth. That what she thought and what's really the case are two totally different things but I know the minute I tell her the truth, whatever small sliver of sanity she's been able to hold onto with waking up and finding her memory erased would be gone. No matter how much it might pain me to do so, I have to keep her believing what her mind wants her to, whether it causes me to lose her in the end or not. I could not let her fall apart.

"Yeah Ser Bear, it does."

"We're together?"

"Yes."

"Graham…"

"Not now Gabe. You see the way she is right now. If I tell her the truth it's going to rip her apart. You can think I'm being

selfish all you want but I won't be the one to rip her world apart."

When no response came from the angel I turned my attention back to the girl in front of me whose eyes are now shining as they begin to fill with the water that would turn into tears. The sight of the tears might have scared me before but I could tell that this is a different kind of cry. This time she's going to cry because of happiness, peace and love. All the things she wanted for as long as I've known her and I'm the one giving it to her.

She moved in the bed and threw her arms around me and even though I didn't expect it, I allowed myself to respond in kind, wrapping my arms all the way around her and pulling her as tightly as I could into me.

I knew it wasn't going to last forever but in this moment right here and now I was going to accept it for what it is.

My prayers being answered.

Ryan

I want this feeling to go away. I want someone to tell me that what I'm going through is just some stupid nightmare and that if I just wake up all of it will go away and things will go back to normal. I can't live with the stabbing pain in my chest. I just want to shut it off because this can't be the way things turn out for me.

Standing in a line, getting food for my wife while she sits in my bed alone with her soul mate. Her first love. The one person that stands between me and the life I want so desperately to have with her now that she's back and in one piece.

That son of a bitch had gotten the perfect revenge on me when he wiped her memory. He took away the one thing that matters most to me and replaced it with an emptiness that I had forgotten about since I haven't felt it in well over a year. I should have killed him when I had him alone in hell. Letting him go was going to haunt me for the rest of my life, whether Serenity eventually remembers or not.

The fear in her eyes at seeing me when she woke up still makes me wanna throw up. With everything she had been through

152

over the last year that had been the one look I have never seen on her face, unless it's because she was afraid for me. She has never been afraid of me and knowing that she is now only twisted the knife that much deeper in my chest.

She remembers Graham Hudson just fine which I'm sure was Lucifer's intent when he wiped her memory. He wanted her to remember her soul mate because he'd already been able to manipulate him once and could easily gain access to do it again, something that try as he might he just would never be able to do with me. I'm stronger than that and he knows it so he took a different path. The one that would afford him the most satisfaction.

I should have known that nothing would ever be this cut and dry with him. In all the years I spent being groomed by him you would think I would have learned the way he operates by now but I still trusted him even when there was a pile of evidence so high that proves he can't be trusted at all.

I am the world's biggest chump.

"You and I need to speak immediately. Please remove yourself from the public setting you find yourself in so that I may appear."

Michael.

I knew it was only a matter of time before I would come face to face with the two angels that I fought side by side with but right now was most definitely not a good time. I wasn't sure how much Michael knew but with the way I'm feeling the last person I want to see is an angel. I want to wallow in my own pathetic shit a little awhile longer.

"I cannot allow you to do that. Please do as I ask."

As much as I don't want to do as he asks, the way he says please gets to me. I wasn't sure how often it happened but I have to figure when a being much stronger then yourself is politely asking you to do something, it's probably best to listen. In a way it seemed even more important.

Grabbing the food as the order came up; I made my way out of the diner and immediately ran down into the alley next door. It wasn't the best spot in the world but for now it was going to have to do. It's not like I'm in a rush to head back to my room and see just how close Serenity and Graham have gotten in my absence. As much as I've come to respect Graham, I know that if given the choice, I would choose to make Serenity remember the times with me more than anyone before me. It might be selfish but it's also human and that is something Graham was through and through.

He would want to enjoy as much time with her as he could before her memory returned and as much as I loathe even thinking about it, I understood it.

As the alley lit up I leaned back against the wall and watched as Heaven's strongest warrior appeared in front of me, his wings spanned out so far they took up almost the entire space we now occupied, his face giving away nothing as to his mood. It was time to find out just how much he knew and what he needed to speak to me about so badly.

"She's awake." I state evenly, not trusting myself to say more and risk giving away how it all makes me feel.

"I have been made aware of that. Gabriel is currently watching over her. What I have to speak with you about does pertain to that in a small way but it is not the sole reason I have come to you."

"Then what do you want?"

"It appears as though my fallen brother fell back into old routines and lied to us."

"No shit. It's what he does."

"This upsets you. As much as you want to hate the man that took you under his wing, you trusted that he was telling you the truth as it pertains to her."

It really didn't take an angel or even a mind reader to know that I trusted Lucifer when I shouldn't have, it was more than obvious and I didn't need Michael pointing it out now. I was already giving myself enough shit because of it.

"Yeah it upsets me. Instead of getting her back in one piece, we got her back broken."

"Only her mind is broken Ryan. Her heart is still as strong as ever, as is her body. She is not as broken as you believe her to be and all will be rectified in time."

"Is this where you tell me to just hang in there and have a little faith because honestly Michael with the way I'm feeling right now, I'm not against telling you to shove the speech."

"That is not you speaking; it is the concern, anger and upset. As much as you want to embrace all of what you are feeling I am pleading with you not to. You have come such a long way in terms of keeping the demon within you buried; you must not go back on that now."

So that's the real reason he wanted to see me. He's afraid I'm going to give in to the darkness inside of me. Can't say I blame him considering it did seem like something I would do. The only difference is it was something I would have done, not something I'm willing to do now. I may have to live with being a half demon for the rest of existence but it doesn't mean I have to make it the main focus.

"I'm not gonna go dark side Michael. I'm just pissed off."

"An understandable reaction and one that I will not tell you to stop feeling. I do believe you being pissed off as you say will work in your favor moving forward."

Now I'm confused. Is he really telling me that it was alright to be pissed off even though being angry usually led to the very thing he just told me not to embrace?

"It would appear as though Graham Hudson is not as pure as I once imagined him to be. In an effort to protect Serenity he is going down a very selfish road and in doing so making our job that much harder."

"What the hell does that mean? What is he doing?"

Now he had my attention. I expected Graham to take advantage of the situation but if he is doing something more then that I wouldn't be responsible for what I did to him when I saw him again.

"He has informed Serenity of their relationship. Not the soul mate bond but that of the very real human one. She is currently under the impression that the two of them are in a relationship. I know that this will anger you but you must know so that you can work with us in an effort to rectify what Lucifer has done."

"He told her that they're dating?"

"It would appear that way yes. Gabriel told him to keep her as calm as possible given that she is still healing and whether done selfishly or not, he proceeded to tell her this. It would appear as

155

though the ability to sense deceit has been shut down inside of her during her stay in Hell because she accepted it without question."

"That son of a bitch!"

"I know you are angry with Graham but…"

"No I'm not talking about Graham." I snap cutting him off before he can say more. "I expected this from Graham, I'm talking about Lucifer."

For the first time I'm getting to see what an angel looks like when they're shocked. I could tell Michael wasn't expecting that to be my response. I might be inherently dark but I knew where the real blame needed to be and it wasn't on Graham. He was just doing what I would do in the situation if the roles were reversed. He loves Serenity, of course he's going to want to be with her any way he can. I definitely couldn't fault him for that.

In fact I was actually jealous that he was getting to do it and not me. I would kill to be in his position right now, even if it was only for a short period of time.

"You want me to work with you and your brother in order to fix this. Tell me what you need me to do."

"For the time being we need to you accept the way things are and try your best to go along with them for her sake. Lucifer did this for a reason and I am going to find out why because it means something is coming but I am going to need time in order to do that."

"You want me to sit back and let Graham have his way with my wife?"

"Unfortunately yes, that is exactly what I want you to do."

"I don't know if I can do that. You know how I feel about her Michael, do you really expect me to just sit back and let Graham lie to her and make her believe something that's not true?"

"No. I do not expect you to just sit idly by and let the soul mate take her from you but in order to make sure things happen the way they need to it is something you must at least try to do. You must realize Ryan, the woman that you love recognizes you deep inside of herself. Her heart is still very much yours even though her mind cannot place it. She will not let this go on for any longer then it has to."

I have no idea what he's saying. None of it made any sense and I felt like I was right back where I had been months before. Trying to figure out the angel riddles.

"You must open your mind to what I am telling you. Only then will it make sense."

Okay, I can do that. I can look at what he said to me and make sense of it. He wanted me to know that Serenity is stronger than I'm giving her credit for, something I knew he was right about but that I didn't want to admit. He wants me to believe that she would realize the true nature of the life she led and would come back to me before letting things go too far and most important that while she might not remember me physically, the part of her born of the light knew me and would guide her to the right path when the time is right.

"You get it now don't you?"

"Yeah I get it but I still don't like it. Faking it is one thing but downright having to hide how I feel about her and allow Graham the chance with her is just not something I'm ever going to like doing."

"I would expect nothing less. There is one other thing that we need to discuss though as it pertains to us moving forward."

"I'm all ears. "

"That is inaccurate as you are more than just ears Ryan."

"Michael what did I tell you about taking things so literal? It's a phrase that's all. It means I'm ready for whatever else you have to tell me."

"My apologies, I am still adapting to the human way of speaking. It is quite confusing." He stated before continuing. "We need to discuss one Emma Daniels."

"Okay, what about her? Are you planning on screwing with her memories again in order to bring Serenity back?"

"No, while that may have been effective at one time I do not believe it will be the case this time around. I do believe it's time that she came out of the darkness her mind has been in."

"You're gonna need to give me a little more than that man."

"We need to inform her of Serenity's true identity and as such, all of our true forms. I do believe that in the long term it will help

157

not only Serenity but all of us moving forward. The time for denial and keeping things hidden has passed. We need all the help we can get moving forward and I do believe the Daniels girl to be made of the light. She can only help and not hinder."

Now that is definitely something I can agree with. It was way past time for Emma to know everything there is to know about the lives of the people around her. I always thought she would be better served knowing the truth and it made me happy to know Michael felt the same. Maybe doing this, we could get things back to normal quicker.

Maybe I didn't have to live without Serenity at all.

"Count me in Mike. Just tell me when."

CHAPTER EIGHTEEN

Gabriel

This is not good.

Not only do I believe my fallen brother to be part of a much bigger plan than I thought possible where Heaven is concerned but now it appears as though I had him to thank for what I am watching Serenity go through now. Whatever his motivation had been where she was concerned I am not sure but I am sure it has a lot to do with the way he feels about his former protégé.

He is already using the power he held to disrupt the flow of the light. His hatred for our father forcing him to use the power he has at his disposal, power at which Heaven has not seen in millennia. He is pulling us apart from one another, one angel and being at a time until he can be sure there is nothing left. I wasn't sure what his end game is past tearing us apart but whatever it is, it cannot be good.

Using Serenity the way in which he is spoke only to his obvious disgust with Ryan and what he perceives to be the ultimate betrayal. Lucifer has never enjoyed when others change their mind away from something he held such a strong belief in so the way he is reacting now is really no surprise.

When the only thing Ryan lived for is the ball of light that he had come to love and even gone so far as to marry then it was easy to figure out just what it would take to bring him down and it would appear that my brother succeeded in his goal. He had not just stripped her mind of the time she spent in hell, he had taken it a step further and taken the very memory of the man she loves and the experiences they have been through from her and essentially from Ryan as well.

I know that Michael is with him now and that my brother would see that nothing came of the anger I am sure will be rising in him but it still didn't do anything for the off putting feeling I still have inside me. I knew what is causing it of course but I am unsure of how to affectively deal with it.

Graham is doing the right thing for the wrong reasons and I have to put a stop to it but in doing so I will be hurting the person that had gone to hell in order to save us all mere months before. There is definitely no good way in which to handle this situation that doesn't end up hurting her in the process. If I came to her given that she doesn't remember me it would only cause a level of fear the likes of which none of us has ever seen. If I let the lie continue where Graham is concerned and it comes out then it would affectively break apart the one connection that is meant to span the test of time.

She needs to be reminded of her life and exactly who she is but I didn't have the first clue how to go about it that wouldn't shatter her like porcelain the moment I did it. She is more fragile than ever now, with her memory as broken as it seems to be and any slip up, big or small could and would spell disaster which is something I cannot afford.

I needed to proceed with caution now and with Michael taking care of things on his end I could only hope that time would be the deciding factor and things would fix themselves quickly. Serenity would come to remember her time before she experienced Hell and we would be able to all get on the same page in order to take my brother down once and for all.

It might be a long shot but it is something I had no other choice but to believe in because any other option was just unacceptable.

In the meantime I had to watch over both Graham and Serenity and make sure that neither one of them steps too far away from the real truth and what her destiny really is. I knew that Graham was aware of what needed to be done but I also know what the allure of having her only remember him is bringing to the table. It is going to be hard for him to walk away from it when he is getting what he wants.

"Brother we must speak. How are things on your end?"

"They are much the same as the last time we spoke. I am giving them time but I am becoming increasingly uncomfortable going along with the lie even if it does mean that Serenity remains in a state of peace and calm."

160

"I know brother but given who she is, I know she will remember in time. We must not make things any harder on her then they have already been. Lucifer has done more than enough already, we must not let him do anymore."

"What is it that you wish to speak to me about?" I ask, putting Michael back on course and attempting to stray away from the truth of the situation taking place before my eyes. I could no longer focus on what is taking place between Graham and Serenity as it is treading very close to a line that would affect me deeply given my feelings for her.

"I have spoken to Ryan and though I am not entirely positive that he is handling the situation appropriately, it appears that he is on the level with me and will help us as we move forward."

"You have made him aware of exactly what it is we wish him to do correct?"

"Yes and he is on board. We are going to the roommate as we speak. It is time that we face what our brother has done head on. There can be no more time wasted and we need as many people willing to stand and fight as possible."

"There is an urgent matter that we must speak about as soon as you are able to break free from your task with Ryan. I have learned information that I believe is imperative to us moving forward."

"When we are done with the roommate I will make my way to you. Until then please do as you have been and keep an eye on the two of them and please stop the Hudson boy before he brings any other false truths to light."

"I do believe he has done as much damage as he can already with what he is letting her believe but I will keep you posted."

It is always easy to tell when Michael cut communication between us. Where to the untrained eye it would appear as though he had just gone silent, I knew better. There is an almost buzz like sound whenever we spoke and when it is no longer apparent it was an easy way to tell he no longer resided in my mind.

Having him inside of my head and keeping me abreast of things as they are moving forward on his end was preferable to what I am supposed to sit here and watch. There had been a time once before where Serenity accused me of having to babysit her. I

161

refuted that statement because it held no merit but with the way I am observing them now it is almost as if it had come to pass. I am indeed feeling like nothing more than an eavesdropping babysitter.

Something she most definitely would not stand for once her memory of who and what I am to her returned. Just the mere thought of the way she would react if she knew I had been watching her from afar filled me with a moment of happiness that over the last few months had been few and far between.

It was in that moment that I knew what it is that I had to do. There is only one way that I could do what Michael needed me to in watching over her much the way I had been from the start. While he took care of things with Ryan, I was going to take care of things on my end by doing my part to help her remember in a way that only I can.

She may not remember a thing about the voices or even our time together before Ryan and the others had come back into her life but she would. If it is the last thing I do, I would bring her back to me, to all of us, much the way she had been before Lucifer had taken advantage of her sacrifices for the greater good.

It is all up to me.

Serenity

True to his word Ryan came back with the food he promised me and as much as I hate admitting it, I was starving. Whatever I had been through, it felt as though I hadn't eaten for weeks, so the burger and fries I seemed to be inhaling felt like my own personal blend of heaven on earth.

After dropping off the food he said a few words to Graham and had taken off. I can't explain it but watching him leave so quickly after just coming back upset me. There's this part of me that wanted to jump from the bed and tell him that he didn't have to leave but even more, that I wanted him to stay. I am taking up space in his room after all. The least I can do is let him stay given that he had been the one to bring me here and pretty much save my life, at least from what Graham told me.

162

The thought of letting him stay though, it filled with me with a sensation I have never experienced before. If I asked him to stay especially not understanding why it is that I want him there to begin with, I would be betraying the man that I know I love more than anything.

Graham had been so attentive and caring with me since I woke up, making sure that anything I need, he got for me, even going so far as to fill in the blanks about our relationship that I still can't entirely remember. I'm still having a hard time believing that he came to Stephenville for me and that we finally talked about what happened that night three years ago.

We had gotten past it and now we're here in this moment and we're together. The boy from across the street that I had loved more than life itself is really here and I can really call him mine. It really is perfect which means that whatever I'm feeling where Ryan is concerned was just going to have to be pushed down. There is no way I am going to ruin things with Graham before I even get the chance to really experience it. Not even for the boy with the blue eyes I can't get out of my mind.

"Earth to Ser…you there babe?"

Graham, calling to me. He left the room when Ryan came to drop off the food and I had been so lost in my own thoughts that I didn't even realize he came back.

"Yeah I'm here, just trying to remember things but it seems that's pointless."

I don't know why I'm hiding what I'm really thinking from him. We never hid things from each other before but just like what I had been thinking about earlier, I'm pretty sure he wasn't going to want to hear that I was thinking about Ryan. I just couldn't do that to him, so hiding the truth it is.

"It will all come back, you just can't push it."

"Since when did you become such a smarty pants?"

"I've always been smart. It's not my fault that you're such a shallow person you never saw past my looks before."

Wasting no time, I moved across the bed quickly and punched him on the arm. At least that's one thing that didn't change during

163

the time I was out cold. He hadn't lost the ability to be a total smart ass.

"You only wish I was that shallow."

"Never! Or at least not that you'll ever get to me to admit." He says with a wink. "Hey, you wanna do something with me?"

"Depends what you wanna do Graham Cracker. You're the one who knows everything that happened to me. Do you think I'm up for doing anything but lounging in bed right now?"

"Doctor Graham thinks you're well enough to be sprung from the bed rest."

"Oh well if Doctor Graham believes it then it must be true."

I couldn't explain it but I missed this. Being this way with Graham is something I enjoyed so much during the two years I lived in Green Haven and the one thing I missed more than anything when I moved away for school. It was so great to finally have it back in my life. It made me appreciate it even more than I had before.

"What did you have in mind?"

"Take a walk with me."

"Is this some lame attempt at taking me out so you can show me off to all your buddies?"

He snorted and I couldn't help but laugh at the sound. Graham had never been the guy that liked to party hard and spend a lot of time surrounded by a ton of other people so my statement about him parading me around is as far from the truth as you can get, which is exactly what I'd been going for when I said it. I wanted to hear him laugh again. It made everything complete.

"Come on princess, you're going to take a walk around campus with me. I think the fresh air will do you some good. Twelve hours in a bed can't be good for that body."

"You're right, it can't." I agreed as I slid myself up and out of the bed in record speed. If he's giving me the choice of staying in bed or being up and moving, it was definitely a no brainer. I'm going to get the hell out of here.

"Take it easy Serenity...you are still recovering."

What the hell was that?

164

"What did you say?" I asked as he stood at the end of the bed waiting.

"I didn't say anything?"

"Very funny. You just told me to take it easy. I heard it clear as day Graham so you might as well admit it or I'm not against punching you again."

"Seriously Ser, I didn't say anything."

There's something about the look on his face that makes me think he knows more than he's letting on but I believe him when he said that he hadn't spoken. I had heard someone speak though so while it might not have been him; there is definitely someone else in the room with us.

"You're sure you didn't say anything?"

"I'm sure, now come on. I want to take you out for that walk sometime today. Stop worrying about the voices and get a move on."

Deciding he was right and that I needed to let it go, I put the voice I heard out of my head and proceeded to make my way toward the closet I had just been scanning for signs of life. I didn't have any clothes with me as far as I knew but with the way I felt standing in the ones I had on, I was in desperate need of a change.

"Ryan said you could use anything in there until we can get back to your dorm and grab some of your stuff."

As I open the door and take in the line of shirts and jeans all hung up in front of me there is this flash in my mind. I recognize some of these clothes. I wasn't sure where from or why I was even remembering it at all but I did know I had seen these clothes before. They feel familiar to me. As eerie a feeling as it was, having a spark of a memory just on the surface I embraced it. Maybe if things were already starting to happen, I'd get my memory back faster then I originally thought.

Grabbing a sweater and a pair of jeans off their hangers, I turned to Graham and shooed him with my hands. We might be dating but there is no way I was letting him see me change. Until I got my memory back there's no way I'm going anywhere near that level of intimacy, no matter how deeply I care for him.

Winking at me, a grin on his face, he did what I needed him to and turned around. It was in that moment as his back was turned to me and I'm left staring at him, questioning the wink and his grin that it hit me.

If I can't remember even getting together with Graham, just how much more of our relationship is hidden from me? Was he winking at me because we have already reached a point where seeing each other naked didn't need to matter anymore?

Just how far have Graham and I gone?

CHAPTER NINETEEN

Ryan

I always imagined that when the time came for Emma to learn about Serenity and by association me and the angels that it would be Serenity that would be the one coming clean. It always seemed more right that way given their history and the love and respect they have for each other. It wasn't that I didn't like Emma because I did, it's just that of all the people that could be telling her this, me doing it is probably the worst possible way we could go.

Just the way it had been when I came to Serenity and told her just what I am and what I had been sent to do, it's the same feeling now even though I don't care nearly as much for Emma and her feelings as I do with her best friend. It didn't help that I was going to be doing this alone. Michael might be ready to appear when I gave him the okay but that isn't good enough for me. I actually found myself wishing I was doing this with Gabriel instead.

"What is it with you humans and my brother? What does he have that I do not?"

Yeah he's here with me all right. I officially have a babysitter while I drop yet another bombshell on an unsuspecting female and lucky for me it's the guy with the complex about his own importance. Somehow I saw us being laughed right out of the room once we explained all of this to her. There is no way she's going to believe this. I couldn't believe it myself sometimes and I'm the one living it.

"Well for one, Gabriel wouldn't ask me a stupid question like that."

"You may have a point but I do not believe the questions are stupid."

"It's been noted man, now look, I'm almost there. I need to make sure of everything we talked about. Are you sure you really want me to tell her everything?"

"Without question. She must know everything that we know in order to be of use to us should we need her in the future. With

Serenity's current predicament I do believe she will be of much use in the days to come, something she could not be without the knowledge we are about to supply her with."

"What if what we tell her pushes her over the edge? I mean they did spend time together in a centre for mental illness man and I do know for a fact that Emma has issues. I'm not sure how I feel about screwing with that."

"What she suffers from will not affect her as far as this revelation goes. You must put the worry out of your mind if we are to move forward Ryan. She is a strong girl, she will be fine. Much like Serenity was when you told her everything about you and the undertaking."

"Alright fine, we'll play it your way. I won't worry about it, at least not as much but if this blows up in our faces, expect me to tell you a great big I told you so."

"I would expect nothing less."

Once I was sure that Michael had gone quiet and I was actually on my own again I made my way into the girls dorm and took the stairs two at a time not really sure what the hurry was but realizing that the sooner I got to the room, the faster I could get this over with. I didn't really want to do it but now that I'm here, there isn't time to turn back.

Making my way to the door I'm reminded of the times I stood in this very spot during my time with Serenity. The first when she had been in the room with Gabriel and he had been telling her everything she deserved to know about herself and just what her destiny is. The second the night Lucifer had shown up during his time walking around in Graham's skin. Both times I had been worried about her and didn't want to walk very far just in case she needed me.

It's different this time. This time I'm coming back but not because Serenity needs me. In fact it's the opposite. She didn't need me at all since she didn't even remember me. I might be here to tell Emma everything she didn't know about Serenity but there's more to it.

This time I'm here because I needed her.

Rapping on the door a couple of times in quick succession, I rocked back on my feet while I waited for Emma. In just a few minutes everything is about to change for the girl on the other side of the door and there was no way I could prepare her for it. No matter how slow and easy I take things, she's still going to be deeply affected by what she learns today and there is nothing I can do to lessen the blow.

Not only had Serenity lied to her in not telling her all of this from the very beginning but she seemingly vanished on top of it. Sure, she's back now and the picture of good health but as far as Emma knows she's still missing in action which means that the only person Emma was going to be able to process this with is me and I am not looking forward to it.

As the door opened and I came face to face with her, I took a breath and tried to swallow the lump that was growing in my throat with each passing second. It was do or die time. The time for turning back is over.

"Oh Ryan! Hey!"

"Hey Emma, look I know you're probably busy but you think I can steal a couple minutes of your time? There are some things I need to talk to you about."

I'm rambling and I know it. I can't help it though. Once I opened my mouth to speak all of it wanted to come out and it was taking everything in me to just say the few words I managed to get out. With as badly as I wanted to get this over with, I had to make sure I at least waited until we were back in the room before laying it all at her feet.

"Not busy at all. Come on in." she answered, moving back into the room and away from the door giving me the entrance I needed.

Making sure the door is shut behind me; I make my way further into the room, taking a seat on Serenity's vacant bed. At least in the time since she's gone missing Emma didn't change anything. While there isn't very much here in terms of personal touch, it's still hers and anything that was hers let me feel close to her, something I need more than ever now.

"So what's up Ry?"

169

"Honestly Emma, I don't even know where to start with this."

"Is it about Serenity? Did you find her? Is she alright? When is she coming back?"

I just sat frozen as she fired question after question at me. I had answers to every single question she had but without going into detail about everything from the very beginning there is no way I could answer any of them. So while she exhausted herself I focused on exactly how I was going to start this conversation.

It's times like this where I really wish Michael could have been the one to do this. I really wasn't looking forward to it. Just like the first time, this time isn't very fun either. I was about to blow yet another girl's world apart and I'm not even sure in the long run it's worth it.

"It's about Serenity yeah but I can't answer any of the other questions. I just need you….I need you to hear me out okay, no matter how crazy it all sounds."

I could tell by the look on her face, much the same way Serenity's had been the first time I told her about who she really is that she didn't know how to take what I'm saying. She isn't afraid of me which I'm thankful for but she is definitely filled with doubt about what she thought I was going to tell her.

"Sure Ry but just so you know, you aren't making a whole lot of sense right now."

"It's not gonna make any sense when I tell you everything either."

"Good to know. So why don't you just spit it out and I'll figure out what to do once I've heard it all."

She's giving me the opening I need. I have to tell her everything now especially given that she seems to be in the frame of mind where she might accept it. Believing it is another story but at the very least she's open to hearing something that might not exactly be on the level.

"How much do you know about Serenity's abilities?"

Right away I knew I worded it wrong. As far as I knew from everything Serenity herself told me, Emma only knew that she could speak with the dead but nothing more. I only hope Emma wouldn't pick up on my poor word choice.

170

"You mean the fact that she's a medium? I know all there is to know about that but why do you want to know that?"

"It matters believe it or not. Serenity isn't your average girl Emma. She's something more."

"No kidding. Ry, you know I like ya but you're not making a bit of sense. I don't think you're trying to state the obvious but that's what you're doing. Just tell me what you need to tell me. I swear I won't freak out."

I underestimated Emma Daniels. Having been best friends with Serenity for the last eight years had opened her eyes far more then I realized to the supernatural, or at least to the possibility of it. I knew she was the first person to believe Gabriel to be a guardian angel and armed with that information as well as her own words now, I knew it was time and I knew just where I needed to start.

"Serenity, she's not exactly human."

"Say what?"

This wasn't going to work. I needed to try a different tactic otherwise I wasn't going to ever get to the point.

"You already know she's got more than just the ability to speak to the dead. You're the first one that noticed it. Gabriel isn't just a spirit Emma."

Where I expected her to be shocked she seemed almost satisfied as I confirmed what she already knew. I really didn't give this girl enough credit, something I was definitely going to change from now on.

"Gabriel is an archangel and he was sent down from Heaven at the same time as Serenity was. He is her guardian among other things. Serenity isn't entirely human because she's actually energy born of heaven."

When she didn't make a move or even an attempt to give me a response I went for broke and continued. The sooner I got this out the sooner she could process it all and maybe the blowback wouldn't be as harsh.

"The reason she's not here right now is because she tried to do the right thing and save Graham from a situation he couldn't get out of."

"What kind of situation are you talking about Ryan? What did Graham get into?"

"He was caught by Lucifer when he tried to save Serenity and well he was possessed."

While she is trying her hardest not to react I can tell she wants to. My power may not be at the level it used to be but it's still there and more than a little useful in the current situation.

"Alright Ryan, I think you need to start from the very beginning because none of this makes any sense."

"Well if you want me to do that then you better sit down because I'm telling you, when I'm done telling you everything you wanna know, it's going to knock you on your ass."

Graham

There has been so many times over the years where I've actually pictured doing this exact thing. It is more than just picturing it though, I actually wished for it more than once. To just be able to be with Serenity doing something as mundane as walking around a college campus, her hand in mine, just a comfortable silence and the scenery surrounding us.

It isn't like we've never done this kind of thing before because during her time in Green Haven we did basic things like this all the time. This time though it's different because we weren't just best friends anymore. The secret we both held on to for dear life was out now and we were together, really and truly together. It made everything I'm experiencing now that much more important.

I'm aware that I'm not exactly going about this in the most up front way but honestly, what rational guy when faced with the situation I'm in does the right thing all the time? In this case with as much as I knew it wouldn't last, I wanted to do the selfish thing and enjoy what it felt like to be hers. It's definitely easier to do that when I know that being with me is what she actually wants.

"You know, I've been here for two years and I've never really gotten the chance to enjoy this place at night before. It's amazing."

"That's what happens when you spend all your time locked away in your room Ser. Life keeps on moving whether you're moving along with it or not."

"There he goes again with the smarty pants comments. Wow Graham Cracker, I never knew you to be so deep before. You've been holding out on me."

She had no idea just how true that statement is. I am holding out on her. I owe her the truth and all I can do in the moment is smile stupidly at her and enjoy it even though my head is screaming at me to do the right thing. I have never hated the way I am before but right now, I was definitely cursing it. Everything always came back to the secrets I was keeping.

"Ser, I don't wanna ruin your mood but I need to ask you something."

As much as I want to stay in the moment I have to know just how much she remembers especially where her abilities are concerned. She hasn't so much as mentioned hearing one voice since she woke up in Ryan's room and I was beginning to wonder if maybe that part of her has been taken away too even though the memories of us hadn't been.

"Well that sounds serious."

"Yeah," I answer letting out a sigh. "I need to ask you about the voices."

Her face instantly turned to stone and I want to kick myself. I'm definitely going to ruin the mood.

"I wondered how long it was going to take you to ask me about that."

"So you remember it then?"

"Of course I do. It's not like I forgot everything. I just seem to be missing the last year or so of my life. Well not all of it but big chunks and people."

"So have you heard any since you came back?"

"You say that like I've been off somewhere Graham instead of just passed out for awhile."

She's confused and she has every right to be. I wasn't making any sense but seeing as I didn't exactly have much experience with

173

memory loss; it shouldn't be that much of a surprise. I was flying by the seat of my pants on this one.

"To answer your question, no I haven't heard anything since I woke up. It's actually kind of strange. Normally I hear them the moment I get up right until I got to bed at night but it's been pretty damn quiet."

"How does that make you feel?"

She smiled and I swear I felt my heart physically flip in my chest. I didn't want to admit it but bringing this up, with her still unable to remember concerned me. The last thing I wanted to do is cause her any pain, especially with everything she had been through.

"Honestly, for the first time I feel relatively normal. I know that being normal is overrated but not hearing the spirits, it's like a dream come true."

I could see the truth written all over her face. She really did enjoy not being able to hear the voices or sense the spirits around her. For as long as I can remember during my time getting to know her, all she ever wanted was to be like the other girls we went to school with. She had been forced to fade into the background for so long because of her ability when all she really wanted was to be out and doing the things that other people her age did.

For the first time since she heard the first voice at five, she looked free.

Maybe what Lucifer had done to her wasn't so bad after all. It was giving us a chance to reconnect on a level I knew both of us want and she is also free of the very thing that haunted her for years. I hated to admit it because after what he had done to me I could never truly be on his side but there is no denying that this really was a blessing in disguise, for the both of us.

"I know this is gonna sound lame but do you think we can go back to the room now. I think I've had all the walking I can stand and I think I need to rest again."

Pulling myself out of my thoughts, I loop her arm through mine and turn her around in the direction of Ryan's dorm. As much as I still want to be out with her, alone and away from prying eyes I know that her health and safety matter more. The selfish

174

need inside of me that wants to keep her close needs to be put in the background. We had all the time in the world to spend time together but she didn't have all the time in the world to heal.

"Alright sunshine, bed it is. Doctor Graham's orders."

Gabriel

Graham Hudson is dangerously close to crossing a line that would not be easy to come back from. The selfishness inside of him is not of his own very human design. It is all courtesy of my brother, of that I have no doubt. Every facet of what is taking place around me was all carefully crafted by Lucifer and so far everything hit its mark.

I may not be able to speak openly about my concerns, at least with the humans but I would continue watching and doing my part in order to change the path that he put us all on. He hadn't given Serenity over willingly and while I might not know exactly what his end game is, I do know I couldn't let him succeed.

In giving her back without her memories he was slowly destroying Ryan, of that I am certain and in giving her Graham, he is changing that young man into someone that wanted to think selfishly and put the needs of others in the back of his mind. The two men he is changing had forged a bond during the time he had held Serenity captive and pulling that bond apart one piece at a time was the perfect way for him to complete his act of bringing the world to its knees.

It is only a matter of time before Ryan came face to face with Graham and the closer that Serenity became to him and when that happened I wasn't sure any of us would come out unscathed. The same way that he is trying to pull Father away from the rest of us in Heaven, he is also attempting to do here on Earth and I need to put a stop to it once and for all.

"Brother, I can spare a few minutes to speak, are you somewhere that I may appear?"

Graham and Serenity true to their earlier conversation had made their way back to Ryan's room and with me now situated outside; choosing not to listen in on their private conversations both for them and myself it is the perfect time for Michael to appear. It was time that I told him everything I learned.

"I'm outside of the dorm room brother and the area around me is clear. You may appear."

With a brilliant flash of light Michael appeared directly in front of me, his wings completely elongated and looking much like the fierce warrior of the light that he is. Seeing Michael this way only made me long for home and much simpler times. We may have fought together during our time at home but it required far less planning and work then what we were currently facing. I desperately wanted things to be that easy again, at least for a little while.

"So what is it that you wanted to speak to me about Gabriel?"

"During my time at home with father I have learned some things and even more it would appear as I came back down here. I believe it is information that you need to know moving forward."

"This isn't about my attitude where he is concerned is it because Gabriel I am not in the mood to hear it."

"This has nothing to do with it yet it does have everything to do with it. I know that my statement will confuse you so please give me a chance to explain so that it will all become apparent to you."

"Do as you must." was his only reply, giving me the opening I needed.

"It has bothered me to no end the ease at which we were able to rescue Serenity from his clutches. It should not have been an easy task and I believe I may know why it happened that way."

"You have my attention."

"I believe that in giving her over to us as easily as he did that he is putting his final plan into motion. He damaged her memory in an attempt to get to Ryan, the one person he believes to have let him down the most. With her not remembering him the way he so desperately wants her to he is opening the door for Graham, a vessel he has now used to further an agenda, giving him the chance to be with her which will only cause discord in our ranks. Add to that the way in which we are pulling away from Father and it

176

appears as though his plan is working out just as it was intended to."

"You believe him to behind the discord with our father?"

"I do. I am more upset that I didn't see it sooner but with the choices Father has been making as of late added to our objections to them and the way it has distanced all of us there can be no other explanation."

"Gabriel I would like nothing more than to refute all that you have told me but I am unable to do so. You may have a point. If it had just been the issues with Father I may have been able to chalk it up to bad decision making but when added with what you have noticed about Serenity there can be no denial. I do believe this is Lucifer's final plan."

"He wants nothing more than to complete his overtaking of both heaven and earth and the easiest way for him to do that is to pull the people apart that stand in his way."

"Ryan has done as I requested and explained everything to the roommate. Now that it has been done he is calling to me so I must go now but Gabriel, now that we have an idea of what he is trying to do we must do whatever it takes to make sure that he doesn't succeed."

As he vanished leaving me again alone with my thoughts I knew there was only one way and one person that could help us take down Lucifer once and for all. She may not realize it but she held all of the power to be able to end this once and for all and while Michael might not agree with my methods, it is time I did something about it.

It is time to help Serenity remember, before it was too late and we are all lost forever.

CHAPTER TWENTY

Serenity

I can't shake the feeling that I've done this before. It's kind of overpowering and I can't explain it but I swear I've heard this voice before, more than once. There is something about the way he came to me when I was about to fall asleep that felt familiar too. I just wish I could remember it since it's obvious that my mind wants me to otherwise it wouldn't have recognized it at all.

I'm actually finding myself missing the constant barrage in my mind because it kept me busy. If I'm constantly dealing with voices then I don't have time to focus on the other stuff going on in my life and right now given that I can't remember much of anything about the last year of that life, I'm really looking for the distraction again.

So I was thankful for the voice when he came to me. It gave me something else to focus my attention on. It also helped that the voice is so low key and relaxing that it was easy to get lost in it.

*****

"Serenity..."

"I was wondering when one of you was gonna show up."

"You have not been enjoying the silence in your mind?"

Of course I had been enjoying it but when something becomes such a big part of your life and suddenly it's not there anymore it has the ability to throw everything off which is exactly what I was feeling now.

"I'm enjoying it but I'm not used to it I guess. So what did I do to deserve this visit from one of you now?"

"I am here to help you remember."

I might not remember much about my life but I did remember my time with the spirits. There had never been a time where one had come to me, wanting to speak about me or anything related to helping me. They were content to only bitch and moan about their

178

own very sad existence. Just who is this voice in my head, because he most definitely wasn't the standard spirit?

"You are correct in your assumption. I am not a spirit."

"You can read my mind too? Geez, that's not creepy at all."

"It is not meant to be creepy Serenity. Yes I am able to see into your mind and read your thoughts but it is not something I enjoy doing."

"Then why even do it?" I ask, sliding myself up in the bed. If he was going to have a conversation with me then sleep is definitely not going to happen so there was no sense pretending it is.

"I want to do anything possible that will help you remember."

"What do you know about my memory loss? Do you know what happened to me?"

"I know everything."

That wasn't the answer I was expecting but it worked perfectly. If Graham wouldn't tell me what happened than maybe this voice in my head could fill in the blanks. I felt better than ever so there was no reason anyone had to keep things from me anymore.

"I am afraid I cannot give you the information you seek. You must remember on your own. I can only tell you that the strange feelings you have been getting in certain situations, you must grab on to them and see them as more than just random occurrences."

"What exactly does that mean?"

"Do you recall the way you felt when you opened Ryan's closet earlier before going out with Graham? It is those instances that you must grasp onto and not let go of. They are appearing as cues to help you regain your memory."

"It would go so much easier if you would just tell me everything you know."

It was a long shot I know but it was valid. If he told me everything I had been through, how he knew me and just why it is that I couldn't remember anything then maybe everything could get back to normal much faster than it is now.

"Your mind would not accept it coming from me. Serenity, we know each other very well. You have always been the person that

179

deals in facts and is able to accept things at a much faster rate if you come to them on your own. That is the way it has to be now."

He was giving me answers without even trying. He just admitted that we knew one another and had given me proof that he wasn't trying to deceive me. I really am the girl that questions everything and has an easier time coming to terms with things when I come to them on my own terms. There is no way that he could have known that unless he was being truthful and did really know me.

"Can you at least tell me one thing?"

"If it pertains to your memory loss I am afraid that I cannot."

"Can I at least ask the question first?"

"Of course."

"What's the relationship between me and Ryan? I keep getting these flashes like I did with the closet earlier and I can't remember what it is exactly but I get the feeling that there is much more between us then anyone is willing to admit to me."

There was a moment in the silence that I knew I asked the right question. If there was nothing between Ryan and me then I have to assume that the voice would have answered back almost immediately and he isn't, which means that there was more going on then I'm aware of.

"Your silence is all the answer I need." I state. "I've got one more question though."

"What would that be?"

"Who are you?"

"I am Gabriel and that is all I can tell you for now."

*****

Gabriel. The name is so familiar and I can feel the knowledge at the edge of my mind but I'm unable to grab a hold of it and make it stick. I can't remember even though I want nothing but. He is something more than just a standard spirit and the proof of that is in the fact that he knew information he shouldn't be able to know.

He also gave me information without meaning to which means now I have a place to start in order to get my memories back. There is a history between Ryan and me and I'm going to get to the bottom of it. I might be with Graham and being with him after spending the last three years apart made me happy but I know I can't move forward before knowing everything I'm leaving behind.

Just what is it about the guy with the cloudy blue eyes that won't leave me alone? What happened between us that even with the memory loss I'm unable to entirely forget? More importantly, why do I feel drawn to him every time we're in the same room even though my heart belongs to Graham?

I need answers and I need them soon because much more of this and I'm actually going to be as crazy as I always believed myself to be all those years.

Ryan

Emma Daniels is quite possibly the only human being I have ever come across that can handle her world being turned upside down with strength and humor. Serenity had been the same way but even with her there had been moments where I could tell she felt the entire thing was unbelievable. With Emma there didn't appear to be any of that. She just accepts it as fact.

"So is there anyone that I hang out with that isn't something supernatural?"

"Well that boy you brought back to your room last week is one hundred percent human."

"How do you know about that? Wait, you know what? Never mind. I don't think I wanna know how you know that."

I wanted to tell her the truth. That the only reason I knew about the guy is because he happens to live in the same place as me and I heard him bragging about it to his friends but the way she was reacting to what she assumed is some ability I had because of who I am, is just too enjoyable to stop.

"I always knew Gabriel was an angel. It was so obvious I don't know how she didn't see it."

"She didn't want to see it."

"Can you really blame her? She spent her life with a mom that assumed she was crazy and then locked her away for almost three years because of it. I can see why she wouldn't wanna believe she was talking to angels."

"Yeah, neither one of us ended up in the right place in the parent department. Only difference with me and her is that my mother actually knew she had laid down with a demon and hated me because of it. Serenity's mom loved her, at least in her own way."

Emma snorted and I couldn't help but laugh. It appeared as though we both share the same feelings where Serenity's mother is concerned.

"There's something I don't get."

Considering all of the information she's taken in I'm shocked she's only now admitting there were things she heard that she didn't get. I had been expecting to hear it much sooner but am thankful that finally there seemed to be something I was going to have to walk her through. Having someone take in the news of angels, demons, the devil and a war between heaven and hell so easy is off putting.

"Why wouldn't she just tell me? I mean she had to know that since I thought Gabriel was an angel that I would understand it? Why keep it from me?"

"That wasn't her choice. She died a little inside every single time she had to lie to you, trust me on that. Serenity is not a liar but the angels told her that in order to keep you safe she had to keep things from you, so she did. It was made worse with them implanting the memories they did during her time away."

"Yeah, I don't think I'm a fan of that. I swear if I see one of those angels that did that to me I'm going to give him a piece of my mind. No one is allowed to fuck with my head but me."

I liked Emma. Now that she knew everything she was going to fit in easily with the rest of us and it had nothing to do with her willingness to accept what she is being told. It's strictly because she was a take no bullshit kind of girl. I couldn't wait for Michael to appear so the fireworks could really begin.

182

It might have been Gabriel that implanted the memories in her mind but since he was off taking care of Serenity and making sure that the situation with Graham didn't become any worse than it already was, it looked like Michael is going to end up taking one for the team.

"Trust me; you're not the only one that feels that way." I laugh. "Just wait until they talk to you in riddles and then tell you that all will be revealed in time. You're gonna wanna do more than just give them a piece of your mind."

She smiled at me but looking at her I could still see the questions in her eyes. There was obviously more on her mind.

"So she's really back now?"

"She is. She's with Graham and Gabriel but like I told you, she doesn't remember much of anything about the last year of her life. Whatever Lucifer did to her in an effort to have her forget her time in Hell scrambled everything in her brain."

"She remembers me and Graham though right?"

"Yeah, that's about all she remembers."

"How do you feel about that Ry? I mean your wife is in your room right now with Graham of all people. You know the history there and if that isn't bad enough she believes that they're dating. You can't be handling it well."

Well she definitely had a way of getting right to the heart of the matter. No, I wasn't handling it well. I wanted nothing more than to go to her, tell her the truth and take her away from Graham, the angels and all of the shit we've been dealing with and spend some much needed time alone with her the way we deserve.

"I don't have much choice but to deal with it Emma. I can't exactly drop a year's worth of information on her right now. Who knows what kind of damage that could do to her?"

"I don't entirely trust Graham with her."

Well we had that in common too. Sure the two of us had formed some kind of a bond during the time we spent together trying to rescue Serenity but he had still been Lucifer's vessel at one point and even though he might be healed from it, who knew what lasting effects it left behind. Not to mention the whole soul mate bond. I didn't trust that one bit.

183

"Is that because of what happened between you guys when he was possessed?"

"Yeah a little. I know he wasn't in control of it but Ryan, if she hadn't come home when she did god only knows what would have happened in here. I want to get over it but every time I close my eyes I can still see it. It's scary."

"Just be thankful that she did come home. You're right, he wasn't in control and he was being driven by Lucifer to do all of that to you, I don't doubt that for a second. He wanted to get to her, damage her in some way and the easiest way to do that other then coming after me was with you."

There is more going on than what she's admitting to but I wasn't sure I wanted to push it. I had seen Graham and her together a few days before and while she did appear to be at least a little bit scared of him there was also something more there. I have no idea what exactly happened in the room between the two of them but it's obvious that it had gotten to her in more ways than just the obvious.

Graham told me that there was nothing going on between him and Emma and I didn't believe him. Maybe it's time that I ask the other person involved. I still had the ability to tell when someone was lying to me and I'd be able to see through Emma easily.

"What exactly is going on with you and him anyway? I saw you two the other day and it didn't seem that you were too afraid of him then."

Her face flushed pink and I knew I had her. While Graham could do the typical guy thing and blow it off as nothing, she couldn't do the same. She was affected by Graham Hudson for whatever reason and with the rosy pink of her cheeks now I realize that it might actually work in my favor.

"Can I tell you something but have it stay between you and me?"

I am not a fan of keeping secrets. I don't see how it serves anyone in the long run because usually the secrets that are kept are ones that when they do come out do an irreparable amount of damage but right now with the way my mind is working, I was

184

willing to hear this secret and keep it. Especially if it's what I thought it was.

"I can't promise that I can keep it to myself if it affects Serenity in some way that's important Emma but I'm willing to hear you out."

"I guess that's going to have to be good enough." She answers sighing loudly. "It probably will affect Serenity so you don't have to keep it from her if it ever comes up."

I knew what she was going to say and I didn't have to use my abilities in order to figure it out. It's written all over her face. There is most definitely something going on between her and Graham, at least on her end. I didn't want to think selfishly but I wanted my wife back and if this information could give me that then I was most definitely going to use it.

"I never told Serenity but I always thought Graham was pretty cute. I would have never made a move, I mean he is the guy that my best friend was in love with but then you came along."

There would never be a time, no matter who is speaking about it where Graham being Serenity's first love wouldn't piss me off and bring the anger up inside of me. No one gets lucky when they fall in love, there is always a person in the past that affects them so I really shouldn't look at it any other way but it's hard not to. I wanted to be her one and only love.

"He said some things to me that day here and he wasn't entirely wrong."

"What did he say?"

"That he could tell I liked him and that even though I was afraid my body still responded to him just like his did to me. It was gross but at the same time it wasn't a lie, I mean it did happen."

Shit. Lucifer was definitely a sick son of a bitch. He had somehow figured out that Emma would react to Graham and used it in order to further his plans. Serenity didn't know anything about the way her best friend felt for Graham but it was only going to be a matter of time before it spilled out. If Emma is telling me this easily then I don't doubt she'd end up doing the same with her soon.

"Psych class actually comes in handy after all."

185

"What's that supposed to mean?"

"I can't believe I'm actually going to say this but the way you reacted to Graham that day is actually pretty normal. I mean there are cases of rape victims being turned on during the attack and it's not because they like it or anything, it's just the bodily response. I think the same thing happened with you and Graham."

I really couldn't believe that I am sitting here saying this. Five minutes before I had been wanting her to admit to liking Graham because I could use it to get Serenity back and now here I am trying to make her feel better for feeling the way she did. Letting her know it wasn't entirely her fault. How screwed up is this?

Before I could question it anymore, the room filled with light as Michael finally made his appearance. Now that he knew Emma was aware of everything, he didn't have to warn about his impending arrival and just like in the past, I again had another female falling to the floor in front of me from the shock of it. It was easier to see why Emma and Serenity got along so well now.

"Jesus Christ!"

"Yeah you're not gonna wanna say that."

"Big bright light, enormous wings and a body so tall I can barely make out its face and you're telling me you weren't thinking the same thing?"

"Oh I am but they don't like it when you use those words."

"The use of my father's name in this regard means little to me Ryan. The girl is fine."

Well that's something new. Anytime any of us had ever used the words before we got told off about it. What made Emma so special?

"She isn't all that special; I am just not in the mood to debate right now. It is my understanding that the girl is aware of everything now?"

"Yeah I know everything and before you say whatever it is you're gonna say next I have a few things I want to say to you."

Well it looks like Emma isn't going to waste any time. Michael is going to be in for a shit storm and as much as I want to keep things serious given what we face now, I couldn't hold back the laugh that was building.

186

"I am unsure what you are talking about."

"Putting memories in my head that never happened just so you could keep the truth about my best friend from me? Just who the hell do you think you are? What kind of angel does that kind of thing?"

"Well that would be my brother Gabriel you are referring to but to answer your other question, I do not think I am anything, I know what I am. I am a being made of the light, Heaven's warrior and you would be best served remembering that."

Where Emma had been ready for a fight only seconds before, something in Michael's tone seemed to calm her and as she got back to her feet, she distanced herself even more from the angel. I have been on the receiving end of Michael and his crisp tone and much like she was now, I backed down too. No one messed with Michael that was for sure.

"Gabriel is the one that put the memories in my head?"

"Yeah. Michael was too busy babysitting me back then to do it himself. You're getting pissed at the wrong guy."

"Well shit. Now I actually feel bad. Sorry." She apologized as she turned to face the seemingly irate angel.

"It is of little importance to me young lady. There are more pressing issues at hand."

"Like what?" I asked intrigued to find out what he had learned while he had been absent.

"Gabriel has come across some information that changes things considerably. I think is it imperative that we take Emma to Serenity now in an effort to spark her memory so that we may move forward."

"What kind of information?"

"We believe that it was his intent all the long to erase this much of her memory. That it was done in an effort to break you and Graham."

"He's trying to turn us against each other isn't he?"

"It would appear to be that way yes. Add to that the growing tensions he has created in Heaven with our father and it would appear ripping us apart one by one is his end game."

There is nothing that anyone can tell me about Lucifer and his plans that will shock me. There might be a part of me that puts some trust in him even after being shown otherwise but nothing he ever did shocked me. Where his plans before had always been about attacking the group as a whole, I had to give him credit now. Going after us one by one in the ways that would most affect us is brilliant.

It was just too bad we were on to him now. He wouldn't be expecting that given just how far behind everything we always seem to be during our earlier run-ins with him.

"So what do we do?"

"We get her to remember just who and what she is. All of this surrounds her in some way and the sooner she gets her memory back the sooner we can end this once and for all."

"Do you think there's something from her time in hell that might be able to help us? Is that why you wanna rush her to remember?"

"No, my brother would not have been that careless. He would have realized that she could regain her memory of that time any moment after we got her out so he wouldn't have revealed his plans to her. We need her if we are to fight, plain and simple."

A few months ago God had been willing to put me on the chopping block in order to stop Lucifer once and for all. The way Michael sounded now was like they wanted to do that very thing again but this time with Serenity. I'm not sure how I felt about it. We had done more than enough sacrificing for the greater good over the last year, isn't it time for someone else to step up to the plate?

"I understand your concerns Ryan but this is not about her sacrificing herself this time. This is about having as much power as possible between us to end his reign once and for all."

Now that is something I could get behind. If we were all going to face this together just the way we did when we ventured into hell only days before then it is definitely possible we can end this once and for all.

"So where do I fit in here? I mean doesn't knowing everything now make me a target?"

188

I hate admitting it but when Michael and I started talking about everything he learned I forgot she was even in the room with us. She brought up a valid point though, was she in danger now that she knew all there is to know?

"I do not believe Lucifer will come back to the girl but she is needed for her relationship with Serenity. If we have any hope of her regaining her memory we are going to have to use whatever we can and right now that is you Emma."

"So you just want me to go see Serenity?"

"No, we will bring her back to you. She will be under constant protection, just as you will be and hopefully during her time with you she will begin to remember."

With the new information we have everything we planned on before seemed to be changing and now I had more questions than answers. I wasn't ready to move forward with this plan until I got what I needed. I only hope Michael is willing to give it to me.

"What happens when Serenity starts slamming her with questions?"

"Serenity is under the impression that Emma knows nothing so she will be forced to remember her past on her own with no help from the girl. She does not have that same ability with you and Graham. This is where she needs to be. I am positive this is where her memory will return to her because there will be no pressure."

I want to tell him that she wouldn't get pressure from me either but that wasn't entirely truthful. I wanted her to remember so badly that it was inevitable that I would put strain on her any time I was around her. Michael is right, if she was going to remember on her own and help us in the war that's coming with Lucifer, she would have to do it here. It's the one safe place we had.

"What about her relationship with Graham? Are we gonna let that continue?"

"For the time being we do not have a choice. It is what she wants, at least what her body and mind want. Only when she accepts what her heart is trying to tell her will she truly be ready for the truth."

I will do whatever it takes in order for everything to go smoothly but there was the selfish part of me that prayed that her heart reminds her of who she really wants sooner rather than later. I was afraid of what might happen if it didn't.

CHAPTER TWENTY ONE

Gabriel

There are few moments over the last year guarding Serenity that I had cause for celebration. With the way things seem to be moving forward now, this is one of them. For the first time in a very long time it seems we are one step ahead of Lucifer and whatever it is that he is planning.

With Emma now in the know as it pertains to Serenity and the life we have all been living around her we are only made that much stronger. Michael informed me that she accepted everything easily though she has some anger towards me as it pertains to the work I had done on her mind months prior. I could handle that as long as she is willing to stand by her best friend and help.

I needed to get Graham alone and inform him of everything that is now taking place but with the way he seems to loom over Serenity during her every waking moment it is increasingly difficult. I could have easily used the times at which she slept to come to him but given that I didn't have many hours where I could reach out to her and guide her back to remembering I chose to spend the time with her.

His time with her would soon be coming to an end and he needed to come to terms with that even though I knew it is the last thing he would want to do. Even when you make a decision to do the wrong thing for the right reasons there is still a level of understanding in it at least for me. I understood what Graham wanted to achieve and while I know it was wrong I could not begrudge him the time with her that he desired. If I had been in his place I surely would have done much the same thing.

Now though it is time to inform Father of everything that has been taking place. I am sure that he already knew the steps we have taken in an effort to get ahead of our fallen brother but I found myself wanting to be face to face with him again. It is easy to become lost in the human way of life and I am finding myself longing for the comfort that home always brought me.

"Gabriel, my son, it appears as though you have been quite busy since the last time we spoke. It pleases me to see you taking such action."

"Well you did tell me to get in front of this; going on the offensive did you not Father?"

"That I did my son. I was also able to witness your conversation with Michael and while I am aware that he is still not quite as accepting as you are in forgiveness as it pertains to me, it pleases me that he has not completely disregarded it."

"Michael will come around Father. This has been a trying time for us all but we are finally at a place where we can come together as one again moving forward. We have much to be thankful for."

"How long do you believe it to be before Serenity recalls her life?"

I want to be able to give him a time frame but given that there is still much work to be done in that regard and we want it to be as natural as possible for her own mental state, I cannot. All I can promise him is that it would happen and if I have my way it would be sooner rather than later.

"With Emma Daniels on board with us I do not foresee it being much longer. They have quite a strong bond as you well know and through her I do believe Serenity will begin to pick up more of her memories and be able to come back to us much the same way she was before Lucifer got his hands on her."

"This pleases me Gabriel. It was always my hope that you would realize your true place both here and on the planet and watching you now, with as strong as you have become, it is almost as if my wishes and hopes have come to pass."

I have seen my father in many ways over the years together both when he had been angry and disappointed with me and also when pleased. It saddens me that the moments he was truly pleased with me are few and far between. It is my hope that through doing things the way I have been there would be more of these moments in the future. I rather enjoy these times with him.

"There is only one request that I want to make moving forward my son."

"What would that be?"

192

"I have noticed that you have begun reaching out to your beloved through her mind again and while I find no fault in that I only ask that you tread carefully."

He isn't saying anything that I haven't already thought of myself when I made the decision to do it. I would treat Serenity with the highest level of care so that my time in her mind would not come back to haunt her in ways that I would be unable to fix. She may be my beloved but more than that she is my family and as such I would go to the ends of the earth to make sure she was not harmed.

"You have nothing to fear Father, I know what I am doing as it pertains to the ball of light."

"I know that you made this trip home in order to make sure I am kept abreast of everything that has been going on down there but I have to say that I am also glad you are here because there is something that I feel I also need to share with you."

Over the last year there has not been many times where he wanted to share much of anything with me and while I understood why, it pained me deeply. Now that we are aware of what is going on deeper under the surface, I am willing to forgive it. Anything that needs to be done in order to succeed moving forward I would do.

"What is it?"

"While you and your brother have been working diligently in order to stay one step ahead of your brother I have felt the rumblings of a power almost reaching mine in magnitude that is making its presence known."

"Do you mean to say that you can feel Lucifer rising?"

"It would appear that way yes. It is not yet strong enough for me to say with certainty that he is again topside but I do ask that you keep your guards up and warn all of the people under your charge to do the same."

"Of course Father."

The last time he had information on Lucifer he kept it from Michael and me and in doing so turned us against him. We chose the path of free will in an effort to do what we believed to be right given that Father seemed to want to jump first before thinking things through. The respect he is showing me now spoke volumes.

Lucifer would most definitely not win this battle of wills. We are stronger than him and whatever he wants to throw at us and it is time that we stood up and showed him just how much.

"You do know my son that she is going to be the very thing that defeats him this time?"

""I am aware of it but why do you speak of it now?"

"As you know, I am aware of how things will turn out. Though I do not speak of them in an effort to make sure that nothing that is destined to happen changes, I want to be sure that you are aware that the fate of the planet and even Heaven itself falls on her shoulders. It is her time Gabriel and we must help her reach her destiny."

The undertaking. The very reason I had been sent down to begin with twenty two years before. It is going to happen this time. Even though we prevented it twice already, it would seem that the time for prevention was over and now it is time for action.

"She will reach the destiny as it has been mapped out for her Father. I will succeed in my task of making sure that it comes to pass in its true time, of that you can be sure."

"It would appear as though the moment you have been waiting for has arrived Gabriel. Make your way down to the humans again. It is time you informed the Hudson boy of exactly what happens next. He has finally been freed from his guard of Serenity."

As I watched I could see what he witnessed and Graham is now being freed of his obligation. Ryan had arrived back in the room which meant it is most definitely time for me to get back. The last thing I want to happen now is for these two men to come to blows over the current situation they found themselves in. It would surely tear apart all of the groundwork that had already been put in place.

"Keep me informed of all changes or issues Gabriel and I will help you in any way that you need. Focus on what needs to be done there and if I hear anything more from Lucifer I will call for you immediately."

CHAPTER TWENTY TWO

Ryan

There is something to be said for walking into your room and seeing your wife lying across your bed dressed in nothing but your clothes. Where my heart had been taking a beating since the moment we got her out of hell and she woke up without a memory of me, this was definitely a mood lifter.

I wasn't sure what I expected to see when I got back to the room but this isn't it. I know Graham let her continue to believe that they were together and while I had to go along with it until Serenity could remember, I didn't like it and feared that at any moment I would walk in and catch them doing something I wouldn't be able to erase away.

It wouldn't be the first time I caught them in a position that I didn't like of course. A few months before I'd come back from Heaven just in time to witness the two of them making out on Emma's bed. I tried not to think of that often but with what we were all going through now it was hard not to go back to that time. The last thing I want is for history to repeat itself.

Sometimes I wonder if I've really dealt with what happened that day. I mean I know we talked through a lot of our issues back then but with the way I still felt ripped apart inside just thinking about that day I wondered if maybe I'm still harboring anger and resentment toward her for what she put me through. I might have forgiven her but forgetting is a whole other ballgame and I honestly don't know if I ever will.

"Hey Ryan."

The way my name sounded falling from her lips still drove me as crazy as it did the first time I heard it. With her, no matter how much time passed it seemed my reactions never changed. Whether it is the fifth time or the fiftieth time it seems that it affects me just as deeply. This woman really did own every single part of me but most definitely my heart most.

I know I should be answering her but I can't seem to do that because I'm too busy looking at her. The way her hair falls around her face as it's covered by one of my hoodies is breathtaking. She looks comfortable, happy and more than that, completely at peace. This is my Serenity, my first love, my first lover and the first person to show me that I even had a heart to begin with. She's everything to me.

"You okay Ry?"

My heart leapt in my chest at the sound of my shortened name being spoken. She hadn't called me that since she woke up in my bed days earlier and part of me hopes that in doing it that she might have remembered something during my time away.

"Yeah I'm fine. Actually I need to ask you something."

I'm aware of Graham in the corner of the room, his eyes locked on me even though I'm not able to see them. I can feel them and that is more than enough. I know he didn't like me being here because it slammed the reality of the situation back into him but he was going to have to get over that because things need to change.

"Sure, what's up?"

"What do you think about getting out of here and going to see Emma?"

I could tell by the way her hazel eyes began to glow that I gave her something she's been wanting. Something that Graham for all he had done for her hadn't been able to do. I knew it wasn't a competition but I sure did feel like I just scored the first goal with the way she lit up in front of my eyes.

"Seriously? I can go back home?"

"Yeah you can pretty girl. I think I've kept you here long enough. Emma misses you and I have a feeling you miss wearing your own clothes, though I don't think I've ever seen that hoodie look so good before."

She blushed and I smiled. She might not remember me but that wasn't going to stop me from getting as many reactions out of her as possible. I lived for her and the expressions she made.

"I'll take her over." Graham spoke up, reminding me again that I wasn't alone.

196

"Actually man, if you don't mind I'm gonna let you get back to whatever you've been putting off for the last few days too. I'll take her home and you can meet up with her there later. If that's okay with Serenity anyway."

"More than okay." She squealed jumping from the bed and spinning herself around. If I wasn't witnessing it with my own eyes I could have sworn I was dreaming. This is a side of Serenity I have never seen before but man, do I like it.

"Okay pretty girl, take it easy with the spinning, you're still healing. I'll give you and Graham a couple of minutes and when you're ready, meet me outside okay?"

There was this moment before she made her next move that I ached to hold her so when she threw her arms around my neck and pressed her body into mine I swear I died and went to Heaven. What were the odds that the minute I thought about what she would feel like in my arms she did it? Is it possible she's somehow recalling the connection between us and read my thoughts?

"Thank you for this Ryan. I appreciate everything you did so much. I don't know how I'll ever be able to thank you."

Little did she know that she had already done it. In wrapping her arms around me and putting her body in direct contact with mine she thanked me in the only way I ever want her to. She gave me the one thing I've been missing since she'd woken up two days before.

Hope.

Graham

I knew I had it coming but did he really have to be so obvious with it?

It's no secret that even with her memory loss there is a connection with her and Ryan but for the last little while I didn't have to see it in front of me. Now, here he is and it was making itself apparent. She might not even realize that it's happening but she doesn't have to. I could see it quite clearly all on my own.

I realize that none of this would be happening if I didn't lie to her from the start but can't he see it for what it is and give me just

197

a little time with her? Why did he have to put himself right in the middle of us?

"He is only doing what has been done to him Graham."

"Really Gabe?"

"You and I need to speak when they leave. So say your goodbyes to Serenity and prepare accordingly. There are things going on that you need to be made aware of and you need to store your pity party. You brought it on yourself Graham."

Of course everything he just said is the truth. I had to see this coming because Ryan is only doing what I did to him. Instead of telling her the truth right from the beginning I chose to embrace the selfishness and enjoy time with her, knowing it wasn't going to last long. I just wasn't ready for it to end quite yet.

"Graham where are you right now?"

"Nowhere Ser."

"Why don't I believe you?"

What am I supposed to say? That I'm talking to an angel inside of my head? I want to tell her the truth because honestly not being completely honest with her is just not something I'm all that comfortable with but doing it would only make everything worse. She would realize just how much I've been holding back from her and probably end up hating me. There is no way I am letting that happen.

"Honestly Ser, I don't know how I feel about you going with him."

I might not be able to tell her the entire truth but I could tell her at least some of it. I really didn't feel right about her going with Ryan so for once I don't feel like a heel for hiding things from her.

"Why? I mean we're friends right? All he's doing is bringing me back home."

She really didn't remember him. I could see it all over her face. She genuinely thought that Ryan is only going to take her home and leave it at that. As much as I love the innocence she has since losing her memory I want her to remember just so she would know what I'm worried about.

"You really don't get it do you? He's doing more than just taking you home!"

I don't know where it came from but there was no taking it back once I started. I didn't want her anywhere near Ryan. He could take her away from me. All I wanted for the last four years at least was to be with her and now that I have it, I'm just not willing to give it up.

"Okay I seriously have no idea what you're even talking about but can you stop yelling at me?"

"I'm sorry."

"You don't need to be sorry; you just need to tell me what's going on."

"Ryan, he doesn't want to be your friend Serenity. He wants more."

I thought telling her that might spark something in her, some form of a reaction but when none came I realize that the memory lock is still firmly in place and is showing no signs of breaking.

"Well last I checked who I wanna be with is up to me just as much as the other person and I am with you. So can you please stop worrying about his intentions and just enjoy the break? You'll see me as soon as I'm settled back in my room I promise."

There's the innocence again. She believes every word she's saying and I want to believe with her but I know better. It's only a matter of time before everything comes back to her and the minute it does everything is going to change. I would lose her again and this time for good. No going back.

"I love you Graham Cracker." She said placing her lips to my cheek. "I'll see you soon."

It hit me the minute she turned from me. I might have to get used to going this alone because as she walks away from me and toward Ryan who is waiting outside it's becoming harder to ignore.

All I would ever get with her was her back as it retreated from me.

CHAPTER TWENTY THREE

Serenity

"Ryan, he doesn't want to be your friend Serenity. He wants more."

I didn't want Graham's words getting me considering I am finally going home to my own bed again but no matter how hard I try that is exactly what happens. The voice in my head the night before already told me the same thing just in the way it remained silent but Graham saying it just gave me that much more to go on.

There is definitely something more than just a friendship between Ryan and me.

I'm not sure how I feel about that considering that I'm with Graham and for the most part I'm happy. Did I need to talk to Ryan about it and clear the air or do I just treat it like business as usual?

I can't deny that I was excited about him being the one to take me home. For some reason it just felt like it was the right thing to do. It isn't that I didn't want Graham to be the one to come back home with me but with how happy he seemed when he told me I just felt that Ryan is the one I want to do it.

"Penny for your thoughts pretty girl."

"They aren't worth that much trust me."

I'm starting to notice a trend when I start remembering things. My body, from head to toe gets this all over warmth, like it recognizes something and I focus all of my attention on it because I know that at some point a memory is going to pop up and I don't want to miss it. I've said something like this before, I can tell.

"Somehow I doubt that. Try me."

There is no doubt about it. I am the worst girlfriend on the planet. I turned when he spoke to me and now I'm getting a full on view of his face and I can't help but lose myself first in the lightness of his eyes, even if they do have the black tint to them and then his lips. Watching words fall from someone's lips has never been so appealing to me before but with Ryan I can't seem to help myself.

The way both rings sit on his lips and the way they move just slightly as he runs his tongue along his bottom lip is threatening to send me into what I can only assume is a heat induced coma. God he even licks his lips in a sexy way. Why I'm having this kind of reaction to him I can't say but damn, it feels good.

"Pretty girl, you need to stop looking at me like that."

I have no idea how I'm looking at him to be honest but it's most definitely something I didn't want to stop, especially if it made him smirk like that. His forehead creased and before I knew it he was laughing and I joined in.

"I don't know what you're talking about." I say coming up for air. "I'm not looking any way at you."

"I beg to differ. You've got this look in your eye that just isn't right for a girl that's taken by another guy."

Shit.

It's obvious that the heat I felt watching the way his tongue ran across his snake bites is making itself apparent on my face. He's right, I'm taken by Graham, there is no way I should even be thinking about Ryan this way yet I can't seem to help it. Just what is it between us that I can't seem to pull away from?

Turning my gaze down, away from his face I continue walking, praying that he doesn't say anything until we reach the room so that I wouldn't have another reason to look at him and get lost in him the way I just did. I had a boyfriend that I needed to think about. All I'm doing looking and reacting to Ryan this way is making every fear Graham has that much more valid.

After walking for about five minutes without so much as a word back and forth between us, I stopped, realizing that he wasn't beside me anymore. Turning around I saw him and the look in his eyes told me that whatever is on his mind, it isn't anything good. The only thing missing in the moment is a scowl.

Just what the hell happened?

"Ryan, are you okay?" I ask, jogging the few paces back to where he stood, seemingly frozen in place.

"I am most definitely not okay."

201

"What's wrong?"

"I can't do this shit with you Ser. I want to touch you, wrap my arms around you and feel the way you feel when your body is pressed to mine. I can't sit here and pretend anymore."

I have no idea what he's talking about but he did manage to stop my heart for a few seconds with the vision of him with his arms wrapped around me. Whatever had taken place between us, it's obvious both of us weren't ready to let it go. I might not remember it but my body sure seemed to and it's becoming harder to deny and ignore with each passing second we spent together.

"I don't understand…how are you pretending?"

He pulled me to him and the minute his lips touched mine it was like an explosion went off inside of my head. Memories came flooding at me in rapid succession, so many that it became increasingly more difficult to keep up with them. Ryan and I most definitely have a past together and all it had taken was the feel of his lips on mine, the way the rings dug into my bottom lip for me to realize just how much.

Breaking away from the kiss, my fingers immediately going to my now swollen lips I look up at him and the look in his eyes speaks volumes about what he's feeling and just what that kiss meant to him.

"I'm sorry Ser. I know you're with Graham but I can't hold back anymore."

I want to be mad at him, to tell him in no uncertain terms that what he did kissing me that way had been wrong but the words just wouldn't come. As wrong as it may have been, it just isn't feeling that way. The guilt building in my stomach is very real though and it caused me to look away from him and start walking again.

It doesn't matter what is between us because whether we like it or not, I'm with Graham and there is no way I can hurt him that way. As perfect as it felt kissing Ryan it couldn't happen again.

"Let's just get back to the dorm okay?" I state as he caught up to me and began walking at the new pace I set.

"Actually I'm actually kind of hoping you'll take a detour with me."

After the kiss we shared I want nothing more than to take the detour he's offering but I know if I did, I'd just regret it the minute I saw Graham later. No, I have to start thinking less like a hormonal teenager and more like the very committed woman that I am.

"I don't think that's such a good idea Ryan..."

Even to my own ears the argument is weak. My body and my heart wanted nothing more than to betray my mind and I am dangerously close to letting them.

"I know you remembered something when we kissed Serenity. You might not know everything yet but you know now that there's something between us. So please, for the sake of what you can remember will you please do this with me?"

His eyes are pleading and impossible to say no to. There is no doubt about it; I am definitely going to go to hell for this.

"Fine," I say sighing "Let's take your detour."

Gabriel

Graham Hudson from the very first moment I laid eyes on him has always been the perfect visualization of Heaven on Earth. He embodies the traits that I believe had been Father's intent in making the planet that he did. It is this way of being that made him the perfect vessel for me in the times that I have used him. Even now given everything I know has taken place since Serenity's return he is still very much the same being to me.

Every being in creation has the ability to falter and make mistakes. It is in the learning from those mistakes that we make the most impact. One must always be in a perpetual state of motion, moving forward until every goal has been reached, whether good or bad in nature. There is a great deal of Heaven that believes that mistakes and failing only fall on the humans as it is perceived as human nature but that is not accurate.

It can affect even celestial beings and I am living proof.

Graham made a choice in not revealing the truth to Serenity, one that even now I know he will argue and stand by because he believes himself to be doing the right thing no matter how selfish it may be perceived to be. I cannot fault him for this action because it is one that I have also used on more than one occasion where the ball of light is concerned.

I have walked that fine line in my feelings for Serenity that opened me enough to be taken advantage of. Where I believed myself to be doing the right thing for the right reasons it was not always the case. We all have the ability to falter but we can always come back. All we have to do is learn and that is what I want most with Graham right now.

Yes, I need to inform him of everything that has been learned in the few days he has been with Serenity and I would most definitely get to that before our time is through but first I feel I need to focus on making sure Graham could handle what is going to come next and learn from it. Graham in the form he is now is as close to perfection as humanly possible but Graham with the knowledge and power that comes from learning from one's mistakes, well that makes him unstoppable.

"Don't even say it." He states as I appear before him.

"I am unaware of what you mean."

"You're going to tell me again what a stupid move I made with her and that I'm going to end up paying for it. Save it because I already know it."

"That is not at all what I am planning on saying to you."

"Oh, so you're not going to be like Ryan or your own brother and tell me what an idiot I am?"

"I was not planning on it but if it is something that you desire to hear I am sure I can accommodate you."

I am not here before him now to tell him about his mistakes. I have to figure that he is aware of them all on his own. I will point out the common sense facts in any given situation that is placed before me but belittling someone or making them feel horrendous has never been my style and I would not employ it now. If he wants that then he is going to have to do it on his own.

"Well if you aren't here to tell me how wrong I am why are you?"

"As I stated before, there are some things that I need to make you aware of as they pertain to how we move forward but there is something more pressing at the moment that I believe you may need to hear."

"Oh yeah? What would that be?"

His emotions were guiding him which I know is the cause for the attitude that is now spilling over into his every word. Serenity leaving with Ryan is again forcing the door open on the reality of the situation before him and just how big of a mistake he made in not handling things differently.

"You must learn from what you have done. You cannot go back and change that which you have already put into motion but you can look at it, see it for what it is and move forward differently."

"I thought you weren't going to tell me how badly I screwed up?"

"Where in my words did you hear me say that you screwed up? I am unaware of such a time where that took place."

"Gabriel look, you know I like you and I respect you but man you're confusing the hell out of me. Just tell me what you want me to do."

"I want you to forgive yourself for the errors you believe you made, learning from them and using them to make a much better outcome in the future."

"She's going to remember everything isn't she? I mean that's why Ryan came here and took her away because even he knows that she's ready to come back to him."

"I do believe that it is her time to remember her life Graham but that has nothing at all to do with Ryan and why he made the choice he did in coming here and being the one to escort her. I am aware that just as my brother does and even you do, that he would like nothing more than for her to remember but he also understands the magnitude of the situation once she does and he would never do anything to intentionally put her at risk."

"Looks like you got over your hatred of the demon pretty quick."

"Until a few short days ago I could very well say the same about you."

When you tell a human something they do not want to hear or at the very least are not ready to hear they will revert to the only way they know of to cope and Graham for all of the light inside of him was no different. He put himself on the defensive and is not willing to hear the real truth that I am trying to tell him.

"I'm going to lose her aren't I?"

With one simple question we easily get the heart of the matter. Where Serenity knows nothing of the bond that actually exists between the two of them, he did remember and is even now constantly being guided by it. It is the purest part of him and the very thing I need to get in touch with in order to get him over what would come next for him.

"Deep down I believe you know that she was never really yours to begin with. I am fully aware of the bond between the two of you, just as I am of the one I also share with her but she has never been ours to hold. It has always been Ryan and it is time we come to terms with that and move forward doing what is expected of us."

"What would that be?"

"Supporting her and loving her the way that she needs us to. I am starting to believe that even the strongest of bonds has the ability to be broken."

"So I need to suck it up and get over her now before she gets her memory back so that I can support her and Ryan even though I'm supposed to be the one with her?"

"In a way yes but the way in which you word it is not appropriate. It is not going to ever be that cut and dry. You are speaking to her beloved Graham, that is a bond that even yours cannot touch."

"I thought soul mates were stronger then the beloved?"

"In a very human way they are but when you look at them the way one is meant to, you see that they are nothing alike and they are their own separate entity. I am able to have Serenity when her time on the planet is done, at which point you will become one with her. You will cease being two beings and become one."

206

"So you get the both of us?" Graham asked his nose scrunching up at this disgust that came from what his mind is now visualizing.

"In a sense but you must not allow yourself to picture it that way though I see nothing wrong with the image. I understand the human impulse but you must refrain."

"I feel like we're talking in circles again, so just tell me something. How much time do I have left?"

It would be easy for me to lie to the man and make him believe that he has more time but I did not have that in me. We have come this far, the group of us because we were able to finally open up with one another and be honest. There is no way I am going to go back on that now just to give him some false sense of hope.

"A day or two at best."

"Shit." He cursed under his breath. "When she remembers, she's going to hate me isn't she?"

"I cannot speak to what she will do Graham but whatever avenue Serenity takes you must not let it consume you. You need to rise above that for the greater good. You are much better than what your human mind wants you to believe. It is time you embraced that, especially with what is to happen in the future."

"Back to the real reason you're here again huh?"

"It cannot be ignored, no matter how bad you feel."

"So what do I have to look forward to this time?"

"You must be aware that every step Lucifer has taken right from that first moment in the church when he bonded Ryan and Serenity together has been part of a grander plan. One in which he would finally succeed in tearing0 the world apart and Heaven too."

"You're saying that my possession and even her memory loss wasn't just him making up plans as he went and somehow failing before he could see them through?"

"That is exactly what I am attempting to explain to you. Every move he made has been to lead him to now. This is where Serenity is needed more than ever. This is the undertaking."

I can tell I'm losing him. While I used him as a vessel previously and even explained a great deal to him during our time together I have never given everything. It is now time for me to do that.

"When Serenity was created by my Father you know it was to aide in bringing about peace to the world and also Heaven at the same time. We failed in previous attempts so this time Father created the undertaking in such a way that it could not fail. Lucifer did attempt to stop us but failed. The time is upon us now. The very reason for Serenity's existence is for this moment in time and we must do everything we can to see it through."

"I follow you man but what does her memory loss mean?"

"Lucifer wants nothing more than to separate all of the people he believes can cease his master plan and as such he has gone to great lengths both here and in Heaven to tear us all apart from one another. He made it so that Michael and I stepped away from our father and also that you and Ryan were broken as well."

"I knew I should have killed that son of a bitch when I had the chance."

"While I admire your tenacity Graham you know as well I do that any attempt on his life would have been for naught. You alone are not meant to take him on and win. It has to be all of us or none of us."

"So he erased her memory so that he could what? Make Ryan and I hate each other again?"

"I am sure that is a small part of it but no, I do not believe that to be the motivation. Serenity being unable to recall the last year of her life means that she will not remember Ryan and as such it will destroy the man just as he tried to do in having Ryan take her life originally. He wants to torture the boy he groomed to be his successor. Knowing you as he does since your time together he knew you would seize the opportunity to be with her."

"So I played right into his hands again?"

"Yes but you must not look at it that way. We all played into his hands in the exact way he needed us to. We are all at fault for the way that we let things play out. It is all about what we do now to rectify it."

"So now we're back to the earlier thing you were trying to tell me."

"It would appear that way. So tell me, do you know what you must do now?"

"Yeah I do, I just hope I haven't screwed it up so bad it can't be fixed."

"It can always be fixed Graham; you just need to do the one thing that until this moment you have been avoiding."

"And what's that?"

"Believe."

CHAPTER TWENTY FOUR

Ryan

There are so few things that bring me true joy. I'm not sure if that's because I've just trained myself not to feel over the years or because no one has ever come along and touched me in a way that inspired the joy in me. I just have never had many chances to enjoy pure joy and what I assume to be true bliss.

Getting to watch Serenity as she took in the scene in front of her now is definitely one of those true bliss moments.

When we kissed minutes before and she had taken a step back, the feelings she had for Graham again coming to the surface, I thought I lost her and I could feel the emptiness start to grow again inside of me. Seeing her now though, the way her eyes went wide, complete with the glow that happened whenever she's truly happy, my heart is again filled with hope.

She might not have expected this when I said I wanted to take a detour but this is obviously something that pleases her. I only hope that it helps her memory. I didn't want to rush her but with the kiss we shared, it is definitely do or die time for me. I need her to remember me, us and all that we shared so that the next time I put my lips to hers it would be forever.

"Ryan, oh my god!"

There it is. The squeal of excitement that only she can do. It makes everything that I put together before going to pick her up that much more worthwhile. It didn't matter what happened next because honestly the moment she squealed and jumped up and down, I was completely done. It would be burned into my memory forever.

It wasn't much but recreating the day we had our picnic in the quad was the easiest way I could think to share a part of myself with her as well as possibly help her remember everything that Lucifer had stolen from her. I laid everything out the way it had been that day, complete with the ratty blanket and picnic basket even though we could have just sat on cardboard and it would have meant just as much to me.

I didn't want any details forgotten because this is my way of going all in. I know I'm supposed to be settling for the way things have to be right now but I can't do it without a fight.

"Is the picnic basket filled?"

God this girl never ceases to amaze me.

"Yeah pretty girl it's filled."

Before the words even drop from my mouth she runs forward and drops herself down on the blanket, right in the exact spot she had been the first time we had done this. Michael was definitely right. Her mind might not remember everything that I want it to but her heart damn sure did. There is only one thing missing.

Me.

After making myself comfortable, leaning back on the blanket much the way Serenity herself had done the first time, I looked up at the stars and found myself wondering just what it is she thought about when she did this. I watched her lean back this way the day we spent together and as much as I was focused on just how peaceful she looked I always wondered if in looking up at the sky she was attempting to find answers.

When I heard her laugh it brought me back and I leaned up, looking at her. I haven't gotten to hear her genuinely laugh since we brought her home but now it seems to be all she is capable of doing. I wanted nothing more than to make her feel this way forever. The world didn't seem like such a horrible place when you had Serenity happy and laughing in it.

"What's so funny?"

"You." She chokes out between giggles which only makes the smile I'm wearing that much bigger. "I don't mean it that way I swear!"

"What? You mean to tell me you don't find this face funny?" I pout. "Well now you've offended me pretty girl."

"Shut up! I'm not falling for that buddy."

"Falling for what?"

"That cute little pout you're doing to make me think you're actually hurt. Not working on me, no way."

211

Yes every single person in the world needed their own Serenity the way she is right now. I can see now why she is meant to save the world. Her smile alone could do it. I'm living proof.

"You think I have a cute pout huh?"

She blushed and unable to contain it anymore I laugh. She really has no idea what the hell she does to me. It's also amazing to me just how much I missed this during the short time I lived without it. How much I missed her.

"You're bad."

"I've heard worse."

I didn't know when exactly it happened but she went quiet and her entire expression changed. She had been carefree and light only seconds before, now she looked serious, almost as if she's deep in thought. What exactly did I say?

"We've done this before haven't we?"

I've never experienced what it feels like to be shot in the heart but if the way I felt in that moment is any indication, I have a feeling I'm about to learn all about it firsthand. The reason for her silence, the change in expression is clear as day and it isn't something I said but more in what I had done.

"Yeah Ser, we have."

"Ryan...can I ask you something?"

There was a hitch in her voice after saying my name and I wonder what caused it. I knew that none of us had been entirely open with her since she came back but I didn't like that there is a moment at all in her mind where she felt she couldn't ask me anything. It didn't sit right with me.

"You can ask me anything, anytime Serenity."

"What happened between you and me?"

Shit. The one damn thing I can't answer.

I want to tell her everything. What happened between us and what still has to happen but I can't do it. As much as I love her and want to be honest with her, I cannot be the very thing again that tore her world down around her. I did it once before and I'll be damned if I want to repeat it.

"I lost you." I choke out, praying that would be good enough for her. It's the only thing available to me to say that is still rooted in truth. I did lose her, more than once.

"I'm sorry…"

The actual truth in her wounded words is enough to undo me completely. She has nothing to be sorry for. The only one that has a reason to be sorry is Lucifer and I would most definitely be making him sorry the minute I saw him again.

"Please don't do that Serenity. You have nothing to be sorry for."

"I do though!" she exclaims moving on the blanket until she's on her knees and completely turned and facing me. "I can't even remember you!"

Jesus Christ. Even telling her three little words had completely torn her apart. I needed to fix this and I had to do it quick.

"Why did you laugh at me earlier?"

"What?"

"I can't sit here and listen to you say sorry for something that is not your fault, so I'm going to go a different way. Why were you laughing at me earlier?"

"The way you were laying on the blanket, it reminded me of something."

Content that I had done the right thing with the subject change, I decided to keep it up and push it a little further.

"Like what?"

"When I lived in Green Haven I used to head out to the park a lot, especially at night. There is just something about lying on your back, looking up at a star that's humbling. When I couldn't handle the voices in my head or the way my mom would look at me I'd go there and I don't know, I guess seeing you doing the same thing, especially with the stars and all it was funny."

I knew a lot about her past, especially the time with her mother because we spent a lot of time comparing what we called our horror stories but hearing the way she talked about looking up at the stars showed me yet another side of her I hadn't been able to see yet. It is humbling looking up at the sky because with a sky so

213

vast in front of you, it made your problems seem all that much smaller in comparison.

If I didn't already love her more than humanly possible, I swear I would have fallen again in that moment.

"I did it the last time we did this. I looked up at the sky except it was during the day."

"Yeah you did it then too." I said, stunned at the recall of our time together but not wanting to waste a moment over thinking it. I had all the time in the world to go over the implications of what her remembering now meant, right now I am going to enjoy the moment for what it was.

"Can I ask you some—?

She cut herself off before finishing, blushing, which only made me go even crazier inside then I already had been.

"Sorry, I seem to forget that I already asked you that."

"It's okay Ser, like I said, ask me anything."

"Do you ever miss…" she cut off again and my heart died a little inside, wanting desperately to hear the end of the question. If she is bringing up missing in any regard then I was damn sure going to want to answer her.

"Do you ever miss us?"

"Every single day."

I have never been the type to wear my heart on my sleeve but right now that is exactly what I am doing. I knew there was a line I didn't want to cross but there is no way I'm going to lie to her about this. I would just have to deal with the fallout, if there is any, later.

"Then why did you let me go?"

"I didn't. You were taken from me."

I hit the line. I couldn't say anymore without opening myself up completely and telling her everything. As much as I didn't want this moment between us to end I knew it had too. I needed to take her to Emma and I had to do it soon.

"God I can't do this. I'm sorry. I have no idea what the hell's gotten into me. I shouldn't be asking you this stuff. I'm with Graham and it's really none of my business anymore."

214

Oh no, it wasn't going to go down like this. No fucking way. I might not be able to tell her everything and I might want to get her out of here before I did let something slip but there is no way I'm going to let her blame herself.

Moving as quickly as possible I pulled myself up on my knees and inched closer to her, immediately grabbing her hand and placing it in mine, using my free hand to lift her head until it is level with mine. What I was about to say next she needed to not only hear but see as well, even if she wasn't entirely ready to believe it.

"It will always be your business pretty girl because you are the only one that will ever own my heart."

CHAPTER TWENTY FIVE

Serenity

I don't know what bothered me more. Ryan leaving pretty much the minute Emma opened the door or the fact that it even bothered me that he did it. All I know is that the awesome homecoming I am supposed to have with my best friend has just been blown to shit. I look at her smiling, happy face and I can't match it with one of my own no matter how hard I try.

The entire way back to the dorm from the quad I keep having these flashes of memory and I'm now even more certain than ever that whatever happened between me and Ryan isn't over. Of course I already knew that based on the words he said that I can't get out of my head and the way he was with me the entire walk back to my room but the flashes somehow made it all seem more real than just words can.

I've seen him looking straight into my soul on more than one occasion, the weight of those blue eyes on mine and being unable to look away. I've seen us holding hands, him pulling me toward an unknown location his face serious and determined yet full of tender loving care. His smile focused solely on me warming my body as I saw it just the way he had done numerous times already tonight.

Seeing him as tears fell from his eyes had to be the worst of the visions because even though I can't entirely remember what caused it, I know beyond the shadow of a doubt that the last thing I ever want to see is this man cry. Even though it's only just a vision I want nothing more than to reach out and stop the tears with my own hands, somehow taking it all away from him.

I am losing my mind. That's all there is to it.

Every word spoken after he packed up the picnic and steered me in the direction of the dorm haunts me and even though I belong to another, all I can seem to think about is how much I want to be owned by him and him alone.

216

*****

"You haven't said much since I mentioned bringing you home. Is everything alright Serenity?"

I didn't want to tell him the truth. That no, everything is not okay and it's all because of him. That I hate myself because the very thing Graham had been worried about with me leaving is actually happening. Ryan McGregor is getting to me just as my very real boyfriend fears and I'm powerless to stop it because I want it to happen.

"I'm fine Ryan."

"I don't believe you."

"That's really not my problem now is it?"

"Serenity stop." He called as I began to speed up and move a few paces ahead of him. "Why are you acting like this?"

"You wanna know why I'm acting like this Ryan?" I yell, spinning around, guided by the red hot rage boiling over inside of me and coming face to face with him. "Being around you makes me betray everything I've ever believed in and no matter how hard I fight it, I can't help myself."

"You're not betraying yourself or what you believe in." he whispers, his breath warm against my cheeks.

"How do you know that? How well do you even know me?"

"I know you better then you think."

"Oh really? So if that's true then you must know that wanting you the way I seem to is ripping me apart inside. That being around you for longer than just a couple of seconds makes my head so confused I wanna scream. That even as I'm standing here yelling in your face I want you to reach out and kiss me to shut me up."

He reaches out to me but before I let him recreate the very real image in my head I take a step back. Kissing him, no matter how badly I want to do it, can't happen right now. Not when I was this off kilter. It wasn't fair to anyone, not us or Graham, who is back in Ryan's room trusting that things wouldn't be going to the very place they were so obviously going.

217

"Fuck! I can't take this anymore Ser!" he yelled back the minute I step out of reach. *"You need to know the truth. I can't handle it being this way. I can't handle what it's doing to you."*

"Then tell me. If what I'm feeling is so wrong then tell me what the hell is right because I don't have a clue and it's killing me!"

I could tell he wants to do what I'm pleading with him to do but his mouth remains closed. God this is getting me nowhere. I need to see Emma. She would give me the answers I wanted, if there really are any to be found other than the ones I already know.

"I love you Serenity..."

"That's not enough Ry, not anymore."

*****

"Are you going to tell me why you're staring into space with that sad look on your face?" Emma asks, bringing me back out of my thoughts and back to the reality around me.

For the first time since I found myself in Ryan's bed two days before I finally feel more like me again. I had a habit of getting lost in my own thoughts before the accident, especially with the voices all the time and somehow tuning out all the other people and places around me and doing it now with Emma just reminded me that I wasn't altogether screwed up. I was still very much me.

"It's nothing really. I've just spent the last two days trying to get a grip on all of this time I seem to have lost and it's getting to me."

"Ser, that doesn't sound like nothing to me. Why don't you lie down, get comfortable and tell me everything going on in your head. I know you can't exactly remember much about your life for the last year or so but maybe I can help you fill in some of the blanks."

This is why I love Emma so much. She might be flighty and more than a little boy crazy but when push comes to shove she is always there for me and has my back. She just always wants me to

218

be okay the same way I do for her and right now I couldn't be more thankful for it.

Following her advice I made my way over to my bed and threw myself down onto the mattress, not even bothering to pull the blankets back first. Right now that was the least of my worries.

"I did something so completely stupid and I'm pretty sure I'm going to hell for it."

I'm not sure she's even aware she's doing it but the minute I say the words Emma's eyes immediately go wide and it confuses the hell out of me. Before I can ask her what I said though her expression changes and she smiles weakly. If I didn't know I was completely awake and aware I would have thought I dreamed it.

"Somehow I doubt you did anything that bad."

"Oh you don't even know the half of it."

"Then tell me Ser. It's obvious that whatever you think you did is eating at you so why don't you just put it out there."

"I cheated on Graham."

She coughed, caught herself by clearing her throat and looked up at me again, this time her eyes again going wide. "You did what?"

"I kissed Ryan and before you say that you don't think that's cheating let's just agree to disagree. I have no idea what is happening to me but I never would have done this before."

"No, I agree. It's definitely not something you would do but then again up until recently you wouldn't even look at a guy so I suppose even looking to you would be cheating."

She was definitely right about that. I have never been the girl that gets the attention of a lot of guys and my dating experience is limited to say the least. Graham had been the one and only boy I'd even remotely thought of that way. It's because of this that I couldn't help but laugh at her words.

"You're right but seriously Emma. I think when I hit my head; it screwed up more than just my memories."

"Serenity, you know I love you but you need to stop thinking like that. You're not screwed up. You weren't screwed up when you fell for Gabriel and you're most definitely not screwed up now. Trust me, I've lived with you for the last three years, I would know."

Gabriel.

At the mention of his name I feel the room begin to spin again much the way it did when I had been looking in Ryan's closet and again when I had the memory recall in the quad. What is it about that name?

"Serenity? Are you alright?"

I didn't exactly trust myself to speak so I just nod. I hear Emma say something else but where she had been clear seconds before, now I'm having a hard time making out the words. She sounds concerned but what exactly she's worried about is beyond me.

"Serenity..."

"No. You don't get to do this. If you're going to keep coming to me every night then we better get some stuff out of the way right now."

"I'm unsure of what you mean."

"Who are you, and don't you dare give me that line that you will reveal it all at the right time. Right now is the right time."

"I am Gabriel."

"Serenity, for God sakes answer me!" Emma yells as I feel her shake me.

"Ems…you can stop."

"Where the hell did you go just now? One minute you're here and you look comfortable and the next you look like you're in a trance or something."

"Memories…" was all I could manage to get out. I wasn't even entirely sure what just happened to me so explaining it to an equally freaked out Emma was going to be pointless.

"What did you remember?"

"Gabriel. You said his name and all of a sudden I remember who he is. Or at least something that happened between us."

"Wait, how much did you remember?"

"Not much. I mean it seems like I knew him before the conversation yet all I learned was his name."

"You did know him before that Ser."

That's right. I remember now. Emma said something about me falling for him which meant that he wasn't just another voice in my head. He is someone more, or at least something more.

"What did you mean by what you said about me falling for him?"

She sighs and I know that like Ryan, this is something she didn't exactly want to get into with me. Whatever the reason is for keeping my past a secret from me, it's really getting to a point where it is pissing me off now. Why couldn't any of the people I care about just tell me the freaking truth already?

"Last year before everything happened Gabriel came to you. First he talked and eventually he starting singing you to sleep. I made a joke when you first told me about it that you were falling for him. Turns out that eventually the joke became reality, because you did fall for him."

"For the voice in my head?"

"Yeah Ser, you fell for the voice in your head."

It bothered me to no end that I had to be the girl that heard spirits. Voices in my head at all hours of the day constantly pulling me away from the feeble attempt at a normal existence. Right now though, hearing that I fell for one of those very same voices ranked higher on the crazy scale I judged myself on.

"Well that's something you don't expect to ever hear come out of your best friends mouth."

"How do you think I feel saying it then?"

"Point made."

"If I fell for this Gabriel guy then where is he now? I mean I've only been able to hear one voice since I came back and I'm pretty sure he wasn't it. Wouldn't the guy you fell for make an appearance more than just once?"

Emma shrugged and I resigned myself to the fact that as far as the voice of Gabriel is concerned, I might not ever get the answers I wanted until I remembered what the voice from the other night said to me. At that moment it all came together.

"Where does Ryan fit into all of this Ems? I mean I'll go along with the fact that my crazy ass fell for the voice in my head but

221

why is it that every single time I get within a foot of that guy, my head and my heart seems to turn to complete mush?"

"That's easy. You love him."

Gabriel

Michael had been the one to bring up explaining everything to the roommate. His argument for why he believed it to be the right thing to do could not be denied or fought against. It did indeed make the most logical sense. In the fight that was coming we did need all the help we could get, especially from those few humans we knew carried the light so purely within them.

Emma is indeed a carrier of the light, much the same way that Graham was before her. Truth told it made them quite a powerful combination if they could both overlook the lot they received in life and come together as one. It pleased me knowing that with informing Emma of everything that she had been kept away from we would be able to see that power take form.

The only problem that I had foreseen when Michael came to me was the ramifications that the immense amount of knowledge would have of which is now playing out right before my eyes. Emma having the knowledge she did gave her the ability to inform Serenity of more than just the parts of herself that she is missing. She had the ability to reveal it all and it is my hope as I stand here listening that she does not take it that far.

It is imperative that Serenity remember things on her own, in her unique way so that she will be better equipped in handling everything moving forward. I did not want it rushed for any reason because in my mind doing so could spell certain death for all of us. Serenity needs to be at the top of her game moving forward, ready and able to take on the very man that had done this to her to begin with.

I want to be angry that Emma had been the one to remind her of me but I found myself unable to do so. It looked like Serenity had been in a trance for Emma but what I had seen was far different. I saw the memory of our time together as she remembered it vividly in her mind. It may not have been one of the larger moments between us but it is the time at which she learned of my name and that was the start.

It was shortly after that where I learned of our connection to one another and my care of her almost became obsessive with the need it sparked in me. Though the times that we went through after that moment were not easy it was a gift to be able to see even the smallest of moments between us through her eyes again. She is able to recall me now and my heart soared at the possibilities.

It would not be long now before she came back to me, to us.

Michael has also been right in his assessment of the way her heart would react to Ryan. Though it might be a struggle for Serenity given what Graham led her to believe, it is indeed happening the way that it is intended to. She must remember everything and a good portion of that will be her relationship with Ryan, complete with all of the moments they shared. Her recall of him has not been similar to that of the way she remembers me but she is aware there is more under the surface and we have her heart to thank for that.

A bond between two people is only at its full capacity and strength when it is felt by both parties. For whatever reason she could not recall the bond with Graham but her heart most definitely recalled in graphic detail the way she felt for the half demon turned pure angel. It is what guides her now, much the way the soul mate bond guided her in the struggle she faced to save Graham.

We needed her to feel that, to be guided by it because it is building within her a strength that we have not seen since right before Lucifer had taken her. Serenity is and will always remain a ball of light from Heaven, an eventual angel in a human disguise and it would be that strength and the light inside of her that would bring her back from this. Just as Lucifer wanted me to embrace the fire within me when she first connected with Ryan McGregor, I need her to embrace the light now in order to strengthen her for what is to come.

"It would appear as though informing Emma the way in which we did has actually helped things move along nicely, wouldn't you say brother?"

223

"If that is how you want to look at it Michael. You can see just as I can what is taking place down there. It is only a matter of time before the girl spills all and while you may believe it to be something needed; I see nothing but chaos on the horizon."

"Gabriel you worry too much. Emma is aware of the dangers in telling Serenity everything but do you really want to begrudge her the chance to bring two lovers back to one another? Even you cannot deny it is one of heavens greatest strengths, that of real love."

My concerns with the situation were merited whether he believed me to be worrying too much or not. With everything we learned where our fallen brother is concerned, there could be no room for error so until such time as the undertaking came to pass and we came out the victors I would continue to be concerned.

"Of course I want Serenity to realize her connection to Ryan, it is not that I am concerned with, it is what a thin line we all walk from that to the more important information."

"You think she's going to blow your cover?" Michael asked with a chuckle, a sound I still had not come to terms with hearing. It is just so unexpected given who he is.

"My cover has already been blown brother. Serenity recalls me. That is what you have missed in doing whatever it is you have been doing since we spoke last. It is not even me that I am concerned with so you may cease your laughter at the situation."

"Then tell me Gabriel, what is it that has you wound so tightly when we should be celebrating our successes thus far?"

"Serenity is the key to everything. Lucifer wanted her memory erased for a reason and I am beginning to wonder if it is not for more than just the ability to tear us all apart."

"What more could there be?"

This is where things became tricky for me. I felt secure in the knowledge that he was indeed trying to pull all of us apart one at a time but I have no real facts to back this particular thought up. It is just a feeling that no matter what I do, I cannot seem to shake. I wasn't entirely sure how comfortable I felt giving it to Michael without facts to complete it.

"What if he still has a claim on her? We still have no idea what has been done to her during her time there. Her physical body remains intact but what if he has somehow branded her again, only this way in the reverse."

"You believe him to be bonded to her in some way?"

"Yes. It means anything that Serenity overhears or learns about, either on her own or with the help of others is fair game to him. Even our knowledge of what it is that he is planning."

I could easily see that everything I am questioning made sense to Michael, him knowing Lucifer just as well as I did and knowing not to put anything past him but it is also obvious that for now it was all just conjecture. There is really no evidence at my disposal to support my newest theory.

"How would we be able to tell if that is indeed the case?"

"She would have a mark for one. It is the only way that I have knowledge of that would be able to give up the proof we need. The mark though, it doesn't have to be a physical marking, not one the naked eye can see."

"You mean he marked her mind?"

I only nod. There is also one more part of her that he could mark that would go unseen by the naked eye but one that Michael and I could easily access if given permission. I am just not sure if I want to actually speak of it aloud.

"Well then I guess we know what we need to do next."

"Wait Michael," I called before my brother could continue any further. Whatever reservations I have where Serenity is concerned, I had to let them go, Michael needed to know everything if we were indeed going to move forward with proving this new theory. "He could have easily marked her heart as well."

"That changes nothing other than the need for both of us to be available to get the answers. As she begins to remember more, I will attempt to gain control of her mind while you work on her heart."

"I don't think I can do that brother. You know how I feel about her."

"Precisely Gabriel. It is that knowledge of the way that you feel for her, the bond that the two of you share, that means it can only be you that does this. If you want to save her and bring her back to us completely, in the purest form possible then you have to do this."

I know he's speaking the truth but it doesn't make it any easier to handle. During all of this time I spent on the planet with Serenity, guiding her to this point the one thing I prided myself on most is never becoming entangled with her heart. I always gave her the free will to make her own choices. If Lucifer marked her there in an effort to keep it concealed it is the very thing that would be my undoing.

I would have to breach and break her heart.

"It can only be you brother."

CHAPTER TWENTY SIX

Graham

The more time I spend alone now that both Serenity and Gabriel left me the more I realize just how right the angel had been with everything he said.

Even as I told her that we were together, putting my own selfish needs above all else, I knew it was wrong. For the last two days that I kept up the lie I have been struggling with it even though to Serenity it would appear as if it's business as usual. I didn't like what I was doing but I also didn't want to stop it because if I did that then she would find out the truth and I would lose her anyway.

It's like I was damned if I did and damned if I didn't. No matter which road I chose here someone got hurt. I got hurt. It all did come back around to me and the choices I made. Gabriel is right, I could choose to wallow in that or I could stand up, choose to do the right thing now and deal with the fallout later.

Lucifer is not going to have his way with me, pulling me away from the angels and even from Ryan and Serenity this way. He might believe that because he had become a part of me at one point that he could control the outcome but it's time for me to show him just how wrong he is. He will not do this to me. I will make the things I've done right even if it takes the rest of my life to do so.

It's only a matter of time before Serenity remembers everything and the world I managed to build for myself for the last two days would come crashing down around me so it's imperative I do everything in my power right now to make the devastation that much less than it is setting up to be.

The first step in doing that is going to Ryan. I know he's not with Serenity anymore because as much as I still had to learn about the whole angel and demon thing, I already knew more than I needed to about women. There is no way he is going to be able to stomach more than five minutes in the room with the two of them as they caught up with each other. In fact I'm banking on it.

I screwed things up royally with the guy that fought by my side and it's time I fix it. Lucifer be damned. Serenity has her part to play in taking him down and out for good but so did I. I'm going to show him that he doesn't have the control over me anymore that he thinks he does. It was time to do the right thing.

The Graham Hudson thing.

Clear on what my next stop is, I grab my jacket and make my way to the door but as I open it, I come face to face with a serious wrench in my plan.

Emma. Alone. Standing on the doorstep looking conflicted.

More proof of all of the mistakes I made since I came to Stephenville for Serenity. This is definitely not something I want to deal with right now but the look on her face pulled at the side of me that is just unable to walk away. She needed to talk which meant we were going to talk.

Ryan would just have to wait.

"Emma, what are you doing here? Why aren't you with Serenity?"

"Can I come in?" she asked, motioning behind me to the inside of the room. "She's sleeping so I figure this is probably the best time to do this."

"To do what?" I ask as I back away from the door and watch silently as she breezes past me. "What do we need to talk about?"

Closing the door behind me and turning to face her I can see by the way her eyes squint and her body sags that there is a whole lot she has to say to me and none of it is going to be good.

"How could you do it?"

"Come again?"

"How could you get Serenity back and then lie to her?"

Well now it all makes sense. Now that the angels and Ryan told her everything she's here to be the first person to give me shit. Yeah I definitely wasn't in the mood for this.

"She trusted you even more than she did me Graham. Did you know that? I've lied and hidden things from her before and hurt her when she found out about it. You though, you've never once been disloyal or dishonest with her and it's one of the reasons she loves you so much. So why did you do it?"

"Because I'm a selfish prick Emma. That's why."

She flinches at my words and it actually intrigues me why. I would have thought that hearing me admit to being what she believed me to be would have made her happy, not this. She almost seems bothered by it.

"She kissed Ryan tonight. She's remembering things Graham, a lot of things but because she believes you two are together she is pulling herself apart from the inside out. You wanting to be with her and being a so called selfish prick is killing her."

I don't know what hurts more. Hearing that she's remembering things and is beating herself up over it or that she kissed Ryan. They both ranked pretty high on the ultimate pain scale for me. I didn't want her hurting over getting her memories back but I also didn't want her turning back to Ryan even if it is what needed to happen.

"What the hell do you want me to say Ems? That I'm sorry? That I love the girl so god damned much that I wanted to experience what life would be like with her, even if it was for only a couple of days or a week at most? Would that make everything better for you?"

"No it wouldn't make me happy and I don't want to hear about why you did it anymore. I thought I wanted to know but I just can't hear it anymore."

"What the hell is that supposed to mean?"

"How much do you remember of the time you spent with Lucifer?"

She is hitting on another topic I'm not ready to confront and it took everything in me to keep my feet planted on the floor in front of her when all I wanted to do is get up and leave the room, get away from the accusations and the memories of things better left forgotten.

"Everything. Every single thing."

"Did you mean what you said to me a week ago?"

Has it really been a week since I caught up with her on the way to class and tried to earn her forgiveness for what happened between us? I thought I had seen it all with the way time seemed to move during my time under Lucifer's control but apparently not. It felt like even longer than that.

"I said a few things to you that day Emma, you're going to need to be more specific."

"Ugh, god, this is not coming out right."

"Then take your time, get your thoughts in order and then ask me again."

I had no idea what it is that she wanted to ask me but given everything that we've been through together, both when I had been under the devil's control and then again right before I left to work with the angels to save her best friend, anything could come out of her mouth now and I needed to be patient with her. It's obvious by that same conflicted look on her face that whatever she had to say isn't easy for her.

"How much was you and how much was him when you talked to me that day in the dorm?"

Shit.

When I thought she wanted to bring up the conversation we had outside class I actually felt pretty confident about it but now all of that confidence is draining away. I didn't have a leg to stand on going back to that moment and reliving it. I may have been possessed and being controlled by the bloodlust he inspired in me but everything that happened, the things I said had been all me.

No matter what way I answer this, I'm a dead man.

Bringing up that day in her dorm only made me relive it, moment by moment and it made me sick inside. I want to tell her that it was all him so that she could leave here with the knowledge that I wasn't really that sick son of a bitch she believes me to be but I couldn't.

*****

"You know," I continued, smiling "That day you found us in your bed, I always wished it was you with me instead of her. I think the two of us would have had a lot of fun together."

"You sick bast—

230

"No need for name calling sweetheart, just stating fact. I distinctly remember your hand slapping my ass so I bet you've given it some thought too."

"You're delusional."

"No actually I'm a realist. Why don't we just skip all the bullshit and admit it."

"Admit what?"

"You want me."

"I want you out of here."

Pulling her to my body again I hit pay dirt. She may want to pretend she didn't feel anything towards me but I knew different. The hard buds of her nipples peeking through her shirt spoke the truth where her mouth could not.

"You forget...I can feel it. You wanna try lying to me again?"

*****

"It was all me Emma."

"Say what?"

"I said everything and I'm not going to lie to you and say that it was Lucifer. Actually he was the one getting pissed at me because I wanted you so badly."

"You...wanted...me?" she choked out.

"Yeah, I did."

I'm not being entirely honest with her but right now having this conversation is just not something I need to be focusing on. I need to put my mind back where it was before she showed up and I need to start taking the right steps instead of always following along with the selfish and wrong ones in the mistaken belief that I'm doing the right thing.

This was going to have to wait.

"Emma look, I don't want to make light of this and I do think we need to talk about all of this, especially now that you know everything going on but I need to see Ryan. It's important. So can we just store this until later?"

She stood in place, her eyes locked on the bed in front of us her eyes not even blinking and the more I look at her this way the more worried I get. Did what I say stun her into silence? The way she looks now reminds me of Serenity, not of the blonde bubbly college student I knew Emma to be.

Shaking off whatever it was she was thinking about she looks up at me, smiling weakly.

"Yeah we can but Graham?"

"Hmm?

"I know something's coming. Ryan and the angel told me that much, just do me a favor okay?"

"I'll try…"

"Be careful."

CHAPTER TWENTY SEVEN

Ryan

When Emma called me and told me she needed to go out and that with everything going on she didn't feel right leaving Serenity alone, I did something out of character for the way most guys are. It's not entirely out of character for the way I am but if any other guys witnessed it, I'm pretty they would enjoy calling me whipped. I took my shot at getting alone time with her.

Sure she's sleeping so it means there's not exactly going to be a lot of interaction going on between us and it might even rate on the creeper scale me wanting so badly to just sit here in this painfully hard computer chair and watch her but I just don't care. Getting to see her this way is just another thing I've missed in being separated from her and I'm going to enjoy every second of it. Creeper or not.

Knowing her the way I do, I know there hasn't exactly been a ton of moments where she can be at peace. That the only real time she gets a break first from the voices and then the problems with Lucifer is when she's resting like this. Every move I make from the moment I show up and Emma let me in, to the spot I now found myself in has been done gingerly, in an effort not to ruin the relaxed and peaceful expression that now covers her face.

She is so god damned beautiful it takes my breath away watching her like this. I find myself thinking about what she could be dreaming of, if she's even in the dream state at all and if it's about me. If somehow what she can't seem to grasp during her waking hours she is somehow holding onto in the sleep state. Can she remember our relationship this way and somehow realize how much we mean to each other and will it affect her when she does wake up?

Serenity isn't the only one that wants to remember. I've been using her memory loss as a way to reconnect with everything we've been through and shared together too. We haven't been together all that long and we've been through more than most

233

couples our age but I have to figure that doing it this way is a good lesson to learn now. I don't ever want to get to a point when I'm older where I forget the way I felt when I fell in love for the first time. The racing heart, the butterflies in my stomach, the way her lips feel against mine when we kiss for the first time. I want to remember all of that always.

So that's what I focus on while she sleeps. I remind myself of the small moments together, the things that will define us for years to come. The genuine and true feeling of love that I have for this girl. Her heart may be able to recall all of this in graphic detail even though her mind can't but it doesn't matter to me because I am going to experience all of it again with her. It can only strengthen us even more when she does remember. She will not have gone through it alone.

I know beyond a shadow of a doubt that no matter what we go through or what happens to me in the process I will always love this girl just as strongly as I do in this moment, if not even more so. I could have my sight taken away and I would still see her. You could rip away my hearing so that I would never again hear her say I love you and I would still hear it. The way I feel about Serenity is about so much more than the experience I get from the senses. It transcends all of that. My heart will always call to her and her alone.

Do I believe that everything will always feel this way and that we won't ever have trials in our relationship that will cause it to develop cracks along the way? Of course not. I might not have ever loved before this serene being walked into my life but I am not without knowledge. I know that there are going to be times where we can't stand each other, and times where walking away might seem like the easiest option but there is something more that I know and it's her that taught it to me without even realizing it.

The fun is in the fixing.

It doesn't matter how broken we become along the way because at the end of the day, it will be how we stand our ground and fight to fix it that will define us. No matter how hard things get I am determined to live my life by the lesson that her father taught

234

her years before I had the chance to know her. The fun will definitely be in the fixing.

"Ryan?"

Looking up I'm met with her stretching and beginning to sit up in bed, her eyes on me as she attempts to get them completely open, the disheveled nature of her hair reminding me of the last time we had been together alone in the room this way. I am the luckiest bastard alive. I get to be here as an angel wakes up again.

Man, even to me I sound whipped.

"Hey pretty girl."

"What are you doing here?"

"Emma needed to run out and do something so she asked me to stay with you. I hope that's alright."

"It's fine, "she says her voice trailing off. "I don't even remember falling asleep."

The way she kept pushing her hair out of her face as it fell into her eyes made me want to jump from the chair and hold it in place for her. The only thing stopping me is the knowledge that she wasn't quite there yet and while I seem to have been able to break through to her lately, the last thing I wanted to do is set us back.

"Emma said you had a bit of a rough night."

"Yeah, I guess I did. I remembered some things and she told me some stuff and I guess it was just so much I passed out."

"What did you remember?"

"Gabriel."

Well it wasn't what I wanted to hear but it is definitely something that could only work in our favor for what the angel believes is coming for us.

"What about him?"

"I can speak to angels. Gabriel is an angel. I remember talking to him a couple of times but according to Emma there is a hell of a lot more but it's a start I guess."

How did she know he's an angel? Did Emma go against what Michael and Gabe wanted and tell more then she should have?

"How much did Emma tell you?"

"Not a whole lot honestly. Most of what I can remember now is because these flashes won't stop happening in my mind. I can be in the middle of a conversation and suddenly I'm just lost and I'm reliving things."

I didn't want to push her but I'll be damned if I don't want to know exactly what flashes she's been having. Just how much did she remember since I left her here before?

"She told me some things about us Ry. I don't want you to be mad at her but it wasn't like I gave her much choice. I sort of freaked on her about what happened with us earlier and well she filled in some blanks."

"What kind of blanks?"

"We didn't just date for one. We were in love. At least according to her and honestly with the flashes I was getting during our time together in the quad, I believe it. I don't even think I needed her to tell me, it's just something I've always known. It explains this weird magnetic pull between us."

Oh sweet Jesus, she remembers us. Sure it wasn't all the way but it didn't need to be. This was more than enough for now. Her heart had overridden the corrosion in her head and is allowing her to remember what's most important to it.

"I think I know now why no one wants to tell me anything."

I need to calm myself. I can feel the excitement from her words building inside of me and if I'm not careful it's going to spill over onto her and I'm not sure she's ready for that yet. It was so bad that I almost didn't hear what she said next. I need to get myself under control.

"Why's that?"

"You want me to remember on my own and I'm starting to but I don't think you guys need to worry about it hurting me if you tell me. Emma told me that I loved you earlier and just with something that small I was able to remember that much more. It's not that you're giving me my memory back, you're just helping it along."

It didn't take my feelings for her to know what she was trying to do. She wants more answers and she is trying her hardest to make an argument that makes it okay for me to tell her. The thing is, she's going to get her way. I'm starting to think she's right and that in giving her just small things it might actually help her more in the long run.

236

"What do you want to ask me Ser?"

"When did you first realize you loved me?"

"The first time I laid eyes on you?" I say grinning. It wasn't the truth but it seemed like the romantic thing to say. At the very least it wouldn't be something she would expect if she really is remembering us the way she claimed.

"You're gonna make me wade through the bullshit this early in the morning?" she shot back which only confirmed what I already knew. She was definitely remembering us.

"No, though you gotta admit, it is a damn good answer."

"Maybe if you're trying to get into my pants it is. I want the truthful answer though."

This is extremely easy for me to talk about because just like she wants to know in an effort to remember I want to tell her because I want to relive it, vividly. It is a moment in time I don't think I'll ever forget.

"When I told you everything about me and you accepted it. That was the moment I knew I loved you."

She smiled and I swear I felt my heart melt inside my chest. This is the perfect example of what most guys needed to learn. You could try and bullshit in order to earn the girls trust and eventually her heart but eventually she would see through it and the only thing that can save it is the truth, even if it's not the most beautifully crafted picture.

"Thank you."

"You don't need to thank me Ser. You wanted the truth and I'll always give you that even if I do try and joke beforehand."

"There's actually something else I wanna ask you but I need to show you something first."

This is where she lost me. What could there possibly be in this room that I haven't already seen a million times before that had something to do with helping her remember?

I didn't have to wait long for the answer as she slipped out of the bed and made her way over to Emma's dresser, lifting the lid to the jewellery box and slipping a piece into her hand before turning to face me again.

"What can you tell me about this?" she asks, slipping the ring from her hand until it rests on the tip of the very finger I placed it on months before.

Shit, we were venturing into dangerous territory now. If I told her the truth about the ring then it means I need to tell her about Lucifer. She might not believe that the knowledge would damage her but there is no way that learning about living through the devil's hell can't have that effect. I did not want to be the one to bring that on her now.

I also couldn't lie to her either.

"It's a ring."

"Yeah thanks smartass, I kind of figured that out on my own. What does it mean?"

"It's your wedding band."

The look that came across her face should have hurt me, at least a little but it didn't. I actually expected it to be worse than just a look of shock. I'd been expecting disbelief or even disgust but shock I could definitely handle.

"My wedding band?"

"Yeah."

"I didn't marry Graham."

The way she answered that as a statement and not a question did things to me I don't think I've ever felt before. Even with her memory as broken as it is she still knew that she didn't marry her first love. It is something she couldn't accept and I am beyond thankful for it.

"No you didn't marry Graham."

"I married you."

I nodded, unable to trust my own voice anymore. Her realization of what we had been through is almost too much to take. I'm not even sure I can form a rational thought with the weight of it hanging there between us.

"Well finally!" she exclaims which only causes me to look back up at her in confusion. This is definitely not going the way I expect. "Everything makes sense now."

I'm glad it made sense for one of us because I literally had no idea what the hell is going on. I only hope she didn't make me wait too long to find out so I could share the moment with her. I hated being this lost. I'm starting to think I'm the one with the memory problem.

"No Ry, that's still me."

"What did you just say?"

"I said it's still me. No worries, your mind is still very much the only one working functionally in the room right now."

She just read my mind.

"Pretty girl, I didn't say anything."

"Of course you did. You said that you thought you were the one with the memory problem. I heard it clear as day Ryan."

Shit. She has no idea she's even doing it. I've got to tell her everything now.

"You wanna tell me why you think everything makes sense now?" I ask my final attempt at not having to drop everything on her for the second time since I've known her. What the hell is with me being the one to do this with people? Is this Heaven's idea of a sick joke?

"It's actually a combination of things really. I mean you said something last night that honestly, I haven't been able to get out of my head and then there's what Emma said last night too. It goes against everything I've been physically feeling which with what you just told me makes everything make sense again."

"What did Emma tell you?"

"That I am in love with you for one and then that despite what I believe, I didn't cheat on Graham when I kissed you."

If she wanted an argument to what Emma told her she wasn't going to get one from me. Emma told her the truth just like I tried to earlier in the night when she found herself so freaked out with the way she felt towards me.

"It's true, you didn't."

"I'm not really with Graham am I? He isn't the one I cheated on last night because I've been cheating on you with him."

I wouldn't put it that way and I wasn't going to allow her to do it either. As much as I hated what Graham led her to believe, it isn't her fault and she isn't going to spend another second on my watch treating herself as if it is.

239

"You didn't cheat on me Ser. You just didn't remember. There's a difference but no, you aren't with Graham."

I could tell she didn't want to accept what I'm saying. It's one of the ways we're most alike. We have the uncanny ability of always putting the blame on ourselves just as easily as we seem to always want to sacrifice ourselves in an effort to save people. She wanted to take the blame for this instead of putting it where it belongs.

With Lucifer.

"You're just saying that because you love me."

"Pretty girl, if I really believe that you're at fault for this I would have no problem blaming you no matter how I feel about you. I'm a big believer in owning your shit when it happens but in this case you didn't cheat on me, trust me. This is not your fault. None of it."

"It's Graham's."

I shook my head. Nope, as easy as it would be for me to blame him, I couldn't do that either. I wanted to though, god how I wanted to. That asshole deserved to have her hate him for what he made her believe.

"No it's not his either."

"Well if it's not my fault and it's not Graham's, considering he's the one that said we were together when we aren't, then just who the hell am I supposed to blame?"

Here it is. The time has come now. I had to tell her everything, no matter how deeply it affected her or the ability to remember it on her own. There is no way I can answer her question in a way that doesn't bring everything back to the surface.

"I think you need to sit down if you want me to tell you that because pretty girl, it's not a pretty story."

My last thought as she did as I said, sitting back down on the bed, the ring she'd been holding at the tip of her finger now firmly back in place where it belongs is simple. I really hope I didn't live to regret this.

CHAPTER TWENTY EIGHT

Serenity

It all started happening last night during my talk with Emma. I didn't go into any more trance states but the memory flashes became more than just scenes in my mind and I actually experienced them willingly as they came. There were still instances that I couldn't make out but for the most part I felt like I was remembering everything in just the right way.

What Ryan needs to tell me now I can see is hard for him but I won't stop him. I remember everything about us now and I know that as much as he hates being the one to give me bad news, he would never hide it or lie to me in an effort to soften the blow. It is the one real thing I believe in moving forward. I needed him to be my Ryan now so that whatever came next we could stand together and fight.

I remember Lucifer. I want to tell him this so that he won't feel the need to go into such graphic detail about my life up until this point but if I do that then he might shut down completely and not tell me the real things I want to know. I need to know where I've been for the last few months and how despite remembering everything else I am unable to with that. He has the answers, I just know it and if it means that I need to be less than forthcoming with him in an effort to learn then so be it.

When the time came for Gabriel and Michael to give him shit for telling me things I know they want me to learn on my own the blame would not be placed on him because I deceived him. I hate doing that with Ryan given how honest we always seem to be with one another but I had to do it to learn and protect him in the process. I would deal with the fallout that might come later. Right now I just needed answers.

"How much do you really remember Ser? I mean other then the stuff with us; do you know anything about who you are?"

"You mean do I know I'm made of Heaven? Yeah, I remember that much. I'm a little hazy on a lot of the actual details

241

about it but I know what or who I am. I also know who Gabriel really is to me and Graham too."

"You remember the bond?"

"I do."

"You know what Lucifer put us through?"

"Well I know we're married and since I don't think either of us were jumping at the chance to do that a few days after we met, I have to assume he made that happen."

"God you're actually making this a whole lot easier than I thought it would be."

"Always glad to help angel."

I watch him freeze in place at the nickname and I wonder why. I knew it wasn't a nickname that I used before but there is no reason for him to act this way in response to it. It didn't make any sense. My confusion must have been evident because he wasted no time speaking again.

"You don't remember that part do you?"

"What part? All I know is apparently me calling you angel freaked you out."

"It didn't freak me out Ser, I just wasn't expecting it. More a shock reaction than a freaked out one trust me."

"Alright so there's some stuff you want to tell me?"

"Need to tell you, not want, pretty girl."

"Whatever, you still need to tell me why you don't blame Graham for anything or me for that matter, so I'm just going to let you do that."

My urge to get the answers for the last few months of my life overrode my plan of keeping him under the impression that I am without actual knowledge of everything we've been through. I wanted to keep it hidden from him but not only did we not work that way with each other despite every attempt at making it so but I didn't work that way either. I just don't have it in me to lie, at least not convincingly, especially with Ryan.

"I don't blame Graham, or you, because Lucifer caused this. He caused it the same way he's been causing everything that's happened with us from the very beginning. No matter how much I try and deny it, he is the supreme puppet master Serenity and he's been controlling all of us the entire time."

"You're going to need to give me a little more than that."

"Do you remember much of Graham being possessed?"

I actually don't. I remember being in Green Haven for the wedding and for what came next and even remember a good portion of my time in Heaven watching Ryan recover from what had actually killed him but I didn't really remember a whole lot of what came next. Bits and pieces here and there that made no real sense is all I had. I definitely needed Ryan's help with this part too.

"Not really. I know it happened but how and why and what happened next is all just a bunch of blurry images in my head."

"Graham tried to save you from marrying me that day. Lucifer caught him and tortured the hell out of him. I guess it happened before Gabriel came to the rescue because he didn't even know what happened at first. Under Lucifer's control Graham came back to the school and tried getting close to you and um, the two of you bonded."

"Bonded how?"

"Soul mate shit really but it was the only way that Graham could counteract what Lucifer was doing with him."

I really wanted to remember what happened during that time period. I can tell by the pain it caused Ryan that it hadn't been anything good. That somewhere along the way something had happened between Graham and me that obviously still hasn't been healed. I never want to cause Ryan or hell, anyone, any pain and knowing that I did it and to the man I love no less tore me up inside.

"Graham's okay now though." I state trying to get back on topic and away from the reality of what I'd so obviously done. "I mean that's how he looks anyway."

"Yeah he's okay but that's only because of what you did."

"What did I do?"

"You exorcised Lucifer from him before he could kill him. At least that's what I think was the end result. I don't think he ever planned on letting Graham live the way he explained to you but I guess that's something we'll never know."

We were getting to the heart of the matter now. He is going to tell me what happened to me by Lucifer's hand that made it so that I can't remember the last year of my life. If I wasn't so damn eager for answers I might actually see all of this for the evil it really is.

"It was supposed to be me Serenity. We planned it all out with Michael and Gabe and we went in with a plan but you changed it all in the last second. You saved Graham but whatever your end result was you didn't think it all the way through. He was able to possess you before me or the angels could get to you."

*****

"Graham if you can hear me, fight! Fight with everything you've got!"

"It is pointless Serenity." He choked out. "He is already dead."

"I don't believe you! I will never believe that!" I screamed as my hands began to slip down from the top of his head until they were almost covering his ears.

I can feel his body weakening to mine, the power inside of me overtaking every part of me until all I can feel is the fire inside of me. I start chanting the words then, the ones I looked up and memorized as quickly as possible earlier that day when the others had been out. I only hope that I learned them correctly and this worked, otherwise Graham is doomed.

*****

"Serenity! Baby can you hear me?"

Looking up and seeing Ryan's clouded blue eyes looming over mine I just nod. Where I had been sitting up only seconds before, I now found myself flat on my back. It looks like the trance affect is still possible after all. So much for feeling normal again.

"What did you just remember?"

244

"Saving Graham. You're right. I didn't stick to the plan. I did my own thing. Ryan I'm so sorry! I could have gotten us all killed."

He pulled me up and into his arms and I felt myself grabbing on for dear life. I remember now what I did and it made me sick. Not only did my stupid decision end up getting me caught up in Lucifer's web but it had almost gotten everyone else killed, the very thing I had been trying to prevent all along.

"You have nothing to be sorry for Serenity, you only did what you thought was right." He said, his voice quiet and soothing as he ran his hands up and down my back in an effort to calm my racing heart, now pressed into his chest.

"I remember it all Ryan, at least what happened that day."

I felt him tense yet he didn't stop the movement of his hand on my back. I knew why he tensed and I wouldn't blame him if he wanted to pull away. My decision caused him to do something that even now I can tell he is haunted by.

He had to kill me.

"Michael told me what I had to do and I swear to god I couldn't do it. I wanted to just give up and let him have me. He just told me the one thing that I couldn't argue with. I'm the one that needs to be sorry."

Pulling away just enough to be able to see him again, I place my hand to his cheek and move in as close as possible until our eyes are directly locked on each other. He had done exactly what needed to be done and just like he couldn't let me blame myself for everything that happened with Graham after I woke up a few days before, I can't let him blame himself now.

"You did what needed to be done."

"Killing you is not what needed to be done."

"Look at me Ryan and I mean really look at me. I'm here. You didn't kill me and I'm going to go out on a limb and figure you're the reason I'm even sitting here at all right now."

The minute his eyes shifted away from mine I knew I had my answer. I still might not remember what happened to me, at least as far as events went but there is no doubt as to the real reason I am here now. Ryan hadn't given up on me.

"You would have done the same thing for me." He said his voice now a whisper. "I just couldn't accept that you were gone."

I knew it wasn't the right time to ask it but given everything we just discussed and the way it affected me, I needed the answers more than ever now. I need to know just what Lucifer had done to me, once and for all.

"What did he do to me Ry? Did he take my memories?"

"Yes Serenity, he took your memories."

Before he could say more, I heard the light rapping sound on the door, three times in rapid succession. Knowing that it wouldn't be Emma because she would have just used her key, it only left two other people it could be and one of them, I didn't want to see, at least not until I knew everything there was to know.

It is possible that now that I'm remembering the last year of my life that Lucifer is back to take it all from me again?

Graham

There was this moment when I was standing outside Serenity's dorm room that I swear my life flashed before my eyes. Could have been a bit of an overreaction to what I knew I would find on the other side of the door when she answered but hand to god that is exactly what I experienced.

I have to face the things I've done, just the way Gabriel said but it didn't mean I had to enjoy a second of it. I knew what I would find when the door opened and it wasn't the face of my very happy girlfriend the way it should have been. No, I am definitely in for something much worse and she did not disappoint. At first though, the words out of her mouth did lift my spirits.

"Thank God it's you Graham."

Giving me a loose hug she immediately pulled away and made her way back to the bed where none other than the man I had come to actually see sat, his face giving away nothing of the enjoyment I was sure he is feeling with my upcoming downfall. If Gabe had been right then Serenity knew everything now or at least would soon enough. It's something Ryan had to be enjoying to no end.

"I was wondering when you were gonna show up."

"Missed you too man." I shot back puckering my lips and making a kiss noise in his direction earning the eye roll I'd been expecting.

"I told you it wouldn't be him Ser. It's not time yet. He has to figure by now we'd be expecting him." Ryan whispered as she sat down beside him again, their hands immediately coming together causing my stomach to turn over.

I guess I know where everyone stood now. There could be no more doubt. Serenity had gotten her memory back and is now back where she belongs. As upset as it made me witnessing it this way, I was also happy at the same time. I hated lying to her and making her believe something that was untrue, even if it did make me happy for a little while. She deserved to know the truth always.

"I don't know what to expect anymore, obviously."

The comment was deliberate and it hit its mark. With the knowledge she has again it's already beginning. I had broken her trust and faith in me and she's not wasting any time making sure that I know it. Message received loud and clear. Again I'm being nominated for World's Biggest Asshole all because I love the girl.

I would never feel guilty for the reason why I kept up the lie, only for the lie itself.

"So you know everything now?"

"Not everything but I do know enough to know that the person I trusted most in the world kept things from me."

"We all kept things from you Serenity. Considering what you went through can you really blame us?"

"Graham—

The minute Ryan cut in I realized it. She had been right when she said she didn't know everything. She obviously hadn't remembered just what she'd been through over the last several months. Apparently Ryan hadn't gotten around to telling her since it was obvious with the knowledge she had of what I'd done that he'd been the one to tell her.

"He was just getting to that actually. I'm aware that you all kept things from me and I'm actually okay with that considering but Graham, you outright lied to me instead of just being honest and telling me the truth."

What argument could I give here? She's right. I did do the very thing that I swore to her years ago I would never do. Admitting that we weren't dating wouldn't have done anything to her mind other then push her right back into Ryan's arms so it was just another reminder of how selfish I'd been throughout.

"I did. I lied to you. I can sit here and tell you the reason why I did it but it's no excuse. I did it and I can't take it back. I can tell you I'm sorry though and I am. Sorry. More then you'll ever know."

"It's not good enough Graham Cracker."

Her use of my nickname in that statement really didn't make sense. All I had to go on were the times when my mom was angry with me. She never called me by a nickname during those times, only my full given name and I guess I expected it to be much the same with Serenity now. Why use a term of endearment when you're pissed?

"It's not good enough because it isn't just me that your actions hurt. You hurt Ryan. You pushed him away from me so that you could have time with me. I get why you did it and I'm pretty sure he does too but really? With everything you know about me do you really think that is the smartest thing to do?"

Man she really did sound like my mom right now which only made the ache in my chest even worse. I would give anything to hear my mom yell at me again because then at least I would know she was still here, something she isn't anymore.

"I'm sorry Graham."

"Okay now I'm really confused. What are you apologizing for?"

"She read your mind Graham, don't question it just go along with it." Ryan said laughing.

With the way he sounds it's as if she did the same thing to him since her memory returned and he just found it funny now that it was happening to someone other than him. In an effort to stay on track though, I ignored the laughter and got back to the issue at hand.

"I know I didn't just hurt you Ser. That's actually the reason I'm here now. I came to talk to Ryan."

"I'm not going anywhere." She stated her eyes still showing the disappointment that I alone had put there.

"I don't need you to go anywhere Ser Bear. You're his wife; you're right where you should be. I'm not the angels. You both need to hear what I have to say."

"You actually don't need to say anything man." Ryan interjected before turning toward Serenity. "I know you want to be angry with him for me but you don't have to."

"He lied to me and from what I remember seemed to enjoy it. How can you sit there and tell me that I don't have to be angry with him?"

"I think we need to continue the conversation we were having before Graham showed up in order for that to make any sense."

"Then let's do that because until you explain I'm going to stay the same level of disappointed and angry I am right now."

"Just let her be angry at me man. She needs it. It will help her with everything that's coming."

"Both of you just shut up alright!" Ryan snapped immediately causing both of us to look to him and give him what he wanted but shutting out mouths both literally and figuratively. "We are all on the same page and if we don't stay that way then he is going to win."

As strange as it is to admit, I like that he was standing up this way and putting us in our places. He reminded me of Michael and even Gabriel in the moment which just leant more credence to the fact that buried deep Ryan is indeed an angel of the purest form.

"Serenity, I know you want to hate him but there is some shit you just need to know before making your final decision. I wasn't alone in my attempt to save you. Graham was with me too, just like Michael and Gabriel were. We put aside all of our differences, both angelic and human alike because we all wanted nothing more than to bring you home."

Putting his hand up as her lips parted he continued.

"What Graham did, I can't hate him for because if put in the same place I can't actually sit here and tell you that I wouldn't do the same thing. He loves you, just like I do, if not more because of the bond that the two of you share and because of that it doesn't

249

exactly make even the most holy of men think straight. He made a mistake, one that sure, I don't agree with but it is just a mistake. We've all done that."

"Can I talk now?"

"Yeah you can talk now pretty girl. I'm done."

"What exactly did you save me from?"

I needed to be the one to tell her this. I couldn't explain why given that right now Ryan is the only one in the room she really trusts but it just has to be me.

"Lucifer took you to Hell. We went there to bring you back."

She didn't want to believe me, which is why it wasn't a shock when the truth didn't even level on her face. At least it didn't until she turned to Ryan for confirmation. It was only when he nodded his head in agreement that it all came full circle and hit her in the way we had all been avoiding from the start.

Before I had a chance to react the room lit up around us, causing the light directly above my head to burst and with barely a second to spare, I reacted and immediately threw myself to the floor, making sure to cover my head from the shards as they burst and fell around me.

"Do not say another word. You have already said more than enough."

Peeking out from a crack in my hand I saw not only the angel that the voice belonged to but also the face of the other more pissed off angel that stood beside him, lighting the entire room up with their glow. The only thought that could break through as I watch the two of them now didn't even have anything to do with the reason they were there, which only made me wanna share it that much more.

"Way to make an entrance guys."

CHAPTER TWENTY NINE

Gabriel

It may not have happened the way that I intended from the start, especially since I didn't get to play as big a part in it as I wanted but I am happy that Serenity has been able to remember the events of the last year of her life, only because it means that she can finally begin the true art of the healing that I had done on her only days before.

I could not stand by though as both men in the room with her came dangerously close to spilling the extent of what she had been through. I could feel her reaction even from my positioned place outside of the college itself. Her mind was dangerously close to reaching a limit to which she would be incapable of coming back from given her current state and her body was quickly following suit. I could not allow that to happen.

The very reason I appeared in the room now, with Michael by my side. Any further action taken from this point on had to come from us but not before we did what needed to be done.

As uncomfortable as it is going to be for her, Michael and I need to both become one with her in order to find out whether or not my theory of an attachment with Lucifer was indeed true after all. If she reached the full capacity for knowledge in her path to remember everything that happened over the last year than any chance we would have at gaining information and keeping ourselves ahead of the fallen angel would be for naught.

Something we could just not allow to happen.

"I'm sorry to just appear this way but this conversation needs to cease. There are more pressing matters at hand."

"Pressing how Gabe?" Ryan asked, immediately pulling his hand out of Serenity's and standing to his feet, his stance proving he was more than ready for the inevitable showdown with his former master.

"Sit Ryan, is it not that kind of pressing need. Lucifer has not yet made another appearance. It does pertain to him in another way though." Michael stated.

"If he's not back then what the hell is so pressing you had to come in like that and make the light explode above my head?" Graham asked, finally beginning to move from his crouched position on the floor, his expression none too pleased.

"We believe that he has not yet made an appearance because he is in some way connected to Serenity and is awaiting the moment when she comes to terms with everything that has happened to her. Most importantly, the time she spent with him in hell."

"Connected how?" she whispered, the fear evident in her eyes. I wanted to say some words that might comfort her but I knew that there were none. This is going to be uncomfortable no matter what pretty words were uttered beforehand.

"You think he branded her somehow don't you?"

Having Ryan part of the light continued to have its advantages. There is never a need to go into a great amount of detail because during his time with Lucifer he had learned and seen it all. He would know all about this reverse type of branding better than even Michael or I did.

"That is exactly what we believe. So before you continue to explain what's happened to her we need to find out if our suspicions are correct or not."

"How exactly are you going to do that?" Serenity asked again and this time I turned my attention solely to her. No one else in the room needed to matter but her since everything that came next would affect her alone.

"You need to give Michael permission to join with you. He needs to be able to reach inside of your mind in more than just a traditional way. He needs the connection that being a vessel brings. It is the only way to accurately detect if the branding has indeed been placed on your mind."

"There's more you're not saying…"

It shouldn't have come as a surprise that with the reoccurrence of her memories that her abilities had also resurfaced but that is exactly what it was. I had not been expecting her to be at this level so soon. Remembering maybe but to be able to also use her abilities to see inside of my mind and past the words I spoke should have been impossible.

"I need to speak to your heart Serenity."

"I don't wanna sound like a total bitch but shouldn't Ryan be the one to do that?"

"He cannot do it. Even though it appears as though he is an angel of the purest order, because of the bond between you and Gabriel it must be him." Michael answered in way of explanation which only made Serenity lean back even more on the bed and away from the both of us.

She is now beginning to see it as the invasion that it would be and is not entirely positive she wanted to be a part of it. A reaction that I could not fault her for. There would be nothing pleasant about what was to come and she had every reason to fear it.

"Okay, the rest of you seem to at least grasp a little bit of this but I seriously don't get it. I know what Mike's gotta do but how the hell is Gabriel supposed to reach out to Serenity's heart?"

"Thank you Graham, you took the words right out of my mouth." Serenity answered before turning to Graham and giving him the weakest smile.

"Gabriel would have to force the Beloved bond on her." Michael answered again which I could only believe in some small way is his way of helping me out given just how close to the situation I truly am. "To put it in terms that all of you will understand he will have to reignite the feelings that Serenity once had for him and push them to their limit."

"He's going to rape her heart?"

"I will do no such thing!" I snap the wording used pushing me to my limit. It is no secret what all beings of the light felt for that word and not to mention the action itself. It is something that was created in the darkness by my brother and I would not stand by and let the very human that had at one point been his vessel speak of it so callously.

"Sorry Gabe. You know I didn't mean it like that. I just don't know any other way to word it."

"He's going to make Serenity fall in love with him Graham. That's how you say it. Geez man even I know that and Lucifer is the king of rape and pillage."

"Fine, I screwed up but that still doesn't tell me shit. As much as I hate admitting this for personal reasons, she is head over heels in love with Ryan. She might not share a bond with the guy but her heart damn sure knows him. How exactly are you going to make her fall in love with you and ignite this bond or whatever?"

"He's going to have to do the very thing we want to make Lucifer pay so badly for."

Again Ryan came forward with his knowledge, making any words Michael or I could come up with to explain pointless. He is indeed correct in his explanation as well. I would indeed have to enter her mind and change things. The only difference is, while my brother chose to erase things for a reason, I would do it and put everything back the way it is supposed to be when completed.

"If you can pull apart my mind and my memories and put them back together, how come you didn't just do it four days ago when you got me out of Hell?"

"He needs your permission Serenity and at that stage you were not in the right frame of mind to be able to give it. There are instances where we are known to just take what we need but they are few and far between and usually done by the very brother that was cast out. We always give a choice unless there is no other alternative."

"This is the only way to know for sure that Lucifer branded me?" Serenity asked, her voice barely above the decibel of a whisper, making all eyes in the room to turn back to her and just what effect our very words were having on her.

"Yes Serenity. If there was any other way we would have already done it."

"Then what are we waiting for? Michael, if you don't mind I'd like to start with you first. It seems the least painful of the options I'm given."

I could not let her continue without first letting her know that she still had a choice in all of this. If she did not want to go through what is needed with me then all she had to do is say no.

254

We would face whatever was coming head on, with or without the advanced knowledge. I told her before on many an occasion that she would always have a choice and I stood by that now more than ever.

"You can choose to say no Serenity. I will never take your choice away."

"It's not you taking it away. It's me. If doing this helps us in any way figuring out what comes next then I want to do it, even if it hurts me."

"Then let's begin."

Why did I feel as I watched Michael move toward her that what came next would be the thing that would define the rest of our lives and our time on the planet as a whole? Why did it all seem so final?

Serenity

There has to be a time when the craziness takes a backseat and the lives of every single person in this room with me right now can reach a point of normalcy. We all needed it but more than that we deserved it. We've been going non-stop for a year, though really looking at everything we have been through it seems far longer than that. We were due a little bit of a reprieve.

When they said I needed to join with Michael I have to admit, I thought it would be the most awkward experience of my life and you're talking to the queen of those. Graham is the only person in the room with me now that truly understands what it is that I'm feeling as I lay here with Michael doing whatever it is he needs to do inside of me. I could feel him there but it isn't weird at all, in fact I think for the first time I actually feel entirely complete.

I figure it's got something to do with who I really am. When you strip away the humanity and the life I've lived, what you're left with is the ball of Heavenly light that I am underneath. Michael being inside of me this way could be looked at as an invasion but for me it is so much more than that. He is just reminding me of what I should have never lost sight of the entire time.

255

I am so much more than just Serenity Richards.

"I gotta know. What exactly does it feel like for you Serenity?"

I actually expected Graham to ask me this. After being a vessel for Gabriel and then unwillingly becoming one for Lucifer, he had a lot of firsthand knowledge of exactly what I'm going through. It's only natural that he would want to know how it felt for someone else. Ryan could give his experience but considering all of his had been unwilling and dark in nature, it wouldn't be the same.

"It's like I'm full."

I didn't register his laugh at first but after a few seconds I caught on and realized just how wrong it sounded.

"Gross Graham Cracker! Not what I meant at all."

"I know but come on; you gotta admit that was a classic sex line."

"I admit to nothing." I cracked, unable to keep the grin from taking over my face. "How long is he going to be inside me?"

I heard Graham laugh again and I knew there was just no way of asking what I wanted to know without having it come out perverted. With as serious as the entire situation is, it was actually pretty nice to have something to laugh about. It made me focus a little less on the next step and more on the happier aspect of the entire process.

"He should be extracting himself at any moment." Was Gabe's clipped reply. It is always business as usual. I had kind of been hoping that at some point the angel would have joined in on the jokes. He looked like he needed it even more than I did and I was the one currently having an angel ride around inside of me.

Holding true to his statement, I felt my body being pulled forward as Michael attempted to break himself free of me. This is definitely the part I hated most about the entire process. If it's possible to have your body ripping from the inside out that is how I would explain the way it felt now. After a few more minutes my body went limp and relaxed as Michael again appeared in the room.

"There is no branding on her brain or for that matter on any aspect of her mind. In taking away her memories he did not intend to track her progress in this way."

I want to be relieved but I can't bring myself to feel it. Not when there is still another avenue that needs to be checked. I had come to terms with what Gabriel is going to have to do but it did not mean I completely understand it. In order for Lucifer to access my heart it would mean that at some point I had to have given myself over to him, or at least given him a large enough portion of my heart for him to brand it.

It's something that try as I might I could not remember him doing during my time in hell, though since I couldn't exactly remember anything other than arriving there at all it stood to reason that anything was possible.

"I need to ask this again because time is of the essence here but Serenity are you sure this is what you want to do?"

"My answer is still the same Gabriel just please, put everything back the way you found it. I don't think I can handle not remembering everything again."

"I will make sure that when this is over you will be even better then you were before we began bella ragazza."

"Nice one Gabriel. Try using your own words next time." I heard Ryan call which only made the smile Graham put there earlier come back in full force. No one else is allowed to call me pretty girl but Ryan. I can't help it, I'm a girl and it makes me feel incredibly special even if it had been said as a joke.

It is more than just special I feel though because it also reminds me that I'm loved.

"Before we begin I feel the need to warn you that she may say some things or even do things during the time frame that she is locked in the bond that you may not like."

I wasn't sure who the comment is directed more toward, Ryan or Graham but I was beyond thankful that he said something before just jumping in and having it happen. It is always easier for me facing things I don't like if I know exactly what is going to happen moving forward and I have to assume that it works the same way for both of the men that I had come to love over the years.

Knowing really is half the battle.

"Don't worry, I get it Gabe. Anything said or done will not be held against her in a court of law when you finally give her back to me."

"Your ability to make jokes at a time such as this confuses me to no end and your statement makes no logical sense but it is not of consequence as we are now ready to begin."

As Gabriel made his way toward the bed, I made myself a silent promise. I would make Gabriel and even Michael learn the art of the figure of speech and even how to joke. They obviously needed it more than they care to admit and if it is the last thing I do before my time is up I will see it happen.

The time for talking and joking over, I felt him place his hands on either side of my head and everything around me started to go fuzzy. I had been able to see the room, or at least the parts of the room that surrounded me clearly only seconds before, they are all becoming a blur now. I also felt the pressure right around the place where his hands lay and knew it as the power that he is now using in order to complete the task.

As he spoke to me, his voice a mix of the deep tone of his voice mixed with the melodic sound I had come to recognize as distinctly his, I felt my chest expand and my heart begin to grow warmer with each passing second. I welcomed the feeling because even with as heavy as the heat itself felt, my body and mind felt nothing but light.

"Serenity, dimmi che cosa è che il vostro cuore si sente per me. Parlare non solo al mio cuore, ma per la mia anima."

"Someone wanna tell me what the hell he just said to her?" I heard a voice whisper in the background yet unable to make out just who or what had spoken the words.

"It is not of import human. If what Gabriel has done worked then her answer will be our confirmation."

"Okay man you don't have to be such a dick about it."

"Shut up Graham. Just let them do what they need to do."
Another voice hisses, this one infinitely angry but one that I did in
some way recognize, even if in a fleeting way.

"Il tuo cuore è sotto stress come la mia amata. Devi lasciar
andare il dolore e abbracciare di nuovo la luce. E 'la luce dentro di
voi mi lega a te e lo farà per sempre. Voglio solo la perfezione
della vostra anima. Ogni stella brilla con il mio amore per te
Gabriel."

The other people that I could sense and see in the room were
now glowing with the brightness of light that surrounded not only
me but Gabriel as well. He has never looked as beautiful and
picture perfect as he does in this moment and it is that perfection
that is making everything around me alive again.

I have ached to feel this very way for as long as I can recall
and experiencing it now and with the keeper of my soul, the owner
of the very life force that ran bold and strong through my veins
completes me. It is breathtaking to behold. It is an experience that I
never want to end.

"Desidero guardare nel tuo angelo anima. ho bisogno di essere
sicuro che siete al sicuro e nulla ha rotto quel bel cuore che batte
solo per me."

"Fate come si deve se nulla può mai rompere la mia
adorazione per te amore mio."

The pressure in my human body became even more powerful
then and I knew that Gabriel was doing as he had mentioned and
was checking me for any signs of a breach on the very bond that
we shared. I am sure there would be no such breach found as even
now, as I lay in this position I want nothing more than to reach out
to him, bring him to my breast and consummate our love.

I have finally found it and now I never want to give it back
again.

True perfection and beautiful peace with my beloved.

CHAPTER THIRTY

Ryan

Gabriel did warn me that things would get uncomfortable and that I needed to keep an open mind no matter what I hear or see during the time where he reached into her heart and soul. I thought I'd been doing an awesome job of taking everything with a grain of salt until she began speaking back to him. It's in that moment that as much as I hate admitting it, a little part of me died.

I hate this bond crap. It had been drilled into my head at an early age just how powerful the bond of the soul mate really is and with the way Serenity's feelings for me had overridden it with Graham I felt secure with it and hoped it would be the same way with the bond her and Gabriel also share. I was wrong though, this one is definitely far worse because she has absolutely no control of it, at least not right now.

They are speaking in Italian which is the reason Graham had a hard time understanding any of what was said and wants a translation so bad. If he expects me to be the one to give it to him, he's going to be in for a rude awakening. I would never repeat the words I heard Serenity and Gabe say to each other, the bond more than a little noticeable between them. No way in hell I'm ever repeating that.

He's done with her now and is going through the motions of putting her heart and her mind back to the way it appeared to be before he began. I should be happy, knowing that the truly torturous part is behind us, allowing us to move forward but I'm not. After everything that happened with Graham the last time she had her mind played with, there is a part of me that is expecting Gabriel to do the same thing.

Angel or not the pull, especially when there is a bond involved, is very hard to ignore. I've seen bonds over the years, have even had the pleasure of breaking quite a few and what Gabriel faced now I wouldn't wish on my worst enemy. The minute he put her back together again much like Humpty Dumpty, he would be faced with the knowledge he may never have her again, at least not in the way he wants most.

Her heart belongs to me and while he may own that portion of her soul that I could not reach, I am determined not to give it back to him without a fight. Once we got through all of this with Lucifer this one final time and her destiny is reached, I am going to take her away from here, and make her mine in every way possible. We've waited far too long already for our lives to begin. I wouldn't let an angel come between that.

"You must not worry Ryan, my brother knows what he is to do and he will follow it to the letter. He will not betray your trust or hers in this process."

"Is there ever a point Michael, where you actually think before you read someone's thoughts and realize that maybe its better not knowing?"

"That happens more than you realize. I have had that same feeling where you are concerned three times now and neither time did it become an easy decision but I happen to be quite fond of you and want to make sure that what you are witnessing does not affect you in a negative way."

"You sure it's not just because you know if I get angry I might turn green and end you all?"

"What is with you humans and this turning green nonsense? I am well aware now that it is not even remotely possible Ryan so please refrain from speaking of it as if it is."

"Thanks Mike. I needed that." I say in between laughs.

I knew he would have no idea what I'm talking about and what exactly it is that he did that I needed so badly but he would accept the thank you for what it was. He's right, he did the right thing reading my thoughts because right now with the road they're taking, it's definitely not going to end up anywhere good. I let Gabriel, Serenity and their bond affect me more than I wanted to.

"You are most welcome Ryan. Do not fear anything, she still remains very much yours and I will see to it myself should that change anytime in the near future. At least in a way that pertains to something I am permitted to fix."

261

Listening to him say things made me start to question when this became my life. For so long now I followed Lucifer blindly, not giving much thought to the real evil we were creating with the things we did and yet here I am now, standing in a room with not one but two angels both of which were on my side. If that isn't enough, I'm also one of them, at least somewhere buried pretty deep. They accept me, my past and the mistakes I made without a second thought. We were on the same page.

It's strange but for the first time in my life I think I know what it is that I have now, besides Serenity and everything that she brought to my life.

I have a family.

Before I could respond to him though, if only just to say thank you for the obvious olive branch built around kindness he was giving me, Gabriel stepped away from Serenity, whose eyes were now closed, looking just as peaceful as she did the day she woke up in my bed less than a week ago. It wasn't time for pleasantries anymore, it was time for answers.

"Why isn't she awake?" Graham asks, bringing my attention back to the rest of the room and away from just the private conversation I had been having minutes before with Michael.

"What she just went through both with Michael and again with me, her body needs the time to adjust and recuperate. She is merely sleeping soundly and will wake soon."

"Brother, what if anything were you able to discern during your time within her soul?"

The look on his face told me everything I needed to know. Lucifer opted not for branding her mind but for going to the one part of her that would be hardest to heal. He branded her heart. My heart.

"It is as I feared. He has indeed branded her heart. Her recall of what she endured during her time in hell shouldn't cause her any residual damage unless it is in fact related to feelings that her heart would have felt regarding him. I do believe Ryan can tell her as much as he is able about her time there and from there her memory can do the rest."

"How does this affect things moving forward?"

262

"He will make his appearance Ryan and he will do it soon. It is his way. We must not allow him to trigger anything remotely related to her heart and her time in hell as it pertains to him. If that occurs then Serenity can and will be turned against us."

I understand what he's saying but I didn't want to believe it possible. I always assumed that during her time with Lucifer she would have been fighting tooth and nail against anything he would throw her way but is it actually possible that at some point just as he did with Graham he had broken her too? If he did break her down, he could have abused the pureness of her heart in such a way that turned it around on us.

He could have gotten her to fall in love with him.

"That is a possibility we must consider Ryan. We have no idea of the horrors that she endured during her time there and though she is built of Heaven's light, she is still very much a human girl, he may very well have broken her."

"This makes me sick." I said quietly almost as if I didn't want her to hear me even though she was sleeping. "If this really is the undertaking and she is supposed to be the very thing that saves the world and all of us, including Heaven, how are we going to deal with it if she turns?"

'We prepare accordingly beforehand and cross that bridge when we face it. Until then we hope and we pray that what we believe is not the case."

That is going to be easier said than done. I can't just ask her when she wakes up to tell me about her time in hell and whether or not her and Lucifer actually grew close. It would be those kinds of questions and prodding that would be our downfall if it was true. I just couldn't go forward on blind hope and faith though, no matter how badly I wanted to. I'm not like the angels.

"Frickin Lucifer!" Graham snapped. "Every single time we think we might be ahead of him, we find out we're not. Why the hell didn't we just take care of this shit when we had the chance?"

His question was valid. If we had just done something after rescuing Serenity then maybe we wouldn't be facing all of this now. We could have been the ones to end this once and for all.

"It was not the time Graham. I do believe I speak for everyone in the room when I say that it should have been done and that it would make things all that much easier moving forward. You know as well I do though with as damaged as Gabriel was when we reached him and our overwhelming desire to get her out safe and sound that we would have perished if we did attempt it. All of us, Serenity included."

I had heard more than enough. I could feel it inside me that limit being reached. Not only did I have to think about Lucifer branding my wife in a way that she might never be able to come back from but I also had to think about what could happen if he did get his way and is able to turn her against us. His plan to tear us all apart hadn't worked so now this was his last big hurrah.

I didn't want to talk about what we should have done anymore but instead focus on what we need to do moving forward. Gabriel is right. He will make himself known sooner rather than later and we had to be ready for it, even if Serenity did become a wild card we couldn't entirely control.

It's time for a little less conversation and a lot more action.

"So where do we go from here, knowing what we know?"

"It's time for us to make our way home. It is time we speak with our father again and get any plans he may have moving forward. In the meantime Ryan, I suggest that you stay here with Serenity and watch over her. I believe given the information you above all others have received today; you may be in need of the time with her before we move forward."

I couldn't argue with that. With everything I heard, especially the parts where Gabriel connected with her, I wanted nothing more than some alone time with her. She only just got her memory back and with everything we know now she wasn't even going to get the time to adjust to that before being thrown right back into another face to face with the very devil we wanted to see dead. We both need the time, even if it isn't all that much.

"I'm going to find Emma." Graham spoke up. "If he ends up showing up, now that she knows everything she's in as much danger as the rest of us. When I find her I'll bring her back here and we can all wait for word from you two."

"Yeah man, do that. Right now I'll feel a lot better knowing that she's safe too since I'm the one that put her in this mess."

I didn't want to hear anyone in the room tell me that I shouldn't take the blame for this. The reason Emma didn't know anything about the lives we've been living over the last year was because we all wanted to keep her safe. Now that she's in the loop it put her just as much at risk as Serenity. Realizing that did nothing to help my already downward spiraling mood, in fact it just made it that much worse.

"Well, we all have our orders then. Prepare yourselves in the meantime because once we do come back it will be time to begin."

As both angels disappeared from the room leaving nothing a trail of blowing dust in their wake, Graham turned his back to me finally and made his way to the door. Just as Gabriel suggested, I was about to get my alone time with my peacefully sleeping wife. As much as I wanted to enjoy the moment, watching her sleep the way she is now, I knew it wasn't going to last.

The minute she woke up I am going to have to explain to her that we are going to war.

Again.

CHAPTER THIRTY ONE

Gabriel

I love and cherish my brother almost as much as I do our father but if he asks me one more time if I am handling things alright I will show him just how much being on the planet we had just retreated from has changed me. In the blink of an eye that it takes us to move from realm to realm he must have asked me the same question thirty times.

Of course the reasoning behind it is completely understandable. It is not every day that you witness your brother connect on a level with his beloved. Those moments at least for the brothers that have gone through it has always been a very private affair. No visitors allowed. Since nothing thus far in my existence has ever followed a proper path though, it is no shock that this didn't either.

He had legitimate concerns as it pertained to my current mental state but it didn't mean I want to in any way discuss it. All he needs to know is that I did what needed to be done and would repeat it again in a heartbeat if it got us the answers we needed moving forward.

How I really feel about it is for me only. The way I can still feel the pull of her heart to mine even though she has been back to normal for more than a few hours now. Her words play over in my mind as if she is speaking them to me even now. As I told her, I ache to see inside of her heart and just because the connection had been broken on her level did not mean that I did not still feel that same way. This is an agony like none I have ever known and I just want to shut it off and focus on the task at hand.

We were here to speak to Father and put together a plan of action moving forward. I want to know if he has any new information regarding Lucifer's arrival and if so just what kind of timetable we have to put everything together. That is where I need to be putting both my heart and my mind. As much as I wanted

266

nothing more than to stay locked in that moment with Serenity, it is just not something that can be done.

"So you had to make me do it."

"I did not make you do anything. You chose not to take my answer as fact and did what you wanted. Do not place blame at the wrong doorstep brother."

Of course he stepped inside my thoughts. Father may be the all knowing and seeing one but he did not leave us without any defense against a mind unwilling to let us in. It appears though that we seem to use this particular ability on each other much more often than other beings, such as the humans we are in charge of protecting.

"At some point brother you are going to have to come to terms with what you just went through and not to sound human or anything but speaking about it is the natural way of handling situations such as this."

"You want to have a heart to heart talk? Really Michael? Since when did you become so in tune with your emotions?"

"I do not have emotions, you know this Gabriel."

He's wrong, I do not know that. I have seen the way Michael reacted during the period of time Serenity had been taken from us. He could stand here and tell me that he didn't feel anything until he ran out of breath but it wouldn't change the facts. As much as we all were of the belief that we did not feel, we did in fact feel everything just as the humans did. A lesson I had learned just recently as I guarded Serenity.

"I am also of the belief that warriors such as us do not lie, yet that is exactly what you are doing with me right now."

Taking his silence as the blessing it was, I continue walking until I see the outline of our father standing off in the distance. Even from the vantage point we held he is remarkable in his beauty. The picture of perfection whether it is here in Heaven or during his excursions to Earth. There could never be another being like him.

"It appears as though we have much to discuss my sons. I am aware of everything that you have learned during your time with

Serenity and I do believe I have a plan of action moving forward that will bring about a positive end for everyone."

There had been a moment when Michael came face to face with our father that I had been worried that we would still need to tread carefully. It being the first time Michael has come home since the day he stormed out in anger, I chose to go into the situation looking at it as the worst case scenario. As it appears though, both beings are back on solid ground, connected as we all were with finally reaching the end of our long and winding road with the leader of the fallen.

"It appears as though your brother is indeed making his appearance known. It will only be a matter of hours before he touches down on the planet. The power levels I have been tracking seem to have reached a level that only speaks to him running at full capacity."

"What do you believe his first move will be Father?"

"He will go to Serenity, of that I have no doubt."

"Why can't we just stop him the minute he appears?"

"To assemble not only your brothers but the humans as well as Ryan and Serenity would take far longer than the time we have left before he arrives. I would like nothing more than to put an end to his reign of darkness before he reaches the very woman he yet again branded, it is just not a wise decision and could end up creating far more fatalities than I am prepared to have on my conscience."

"So we just wait until he goes to Serenity and turns her?"

Not capable of emotion my ass.

It is clearly evident that he did not like nor support this method of action which only made his earlier words now a mute point.

"There is no information available that says she will be turned from any visit he makes to her Michael. Where there have been moments where I doubted both Ryan and Gabriel's faith in the ball of light I created, I never expected it of you."

"I have more than enough faith in Serenity and the level of power that she wields under the surface Father. That is not in question here. What we do moving forward is, keeping in mind

268

that we do need to keep her and everyone associated with her protected."

"The issue at hand is not Serenity and her abilities. We need to focus now on what we do moving forward." I interrupted, making both men turn to me and with that bringing the conversation back to where it needed to be. I could sense another argument on the horizon and I am definitely not in the mood for another go round with the two most stubborn beings alive.

"From the very beginning Lucifer has wanted nothing more than to end existence as we all know it in Green Haven. It has significance to him due to the fact that it is where he fell originally. That is where we will put our plan into motion and take him down once and for all."

I agree with Father. Lucifer would want all of this to end in the very place that it all began which meant in order for Serenity to reach her destiny and for us to end his reign once and for all it would have to be done there. I just wasn't entirely sure what he had in mind going ahead.

"Raphael and Uriel are at your disposal for what is to happen next Gabriel. I believe that moving forward we need to trust in Serenity to guide us. She will be the very thing that ends him so in her we must place our trust. She will know what to do."

"All due respect but don't you think we need a little bit more than that moving forward? You cannot just tell us that we have to trust in Serenity to make the decisions when she has been branded by the very entity we are attempting to stop." Michael responded, his irritation level rising as evidenced by the steely look in his eyes.

I understood his concerns but I also understood the point Father is attempting to make as well. Again, as before, I seem to be stuck in the middle. In times before when this happened, I just seemed to adapt but this time, that wouldn't be the case. This time I am going to have to decide just what side I stood on and go from there.

One of the lessons that I took away from what happened to Serenity in the church months earlier is that we all have a lesson we need to learn and mine had been to exert more of my own free will. I did not want to follow Father, nor Michael blindly anymore. I would take both arguments, look at them rationally, giving them both the time they deserve and I would make my next step from there.

"Michael, you need to find and prepare Raphael and Uriel for what is to come. Father, continue doing as you have been and inform us if at any point there may be a flaw in the design of which you have masterfully created. In the meantime I think it is time I went back down and did the one thing I have been tasked with from the very beginning. It is time I guard Serenity."

If Father is right and all of the answers lie with her then standing around Heaven and debating what the right movements were is nothing more than a waste of time. It is time that I could very well be using to move forward and help Serenity achieve her true destiny. With one final look between both of the men I love and respect most in life and here at home, I prepared myself for departure.

It is now time to turn our reaction into actions. It is time to prepare for war.

CHAPTER THIRTY TWO

Serenity

When I woke up and Ryan told me there was somewhere he wanted to take me or more, something that he wanted to show me I couldn't help but feel excited. It seems that since I came back I'm different, because where I used to always want to stay in before, now I can't wait to get out and experience my life. I suppose it has something to do with losing a year of my life but whatever the reason really, I'm just happy it's here.

I've come to terms with the fact that there will never be anything normal about me but as far as my life goes, right now in this moment I feel the most normal that I've ever been and I don't want to do a damn thing to change it.

He wouldn't tell me where we were going so when I finally felt ready enough for a road trip and we'd gone outside I'd been more than a little prepared for a walk or at the very least a ride on the city bus, an experience that up until now I've been avoiding like the plague. It's only when he dragged me to the parking lot that I knew things were definitely not going to be the way I imagined them.

*****

"Why are we going this way? Didn't you say you wanted to show me something in town?"

"I did say that but in order for us to get to town, we've gotta go this way." *He answered with a grin, the same grin Emma used when she knew something I didn't.*

Just what is he up too?

He stopped midway through the parking lot and as we both stood completely still I tried to figure out exactly what was going on. When his hand slipped out of mine and headed toward the side of the car in front of us, I finally put it together.

"Holy crap."

"I didn't even know that was possible."

"Smart-ass."

"Always. You gonna get in or what?" he asked, slapping the top of the car before sliding himself down inside of it and closing the door behind him.

Quickly following suit, I grab the now opened door that he is stretched across and holding and slid myself down inside.

"Since when do you own a Firebird?"

"Um...since now?"

"Funny guy. You have the keys so I know you're not stealing it so come on, tell me!"

"About three weeks ago. I stayed in my room a lot when you were missing but there were a lot of times when staring at my walls started to eat at me so I thought it was time I went and got myself some wheels. Well that and I knew that once you came home the only way I'd ever get you in the backseat the way I want you is to actually have a backseat."

Reaching across as he put the key in the ignition I slapped him playfully.

"Pervert."

"I prefer to think of myself as realistically dirty."

"Of course you do." I shot back rolling my eyes and laughing. "So you gonna tell me where you're taking me now?"

"All will be revealed at the right time pretty girl. For now just sit back and enjoy the ride."

*****

Of all the places I could have imagined Ryan wanting to take me, this is definitely not one that made the short list. The mall had been the first thing I came up with even though it is one of the places that given the crowds, I somehow knew he hates as much as I do. The park near the school was the other option but not this.

"Say something pretty girl."

"Why did you want to bring me here?"

When we got out of the car and walked over here, his eyes seemed to stay locked on the building in front of us but now, me asking him to explain why he brought me here, his gaze is again locked on mine and I can easily see the answer to my question resting right there in them, without words even spoken.

I might be able to read him the same way that I can with everyone else but I didn't want to. I didn't want to know all the answers the easy way. Sometimes the best things in life came in the hardest times and my time with Ryan is no different. I wanted to have him be the one to tell me things instead of cheating and going into his mind to find out. If the harder way meant listening to his voice as he said things especially when they pertained to us then I definitely like it hard.

I blushed with the way my thoughts sounded and before he opened his mouth to speak it became obvious he caught me.

"Why are your cheeks so red Ser?"

"No reason."

There is no way I'm explaining this to him. I'm not entirely sure I can explain it to myself. It seems that ever since the back and forth with Graham earlier, my mind immediately jumps to the dirtier end of things, something I didn't exactly want to brag about.

"I'll make you tell me eventually, you always do."

"That predictable huh?"

"No actually there isn't a predictable thing about you. I just know you suck at keeping secrets, even ones that are of your own making that make you blush."

"I do believe you might be attempting to delay answering my question McGregor."

"You might be right about that McGregor."

Damn. I felt the heat rise in my cheeks again the minute I heard him use his name for my own. At the rate I'm going I would never turn back to my normal shade of pink. I might be stuck with this rosy red forever. In this moment though it seemed almost fitting given that it's the first time he ever called me by my now very real and legal name. I am indeed Serenity McGregor and just knowing that alongside of feeling it did strange things to my insides.

"So why did you bring me here? Of all the places in Stephenville you could have taken me, this is the place you choose?"

"Well honestly it's kind of a two part reason. I needed to do this to face a fear."

"What fear would that be?"

"Until the day in Green Haven I had never actually been inside of a church, so the only real memories I have of them are bad ones. At least that was true until recently."

"Good save." I say laughing.

"I actually didn't even think about it that way. I'm sorry. I just meant that I've been in a church a total of two times in the last year and both times I literally looked death in the face. It occurs to me that I don't want it to always be like that. If I actually want to follow through with a plan I have for the future, I need to face my fear now."

I actually like his reason for bringing me here, at least the first one in his two part answer. I had been in churches as a child so I'm able to see the good in them as opposed to the bad but I also felt the same way, at least partially. It is hard to look at it any other way when both times that you've been in one recently; death has been the only card on the table.

"What's the other reason?"

"Well that one Mrs. McGregor is a much happier reason. I wanted to bring you here because there's something I've been meaning to do for months now and it's just never been the right time."

Oh how I hate being a girl. I could easily make the total female assumption of what he is getting at or I could be totally cool about it, waiting patiently for him to actually get around to telling me. Instead of going the rational route that I wanted to, I chose the one that made my head so giddy I wanted to explode.

"Oh really, Mr. McGregor, what exactly would that be?" I ask all the while attempting to keep my brain in check with my mouth so that the words would come out properly and not all jumbled the way they were in my head.

He started digging around in his pocket and the sleeve of his hoodie slid up his arm and I came face to face with something new, something that had definitely not been there the last time I saw him with his shirt off. In the same way the car is a new addition, this obviously was as well.

Just how many more surprises did he have in store for me?

Before I could question the newest addition to the artwork that already covered the majority of his arm, he got down on one knee and brought my attention straight back to what he had been trying to explain to me seconds before.

I retract my earlier statement now. I actually LOVE being a girl.

"Ry, get up. You don't have to do this, you already bagged the girl remember?"

The reaction I'd been going for stared back at me and I swear if I could do it, I would have cried at the sight of it. I would never get tired of seeing the way his entire face lit up when he smiled at me. It only made the brightness surrounding him that much more so. I want to be surrounded by this for the rest of my life, of that I'm sure.

"I realize that pretty girl but it didn't happen quite the way I imagined it would. So this time I'm going to make sure that it does. So Serenity Richards-McGregor, will you actually make me the happiest half demon, pure angel, head over heels human on the face of the earth and marry me again?"

He fumbles with the ring box and watching him, just the natural way it's all happening, I felt the tears that I couldn't cry seconds before actually begin to fall. It might not have been one of those proposals in the sky, it wasn't even one done in front of family and friends but what it most definitely was, is the most natural and pure, from the heart proposal I have ever heard in my life and with only my knowledge of movies to fall back on, I had a lot of experience with them.

From the way he smiled up at me as he said the words, to the fumbling of the ring box itself as he tried to open it to present it to me, it is all so perfectly Ryan and just knowing that, there could be no other answer.

"Yes Ryan, I'll marry you as many times as it takes as long as you promise you'll never stop looking at me the way you are right now."

Ryan

Of course I set the perfect scene, or at least the perfect scene for us and the stupid ring box won't open. The minute she gave me her answer though, I didn't give a crap about the ring still sitting in the box that I apparently can't even open. All that mattered is that again, just like the first time she said yes to me, despite everything we were going to face.

The ways I love this girl knew no limits. There were no boundaries on it and more reasons and ways became apparent with each passing day. It only took someone sitting down and looking at the life I led before she came barrelling into my life like the hurricane I truly believe her to be to see it. I was destined for a life of pure darkness and the ultimate level of evil, becoming one with the Devil himself. Where most people my age are moving forward or looking skyward, I was always looking down or backward.

Serenity gave my life purpose but more than that she finally gave it a direction. She is so much more than just an answered prayer to me now. She transcends anything Heaven could even create despite being made of the purest parts of it. Even knowing that at any point everything could turn on its axis she came and never left. She has been with me the entire time. One lifetime with this woman would never be enough.

"Say something Ry because I swear, you're not the one that's supposed to be speechless here."

"Since when are there rules about that?"

She shrugs and I laugh, finally allowing myself the chance to get back off the hard sidewalk and pull her into my arms. I might not have the words to say right now but I could damn sure do this and show her what her answer means to me. Shit, even the way her body feels melted into mine there aren't words for. Soul mate bond be damned, what I feel right here in this moment beat that by a mile.

276

We are connected on a level that is so much more than physical. It's emotional, spiritual and all encompassing. Holding on to her now I can feel it. We are completely one with each other. Nothing can tear us apart, not even the devil himself. There is no way I would ever let him near here again, brand or not.

"Ry, as much as I love the comfortable silences, can you say something?"

"I can't lose you again. I barely survived it the last time."

"Why would you be worried about losing me? It's not like Michael and Gabriel found anything right?"

Of course this is how it all plays out. I am left again with the task of telling her bad news. At some point this crap would have to fall on someone else because I have seriously reached my limit with it. It almost seems that for every good moment I'm able to give her, I have to turn around and give her an equally damning one.

"After Gabriel connected with you, he wanted your body to heal so he put you to sleep. They left to go deal with stuff before they had a chance to tell you exactly what they did find."

"So Gabe did find something?"

Pulling back a little bit more from the embrace, I ran my fingers down the length of the stray hair now blowing in front of her eyes, holding onto it at the end and placing it behind her ear as I nod slowly. As has always been our way, I wanted her to see me, my face and my eyes clearly so she would know beyond the shadow of a doubt that I was being honest and open with her.

"What exactly did he find?"

"Lucifer branded your heart Serenity. That's all I can tell you without starting something I'm not entirely prepared to deal with right now."

"Okay, good. I'm not really in the mood to talk about that anyway. So how about for the foreseeable future we just focus on us?"

I've been noticing subtle changes in Serenity since we brought her back from Hell but haven't given them much thought before now. Seeing the ease at which she switched gears and knowing just how unlike Serenity that really is made me wonder just what else had changed besides the things I already notice. In a way it's almost like she has finally come into her own, all of the things different about her, all things that just made her that much stronger.

"I can't think of anything better, so pretty girl, you ready for your next surprise?"

CHAPTER THIRTY THREE

Lucifer

For centuries there has been much talk of me and my true motivations. It is during this talk that misconceptions are born. I have never had much time for conjecture. I enjoy dealing with the cold hard reality and facts of a situation. It serves everyone better in the end though it does appear to be something that most of the human race has not had the opportunity to grasp quite yet.

I have walked a lonely road since being cast out of the only true home I have ever known, or at least one that was not of my own design. There were other angels and spirits that joined with my cause, falling with me but I was not content to let anyone close enough to get past the proverbial velvet rope. No one had what I believe is needed to know and handle the truth. That is until I came across Ryan's father.

He was one of the demons to fall with me originally and after some time wandering the darkness together, became my closest confidant. He became as close as I could permit anyway. His loyalty to me and what I believe my end to be knew no boundaries. The lengths he would go to in order to succeed were unmatched. So when he was finally eradicated, I grieved the loss more powerfully than any other before him.

When it came to my attention that he had indeed impregnated a human woman and that there would be a son born to him it filled me with a feeling long forgotten. Hope. I had hope again that as the boy known as Ryan grew, he would become everything his father had been and so much more. He did not let me down either, giving me everything that his father had done before him as well as a strength and level of power that I could only describe as close to my own. He was the perfect specimen for me moving forward.

I always planned to keep him close and have him be the vessel for me when the time was right. There is no other being alive besides the Hudson boy that could contain the likes of me but him. So I found myself mourning the loss again as he turned on me and chose a much different side then the one he had been groomed for. I attempted to treat my loss with the human, Graham Hudson but that had been to no avail, at least not until that day in Green Haven.

Graham gave me a gift that day though he is unaware of it. Serenity has always been my choice, at least since I discovered her years before and in an effort to save Graham she willingly gave herself to me without a second thought. So I had much to thank the Hudson boy for because if he had not been her soul mate and destined to be in her life in the manner at which he was, then I never would have gotten the treasured gift of my time with her.

All of this history brings me to now, as I stand outside of the college again much the way I did months ago, except this time in a makeshift host that will be dumped and burned once his use has reached its end.

Serenity.

The way time moves between plains has made a week seem like centuries even though that is not exactly the case. It feels as though she has been away from me for far longer than just the week it has been. It is because of this time difference and the ache that being without her creates within me that brought me here now.

I must have her again. It is time for my final act to come to fruition and for her to join with me so that we may go back home and rule together forever. The two of us side by side watching as the world as we have once known it burns to the ground around us, bringing Heaven and all of its goodness and light with it.

Serenity Richards is the only person, the only true entity I have ever exposed myself with. She is the true keeper of all of my secrets and things that the world would be shocked to hear. Ryan's father had known a great deal just as Ryan himself but they didn't know near as much as the ball of light known as the serene one. She knew it all. When she joined with me I had given her all of me just as she had in return.

I have never admitted to needing anything in all of the centuries I have walked both the world and hell alone but I need her. It is a heavy pain in my chest, the desire inside of me to have her near me again. I could not do any of this without her and it is time that she remembered that and again made her choice.

She has already given herself to me once before, becoming one with me in Hell and it is through that bond now that I stand outside the very place where she rests her head. We are bonded and I know that when I show her the life we shared again, that her ultimate choice will be clear. She will turn her back on everything she has been told and she will realize her rightful place by my side.

In times before I may have had to force the choice but this time I knew different. Her heart would answer to me not only because of the way she had given herself over but because of the brand that I placed there as I took away the very memories of our time together.

There can be no turning back now. It is time to realize our true destiny.

Together.

Serenity

I can't remember the last day I had that turned out this perfect.

Before I moved away from my mom and came to Stephenville for college, most days happened the same way. I would spend the majority of my time trying to block the voices, all the while pretending I was just another normal teenage girl. Sure there were the times with Graham and even with Emma that kept me going but for the most part the days ran into each other as I struggled with my gift.

I was happy on the surface but not all the way through. My smile never actually reached my eyes. The sun never really did shine in its true brightness. It was just months and years of going through the motions and just trying to survive.

The struggle to survive is still there, mainly because of what I know about who I really am but today wasn't a day where I felt at all like I was going through the motions. Right from the moment Ryan sprang the idea of spending the day together, I knew instinctively that it was going to be so much more.

After the church he decided there were two other places that he wanted to take me. Things that he said that in order to truly live I just had to experience. Now that we've done them, I'm not

281

entirely sure that I need them in order to really live but the way he lit up at each place, I know it is what he needs to live and that made it all worth it.

*****

"So I haven't really lived until I've watched college guys play hockey?"

Continuing to guide me down the steps until we were directly in front of what looked like a plexi-glass jail cell, I heard him laugh.

"Well not college hockey but seeing as it's not even pre-season yet, this is the best I could do on short notice."

"I never pictured you for a hockey player or even a fan really."

"More generalizations on my appearance Ser? I thought you learned not to do that by now. Some doctor you're turning out to be."

Laughing and slapping him playfully he pointed in front of us, his expression turning serious.

"For that you need to get your cute butt in the penalty box."

"Is that like time out for hockey players?"

I know how ludicrous I sound but I really have no clue about anything sports related. I was going to need a whole lot of help if this is his idea of living.

"That's one way of putting it. Now get in. Slapping earns you a time out."

"Fine I will but on one condition."

"You don't get to barter with me about this pretty girl. You commit the crime, you do the time."

"I see a courtroom in your future McGregor."

"No changing the subject either. What's your condition?"

"You. In the box. With me."

I can tell by the grin he isn't going to deny me. I don't think he would ever deny me, unless of course it had something to do with life or death situations but since I knew we wouldn't find one of these here, I had him.

282

"That's not exactly a time out for bad behavior now is it?"

"Well if you come in with me, it's most definitely going to be about bad behavior. That's close enough right?"

*****

From the arena he took me on another date that as it turns out was yet another first for me and one I actually found myself really excited for. Emma told me about it once, when they opened it about six months after we started school but me being me, I never actually got around to experiencing it. Now with Ryan, its happening and I couldn't be happier.

There is something about pulling up into a wide open field in Ryan's relatively new car and getting to watch a movie that actually made me want to squeal with delight. Maybe it was because of all the movie nights with Emma but I always wanted to do this.

*****

"Okay so it's been noted, hockey is most definitely not your thing though you do seem to enjoy being in the penalty box. Judging by your reaction, drive-in movies are definitely more your speed."

"It's a movie and it's on a big screen in the middle of nowhere. Of course it's my speed. It's also my kind of private. Did you see the players faces when they caught us in the box?"

"Trust me; it's not anything they all haven't done on their own before. It's actually a hockey rite of passage to do what they caught us doing." He winked and I felt the butterflies actually do flips inside my stomach.

I wasn't entirely sure what had gotten into me today but I am definitely enjoying it. Even getting caught by a group of hockey players making out with my husband in the penalty box had been a thrill.

"I definitely have a new appreciation for hockey now."

"I bet you do. So you ready for your first drive in experience?"

"More than ready."

As the screen lit up and the opening of the movie began I realized exactly what movie we were going to watch and finally let out the squeal I'd been holding from the time he pulled up.

"Pump Up the Volume, really?"

"A birdie might have told me this is one of your favorites."

"Yeah okay but how the hell did you manage to get it to play here?"

I couldn't tell with the way the screen and the light seemed to cast shadows over his face but I swear I felt a shift in the mood in the car the minute the question fell from my lips.

"I pulled in a couple of favors. No big deal."

"It doesn't seem that way. Define pulling in favors."

It was a risk but even if I couldn't entirely make out his face I knew that there is something more here. Call it the pull between us or whatever but there is something he isn't telling me and that just wasn't going to fly. Not with as perfect as this day had been going.

"Before I met you, I used to gamble. Poker mostly but I did some other stuff too. I never lost. I figure you know why but anyway there were a couple of people in town that owed me so I called it in."

"So you managed to snag my favorite movie in a drive in theatre because the guy running it owes you?"

"Yeah, pretty much. I'm not exactly proud of it Ser but well I wanted to go all out for you."

He has no idea how cool I actually think this is. Sure he seemed to think he'd done something wrong and that I would judge him on it and who knows, maybe I should have but I actually found it entertaining. He had this whole other life before me and finding out about it now, even in little bits is actually pretty fun.

Even if the things he did weren't exactly above board.

"Okay well there's still something I need to know?"

"No pretty girl, I don't do it anymore."

"That wasn't what I was going to ask." I answer, leaning over until he had no other choice but look directly at me.

284

"Well what do you want to know?"
"Please tell me you brought popcorn!"

*****

I'm not sure he will ever understand it but the best part of the day for me had nothing at all to do with the places we went and the things we experienced together. It was the things I learned about him that made the most impact on me and even now, as I lay here alone, it is the single thing that occupies my mind more than anything else.

When I was younger I was like other girls in that I always pictured my perfect boyfriend and eventual husband. Just like I always imagined walking down the aisle the first time dressed in white, I also pictured just what my perfect relationship would be like and after what happened with Ryan tonight I'm positive that I am living my dream.

He shared a part of himself with me, the part that lived without me and even though he didn't want to do it, instead content with being the person he has been since I came into his life, it gave me even more insight into the man that I chose to marry all of those months ago. Reminding me again that even with all of the things he considers flaws, I still made the right choice.

The night wasn't supposed to end so soon but coming back to the room and seeing Graham and Emma both here, their expressions grave and unable to entirely explain to me why they looked the way they did, he chose instead to leave with them in order to talk, giving me some time alone to process the day and everything that came along with it. I didn't exactly want the time alone considering everything that I managed to remember over the last twenty four hours but I wasn't about to make anything harder.

If what Ryan said to me earlier is any indication, right now I'm a wild card. Whatever happened to me during the time I was away had obviously made things harder for everyone moving forward so the least I can do is give them time to work things out on their own until they feel they can tell me, or at least come up with a way to fix what Lucifer broke.

285

It's only when I hear the door open and turn over in bed, expecting to see Ryan, instead coming face to face with the very person that caused them all to leave the room to begin with, that I realize that maybe it wasn't going to be up to them to fix what he broke.

Maybe it's going to be up to me after all.

"Hello again my beautiful belle."

Lucifer

Everything is working out perfectly.

Just as I hoped Ryan had brought Serenity back to her room and a few minutes later exited with not only the roommate but Graham Hudson as well, all three of them getting into his car and heading off to an unknown location making any extra work I would have needed to do in order to get Serenity alone that much simpler.

Making the choice of how to appear to her again had been an easy one. To my knowledge she is still recovering from the trauma of being taken from Hell and Gabriel's healing so in an effort not to put her through any more undo strain, I decide to come to her as any of the humans she surrounded herself would have.

I knew she wouldn't be expecting me on the other side of the door when I entered but witnessing the true fear that registered on her face excited me. It reminded me effortlessly of times before where that very look on her face had been the one I most wanted to break within her.

"Though not much time has passed since our time together, you seem to have grown even more beautiful Serenity."

"That's funny because you seem to have stayed the exact same."

"It is such a treat to see that your feisty demeanor remains. I have found myself missing it greatly during out time apart."

"You keep talking about our time together but here's the thing, I don't remember any of it."

"I am aware of that, a fact that pains me. It was my hope that I would be able to come to you once you recalled our time together

286

so that we might continue where we left off before you were taken from me."

Her laughter surprises me as I am unaware of speaking anything remotely amusing. I had only spoken from what I assume is my heart which is definitely nothing of comedic nature.

"How are we supposed to do that when I can't even remember where we left off?"

"I give you that which you want."

"Really? What is it that you think I want?"

"Your memories back, or at least as they pertain to our time together. I can easily see that you have regained the ones from before."

"So then you know that right now the only thing I really want is you dead."

"It would appear that way yes but you will not follow through with your misguided threat of death, at least not yet. Not when there is still so much that your mind is desperate to regain and of which I am the only one able to give it to you."

As much as I could see she wants to argue with me, her face contorting in such a manner that she is disgusted at the truth in my words, I am also bearing witness to the curiosity that looms just off in the background. She wanted nothing more than to remember the time she is unable to place and I was not going to waste any more time making her wait.

"There is a time where you trusted me implicitly my belle. It is that place at which I would like you to go now because I am going to give you back that which I stole from you. It is time."

"Don't come near me."

"And if I do not heed your words?" I question, slowly taking steps toward her position on the bed, seeing her breath hitch in her throat the closer I came. "What will you do to stop me?"

So close to her now that it would only take me leaning my body into the bed to touch her, I stood watching as she so obviously fought with herself for an answer.

"We are alone here Serenity, the others having taken off with your lover to a place of unknown origin. Even my overprotective brothers who I would expect to be guarding over you are nowhere in sight. You are completely at my mercy. It is now that you must do as I ask and surrender to me."

In a moment I can only describe as perfection, her body went still as she followed my command, the branding I placed on her heart kicking in at just the right moment. I meant her no harm but given that this is my first real experience branding in this way I am marveling at just how well it worked.

"May I fix you Serenity, as only I can?"

Though the fear is still evident in her eyes, her mouth remains closed as her head began bobbing up and down, giving me the answer I so desperately want. It has been far too long since I laid my hands upon this beautiful belle before me and I was going to savor every moment of it as I healed her completely.

Running my fingers down her face starting at her forehead until I successfully worked my way down the outer lining of her cheeks to her chin, I reached back up with both hands and placed them evenly on either side of her head.

It is time to bring my Serenity back to me, in all her deliciously evil glory.

Serenity

I can't explain what's happening to me.

A minute ago I wanted to jump from the bed, grabbing any possible thing in the room that I could use as a weapon and stab the son of a bitch standing in front of me until he couldn't speak anymore and just as easily as I felt it, it changed into something more. I can't move at all and even with as badly as I want to, I listen to his every word and do exactly as he says.

When he placed his hands on my face my body shivered with the touch and not because it was in any way cold to the touch. No I shivered in a way that only Ryan had been able to give me before now. Well Ryan and Graham. My body continues to betray me because I actually like the way his hand felt running along my skin.

What the hell is happening to me?

288

"I will take this as slowly as possible but when it is over you will remember everything that we shared together and you will come to see why I am reacting to you in the manner at which I am. Everything will become clear and your eyes opened once more."

Oh how much I wanted to open my mouth and tell him to shove it. He might have gotten away with doing things to me before, even turning me, in whatever sick way he had but he is not going to do it again. I might not remember everything that happened between us but I did remember enough to know that we were nothing alike and I would never entirely bend to him again.

The flashes started again, beginning with our entrance into what I can only believe is hell and then quickly moving on to my slow acclimation to the way of life he had created for himself and the other occupants that resided with him. The light being removed from an innocent body as well as Lucifer himself partaking of the blood after it had been completely drained.

God I want him to just turn this off. I don't like this movie.

Using every bit of strength in me I attempt to close my eyes to block the visions he is now so enjoyably throwing my way. I could not witness this. I might have already lived it but there is no way I want to do it again. There is a reason my mind up until this point had blocked it out and I knew it had everything to do with the nauseous feeling it is giving me now. I blocked it because it's wrong.

"You have not even gotten to the best part my belle. You must remain focused and see the true beauty that is to come."

As he spoke the words I see it. No longer is it Lucifer removing the light from unwilling bodies and partaking of the blood but me doing so and enjoying the more that it occurred. From the torture he took it a step further, allowing me to see just how close the two of us had become during my time with him and I immediately turned my head away.

"I didn't do that. I wouldn't do that. You are putting your own sick fantasies inside of my head!" I shriek, attempting to pull my body away from his and break the contact.

"You did all of that and more Serenity and it is time that you remember it but more than that, come to terms with it. You must witness it all in order for the both of us to move forward with our ultimate goal."

"No! I don't believe you!"

My attempts at breaking the contact fail as he uses even more of his strength, pressing even tighter into my brain, the images flying by faster now, each one making me sicker than the last. I not only did the very things he's showing me but I had taken it one step further. I really had become his princess, giving in to him completely, something I'm sure I would never be able to come back from.

"We connected Serenity; you can no longer deny the truth set before you. Not only that but you can also see that you did not want to leave when Ryan and the others came for you. You very much wanted to remain in the darkness with me."

It's true. As much as the visions he showed me could be falsified I knew my reaction to them both in my mind and my body could not be. I did everything he was showing me and had even gone so far as to give myself completely over to the darkness. Wanting nothing more than to please him for eternity.

"Surrender to it Serenity, give yourself completely over to the way you feel inside. Allow yourself to become one with me again so that we can move forward."

"Why are you doing this to me? Why now? What do you really want?"

There are so many questions I want to ask of him as I let everything I just experienced wash over me, taking away the perfect day that had been lodged in my memory and replacing it with what was left.

"I would assume that the reason for me doing this would be apparent by now but for you I will explain it again."

As he opened his mouth to speak I saw the spots before my eyes and knew what was about to come next. Just the way it happened before with both Emma and Ryan, it is now going to happen again. I'm going to remember something, only this time it is definitely not going to be something wanted but something much better left forgotten.

*****

"Tell me what you're thinking. I think we've reached that point now."

"Serenity you do not want to know my thoughts on this matter. They are not the most pure."

"I don't care if they're pure and nice or not. I want to know."

"I do believe that you have come to enjoy your time here and as such when they arrive I will defend myself and you. I do not think I can allow them to take you. I know that goes against my earlier statement of wanting to let you make the choice but you did ask for the truth always."

"I know this might sound weird but do whatever you have to do."

"It does not sound weird Serenity but I do have to admit I am quite confused by your response. Just what do you mean?"

"It's simple. Do whatever you have to do in order to keep me here because I don't think I want to be saved."

*****

"You…"

As he looks up at me, I see something in his eyes that up until a few seconds ago I never would have believed possible. Hope is there, making even the blackness of his eyes somehow glow. There is something in the way I spoke that lifted him which only made me want to finish my statement that much more.

"What about me Serenity? What is it that you are remembering?"

Before I could open my mouth to answer him he lifted a finger, his hands now resting as his side and far away from the place they were just resting on my head.

"You must realize that I have seen that reaction many times before. You have remembered something that has changed something deep within you. Where before you were unwilling to accept everything I wanted to show you, now you seem to ache for more knowledge."

291

"I do remember. I remember a lot but it is one thing in particular I seem to recall more so than anything else that you have shown me here today."

"What is it?"

"You love me."

There is a part of me that even saying the words feels they are wrong but I'm unable to tap completely into it. All I can see is the truth of my statement hanging heavy between us and my almost desperate like need to have him tell me that I'm right in what I remember.

"In the way that a being such as myself can love, yes I do, very much so."

"I never wanted to leave you so why did you let me go?"

"Oh my sweet belle, I never wanted to let you go. I know that as you recall it now it is also being filled with other times in your very human existence where you have been left behind by those that have claimed to love you but you must remember that I am not them. I am only me and I never let you go."

"What do you call giving me over to Ryan and the angels?"

"Proceeding with the plan. It is a cold way to look at things and for that I give you my sincere apology but it needed to be done in order to move forward now."

"How does this move us forward?"

"That is a most complicated answer."

"I remember telling you that I wanted to remain with you yet I didn't. In order for us to proceed as you want then you need to do now as you have done before and tell me everything."

"You have always been at the center Serenity. The piece that I need and want more than any other in order to complete the ultimate goal of taking down everything my father built. I am not proud of the steps that I have taken but I used you one final time in an effort to reach this point."

"You used me?"

"Yes. You are not only the center of everything for me but also for Heaven itself and the people that it has since employed in an effort to bring me down. It is through you that I knew I could achieve greatness and you did not disappoint. Your return created nothing but chaos for everyone surrounded in your light which was my intent."

"You wanted to pull everyone apart."

"Yes. The more they were preoccupied with the ongoing issues with each other the easier it would be for me to plan my attack. This brings me to why I am here now."

"It's time to put the final plan into motion." I answer, knowing it all without even having to question it. It could only be this. No other reason made sense.

"Yes, I came back for you as it is now our time to be together and also to begin what will turn out to be the end of creation as my father has known it."

"So where do I fit into your plan now? What is it that you need of me?"

"I have taken your choice from you once before but it is now time for me to give it back. The time to decide once and for all is upon us. You must choose to stand with me and watch as the world crumbles or choose to fight alongside of my brothers in a misguided attempt at saving it, of which you will fail."

Life is a series of choices. People tell you that in any given situation you face that you can stand and fight or you can back down and watch as everything falls apart around you. I have been placed in this type of situation for as long as I can remember and no matter what avenue I seem to take it always turns out differently than the way I hope going in. Choosing to stand and fight with Heaven or to redeem Ryan had been my first experience with it and it had only gone downhill from there.

I faced it again in choosing to save Graham myself instead of allowing Ryan to do what God himself believed to be his destiny which brought me to now. The very man that had taken my choice from me on more than one occasion is giving it back to me now except it wasn't as cut and dry as it appears.

At some point during my time in hell I had given the very best parts of myself to the fallen angel and because of that I felt more than a little drawn to being with him and taken back to the place where for the first time everything had seemed so clear but the light in me demanded that I stand and fight alongside of not only the angels but Ryan and Graham too, especially given the feelings and bonds that were created with all of them.

As hard a choice as it is for me to make, I know what I have to do. It is what I have been made do. It is in this moment right now that everything again seems most clear. I need to do what he has told me all along is my destiny.

I need to join again with my prince of darkness and rid the world of its evil once and for all.

CHAPTER THIRTY FOUR

Gabriel

There are many different scenarios that I pictured finding when I came face to face with Serenity again. I assumed I would find her and Ryan together, or the worst case being that I would come upon her with Lucifer. If I was to be given a choice to which one I would rather, it would have be neither as I don't think my heart could take one nor could my way of being accept the other.

The scene I came upon though as I entered her room, the door having been left wide open is exactly as I wished it in that it is neither of the scenarios that I went over before making my descent but not at all what I wanted to find.

Her room looks much the same as it always had in times past but there is no one inside, something that I knew was wrong. Ryan and Graham had both made a plan before my brother and I ventured back to Heaven and none of that plan is taking place before me now. Not only is Serenity missing but it appears as though the others are as well.

I don't know what concerned me more as I took stock of the room around me. The fact that Serenity was not here as she is supposed to be or that she might be missing because Lucifer had gotten to her before I'd come back. Given that Michael had been the reason I had not been here sooner, I couldn't help but feel as if anything happening to her is actually my fault.

Just like before, I let her down again.

Staying behind and speaking with Michael had been productive, at least in terms of putting a plan together moving forward but it all relied on getting the approval of the other person that was needed in order to make it happen. The very person that is not where he was supposed to be.

Here, now, in this room.

Despite my unwillingness at first to hear Michael out where Ryan is concerned, by the end of it I knew that my brother did have a point and none of the result we wanted could happen without him. Now all I had to do was find him.

*****

"Gabriel wait!"

Just as I had been prepared to disappear from Heaven, straight down to Serenity's dorm, his voice came preventing me from completing what I believe needed to be done.

"What is it brother?"

"I know what it is that you want to do but I think we also need to think of another way."

"You heard our father as well as I did Michael. The answers lie with Serenity. You may not want to use that avenue but I do believe it is the way that we need to proceed moving forward. In the meantime she needs to be protected and as her guardian I would really like to get back to doing my job."

"I do not deny that Serenity may be the one that holds the key to ending all of this but there is another avenue that you are not allowing your mind to process."

"I have processed it Michael. It will not happen that way."

"You need to let that be his decision brother. I understand the way that you feel about Serenity and even more than that, I understand your belief that she is meant to save the world because I believe in it too but if Ryan is the one that is to defeat Lucifer then it would be wrong of us not to look it more closely."

"You want to send him to slaughter? Michael, after all of the time spent with the human can you really allow Ryan to face Lucifer again?"

"In the manner at which I want to suggest, yes Gabriel, I can."

"What is it that you want to suggest?"

"It may sound cruel but I say that we use him as bait and face him again, this time, all of Heaven strong at which time Serenity can achieve her destiny."

"Do you even hear yourself Michael? You want to use him as bait? Since when did we become no better than the brother we are preparing to face? That is a move of his design, not ours."

"You are blinded Gabriel. Things are happening around us at a rapid pace and you cannot afford to live in the dark this way for much longer. Lucifer is coming and he is coming to claim the very person you believe has been sent to save us all. He owns her, at least in a way that we are currently unable to defeat. You must realize that right now all is not clear where she is concerned. We need to look at all available options."

"You do that then Michael because I'm leaving now. I'm going back to Serenity and I will prove to you once there that we can and will do this, once and for all."

*****

Is it possible that in my lengthy absence, Lucifer had come back and somehow captured not only Serenity by Ryan as well? For that matter could he have already done away with Graham and Emma? That can hardly be the case, at least if the room before me now is any indication. There seemed to be no signs of struggle present here and though my connection to my brother is no longer as strong as it once was, I couldn't feel him here either.

Needing answers and sure of only one way to get them, I focused my mind on the four beings that I had come to care a great deal about in varying degrees. If I couldn't figure out where they were on my own then I was going to use the power of Heaven to do so and deal with any complications later.

Focusing on Ryan first I found him and soon found that he was not alone. Graham and Emma are with him and just as I had done with Serenity in the past, I focused even further on their frequencies, immediately locating just where they were, also learning in the process that for the time being they were all together and all safe and sound. There is only one thing I could not ascertain and it caused a chill to make its way through my body.

Serenity was not with them.

"So how did it go brother? Did you get the answers you seek?"

At the sound of his voice I turned to face it, the face of my brother, not in the mood for his sarcasm. If he wanted to bother me as it pertained to my earlier belief, whether I now believe him to be correct or not, it was going to have to wait. We had far more pressing matters to deal with now.

"Now is not the time Michael. Something has happened."

"What do you mean?"

"Serenity is missing."

"You worry too much little brother. She is probably just off with Ryan as she was earlier in the day when I called on them to check in."

This is news to me. When we had been in Heaven I cut all contact with the outside world, figuring that for the time being if Father had not sensed Lucifer, it meant everyone was safe. Finding out now that Michael had indeed taken the time to check in with them, ensuring their safety at certain points throughout the day did not set well with me. Since when did he become the guardian?

"I assure you brother, I am not stepping into your shoes but we are partners in the fight now and as such I will do as I see fit in order to protect everyone involved. You must not concern yourself with such petty things."

"She is missing Michael. I have located the other three individuals and they are fine, even if they are nowhere near here but she is still unaccounted for. Is it common in your experience for a man that loves Serenity the way that Ryan does to leave her at her most vulnerable time?"

"Where is he?"

"Green Haven and I am going to give you two guesses why."

"Son of a bitch."

"Be careful Michael, your human is showing."

"Funny. Well brother, what is our next move?"

"I am going to go to Green Haven and find out just what the hell is going on."

"Green Haven it is." Michael stated before disappearing right before my eyes.

If the others had gone to Green Haven than Michael knew as well as I did that it meant nothing good. Whether Serenity had gone missing before they made their way there and they had taken off in an effort to find her, or they had gone there of their own volition in an effort to stop things before they began is unclear but what is known is that they wouldn't be dealing with it alone.

It is time to end this once and for all.

Ryan

When Graham came to me and said that instead of just hanging around and waiting for the angels, instead getting a jump start on Lucifer on our own, I wasn't entirely sure how I felt about it. I mean there is no doubt that I want to take him out once and for all but to go at it on our own, I wasn't sure that was the right move.

Not to mention the day Serenity and I had just shared. I wanted to end it on a good note, spending the night in her room with her the way we did before when things seemed to go bad, not where I'm standing now but eventually his argument won out and I decided that in order to have more days and nights like this one with her, I had to stand up and fight now.

So here we are, standing again outside of the church of horrors in Green Haven, deciding between us just what we were going to do next. Not that there is a whole hell of a lot that three relative humans can do. Sure I might have the light and the darkness inside me, which did give me more of an advantage but not much of one when faced with going up against the devil himself.

I should have just stayed with Serenity and waited for Gabriel and Michael to come back. Doing this, something didn't feel right about it and with the bad feeling I'm already beginning to get, I know it's only a matter of time before the concern set in about Serenity as well. Leaving her alone in the room with the promise that I would be right back might have been the stupidest thing I have ever done. If something happened to her while I was here following Graham, I would never forgive myself.

"You need to explain what the three of you are doing here and you need to do it now."

Spinning around I came face to face with the two very angels that only seconds ago I had been regretting not waiting for and neither one of them looked all that happy to see us.

"We got tired of waiting around for word from you and decided it was time to act ourselves."

There aren't many times that I wanted to bury my head in the sand and forget that I had done something or been somewhere I shouldn't have but as Graham said those words and even more so with the way he said them, I wanted to do just that. If I knew anything about the two angels, it was that they wouldn't take kindly to being spoken to that way.

"What is it that a human such as you believes he can do, especially as it pertains to the man that I am sure resides behind those doors now? Have you recently developed superpowers that we are all unaware of?"

Score one for Michael. Covering my mouth with my hand I let the laugh that was hanging on the surface loose, immediately feeling much better about the position I found myself in. At least that is until Gabriel spoke and everything came crashing down around me again.

"In your haste to end this you have all left Serenity alone and vulnerable and now it appears as though she is missing. I am sure that between the three of you, it will be easy to figure out exactly what it is that we believe happened to her. If not I can paint you a very descriptive picture."

"She's...missing?" I choked out, hearing the words but not sure I had heard them right. The overall sick feeling I experienced in doing this was finally starting to make sense. It wasn't the guilt I felt at all, it was the fact that I had left her open and Lucifer had most definitely taken advantage.

"It appears that way yes. When I located you three here, I originally thought that you had come to the same conclusion before my arrival, coming here in an effort to save her. Knowing what I do now thanks to the Hudson boy, I can see that is not the case at all."

"We didn't know he was going to show up while we were gone!" Graham snapped. "We just wanted to do something, even if it was just standing here for awhile and staking the place out for the both of you. Anything that would make it seem like we were doing something to move this thing along."

"Well your impatience has cost you all dearly now hasn't it?" Michael asks before turning and facing me, leveling me with his glare. "It is imperative that we speak with you alone."

Nodding and motioning away from where I stood with both Graham and Emma, I follow behind slowly as both Michael and Gabriel begin moving in the direction I pointed toward, more than a few feet away from the others. When they were positive that they would not be overheard they got right down to business.

"Given what has taken place this evening we think it is time that we come up with a plan, the three of us, moving forward."

"What do you have in mind?"

"At one time you learned of your true destiny as determined by Heaven itself. What Gabriel and I need to know now is that if faced with that same situation again are you willingly to give yourself over?"

"To save Serenity? You're damn right I am."

"It is about more than just Serenity I'm afraid. This is also about achieving your destiny and ridding the world once and for all of Lucifer and the evil at which he has been unleashing for millennia."

"Again, you know my answer Mike. Whatever it takes to end this, you know I'll do it."

"There is more." Gabriel interjected. "This time we will need you to not only be the very thing that ends Lucifer but also the proverbial bait in an effort to learn of Serenity's true location."

These guys were too much. I was going to be bait whether I went in looking for information or to end Lucifer. I am the weaker of the angels after all. All the demonic power I could attain in the world wouldn't be enough to stop them when they were at their full power. Well other then Lucifer himself. He would be the only one able.

"So then just tell me where you want me and let's get on with it."

"We need to remove Graham and Emma from this situation first. You must go to them now and explain that they are no longer needed. We must at all costs protect them in this fight."

"Since when are they not a part of this Gabriel? Didn't the both of you say we needed them on our side to be able to do this at all?"

"Times have changed. They are both the very beings that Lucifer wants nothing more than to destroy. If we put them in harm's way I can make no promises that they will make it out alive. It is for their own well-being that we get them out of here now."

I would do whatever it is they wanted from me if it meant that we could find Serenity. I had been the one to leave her this time, something I swore on more than one occasion before that I would never do and it's up to me to get her back. I not only owe it to the two angels but to Serenity herself.

"You will enter the church once they are gone and you will offer yourself up to Lucifer. It is the only way that we can make this work. In an effort to earn his trust back, or at the very least prove yourself to be the weaker of the both of you and find out where Serenity is, you need to do this."

Put myself on a platter and offer it up to Lucifer knowing just what he wanted to do to me for the betrayal he believes I gave him? Of course this is the thing that I need to do because nothing in my life ever worked out to where I wasn't constantly sacrificing everything.

"Why can't it be one of you?"

"Because I do believe he is going to want to tell you where she is and what he is doing to her. He will enjoy it. You know him as well as we do Ryan, can you imagine it going down quite that way if Gabriel or I enter the church instead?"

He had me there. He might want to destroy all of us one by one but with me, he would definitely want to torture me more than he did his brothers.

"No, I get it Michael. I'll do whatever I have to and I won't stop until I get her back. You can trust me on that."

302

"You will not be alone in this. Where we failed the last time in protecting all involved, this time we will not make the same mistakes. When the time is right, Raphael and Uriel will join us and as one unit we will end this once and for all."

They both seemed so sure of themselves that I felt like an ass having doubts. With everything that happened before, every single time we came up against the king of hell this very same way, I just couldn't get it out of my head that this time would be any different.

Letting Michael's statement float in the tense air around us, I began making my way back to where Graham and Emma stood both of them locked on me as I move, waiting to see just what the next move is. The closer I came to them and inevitably my final act in the war we are about to wage I'm left with one thought, one that no matter how hard I try won't leave me alone.

What if he had already won and turned Serenity?

What are we going to do then?

CHAPTER THIRTY FIVE

Lucifer

If there is one thing that is true about the humans it is just how predictable they are.

He seemed to know nothing of what had actually taken place with Serenity but he had come anyway. I couldn't have planned it better myself. The time had come for Ryan and I to come face to face finally and this time deal with the issues that lingered between us. Having Serenity see the path she had taken only a week beforehand had been brilliant because not only had it given her back to me but it also brought about this delightful turn of events.

Given his feelings for the ball of light that is now preparing again to take her rightful place by my side, it is no surprise that he is here now and making his way toward me, his face giving away the true anger that still resides within him. It is obvious he is not here to bow before me though the anger flowing through him now did speak to his ability to accept what he truly is.

Ryan McGregor would always be a demon despite everything he had done in an effort to prove otherwise and the anger is only just the first step in his acceptance. Once he let his anger take control it would be then that the other facets that made him the perfect companion for me over the years would become apparent again. I want him bathed in his sins. It made my heart sing at the thought.

It is entirely possible that I can have the best of both worlds moving forward. First, in taking Serenity as my bride but also claiming Ryan as my own. If things move forward the way they are appearing I could most certainly go back to my original plan and make the man my true vessel. It really would be the perfect ending.

"We need to talk."

Oh this is delightful. He truly believes that we are still in the stages of being able to talk all this out.

"The time for talking has long passed Ryan; I would have thought you more than anyone knew that. I finally have everything I want and there is nothing that can be said to change it."

"You're wrong. You don't have everything, not yet."

The time for talking may have long since passed but I couldn't deny that he intrigued me. I am unaware of anything that I still need to obtain given that I had the greatest gift of all in my possession. The very woman he himself loves.

"Do tell me what it is that you can offer me now that I do not already own or will own once everything has come to pass."

"Me."

"What makes you think that I want you? There may have been a time where I wanted nothing more than to be joined with you moving forward but just as the need to speak has passed, so has that."

"I know you can feel it Lucifer. The power I have in my possession, both from my time in Heaven and that which you gave to me, having me partake of Serenity in the way that I did all of those months ago. You can deny it all you want but you know deep inside that I can still be of use to you."

"You accuse me of having ulterior motives in every decision I make and that is a fact that I cannot deny but I also believe the same of you as you stand here now. So what pre tell do you want in return Ryan?"

"I want to know where Serenity is."

"I am deeply sorry but that will be information you will never learn. You see Ryan, she is no longer yours. She has joined with me willingly in the ways at which you never truly could accomplish."

I can tell he didn't want to believe my words and that was fine. He didn't have to believe them. When Serenity finally made her presence known there would be no denial as she would be the one to end his faith in her once and for all. I would entertain him for just a little longer though.

"Prove it."

"Time will prove it for me my son."

His silence now is delightful. It means he understands my position and can even see where things are headed. In time he would come face to face with Serenity again and in that moment everything I am now saying would become clear. He would indeed lose her forever and it would be to me no less. The very person he had come here to destroy.

"I have the ability to give you the one thing that you have desired for months. I will give myself over to you willingly, no fighting, to do as you see fit with me, whether that be torture or something even more severe. All I ask is that you allow me to see her one last time."

It is no secret that I have desired nothing more than to make him pay for his betrayal since the day we stood in this very church and he chose the side of redemption and light over the plan I had put in place for his life. Standing before him now this way I wanted nothing more than to end him but I also couldn't help but see parts of me in him which prevented me from moving forward.

"You want to give yourself over to me in exchange for one last moment in time with Serenity? Even though I have told you that she no longer sees things in the way that you do?"

He nodded and I found myself mulling over the idea. Maybe it is possible that in giving in to the half demon's request I could kill two birds with the one stone as it were. In standing before Serenity again, for the final time, he would be able to see just what side she resides on kand she might even do what I have been unable to do up until this very moment.

She could end him once and for all.

"I do have reservations in doing this but I cannot deny that the exchange at which you are attempting to barter does interest me. So Ryan, I will give you Serenity's location in exchange for you giving over the very light that burns bright within you, so that I may do as I see fit."

Ryan

I really didn't think it would be that easy. When I walked into the church I expected to find him just the way I had but in giving

306

myself over to him this way in an effort to find Serenity and even one last time trying to save her, I expected much more of a fight.

We don't trust each other anymore. This man that I have looked up to for as long as I could remember is now standing in front of me and agreeing to one last request, despite the lack of trust. All I know is that in agreeing he has given me and the angels that would soon be joining me exactly what we needed moving forward.

"She remains in the location to which we placed her during our first time standing in this very place."

There is only one place he kept her in the church during our first time here and as much as I want to run from the room and go to her now, I know I can't. He was keeping her in the bible study room that had been turned into the place that she used to get ready for our wedding. I don't know why it surprised me but if he had taken her against her will I would have assumed she would be chained and gagged in the basement much the way that he had done with Graham.

Is it possible that he's telling me the truth and Serenity really is here by her own choice?

"I can see the wheels turning in your mind Ryan and what you cannot bring yourself to believe is very much indeed what has come to pass. She is indeed here of her own choice and will remain here in the very same capacity."

If he's right then I have to figure out a way to get her out of here. She might not want to go willingly or even able to given the branding that he placed on her heart but I would do whatever it took to get out of here regardless. I could not let this be her fate. Whatever he had done to her caused this and I needed to make her see that before it was too late. I could not let her join with him forever, not when she is meant for so much more.

The doors to the church blew open then and the light immediately spilled in, signaling the arrival of the other part of my plan. I had done as the angels requested and given myself over the fallen angel himself and now it was up to them to create enough of a diversion so that I could get out of here and get to Serenity.

"As always little brother, you have taken the predictable route again. What is it about this girl that makes you all seem to lose the rational parts of yourselves?"

I expected it to only be Michael and Gabriel moving toward us but now I could easily see that it was not. They were not alone, this time the other archangels were with them, their brothers, side by side, more than prepared to fight. The level of light in the room was unheard of and I was completely taken off guard at the sight of it.

With renewed strength given the immense power that seemed to surround me I turned back and faced the only father I had ever known and this time, my expression was not one of surrender but one of fight and what I could only hope was victory.

"You act as though I did not expect this Ryan and in that regard I can assure you that it will your undoing because as you well know, I always plan ahead for everything."

"Ryan...move now! Go find Serenity and get her out of here."

Just like the way he had been in Hell, I heard Michael's voice in my head as clearly as if he had said the words while standing right beside me. Before I could follow his orders and move out of the way I saw Lucifer open his hands and the bright light take form.

Fire.

Thrown back from the force of the blow, I felt the sharp pain and heat as my body became engulfed in the flames until after a few seconds everything seemed to go numb.

"Ryan, open your eyes!" the voice screamed at me and doing as it asked, I slowly began to pull my eyelids apart even though with each passing second the pain became increasingly worse only making me want to close them again.

"This is one of the times that using elemental power has its advantages I would believe." Raphael said to me, a smirk playing on his face. "Now do as Michael said and find Serenity. We will take care of our brother, at least to the best of our ability."

Placing his hand on my chest, I saw the light begin to take form, slowly starting at the very place his hands lay and moving up until it surrounded me completely. I have no idea what he's doing but wanting nothing more than to find Serenity now, I stood to my feet and with one last look at the angel that had again come to my rescue, I moved, more determined than ever to get to my destination.

The closer I got to the edge of the room I turned one last time and looked behind me as the war raged on between the brothers. Michael and Uriel had taken point nearest to Lucifer, leveling him with not only their power but the brute strength as they attacked him with their blades.

It was as I turned back focused again on what I had to do that I heard the voice crystal clear in my mind, this time not from Michael or even from Raphael but from Gabriel himself.

"You are being protected by the very light of God. Go forth and do whatever it takes to save her Ryan. It is all up to you now."

Serenity

I need to do something. I cannot let it all end this way.

I can feel both of them as if they stand here in the room with me yet there are nowhere near me. I can hear their voices through the door as I stand and wait for what comes next. I know what I have to do no matter who walks through that door and it is only a matter of time before someone does.

It can only be one of two people and I am not sure who I want it to be more. There is on the one hand Ryan who over the last year of my life has brought light and darkness into my life all in the name of love and then we have Lucifer who I am bound to yet even if I wasn't I am not entirely sure I could turn away from.

There is a side to him that no one is willing to see and somehow in my time with him I have been able to see through it all. The façade he puts on in an effort to appear as though he is untouched by everything that he has been through and also that which he has caused the millions of others he had put himself into contact with. I have gotten past his walls and I believe I have seen into the light that still remains inside of him even though it is buried so deeply under years of bullshit and anger.

He did not take away my love for Ryan which even now still burns so strongly inside of me it is as if it is part of the very makeup of what I am. I can feel the pull to him from here, wanting nothing more than to leave this room, run to him and save him from what will obviously be another sacrifice attempt in an effort to do the right thing, not only by me but by the world. Yet I cannot do that, at least not yet. Not until Lucifer and this attachment I feel with him is completely taken from me.

It causes no small degree of anguish being unable to do the one thing I know I can do if just given a chance. If I could have my way right in this moment I would simply wish and want for one thing and one thing only.

To save both of them.

He should have taken that part away from me when he had the chance. I do not want to feel this way, pulled in two different directions by two separate entities that stand for such opposite things yet fight for the same very thing. Me.

It is to be my destiny to end Lucifer's reign yet it is also Ryan's. Somewhere along the way our destinies have clashed and caused what now takes place just outside of this door. In falling for me he has gone against everything that once upon a time he believed in and what made him distinctly him. He is torn apart from the only family he has ever truly known all in an effort to fight for the existence that he should have had within the light. He has to be the one to level Lucifer with the final blow and I need to be the one to let him yet it is something that I cannot do.

The devil himself believes my destiny to be one of a more basic design. That I am in fact not meant to end him but to join him and in doing so we can right the wrongs that he believes so strongly his father created when making the planet I now call home. Somewhere along the way I found myself agreeing with that and wanting nothing more than to be what he needs me to be even though there is still a small part of me fighting and warning me that it's wrong.

It isn't wrong though, not to me. How can someone with the light within them be wrong? Sure he hasn't always done the right thing and his need to get revenge overrides the light more often than not but there is still light in him and as long as that light is there I want to tap into it. I want to use it and be the very thing that ends this once and for all but not in the way that Heaven wishes of me.

I want to use it to save him and bring him home.

"Holy shit…it's true."

Turning at the sound I come face to face with one of the very men I had just been thinking about, his clothing seemingly burnt which only left me questioning just what had taken place before he made his way here.

God I hate this. I can't even figure out who I'm more worried about.

"What's true?" I ask, deciding to leave my concern over his current state until later and deal with the statement that had been made as he entered the room.

"You did come with him willingly."

"You mean to tell me that given everything you have learned in the last twenty four hours that you did not expect that to be the case? It is the very reason you left me alone was it not?"

"What the hell has gotten into you Ser? Why are you talking like that? What did he do to you?"

"He did nothing but remind of exactly what took place during my stay with him."

"You say that like you just went across the street to his house or something. Holy fuck, it's even worse than I thought. He took you to Hell for Christ's sakes, not out for some tea."

"I am well aware of what has taken place Ryan; there is no need to explain it to me like I am some kind of idiot and you would be better served not using those words around me again in the future. I may not exactly agree with it but I do understand the angel's insistence now."

"You're kidding me right? You of all people are going to get on me for using God's name when you're going against him in order to be here with Lucifer and end everything?"

"I am merely here to make sure that things are put right again. The way they should have been all along."

"The world ending, that's putting everything right again?"

311

No that isn't what I believe in my heart will make everything right again but I couldn't deny that it made sense. In taking out the world it would rid it of all the darkness both what hadn't been created by Lucifer and what had. It was horrible and tragic but I could see the need for having it happen.

"What did he do to you? Where is the girl I fell in love with? "

"She is still here Ryan; she is standing before you now. Surely even you can see that."

"No she's not. He did something to her because the woman I love would not go along with this even if she is branded and forced. She would still choose to stand and fight beside me and her family. You do remember them don't you Serenity? The very people out there now, fighting that son of a bitch in order to save you and what he wants to do to the world."

"Please tell me some of what I'm saying is getting through to you and that you haven't been turned completely!" he said, his last statement coming out in a shout, a clear effort to try and get to me.

What he didn't realize is that he is getting through to me even without raising his voice. I knew what is right and what is wrong despite also seeing the other side of things. I did not want to end the world any more then I wanted Lucifer to end the family Ryan just mentioned but I also know there is no other way around it. Everything had to happen this way.

He made a move toward me and though I could have easily seen it for the pleading maneuver that it is I saw it as so much more. If he believes that I have been turned then there is nothing stopping him from ending me here and now and the closer he came to me, his face never changing the more real it became.

Backing up as quickly as possible, bumping into the table as he continued slowly moving toward me, I saw it. Gleaming with the light that shone in from the street lights outside I saw the one thing that could stop him right in his tracks and not wasting a second I immediately picked it up and turned again to face him this time making my position more than clear.

The shock in his eyes told me everything I needed to know. He had known the weapon was there, it wasn't like it was hidden but he can't believe that I would actually pick it up the way I did

312

and turn it on him. Knowing that my choice pained him and due to the close proximity and the way I still felt about him, it pained me too.

"Well pretty girl," he called to me his eyes locked on mine. "Looks like it's time to make a choice."

CHAPTER THIRTY SIX

Gabriel

When Ryan had been thrown across the room under the weight of Lucifer's power I thought that it would be the end of him. That a force that strong would be too much for the half demon and he would indeed perish under the weight of it. It is not the way things were supposed to go but there was no doubt as his body crumpled to the floor that it was indeed what was going to take place.

At least that is how it appeared until Raphael had used his own power to save him. That is when everything changed.

Now it was the four of us fighting against the brother that at one point we wanted no more than to save and I am left here praying that in the meantime Ryan would be able to get through to Serenity and break whatever hold my brother held over her. It is the only way that any of us would make it out of this alive, or at the very least, less damaged than we were going to be.

Fighting alongside Michael, Raphael and Uriel this way should have brought me comfort but it only seemed to tear me up inside because going into this I knew more than they did and I had made a vow to the very person we are now attempting to save not to allow any of them to know even though with their help we might be able to have things turn out differently.

I had located Serenity shortly after Ryan entered the church to sacrifice himself. I had broken away from Michael, explaining to him that I wanted to be sure that Graham and Emma had made it safely back out of the city but in actuality had gone to her instead.

A plan had been formed during my time with her and even though we were still very much following the plan Michael and I had set forth with Ryan, I also knew that I would need to break away at any moment in order to complete my end of the one I had made with Serenity. I could not let what she planned to do come to pass without intervening the way I had promised.

*****

"Gabriel, what are you doing here?" she asked as she caught sight of me standing behind her through the mirror.

"I came to get you out of here. I know that you have been branded but Serenity we cannot do this without you and I am prepared to take you by force."

"You can't do that Gabe."

"Serenity you are unaware of what I can really do so you cannot speak on it. Now come with me willingly or I will take you in whatever manner I have to forcefully."

"No you see, you can't do that and it's not because of the branding. I know all about that now. It's because he knows what you're planning and if you attempt to take me from here he will kill Ryan right where he stands now."

I had not been expecting that. If Serenity is explaining this to me now it means that she isn't entirely under the control of the man that Ryan faced in the chapel. She was still very much guided by the light inside of her but more than that, her love for him.

"What is to happen if I leave you here? Has Lucifer explained to you what he has planned?"

"He wants me to kill Ryan...Gabriel he is going to willingly let him find me so that I have to kill him. I want to fight it but there is this urge inside of me that I can't explain. I need to see Ryan's blood spilled."

"That is the bond between you and Lucifer. His bloodlust has been transferred to you and he has put you in an impossible position."

No matter what avenue we took from this moment onward Ryan's fate had been sealed. It was his grand design to see the very demon that had betrayed him for love destroyed and now it was only a matter of whether he did it himself or he left it to Serenity.

"I know everything now Gabriel, all of it. I chose to be with Lucifer and the only reason I am even here now is because he had a bigger plan for all of us and needed to use me to get it."

315

I had been right all along. It had been my fallen brother's goal to make the world crumble down around us by ripping us all apart one by one and using Serenity to do it. We played into his hands until I learned of it but now just as before it appeared as though I had learned of it too late. The damage, no matter how strong we all were as a unit now was done.

It was in that moment I knew what needed to be done. It all came down to this moment now and in this one regard, I would not fail. I would make sure that both Ryan and Serenity reached their true destinies and that Lucifer was stopped once and for all.

"Why are you looking at me like that Gabriel?"

"I believe I have found a way out of your dilemma but it is not something that you are going to want to hear."

"Will it save Ryan? Will it break whatever this is with Lucifer? Will it save the world? Because if it can even do one of those things then I want to hear it."

"If done correctly it can do them all."

"Then tell me."

If there was any feeling in her now towards me than what I am about to say would upset her greatly but I knew that once she moved past the upset that she would see the logic in the situation and it is my hope that she would come to terms with it and move forward with me.

I wanted to do this but it is more than just a want, it was also a need. I needed to fix everything that from the very moment I had revealed myself to her I had broken. I had to save her.

"We need to continue on as planned, on both of our parts. You must continue on as you have been in your concern for both Lucifer and Ryan. You must do whatever it takes to make sure that Lucifer has no idea that you are faltering in the plan the both of you have agreed on. You must make Ryan believe that Lucifer has indeed won."

"Okay but then what?"

"You must make it seem as though you have killed Ryan."

"No! No way Gabriel. I am not going to hurt him."

"You are conflicted are you not? You want to see Ryan die at your hand yet the love at which you have for him prevents you

from doing it. This is the only way we can fix things and set them right."

"You want me to kill Ryan and then what Gabriel? The minute I do it he's dead. How does that stop anything that Lucifer put in place?"

"It does so because he will not die. I will save him."

"How?"

"Leave that to me angelo ragazza. Just make sure that you do as I have said. I will determine the rest."

*****

I had chosen in the very last moment to keep the real truth from her. It is going to be hard enough for her coming to terms with what she has to do now, I did not want her thinking about the lengths I was about to go to in order to make sure that the proper end is reached. I know her after all of this time and I know that she would never stand for it, whether it saved the world or not.

It was also going to be my gift to the both of them. It had been far too long since the light had blessed either of them and if it took me doing this in the manner at which I was about to in order to bring them some peace then I would gladly do it as many times as needed. There were no other two beings alive that deserved it more.

Lucifer is struggling against the power of my three brothers, all of whom are focused on the singular goal of weakening him just enough so that I can bring Ryan in to finish what he had planned to do from the start. It could only be him to finish off the dark angel and now that my brothers seemed to have things under control it was time for me to put the final stage of the plan in motion.

The final stage that only I know about.

Ryan

Everyone has a list of things they hope to never see in their lifetime and I am now standing face to face with mine.

317

Serenity in front of me with the blade held out in front of her, determination in her eyes is most definitely the one thing in my entire life that I never wanted to see. Yet it's happening and even though in telling her that she had a choice, I hoped she would realize just what she is about to do, it seems as though it isn't hitting home.

"You don't want to do this pretty girl. Please, fight this."

"I'm sorry Ryan, I can't do that. You are the very thing that stands between me and the peace I have wanted for the last twenty one years."

Is that what Lucifer offered her? Eternal peace if she did away with me the way he wanted? Didn't she see through this? There is nothing peaceful about life with Lucifer whether he adored you or not. It was always just going to be an existence filled with pain and agony, even if the world was taken out of the equation. He didn't know any better.

"You're not going to put the blame on me for your life Serenity. It doesn't work that way."

"My life might have been screwed up before you Ryan but until you dropped that bombshell on me a year ago I would have dealt with it. That is your fault."

I can't believe I'm hearing her say this to me and she is showing no signs of it being a lie at all. I can see right through her and she's being honest with me. It's killing me because she is just confirming things I already thought myself. I had been the very thing that had taken her into this life and if I had just left her alone none of this would be happening now.

"You don't mean that…" I say my voice pleading, silently praying at the same time that whatever is making her say these things would be washed away and I could get the woman I love back again. I wasn't a real big fan of the Serenity she had become and it had nothing to do with the truth she spoke.

She began moving towards me, gripping the blade even more firmly in her hands, this time as if she was on a mission. It's clear to me the closer she comes that just like it had been my doing in the church when I had taken her life in an effort to defeat Lucifer, it was now happening again, only this time, in reverse.

318

Serenity would be the very thing that ended me and as the realization hit, so did the fact that if it had to end, this is the way it needed to be done. I wanted her to be the one to end me. Finally coming to terms with what had to happen next I moved myself toward her at a more rapid pace than the one she was taking and as the blade hung out in front of her, I did the only thing I could.

With as much force as I could muster I threw my body into her, watching and waiting for the weight of the blade to slice through me.

I made the ultimate sacrifice.

Serenity

No.No.No.No.No.

This cannot be happening right now. I had been putting it off even after I grabbed the weapon, wanting to go along with everything Gabriel wanted me too in making him believe that he really couldn't get through to me but it still ended up this way.

The minute the blade sliced not only through his shirt but made its way into his body I knew that I had done the unthinkable. What I wanted more than anything, the very thing that fueled me in moving forward before is now crumbling down around me and would never come to pass. I could not save them both, because I wasn't strong enough. I couldn't even save myself.

As he began to fall, his body finally giving into the pain from the blade that now lay frozen in place in the middle of his chest; I grabbed on to him and held on for dear life. What I had been putting off in continuing the conversation and taking slow steps toward him, he had finished off by throwing his body into the blade before I could. As much as Gabriel wanted me to do it, I wasn't entirely sure I would have gone through with it but Ryan had taken the choice away from me, again doing the very thing that made me love him in the first place, sacrificing himself.

Where the hell is Gabriel? I could feel the life draining from him with each passing second I held him in my arms as we had both fallen to our knees now. If the angel didn't show up soon there would be nothing left to save and Ryan would be lost to me forever. As much as I could still feel the connection between Lucifer and me deep inside, I knew that the love I had for Ryan won out over all of it.

It could not end this way. Not when we planned it all so differently.

I felt the tears begin to fall from my eyes, one after the other in rapid succession and felt my throat immediately begin to seize up with the reality of the situation I found myself in. I had made him believe the worst in me and now he's paying for my lie and I hadn't even been the one to plunge the proverbial knife right into his back.

I really am bound for the darkness after all. Nothing can save me now.

Gabriel

The scene I walked into when I entered the room was much the way I expected it to be. Serenity on her knees, cradling Ryan as closely as possible as the blade remained protruding from his chest, the blood within him slowly pouring out around it and making its way down and onto the both of them.

There could be no time wasted in what happened now. In my effort to get away from the battle that still raged beyond those doors I had taken longer than expected and now it appeared as though Ryan himself is paying the price. I could only hope that I was not too late to fix all of this in the way that I wanted.

"You did it."

"No Gabriel, I didn't. I was trying to kill time until you showed up and he threw himself into the blade. He did it but he did it because he honestly thought that there was no getting through to me. He did it again to save me even though that's the last thing I deserve."

"Serenity now is not the time to be filled with doubt. I assure you that you will get your chance to make all of this right again but you must trust me and do as I say from here on out alright?"

"What choice do I have?" she cried and as she attempted to wipe at her eyes I saw the stains that streaked her face and knew

320

that just as I had suspected, Lucifer had indeed not gotten his way with the ball of heavenly light. Even faced with a situation such as this she still chose her love for Ryan above all else.

It just gave me even further proof that what had to come next is indeed the right step to take.

"You need to let him go Serenity…"

"Can't you fix him like this? I don't want to let him go Gabriel."

"Judging from the blood loss and the life force within him draining away, if you want to save him then you need to let him go now and let me do what I came here to do. Please Serenity do this for me."

Not even questioning it she began to stand, making sure as she did that his body fell to the floor softly. Though I knew the man would feel none of this, I understood why she moved in the manner she did and felt even more than ever before just how much love she had for him.

Now is the time that I needed to tell her everything. Inform her of everything that I am about to do so that she would be able to handle it as I saved the man she loves but I found that I could not do it. I needed to take this secret with me to the grave. By the time she realized just what happened I would be long gone, the way that it needed to be.

"I need you to do something for me and you must not question it. Just do it."

"What?"

"Focus your heart and your mind on the very light inside of you. Use that and reach into me and pull out my light. Serenity I know that it will make no sense to you but this is the only thing that can save him now. He is too far gone even for normal healing."

It wasn't exactly the truth but I knew that in showing her that there is no other alternative that she would do as I asked without question, something that if I judged purely based on the controlled look that came over her face now, she was going to do. Within seconds I felt the pull as she reached into the deepest parts of me and pulled at the very light that I needed in order to save the man before me now.

"You must put it into Ryan now Serenity…." I said my voice choking on every word as the very light that made me the warrior I am was pulled from my body, the agony of which is almost too much to bear.

I watched as she proceeded to do as I instructed and placed the light into Ryan's body and the very last thing I saw as the light began to fade around me was Ryan as his body adapted to the life force that is now free to make itself at home inside of him. As his body moved I let myself finally relax and accept what would come next.

I had succeeded in my goal.

Ryan

When I threw my body into the blade I thought for sure that would be the end of me. That the last sight I would ever get to see would be Serenity as she had been standing before me. She may not have been my Serenity anymore but the way she looked, she would always be that girl to me and that is how I would remember her, looking just as beautiful as she had the first day I saw her.

That's not what's happening now though. I can feel it. Something is going on inside of me, a power that I have never known before; giving me a strength I haven't been able to feel since my time with Lucifer. I feel fine. Absolutely fine.

I can hear her voice. It sounds muffled but even if I was completely without hearing I know I would be able to hear it because it belongs to her. She is screaming and out of the corner of my half opened eyes I can see her pounding her fists into the floor and it makes no sense to me. She is crying, I can hear that as her sobs choke the screaming but I have no idea what for.

Is she reacting to what she did to me? Is she really still the same Serenity that I fell in love with and not the dark one of Lucifer's design after all?

"Serenity…" I manage to choke out though even to my own ears it sounds garbled and weak. I need answers to a whole lot of questions now swirling around in my brain and she is the only one that can give them to me. That is, if I can get her to stop wailing away on the floor the way she still seems to be doing.

"Pretty girl please…"

She turns then and seeing me she immediately ceases in her physical action, sliding herself across the floor quickly until she is all I can see in my line of vision. I see the tear stain marks on her face, as well as the drawn in lines on her forehead, the picture of the stress she is under at which I can only assume is her loss of me. Even with all of that she looks as beautiful as ever, my true light in the darkness.

"Ry…oh my god, it worked."

"What…worked?"

"Gabriel, he came and…Oh god Gabriel." She says, the sobs coming again, this time so powerfully I have no idea what to say or do in order to make them stop. If Gabriel had shown up and done something to save me than why is she so distraught?

"What about Gabe?"

"Ryan, he didn't tell me…he did this and he didn't tell me what it meant!"

"Ser...Breathe please."

"He sacrificed himself for you and I had no idea that is what he was doing!" she cried out and the minute the words fell from her lips I knew what they meant. Gabriel had come to her and in an effort to save me for her, given his own life up. That's what the strange feeling of strength is inside of me. It was not healing as I assumed but the power of the archangel himself.

"Gabriel…is dead?"

She nodded, the tears falling down her face again and finally, using the strength that the angel afforded me I began to sit up from my position on the floor, pulling her immediately into my body and stroking her back as she finally let the sobs come forward again.

Only minutes before I had been face to face with the woman I loved and truly believed that I had lost her to the darkness but now I knew differently. Whatever had been said between us before I had thrown myself into the blade hadn't been real. This, now, the way it's happening is what's real.

"You're right you know. None of what I said was real. I only said it because it needed to be said in order for things to happen the way Gabriel wanted."

"What do you mean?"

She pulled away from me and not only did my body feel the loss but so did my heart. Even though I know she's only doing it in an effort to explain to me exactly what happened during the time I thought I was dead, I'm still raw from her words despite knowing deep down that they aren't based in reality.

"Gabriel came to me earlier Ryan. I told him the plans Lucifer made and he countered with one of his own. I went along with it because I thought it would be the only real way to save you but I swear to god I just thought he was going to heal you, not do this."

"What exactly did he do?"

I needed to know. I am aware of what happens to an angel when they die, just as I am aware of the true death as it pertains to the other side with demons and I needed to know if what Serenity witnessed was in fact what she believed it to be. I needed to know if he did indeed die and save me with his own light.

"He told me to use my power, to focus on it and to reach into him…god Ry, I can't even talk about this…"

"I need you to try Serenity, I need to know."

"He told me reach inside him, to pull his light out, his life force I guess. When I did what he said he told me to put it into you the same way. If I had known that doing it was going to kill him though…"

It should have bothered me hearing her basically tell me that if she had known differently she wouldn't have done it but it didn't. That is just who Serenity really is. She cared about Gabriel even if they had never been on the same page in terms of the bond between them and she really did believe him to be the family I mentioned earlier when attempting to stop her from going to the edge. I understood the way she felt because I wouldn't have let him do it to save me either.

"He sacrificed himself for me in order for me to finish what Lucifer started…"

"What do you mean?"

"I need to get back out there. I need to end this once and for all."

"No you don't! It's supposed to be me remember? I'm supposed to be the one to set things right."

 I couldn't exactly argue with it given what I know her destiny to be but given Lucifer's power level and exactly where it originated from, the original plan that should have taken place months before needed to happen now. It had to be me to finish him off but that didn't mean that Serenity couldn't still play a very big part in making it happen.

"Maybe it isn't supposed to be just one of us Ser."

'What do you mean?"

"Maybe it's supposed to be the both of us. Especially now with what Gabriel has just done for me, for us…I think that we need to do this together and I've got an idea how."

"So what's the plan?" she asked, her mind obviously coming to terms with just what my words really mean. It had always been about us, whether together or apart and now is no different. Only this time we were going to come up with a plan together and we were going to make it work in order to end everything once and for all.

This time we would not fail.

Serenity

There had been this one time when I was four that my mother thought it would be fun to take me to the community pool and try to teach me how to swim. It really hadn't been that bad of an idea except that she wanted to do it the hard way. It would just be me and her, no air filled floating devices of any kind. Needless to say that her plan hadn't exactly turned out the way she hoped because in believing that I was indeed floating on my own after holding on to me for a period of time she let me go and I had almost drowned.

325

I had been underwater for maybe two minutes before being saved by the lifeguard that was on duty at the time but in going through that experience it had given me a tool that I am now going to have to use for the first time in years.

When Ryan laid out the plan to me I hadn't exactly been sure I would be able to pull it off but when he explained to me that it would only be a few actual minutes that I would need to actually appear as though I was dead, I remembered that day at the pool and instantly found the strength to move forward.

I don't know how we managed to do it but I knew as he held me in his arms, moving forward into the chapel to where we would find Lucifer fighting against the very brothers that months before had mourned his passing, that as long as I held up on what I knew needed to happen next, we would get through this.

His blood covered my shirt, and the very blade that I had only minutes before used on him is protruding from a delicately placed hole that went straight through to where it barely pierced my skin. It really did appear as though Ryan did what he is about to claim he did and had taken my life.

Even though it's supposed to appear as though I'm not breathing and my eyes need to remain closed, I can sense the lights around me, figuring it to be the battle waging on before our very eyes and I find myself hoping that we do not become casualties of it before our goal can be reached.

"Lucifer stop!" I hear Ryan call out, just as we planned and as we both suspected, the shadow of the lights I have barely been able to sense seems to cease and Ryan continues making his way forward, each step bringing me one step closer to the end.

"You fool! What have you done?"

"Well she put up a valiant fight which I'm sure is exactly what you expected of her but she is no match for me."

As Ryan spoke so coldly of what had supposedly taken place in the room, I couldn't help but get a full view of exactly what it is he must have felt hearing me say the horrible things I said to him minutes before he plunged the blade deep into himself. When we got out of this and we would be getting out of this, I was going to make up for every word I said so that he never doubted my loyalties again.

"As you can see, just as she was the first time, she is as beautiful in death as she is in life. I feel it only my right to bring her to you now as she does indeed belong to you."

I felt him kneel and before I could prepare myself, I felt the cold air blast in around me as he placed me on the floor directly in front of Lucifer just as we planned and took a few steps back.

"Nooooo!!" I hear the fallen angel cry as I feel myself again being scooped up into arms, though not the pure ones I had felt only seconds before. These arms belong to the very man I had been hoping I could have saved and failed at.

He began placing kisses all over my face and I held my breath as long as humanly possible. The minute his lips pressed to mine though, I felt everything begin to shift and I let out the breath I had been holding onto so tightly, which immediately brought his attention to me and my apparently fake death.

"Serenity? My belle…I can feel the breath within you, please fight."

I thought he would figure out what we attempted to do but it appeared as though he still remained very much in the dark, which only worked in our favor with what had to come next. As if perfectly on cue with the thoughts in my mind, I felt the room begin to shift with the power that had just been released and before I knew it, found myself falling until I landed hard on my back, directly at the bottom of the stairs.

Opening my eyes just slightly and taking in the room around me, I saw Lucifer begin to fall from his standing position as more power is leveled at him from all directions. As he fell to his knees directly in front of me, I did the only thing in that moment that I could and I focused again just the way Gabriel taught me and following suit, brought out my own burst of power that took him immediately from his knees to his back on the floor.

"Now Ryan! You have to do it now!" I screamed as I began crawling on my knees quickly, finally standing up when I was far enough away not the feel the damage. As soon as I was out of the line of fire, I saw him move and as if it happened out of thin air, I

327

see a silver blade in his hands as he found himself standing directly above Lucifer, his eyes steeled, all traces of the black lining gone, despite the anger I knew is flooding through him.

"Despite what you think, this isn't for Heaven. This is for Gabriel, you selfish son of a bitch. Burn in the hell you created forever."

As his words came out in a scream, he plunged the blade down quickly but before I could run to him, he pulled it back out, repeating the motion over and over again. It wasn't until he pulled it out from Lucifer's chest one final time, moving it upwards that I knew what was about to come next.

Running to him just as he brought the blade down one final time, the sound of it as it hit the skull of the vessel he had been commanding turning my stomach, I stopped directly behind him turning away from the sight. As much as I don't want to admit it, I had come to care for Lucifer; at least in the most basic of ways and seeing him destroyed, as happy as it makes me, is something I couldn't entirely take. As he brought the blade up in the air again, I reached out, unsure of what was guiding me but knowing it was the right thing to do.

Placing my hand on his arm, I brought it back down from its raised position in the air. It's only as he turned into my body allowing me to hold him that we finally took a breath without fear for the first time since it all began.

Today we have done as Gabriel attempted to a year before. We won because even though we were all at some point shrouded in darkness, we did as God intended all along and just turned on the light.

It's finally over…

EPILOGUE

Ryan

Gabriel gave me a gift.

It's a gift that no matter how long I live from this point on, or even how I live I will never entirely be able to pay back. It is a big enough deal on its own that he gave up his life so that I could spend the remainder of mine with the woman that despite the way it all played out, both of us love. I use the word love because even with his passing, I don't think he will ever stop loving her just as I know beyond the shadow of a doubt that I won't either.

My final words to Lucifer before I took his life still remain true. As much as I know that ending him had been what Heaven wanted, I didn't do it for them. I didn't even do it for me or even Serenity. I did it for Gabriel. For everything he had gone through during his time defending us against the brother at that one point I know he loved more than life itself. I did it for the very sacrifice he made in giving up his life. I did it for everything that he stood for and even though he is no longer with us, I know that from his place, where angels end up when they pass, he is looking down on me with a smile.

With each passing day I am learning just what he did making the decision he made. He didn't just give up his existence in order to save mine. He gave up the very bond that he shared with Serenity, passing it to me instead. I will never understand what brought him to that point where he felt that it deserved to be with me more than him but it is just another thing that I am thankful for.

With or without the bond I would have loved her until my dying breath, I know that. It is just that easy. There will never be another human being alive that can make me feel the way that she does. That can bring out the goodness in me, or as she calls it, my light. She not only inspires feelings in me that I believed to be long dead but she also inspires me in other ways. I now know what I want to do with my life and it is as far away from the original path my life was taking as it can get. I want to be the person that she

329

sees and that I know is inside me, even though up until recently it had been buried pretty far down.

Three months has passed since that day in the church and things are finally now getting back to normal. I have concerns about Serenity and her state of mind moving forward but in the moments when we're alone and she looks at me with that smile, the one she reserves strictly for me, my concerns just seem to fade and I am filled with an overwhelming feeling of peace and more than that, one of love.

I know she is affected by what happened that night just as I am. Not only did she grow to care for the fallen angel during her time with him but she saw parts of him that I have also seen though we differ in our reactions because they are parts that I saw erased in him over time and for her they were fresh and new again. The only way I know to help her moving forward is in allowing her to talk about it. It's hard hearing that the person you love has been so affected by another especially when that other person's sole goal throughout time has been to destroy you but I do it for her because I know that it's what Gabriel would have done and lately I have been feeling more like him than ever before.

Saying that I miss him seems so wrong because in actuality even though our sole purposes seem to be the same, we were always on opposite sides. Not a day passes that I don't miss him. I think it's made worse because Michael seems to have pulled away completely after learning of the loss. I understand why the elder angel is doing it this way but it doesn't make it hurt any less. Whether he wants to believe it or not, we are all family and right now we need each other. It's the only way we are ever going to move forward.

On the other end of things it appears as though there might be another secret revealed sooner rather than later as it pertains to our very human friends. In succeeding in keeping them safe, they are both now free to move forward and I only hope for both of their sakes that it is together, despite the bond that will always remain between Graham and Serenity. In the same way that I have always just known I needed her in my life, I know that Graham and Emma need the same thing and I only hope they are able to achieve it.

It's time.

I can hear the sound of church bells off in the distance and instead of filling me with dread as they have been for the last year, now all I can sense as I hear them is the future and what comes next. In a few weeks I'm going to be taking yet another step toward the light in taking Serenity as my wife, this time in the way I always imagined it for her. There is a difference this time around though and it has nothing to do with a white dress and reciting some vows.

This time it's not only me that gets to marry the girl of his dreams. Gabriel does too.

Serenity

No one knows this but I'm not alright.

I put on a brave face and I go through the motions and appear as though I'm handling everything the way a normal person should but that isn't the case at all and if I don't do something about it soon, I'm pretty sure it is going to rip me apart from the inside out.

When Graham was missing and no one could find him, it felt like there was this part of me missing. Like it had been completely ripped out and I wouldn't feel right until it had been put back where it belongs. In finding him we had done that but this time, it's happening again and nothing that anyone says or does can fix it.

Gabriel is dead and he isn't going to come back and no matter how many books I read about loss or listen to other people speak of it, it just never heals. It gets worse in the times where I remember that he did it and never even warned me. I want to believe he did it to protect me because he knew that I wouldn't let him go through with it if I'd known but because the loss is so heavy I find myself at times mad at him for not trusting me enough.

In the moments where I'm not mad though, I remember exactly what in giving up his life he gave me back in return and it just makes my heart hurt. I want so much to focus on him the way he taught me and call to him, having him appear so I can show him just how well everything is going both with me and Ryan and then

Ryan on his own. I want Gabriel to be able to see just what his sacrifice did.

It's not only Gabriel and his passing that is getting to me. I've talked to Ryan about it as much as I can given he is really the only one around that truly understands it but while it helps a little it doesn't get me to where I need to be. I want to be happy about this, beyond happy really but all I can feel is another tremendous loss on my heart.

His words to me during our time in hell haunt me a lot. The caring way he was with me when no one else was around to see it. God wants nothing more than for me to see it for what it really was but I can't do that. I refuse to believe that the man I viewed during my time there was all an illusion and he only gave me what I wanted to hear and see. Especially hearing his agony when he believed me to be dead in Green Haven three months ago.

No, he felt more than even his own father is willing to give him credit for and that is what I can't seem to let go of. I saw a side of him that not many get to see other than the angels before he fell and that is how I want to remember him. Everyone else though, they don't want me to remember him at all. Ryan wants to support me and I know he will be there for me through whatever it is that I need to do in order to move forward from this but I can tell in the moments alone when we do speak about it that he wants nothing more than for me to just forget.

I'm getting married in a few weeks. Emma has pretty much been up my ass since the minute she found out that Ryan proposed again and even more so because this time she actually gets to be there. Despite my telling her that she really didn't want to be there for the first one, she still feels let down that she wasn't included. I swear with that girl some things never change. So while there might be the dark cloud of loss hanging over me there is this ray of sunshine breaking through, not only in the form of my best friend but also because of the man I am about to pledge my life to again.

Without Ryan I don't think I would have ever faced everything that I have and come out stronger because of it. He still believes himself to be the reason my entire life seemed to implode but what he doesn't get is that it probably would have anyway,

332

despite what I said to him in the church. What wouldn't have happened is all of the other things that came along with the implosion. I would not be sitting here now with this rock on my finger, smiling happily as I think of him, I wouldn't be strong and recognize the light inside of me and more than anything else I wouldn't have been able to take the steps I needed to in order to accept myself, flaws and all.

There is just one thing I can't seem to shake, and no matter how hard I try it always seems to come back around again. With my wedding day fast approaching, I find myself not only wanting to share it with the angels, especially Gabriel, but I also have a wish that I can't tell anyone about. One that despite knowing everything that's happened, I still want to come true.

I really want Lucifer to be there…
TO BE CONTINUED…

THE FINAL LOVE UNITED SERIES BOOK #4: STAIRWAY TO HEAVEN

ACKNOWLEDGEMENTS

To the ladies of the HMC: As always you were right here with me every step of the way. With every word, every paragraph and every page written you supported me, whether you were aware of it or not. Jennifer Ankles, Jenn Lierman, Jennifer Hicks, Savanna Decker, Linda Rabinowitz, Jill Fritz, Faith Walsh, Portia Lowery, Mariah Newton, Michelle Smith, Erin Narr. All of you ladies mean the world to me and I will forever treasure it. Bring on the hot guys!

Mallory: Not only do we seem to enjoy watching the same shows but we have both been bitten by this bug called writing and even though we may hide it away and not want the world to see it because we believe it may not be its best, the world needs and wants to see it. Never stop writing if it's what you want to do and one day, you'll be writing one of these things out for the people that helped get you there, that I promise you. You're amazing, keep at it and when you publish in the future and trust me you will, be ready to have your first official fangirl!

For the girl that turned into the woman that I will always remember as my first best friend, thank you from the bottom of my heart for all of your support and pushing of my work across all avenues. Whether you are aware of it or not, your support pushed me forward, even on the days when I most wanted to just give it all up for awhile. Jessica Van Acker, this one's for you!

Joey. What can I say about you that hasn't already been said? Oh I know! Once this series is done, I think we need to have one hell of a Thor marathon! Seriously now, thank you for being you and for taking me and these books even farther then I imagined in the beginning they would go. You're truly the best. You really have become Graham Hudson right before my eyes.

As always, I cannot write a book and not thank my kids. Not only do I have the four best kids on the planet but I also have one that's old enough to read and love my books and two that are dying to read like their big brother so they can read and love my books too! You guys and gals are the apples of my eye and you will always own my heart. Love you crazy kids!

To each and every person that either picks up a copy of the e-book or paperback version of any of my books. Thank you, not only for spending the money to own them in whatever format they appear in but also for the time that you put into reading it and reviewing it. It means more than the world to me and there just are no words to convey what it truly means to me. Each and every one of you rock my socks!

ABOUT THE AUTHOR

Melyssa is a mother of four from Toronto, Ontario, Canada. Previously spending her daylight hours freelance editing for friends and family, she happily traded in her gig for a rewarding career writing young adult supernatural novels. The best part being that in working from home, she gets to spend more time with her own set of real life angels, and maybe a demon or two as well.

She is currently working on Book 4 in the Love United Series titled Stairway to Heaven, a currently unnamed spinoff book featuring two characters from Holding On To Heaven, and a book filled with positive experiences as it relates to the autism journey.

When she's not writing, you can find her buried under the covers with her portable DVD player, watching marathons of Supernatural and Veronica Mars. When those aren't available, you can find her curled up in a corner with her e-reader and a plethora of books, falling in love with characters written so well she deems them her book boyfriends and girlfriends. If you want to find her, check Facebook or Twitter as she may just have an addiction to both. If those don't work you can always keep up with her progress on her personal site where she more than loves blogging about her various endeavors.

www.ingramcontent.com/pod-product-compliance
Lightning Source LLC
Chambersburg PA
CBHW070643180626
46817CB00006B/2228